Praise for Mark Gartside

'Gartside's warm, thoughtful, emotionally honest treatment of the process of becoming a man, especially handling responsibility for others in the face of loss, is a promising debut from a writer not afraid to show his feminine side'   *Daily Mail*

'Touching, unsentimental novel about single fatherhood'
Sainsbury's Magazine

'A lovely, heart-warming book about a widowed father, his son and the loves in their lives'   *Bookseller*

'*What Will Survive* has all the ingredients for tear-jerking chick-lit but with thought-provoking discussions about class, a strong male voice and an unmistakable northerness, this debut novel has a far bigger reach'   *Big Issue in the North*

'A gripping story of love, laughter and tears'   *Lifestyle North East*

'A touching story about love, tragedy and rebuilding life'
Time Out Dubai

The Last to Know

Mark Gartside was born in Warrington in the 1970s.
He currently lives in Maine, USA, with his wife and two sons.
The Last to Know is his second novel.

Also by Mark Gartside

What Will Survive

MARK GARTSIDE

The Last to Know

PAN BOOKS

First published 2013 by Macmillan

This edition published 2014 by Pan Books
an imprint of Pan Macmillan, a division of Macmillan Publishers Limited
Pan Macmillan, 20 New Wharf Road, London N1 9RR
Basingstoke and Oxford
Associated companies throughout the world
www.panmacmillan.com

ISBN 978-1-4472-0188-5

1 3 5 7 9 8 6 4 2

A CIP catalogue record for this book is available from the British Library.

Typeset by Ellipsis Digital Limited, Glasgow
Printed and bound by CPI Group (UK) Ltd, Croydon, CR0 4YY

Visit **www.panmacmillan.com** to read more about all our books
and to buy them. You will also find features, author interviews and
news of any author events, and you can sign up for e-newsletters
so that you're always first to hear about our new releases.

To Tahnthawan

Acknowledgements

I owe the warmest thanks to many people for their contributions to this book. Gail Kezer, Sarah Singer and Sharon Zink, all of whom read the book early and helped me to see the shape it would eventually take. Jaed, who listened to my concerns and questions all the way to Warmings, and sometimes on the way back. Sam Copeland, who is both a critical eye and a literary agent. Wayne Brookes – it is hard to imagine a more supportive editor – and the Macmillan team, and finally, Astrid Rogers, the value of whose insights and guidance it is impossible to overstate.

PART ONE

Pony Party

At first the gift had just been a way to get me out of a tight spot but now I was getting quite excited about it. I've always been like that when it comes to giving someone a present; I can't stand the wait before you see their reaction. As soon as I've bought it I want to hand it over, and since I have limited impulse control I've given a lot of presents weeks before they were due. Part of the reason is that I am quite an extravagant present buyer. I don't always remember to do it – I forever miss birthdays of cousins and siblings and nieces and nephews, and even, from time to time, Sherry, my wife – but when I give them they're good. And this one was going to be a winner.

It was my daughter Peggy's fifth birthday and the party was in full swing. I sidled through the guests in the living room and made for the garden. As I went through the French doors our neighbour, Lisa, mother of Peggy's best friend Fern and Sherry's oldest high school friend, grabbed my elbow.

'It's a lovely party,' she said, her cobalt eyes and perfect teeth distracting me. 'Thanks for inviting us.'

She said it with the overdone – a cynic would say false – sincerity that was typical of her suburban American type.

I smiled. 'We weren't going to, but it would have been awkward not to, seeing as we share a fence.' I said it with the wry – a cynic would say unpleasant – jokiness that was typical of my repressed English type.

She laughed a nervous, uncomfortable laugh, unsure whether I was joking. This happened a lot to me in the US. She looked at Fern and Peggy, who were playing in the garden. 'It's so nice that the kids have each other. It's like me and Sherry all over again!'

It was nice for them. Fern and Peggy were inseparable. Their bedroom windows faced each other, and I often went in to see Peggy in the morning to find her perched at her window engaged in some sign communication with Fern. I would try and give her a kiss and a hug, then suggest that we go out for breakfast together. Invariably, she would shake her head and ask if she could go and see Fern.

'I mean,' Lisa continued, 'I never thought we'd end up living next door to each other. And now the whole crew's back together. Daniel Faber's back. He arrived yesterday.'

Daniel Faber. The name rang a bell somewhere in my memory, so much so that when Sherry had told me he was coming back a few weeks ago I'd asked her if I'd met him, but she'd said no. Since then I'd heard a lot of talk about him – about how he had been one of their group in high school – Sherry, Daniel, Mike and Lisa – and how they'd not heard from him much in the last few years and how he'd made a load of money in New York and every time I'd had the same reaction. I knew the name. I was sure of it. I just didn't know how. It was frustrating. The memory was there, elusive, rippling just beyond my grasp. And now he was here. He'd moved back.

Moving back. It seemed to be what people did – we had, Lisa had, with her husband Mike, whom she'd met in high school and been with ever since – and now there was another one. I understood the allure of the place, especially for people with children:

house prices were low, the school system was good, there was little crime. I'd been amazed when we arrived to find that most people left their doors unlocked when they went out.

'Well,' I said. 'I'll look forward to meeting him.'

Lisa patted my arm. 'We were such a gang in high school. He's a great guy. You'll like him.'

'I'm sure I will. Anyway, it's time for the present.' I smiled at Lisa and went outside to find Peggy.

She was in her paddling pool, a deluxe model with slides and blow up elephants that sprayed water from their lilting trunks that I had bought for her fourth birthday the summer before. It wasn't expensive – nothing was in America, especially after living in the UK – but it more than made up for that in the effort required to blow the damn thing up and keep it inflated despite the welter of punctures that appeared over it like a case of particularly virulent measles.

'Peggy,' I said. 'Are you ready for your present?'

She nodded, and her eyes widened with that expectant greed that children have. An adult would have feigned polite indifference to the prospect of a present. After all, in your forties it didn't do to jump up and down when someone produced a parcel on your birthday, however excited you felt inside, but Peggy hadn't yet learned to dissemble and I loved her all the more for it.

She stood up and addressed the assembled parents and friends who made up her birthday party. 'I'm getting a *present*.' She looked at me. 'Where is it, Daddy?'

'In the shed,' I said. 'But first I want to give you this.'

From behind my back I pulled out a bridle.

Sherry put her hand on my wrist. 'You *didn't*,' she said, smiling, her mouth slightly open. She'd had a couple of glasses of wine during the afternoon and was in that happy state of benevolent acceptance of the world. I loved her in this mood, particularly

5

because this mood invariably went along with another kind of mood, which I liked even more. I knew what we'd be doing when the guests were gone and Peggy was fast asleep.

I raised and lowered my eyebrows a few times. 'Maybe,' I said. 'Wait and see.'

She laughed. 'Oh my God. I don't believe it. I don't *believe* you.'

I waggled the bridle. 'What's this, Peggy? Do you know?'

Peggy nodded. Did she ever know. It was all she'd talked about since Christmas. She wanted a pony. The idea had been planted by a guy called Gerard, a friend I'd met when he made some cabinets for me years ago. He'd told her at Christmas that Daddy would buy her a birthday pony that summer, if she was a good girl. *Daddy loves you,* he'd said, looking at me and grinning. *He'll get you whatever you want.* Since then barely a day had gone by without Peggy mentioning it. She had the name picked out – Chattasuta, wherever the hell that came from – and told us stories at night in which she and Chattasuta went on long adventures together.

At first I'd thought it was a fad, so I'd tried to wait it out, but after six months that clearly wasn't going to work, so I'd decided to do something about it.

Peggy hopped from foot to foot. 'It's a bridle,' she said. It came out as *bwidle*. 'For a pony. For Chattasuta.' Her voice was little more than a breath.

Gerard, who was there with his teenage son Tyson, gave me a thumbs up. *Nice work*, he mouthed.

I handed Peggy the bridle and took her hand. I led her to the shed, a ramshackle thing I'd built when we moved in before I realized how harsh Maine winters were. It wasn't surviving them very well. Her three friends – Lyle and Lizzie, as well as the ever-present Fern – followed her, their expressions a mixture of awe and unadulterated jealousy. It was hard to suppress my smile.

The shed was in the corner of the garden and we had to negotiate the crowd of adults to get there. Peggy trotted along beside me, one hand loose inside mine, the other clutching the bridle, a cheap plastic thing that I'd bought at the last minute. Originally I was just going to open the shed door and let her see it herself, but then I thought I needed something to build up the anticipation. A kind of *coup de théâtre*. And, cheap and plastic it may have been, but my bridle was doing exactly what I had wanted. Peggy was white with excitement.

At the door I unclipped the padlock and lifted the wooden bar. The door swung open and the shed loomed, the inside dark and cool.

Behind us the guests had gathered, a strange silence upon them. They were as interested as Peggy and her friends. I glanced back and gave Sherry a wink. She lifted her glass of Sauvignon Blanc and raised an eyebrow.

'Well then, Peggy,' I said. 'Do you want to have a look inside?'

She bit her lip. She hesitated. She nodded.

The contents of that shed had cost me a small fortune, although the look on Peggy's face told me it was going to be worth it. When I'd had the idea to get her a toy horse I'd been a bit sceptical of her reaction, picturing a wooden rocking horse of the type I'd had as a kid in the UK – but when I'd bought it I'd been amazed what toymakers could do nowadays. These things were like real ponies. They had thick, lustrous horse hair, long tails, and were perfectly proportioned. From a distance they looked real, albeit a bit small and motionless. Of course, there was no way we could get her a real pony – we had nowhere to keep it, neither of us had the time to look after it, and we couldn't afford it. The stabling fees alone were six hundred dollars a month – but this was as good as the real thing. Or, if not as good, not far off.

My eyes adjusted and in the dark I could make out the shape of the pony. Peggy's eyes must have adjusted too as she gasped. As

I'd hoped, the quality of the toy deceived her and she thought it was real.

'Go on,' I said. 'You can pet it. It's yours.'

Peggy said only one word, but in that word was all the love and longing and faith in the perfection of the world that a child could feel.

'Chattasuta,' she said. 'It's Chattasuta.'

She didn't move, stuck to the spot on the threshold of the shed. Impatient, I reached inside and grabbed Chattasuta's mane. Her – I guessed Chattasuta was a she – wheels squeaked as she travelled the short distance to the door and poked her nose out of the shed to greet her public.

Her public reacted with silence. Someone – Gerard, I guessed – started to snort with laughter but managed to suppress it and turn it into a cough.

I beamed at Peggy. 'There you are, petal,' I said. 'Your very own pony.'

Peggy looked at me, the expectant expression frozen on her face for a few seconds, before the corners of her mouth started to quiver and her eyes creased and she burst – really, it seemed like she burst – into tears.

'It's not a *real* pony,' she said, then ran through the adults and into the house. Sherry made a *don't worry, it's not your fault, you tried* face and followed her.

I watched her go, my heart breaking as I realized what I had done. It had never crossed my mind that she was *actually* expecting a pony, a flesh and blood, grass-eating, manure-producing pony. I mean, surely she knew she couldn't have one? When boys asked for cars they didn't expect to get a *real* car. They expected a remote control one, or a miniature one at best. It was the same with girls and ponies. It had to be. At least, I had thought so until a minute ago.

It was in these moments that you realized that you didn't really know your kids. You also realized how hard it was going to be to be a parent, not least because your kids had no way of moderating their emotions. If you let them down, then you knew about it. With your wife, you got a few chances. A misjudged present – as when I'd bought Sherry a book of famous war photography for Valentine's Day, which I still thought was, if not romantic, at least an interesting present – and she'd forgive you. She was an adult, she knew that people made mistakes. Not so with your kids. One false step and their world crumbled, and it was your fault. They blamed you and you blamed yourself.

'Well,' I said. 'That went well.' I watched Peggy cry through the kitchen window, cradled in Sherry's arms. 'Really well.'

Fern, Lizzie and Lyle walked over to the shed and pulled Chattasuta out of her stable. Her wheels caught on the grass and she tipped onto her side. After a long, contemptuous look at the stricken pony, the three children went back to the sandpit.

'Shit,' I said. 'Now it's covered in grass. I hope the shop takes it back. It was expensive.' I picked up Chattasuta and pushed her into the shed. I closed the door behind her. I didn't want to have to look at it.

Gerard shook his head. 'Shame. It was a good pony.' He paused, the corners of his mouth twitching. 'For a fake.'

'Well, thanks for that. Any other ideas for a present you can put in my daughter's head?'

Gerard leaned forward and passed me a bottle of Coors Light. Normally I wouldn't have touched the stuff but I needed a drink, if only for something to do.

'She'll get over it,' he said. We both knew he was lying.

My Mother-in-law's Strawberry Pie

When everyone had gone and Peggy was in bed, Sherry came and sat by me on the couch.

She tucked her hair, which was a deep copper colour that I had never seen on anyone else, behind her ear. It was a new gesture – she'd recently had her hair cut into a shoulder-length bob, which was the shortest I'd ever known it – and it allowed me to see her afresh, to shake off the familiarity of long association, and see her as the rest of the world did. And all I noticed was how beautiful she was. She always had been; not in a pretty way, like Britney or Marilyn, but beautiful in a striking way, like Ava Gardner, or Angelina Jolie. Tall, elegant, high-cheekboned, with dark, unknowable eyes. When we had met she was almost intimidating; as she had grown older she had softened a little, and matured into her looks. She was, as they would have said in a romance, a 'beauty'.

'So how was Peggy at bedtime? Over the disappointment?' I said, feeling like the worst parent in America, which was not an inconsiderable achievement if you believed what you saw on the news. The more I thought about it, the more I thought that what I had done was a kind of torture, almost designed to cause maximum distress to a little girl. I'd given her the impression she was getting a pony – the greatest dream of her short life – then whipped it away and given her a toy horse. Which, by the way, was back in the shed, where – unless I could return it – it would stay and rot. It was like someone telling me the England football selectors had finally woken up and seen what had been under their noses all along and picked me as centre forward; then, when I was kitted up and in the tunnel, about to make my international debut, a joker popped out and shouted surprise! How I could have been so stupid I had no idea.

'She'll be fine. She's just a little disappointed, that's all.'

'She seemed more than a little disappointed, if the wails I heard from upstairs were anything to go by.'

'She'll forget about it.'

'No she won't. One day she'll tell her husband about it, and what a lousy father I was.'

'It'll be one of those stories that daughters tell about their fathers as a joke, designed to show how much they love them. Don't worry. You're a marvellous dad. Didn't she tell you that, on Fathers' Day? What's on that mug in the cupboard? Do you want me to get it out and show you? World's. Greatest. Dad.' She spoke slowly, hamming it up, with a heavy emphasis on each word as though talking to someone who was a bit stupid. 'It says it on the mug. So it must be true.'

'Fine. But I still feel rotten.'

Sherry turned to face me so that her thigh was over mine. She put her head on my shoulder, her lips against my ear and nuzzled my neck.

'Perhaps I can make you feel better.' Her voice lowered a tone or two. 'So, world's greatest dad, how about you and I try making another kid for you to give crap presents to? It's that week again.'

That week. We'd been trying for another child for a few years, and I'd grown sick of her telling me she was ovulating. The two least erotic words in the English language are 'I'm ovulating'. Every time I heard them they had a direct, and wilting, effect on my ability to provide the sperm to the ovum in question. I'd suggested a few other phrases, but 'It's that time of the month' had unfortunate connotations, 'I'm ready' made it sound like she was about to submit to a gynaecological exam, and she wouldn't accept 'Come and get me, big boy.' So we settled on 'that week'. Not great, but after a while it just became part of the lexicon of our marriage.

And it had been a while. Things hadn't exactly gone to plan with Peggy – who was called Margaret, after my mother, but went by Peggy – so we had waited until she was two before trying again. We figured a three-year-old and a newborn was a pretty good combination. At least there'd only be one in nappies to deal with.

But it hadn't happened. Nothing. Just lots of frantic sex for one week a month, the frequency of which died down after a year or so. We'd tried doctors, had fertility tests and everything was okay: it just wasn't happening. At thirty-two, Sherry still had plenty of time, but it was definitely starting to feel like it was running out, and I could sense an increasing desperation in my wife.

Still, there was always the hope that the next time would be the one.

I turned my head and kissed her. She reached down and unbuckled my belt. Since the early days of our relationship there had been something uncontrolled about her when we had sex; as soon as we started kissing or touching or talking about it, she almost seemed to step out of herself. It was like throwing a switch, as though she had been waiting for it. Sometimes I almost didn't recognize her.

'Let's go upstairs,' I said, and pulled her to her feet. She responded by gripping the back of my neck with one hand and kissing me even harder.

In the end we didn't even make it up the stairs. We did it half-way up them. Between the moans and the banging of our limbs into the wall and staircase there was a lot of noise. Thankfully, Peggy stayed asleep.

'Well,' she said, as we sat side by side on the stairs, hold-ing hands, which seemed an innocent gesture after the violence of what we had just done. 'If that was the one I'll certainly remem-ber it.'

'Not a story we'd share with the kid, though. Imagine, if the kid asked where it was conceived.'

'We'll tell them it was in Venice, or something like that. Sounds better than doggy-style on the stairs.' She stood up. 'Let's go and tidy up.'

We walked down the stairs and into the kitchen.

There was a pie on the table.

We both stared at it. It had a strawberry, carved into the shape of a flower, in the centre. This was Sherry's mum Lauren's decorative trademark, the addition she put on every strawberry pie she made.

'I didn't know Lauren was coming back,' I said.

'Oh my God,' Sherry said, her face as red as the strawberry. 'She went home after the party to get the pie. I forgot.'

'Well,' I said. 'Making love is all part of a healthy marriage. I'm sure your mum would agree.'

Sherry just nodded.

'Of course, you don't have to do it on the stairs, wailing like a banshee.'

'I wasn't wailing!'

I shrugged. 'Not far off. Don't be embarrassed. I'm a very attractive man. Your mum will understand that.'

Sherry groaned. 'This is so embarrassing. I mean, my mum just heard us having sex on the stairs.' She put her head in her hands. 'What if she saw?'

'What if she did? I'm guessing she knows already that you're not a virgin. And she'll forget soon enough.' Gerard's words from that afternoon came back to me. 'She'll get over it.'

I wasn't sure about that, though, and from the look on her face, neither was Sherry.

After the Pony Party

I lay in bed, wide awake. It was two a.m. and all I could think about was Peggy and how disappointed she'd been. *Don't be soft. Get her a pony, if she wants one. Find a way.*

You love your children with an intensity that hurts. It's that that makes it hard to be a parent: not the sleepless nights and the lack of free time and the constant noise, but the knowledge that there is someone in the world who you love more than you love yourself, but who you cannot always protect. I remember the first time Peggy got sick, with some minor stomach bug which made her vomit for twelve hours. I couldn't eat, sleep, think: I was convinced she was going to die, and the fear hollowed me out.

I'd never even liked kids. When I'd been around other people's I'd found it tedious: their speech was annoying, their cute singing discordant, their tantrums selfish and unreasonable. Peggy, though – when she spoke it was charming and delightful, her songs were tuneful and pleasant and her tantrums signs of a quirky and intelligent character. I knew I was just being a typical parent, but I couldn't help it. Even though I knew it wasn't true, in my eyes Peggy was nothing less than perfect.

15

I kicked the sheets from my legs, hot and unable to sleep. Next to me Sherry murmured, then elbowed me in the bicep.

'Go to sleep,' she said. 'Stop thrashing about.'

I propped myself up on my elbow.

'Darling, do you think I should get her a pony? A real one?' It was the obvious solution to my treachery. I'd work out a way to keep it. I'd look after it myself, if that would keep the cost down. At that moment I was convinced that my daughter was scarred forever by my failure to provide a pony, so mucking out at six a.m. every day seemed a small price to pay for some peace of mind.

'Don't be silly. She'll be fine.'

'I know, but – I feel terrible about it.'

'Where are we going to keep the thing?' She pulled the sheets around her and turned on her side.

'I don't like her to be upset.'

'Which is how she keeps you twisted around her little finger. She's fine. Now go to sleep.'

I still couldn't sleep. Doing nothing for Peggy wasn't an option. Whether she would get over it or not, my conscience needed a salve of some sorts. 'How about riding lessons?'

She sighed. 'Fine. Get her riding lessons.'

'You want to go with her?' She didn't reply. 'I hate horses.'

Silence. I listened to her breathing become deep and rhythmic, then I got out of bed and went downstairs to search the internet for riding schools in Southern Maine.

In the end, I fell asleep on the couch. It was too hot to go back to bed upstairs. For someone used to the temperate climate of the UK, Maine had odd seasons. It seemed to wake up from the winter sometime in April, and, eschewing spring in the scurry for some warmth, shoot straight into summer sometime in May. By the fourth of July – Independence Day, and a day on which I heard the same jokes about breaking free of the Empire etc., *ad nauseam*, jokes which were not funny the first time and which did not grow funnier at the thousandth retelling, although, who knew, maybe the ten thousandth was the one – summer had baked itself in, and the days were hot, the nights sticky. The sound of summer in Maine was the buzzing of mosquitoes and the whirr of a fan in the bedroom.

Peggy woke me.

'Hey, Poppet,' I said, and pulled her onto the couch with me. Her hair – she had her mother's coppery hair colour – lay flat on her temple and cheek where she had sweated in the night.

'Why are you down here?'

'I fell asleep on the couch.'

She looked at me. 'You're wearing underpants.'

She had just started to lose the innocence that allowed her to run naked on the beach; now she wanted to wear a bathing suit. I hated it; it reminded me that next would be puberty and boys. When I'd had a daughter my best friend had shaken his head and told me that with boys, you only had one prick to worry about; with girls you had every prick in town. It was not advice I wanted, but it was advice I couldn't forget.

'It's hot.'

She looked at me for a long time, her eyes the same unfathomable pools that her mother had. I never knew what she was thinking.

'I'm sorry about yesterday,' I said. 'About the pony.'

She made a slight movement that was barely a shrug. 'It's okay.'

I didn't want it to be okay; okay meant that she'd come to terms with my disappointing her. I didn't want that. I didn't want to be someone who disappointed my daughter. If she'd asked for a pony right then I would have promised her one and then gone and bought it that morning. But, thankfully, I had another card to play.

'I did get you something to make up for it. It's not as good as your own pony, but you might like it.' I was a soft touch and I knew it. But I liked it. She was my daughter, after all, and if a dad couldn't get his daughter a treat, what use was he?

'What is it?' I disliked the wariness in her voice.

'Riding lessons. They're doing them on Popham Beach. You get to go every day for a week and ride a horse.'

Her mouth and eyes opened wide and all her five-year-old's reserve fell away. She was two years old again. 'A *real* horse?'

'As real as you or me.'

'Daddy,' she said. 'Thank you, Daddy. I love you.'

'Come on,' I said. 'Let's make some breakfast.'

I'd bought her affection, but it was no less sweet for that. And to think we wanted another. We must have been mad.

I put the stack of pancakes that Peggy and I had made, at the cost of a great deal of flour and eggshells, on the counter top and was about to call Sherry when the front door opened. Wandering into people's houses unannounced was a speciality of the town of Barrow, made easier as no one locked their doors. More than once we'd been caught in the act on the couch and had to scramble for our clothes while a neighbour stood in the doorway calling hello and carrying some organic eggs or home-grown carrots. This morning it was Gerard.

'Morning,' he said. 'You making pancakes?'

'I'm making pancakes,' Peggy said. 'Daddy's just helping.'

'In that case I'll have one,' Gerard said. 'If I'm invited?'

I nodded at the plate. 'Go for it.'

'We'll need them,' he said. 'Big day's fishing ahead.'

'Fishing?' I said. 'We're going fishing?'

He nodded. 'We talked about it last week.'

'Did we?'

'Yeah. At the Sea Dog.'

I had a hazy memory of Gerard mentioning something. He specialized in making vague suggestions – *Hey, we could go fishing on Sunday, what do you think?* – and then, unless you said a clear no, showing up on the day in question as though the plans were carved in stone.

'I'm not sure I can go, mate,' I said. 'I sort of forgot that we'd made a plan. I didn't say anything to Sherry.' I looked out of the window. The sun was creeping over the lawn. 'It would be good, though. And it's that or church.'

'Your call, buddy.'

'I'll ask Sherry. She'll be down in a minute.'

I stacked a plate with pancakes, syrup and blueberries. As I picked it up the front door opened again.

This time it was Lisa.

She was accompanied by a man, of her and Sherry's age. He was short, with neatly trimmed blond hair, and handsome in a Tom Cruise way: bland and smooth, but not very lived in. He smiled, revealing a set of exceptionally shiny teeth, and put his hand out. I shook it.

'Tom,' Lisa said. 'This is Daniel. Daniel, Tom.'

'Hi,' I said. 'Nice to meet you. I heard you just moved back to Barrow? Welcome.'

'Thanks,' he said, still clasping my hand. I tried to pull it away gently but he kept it in his grasp. 'Nice to meet you too. I've heard a lot about you. All of it good.'

'Really?' I didn't know what to say; I never do when confronted by the earnestness that some Americans specialize in. I gestured to Gerard. 'This is Gerard.'

Thankfully Daniel let go of my hand to shake Gerard's. It was a much briefer shake, and he barely looked at Gerard; perhaps Gerard's faded baseball cap and cheap jeans put him off. Whatever

19

it was, people like Gerard were clearly not worthy of Daniel's full attention.

Not that it seemed to bother Gerard. 'You back for good?' he said.

'Yes, I am.'

'Why's that then?'

'Oh, you know. Times change, that kind of thing.'

'Where were you?'

'The city.'

Gerard raised an eyebrow. 'Which one?'

Daniel looked like he wanted to run away; I bit my lip to suppress a smile. Gerard was doing this deliberately. It was classic Gerard.

'I was between New York and San Fran.'

I rolled my eyes. San Fran. Like it was an old friend. It was like when people referred to someone famous by a familiar name – *you know, Dave Beckham, he's like, a really genuine guy.*

'And here you are in Barrow, Maine,' Gerard said. 'After all that jet-setting. Must be a bit of a change.' The subtext was clear. *What the hell are you doing here, big-shot? Mustn't have worked out for you, eh?*

'Oh,' Daniel said. 'I could have stayed, but I like it here.' He turned to me. 'Lots of people do, right Tom?'

Gerard winked at me. 'That's right,' I said. 'It's a marvellous place.'

'I love your accent,' he said.

'Thanks.'

'Is it Australian? You an Aussie? Is that what I heard?'

Americans always guessed Aussie. It was like Brits hearing a North American accent and asking if its owner was Canadian; half because they wanted to sound as though they weren't ignorant enough to assume that all North American accents were from the

USA and half because they knew that Canadians hated being mistaken for Yanks.

'British,' I said.

'Oh, I see.' He grinned. 'Here to check on the colonies? We need it.'

A colonies joke. Another thing I heard a lot. In his case, it smacked of false modesty, the hallmark of a smarmy bastard.

'I think perhaps you do,' I said.

The stairs creaked. I looked up; Sherry appeared in the kitchen door jamb. Her eyes widened at the sight of our new guest.

'Daniel!' Sherry walked across the kitchen and hugged him, in the kind of tight embrace that Americans hand out like M&Ms and Brits reserve for their most intimate moments. I hated getting those hugs; the only thing I hated more was seeing my wife giving them to Tom Cruise-a-likes she'd known since childhood.

Daniel pulled out of the hug and looked at her. 'It's great to see you,' he said, his voice loud enough to be decent but quiet enough to be meant only for her. There was a strange intensity in the way he looked at her; it soon passed.

'You too.' Sherry patted his shoulder. 'I can't believe you're back.' She looked at Peggy. 'This is Peggy, my daughter. And I see you've met Tom, my husband.'

'I have. He was telling me that we here in the colonies need some help from the mother country!'

'Hang on,' I said. What the hell was he doing, twisting my words to get a laugh? 'I wasn't at all. I was just answering your question. It was a joke.'

Sherry gave me a strange look. 'Anyway,' she said. 'Do you want to eat? I can get you a plate.'

'I'm having breakfast with Mum and Mike,' Lisa said. 'But Daniel might.'

'Sure,' Daniel said. 'That sounds awesome. I'd love some.'

Daniel sat on one of the stools and put his elbows on the bar in the centre of our kitchen. 'What's cooking?'

'Pancakes,' Peggy said. 'Me and Daddy are making pancakes. Do you want one?'

Daniel clapped his hands together. 'How could I refuse? That'd be lovely.'

I rolled my eyes. This guy was unbelievable. I'd never imagined anyone could be so smarmy. So *unctuous*; that was the word.

I switched the stove back on, retrieved the pan from the sink, opened the fridge and took out some more eggs. There were a few at the back which had been there a while. They'd be perfect for Daniel.

'Coffee?' I said, as I beat the eggs.

Daniel nodded. 'Sounds awesome.'

Everything was bloody awesome. I slid a mug over the counter; the scraping noise seemed loud in the silence.

'So,' Gerard said. 'What did you do in the city?'

Daniel looked at him. 'Oh, finance stuff.' Just *finance stuff*. No more info. *You wouldn't understand if I told you,* he meant.

Sadly for Daniel, Gerard was an expert bubble popper. He raised his eyebrows. 'You're an accountant? Double-entry book-keeping, that kind of thing? If you need some work round here I know plenty of people who could do with a little help. Tax returns, that kind of thing.'

'Thanks.' Daniel's face was fixed in a rictus grin. 'Not quite my field.'

Gerard looked at him expectantly.

'I was more into leveraged stuff. Buy a company, fix it up, sell it on. That kind of thing.'

Sherry wiped maple syrup from our daughter's face. 'We'll have to get you cleaned up before church,' she said. 'Can't have you going with half a pancake on your face.'

'Still go to St John's?' Daniel asked. 'Remember the Sunday School there? With Miss James?'

Sherry nodded. 'She's still there.'

'No way.' Daniel laughed. 'She was a bit of a dragon back then. I can't imagine she's mellowed with age.'

'You want to come along? I can give you a ride.'

'Sure. You joining us, Tom?'

You joining *us*? I was *you* and they were *us*? Something in me tightened. That didn't sound right to me.

Or maybe I was being over-sensitive to what was just a casual expression. Maybe.

I never went to church, in part because I enjoyed the peace and quiet at home once a week and in part because I couldn't stand it. The sermonizing, do-gooder minister, the pillar of the community church elders, the hypocritical congregation who spent their week boozing and swindling and fornicating then showed up for their weekly dose of forgiveness. Apart from anything else, I was an atheist, which in the US was awkward. You could be anything you wanted – Catholic, Protestant, Jewish, Buddhist, Muslim, as long as you believed in something, but being an atheist was not acceptable. It would have been better to be a Satanist. At least it was a position. At least you accepted that there was a world of some kind beyond ours. Being an atheist, though: that offended everyone. It was as though you were laughing at them for having imaginary friends.

Which was what I'd told Peggy, much to Sherry's upset, although not because she was particularly religious. She just didn't want to offend people. Sherry was a sort-of believer, a position that to me was at best lazy and at worst dishonest. Either commit and accept the discipline of a religious life, or give up the whole thing. Showing up each week and pretending because your friends did was hypocrisy, and I didn't see why I should lie to my child just because some bible-thumpers wanted me to. Anyway, we'd learned not to talk about it, after our fiftieth argument.

Today though, I felt in need of some spiritual nourishment.

'Sure. I'd love to come.'

Gerard frowned at me. 'What about fishing?'

I ignored him and gestured to Daniel's pancakes. 'Eat up. Don't want to keep the Good Lord waiting on his special day. He might smite us.'

Sherry glared at me. 'I'm sure we have a few minutes.'

Daniel folded his knife and fork over his plate. 'You're right, Tom. We'd better get moving. Sure I can squeeze in with you?'

I left it to Sherry to reply. She told him it was no problem and that it would be our pleasure.

I loaded the dishwasher as he went outside. From the window I watched him move his car. He drove a small, silver Mazda Miata convertible. It was the perfect car for him. A hairdresser's car.

A few minutes later, we were on our way to church.

It was as though Brad Pitt had come to visit. All through the service people were turning round to look at Daniel, who kept his eyes on the minister and his face arranged in a beatific smile. Quite a few people stared at me and Sherry with what I took to be naked jealousy, as though they were outraged that we dared take up space in his pew.

When the service was over and the collection made – Daniel put in fifty dollars, enough to be generous without being showy; I put nothing in, on the grounds that he'd given enough for all of us – we gathered in the church hall for coffee.

'Daniel Faber,' the priest, a greying man in his fifties, said. 'It's so good to see you back in Barrow. Just visiting?' He took Daniel's hand in between his as he spoke.

'No.' Daniel said. 'Here for good, I hope. Back where I belong.'

'That's wonderful news. Truly wonderful.' A few people were hovering round to listen in on the exchange. When the priest finished speaking they broke into a flutter of applause. It appeared that Daniel was a celebrity in Barrow.

I felt like spitting into the collection plate.

Land Line Phone Calls Are Rare These Days

'Would you like to come for lunch?' Sherry was standing a few yards from me, just inside the church, talking to Daniel. I was by the door, waiting to get away.

'It's been such a long time,' she said. 'I can't wait to catch up.'

I groaned. This was a disaster. Daniel was probably a nice enough guy, but for whatever reason I had taken against him. Maybe I was being unreasonable, but it was what it was. The last thing I needed was him at our house for the rest of the day.

Daniel smiled. 'I'd love to come. Are you sure, though? I don't want to impose.'

'Of course we're sure.'

I groaned again.

'Daddy?' Peggy tugged my sleeve. 'Are you okay?'

'Sorry, darling?'

'Are you okay? You're making a noise.'

'Oh. I'm just hungry.'

'Is that what you do when you're hungry? Uggghhhh.' She clutched her stomach. 'Uggghhh.'

'Peggy?' Sherry said. 'Are you okay?'

26

'I'm hungry, Mom. Daddy said that's what you do when you're hungry.'

I shrugged – a *kids, eh?* shrug, as though I didn't know what she was talking about – and gestured to the door. 'We ready?'

'I invited Daniel to lunch. Hope that's okay.'

'Fine,' I said. There was no point arguing about this. He'd be gone soon enough, and then I could just ignore him. 'Sounds lovely.'

Sherry smiled. 'Thanks,' she said. 'For being so welcoming.'

We had lunch outside. I marinated some chicken and fired up the gas grill. We were just sitting down to eat when the phone rang inside.

'I'll get it,' Sherry said.

'It'll be Mum.' I said. 'It's the landline. I'll go.' My mum was the only person who still called the landline. We kept it for her, along with some deal that meant she could call us for one pence a minute. The line cost us forty bucks a month; we'd have been as well to pay her phone bill, but she had a thing about calling an international mobile phone. She thought she'd be charged hundreds of pounds. I'd tried to explain it to her but she wouldn't accept it. Sometimes it was easier to just to give in.

'You stay,' Sherry said. 'Eat. I'll get it.'

A few minutes later she leaned out of the kitchen window.

'Tom?' she said, frowning slightly. 'It's your dad.'

My dad? I couldn't remember the last time he'd called. It was always Mum who called, and after we'd all talked to her she'd call Dad to the phone and he and I would have a two-minute discussion about nothing.

I took the phone into the living room and sat in my old, cracked leather armchair. The sun streamed in through the bay window.

'You at home?' he said.

'Yes. Sunday lunch.'

'Oh,' he said. 'Call me when it's over.'

'It's okay. I can talk now. What's up?'

There was a long silence. 'It's your mother. She's been taken ill.' He said it just like that; no soft-soaping news from my dad, no attempt to deliver it in a way that would minimize the blow.

Your mother's ill. You know it's coming with your parents, one day. That phone call, either from the parent that's still okay or from the police or hospital or care home or whatever. *Your mother's ill.* Which at her age, and coming from my father meant she was on her way out. Even though you've known it all your life it's still a shock. That's the funny thing about death. It's the one fact we all know and agree on, but it still surprises us when it happens.

'What's wrong?'

'Stroke.' My father had never been a man of many words.

'Is it bad?'

'It's not good.'

'I mean, how bad is it?'

'She's had a stroke, Tom, and she's in her seventies.'

'Did the doctors, did they say – anything?' I meant how long, but I couldn't say it.

He knew what I meant. 'She should recover enough to come home. After that, who knows? A year maybe.' His voice sounded close to breaking, which was the most emotion I could remember from him. I was aware, suddenly, of what this must have meant to him: his wife of forty years was dying. I'd never really considered my dad's feelings for my mum. I'd just assumed he put up with her and vice versa; to hear in his voice that he was worried about her – that he loved her, even – was shocking. It shouldn't have been, and if I'd ever bothered to think about it, it wouldn't have been.

'Should I come?'

'If you want to see her.'

'I meant when. When should I come? Of course I'll come.'

'Come soon. She's got a while yet, but come soon.' He paused. 'She'll be glad to see you. She's expecting you, actually.'

'I'll be there as soon as I can. Give her my love.'

'She had a question for you.'

'Oh?'

'She wanted to know if Peggy's coming.'

Of course she did. Peggy, her only grandchild. The too-distant apple of her eye that she hadn't seen for two years now. It was a long trip, and it was difficult with a young child.

'She's coming,' I said. 'See you, Dad.'

I sat back in my chair. *A year, maybe* . . . I couldn't think beyond those words. *A year, maybe.*

'Problems?'

I turned round. Daniel was standing in the doorway. I wondered how long he had been there, and, more to the point, what the fuck he thought he was doing eavesdropping on my conversations.

'No.' I smiled. Better to rise above. 'Fine, thanks.'

'Sounded pretty dramatic.'

Sounded like none of your fucking business.

We looked at each other – stared, really, like two teenagers before a high school fight – and I got the impression he was sizing me up, wondering what I was capable of. It was deeply unnerving.

The stare was broken by Sherry's arrival.

'Hi,' she said. She handed Daniel a plate of food. There was a closeness, an ease, in their gestures that I didn't like. 'It's so good to see you.' She looked at me. 'And I'm glad you're getting to know Daniel.'

Daniel. She said it in an odd way, with a longer emphasis than usual on the first syllable. And I remembered why I knew that name, where I'd heard it before.

It was in Paris. I'd heard her say it in Paris.

Back in the Day

Sherry and I met in Spain. I was on holiday with two friends, Paul and Jerry, in early summer, before the schoolkids and students turned up and when the clientele were a little older and less annoying, although the basic recipe of sun, sand and sex was the same. The last thing I was looking for, in my life generally and on that holiday in particular, was a girlfriend. I was feeling pretty sorry for myself: at twenty-seven my career as a rugby league professional was over, in some ways before it had really begun. I was what used to be called a 'journeyman pro' – not especially gifted, but hard-working, reliable and intelligent enough to make the best of what I had. People like me tend not to burst onto the scene as teenagers; we make our impact as senior squad members later in our careers. Mine, though, was over, victim of a recurring knee problem. Fortunately, I'd done a degree in Sports Science and had a job working on rehab programmes for post-operative patients in the local hospital. Two weeks in Spain was my way of consoling myself before starting on the rest of my life.

The resort was large, and, like all such places, had different areas with different characteristics: there was a noisy strip with neon bars and cheap booze, where most people ended up, drunk and dancing and looking for girls; there was a town square, which was quieter, and had some decent restaurants; and there was a beachfront area, which was a combination of the two. After a couple of nights on the strip, Paul, Jerry and I had decided to go to the beachfront; the strip was loud and we needed a break; besides, there were some Glaswegian girls we wanted to avoid. Around midnight, I was at the bar ordering a round of kamikazes, some kind of filthy cocktail that we switched to after we'd had enough beer.

I arranged the three glasses into a triangle and picked them up. As I did, someone knocked into my elbow and the blue liquid sloshed out.

'Oh my God,' a woman's voice said, 'I'm so sorry.'

I turned round. A young woman was looking at me, her lips drawn back at the corners in an apologetic smile. She had long, coppery hair, near-black eyes and a lithe, athletic figure. She was also tall; our eyes were nearly on the same level, although that was partly owing to the heels she was wearing.

Had it been a bloke, I would have insisted he buy me another drink. Had it been a different woman, I would probably have waited until she offered and let her buy one. As it was I just smiled.

'Don't worry.' I couldn't think of anything to say. Had I not been half-drunk I would never have dared talk to her in the first place. She was one of those girls that you don't bother approaching.

'I'll get you some more. I insist.' I noticed her accent for the first time; a husky, American drawl. It made her even more attractive. 'What are you drinking?'

I felt stupid saying it. 'Kamikaze.'

She smiled. 'Sounds delicious. I might try one. What's in them?'

I shrugged. I didn't know. 'They're good.' I held out one of the half-empty glasses. 'Try it.'

She took a sip and grimaced. 'Maybe I'll give it a miss.'

'Where are you from?' The great thing about meeting people who weren't from the UK was that you had a ready-made question that sounded interesting and not sleazy.

'I'm American.'

'Whereabouts in the US? I went there once.'

'Really? Where to?'

'Milwaukee. Warrington played Wigan there in an exhibition game.' She looked confused. 'Rugby league. They were trying to spread it to the USA. It didn't work. The players hated each other and ten minutes in there was a massive brawl.'

'Sounds like the kind of thing that might be popular in Milwaukee.'

'It didn't take off. I think they were selling it as family entertainment. So where in the US are you from?'

'Maine. A little town called Barrow.'

'Oh, that's Stephen King country, right? I read *Carrie*, and *The Shining*. I was twelve. I was terrified for weeks.'

She laughed. 'I don't read them. They're too scary. I used to hide behind the sofa when that cartoon duck vampire was on – *Count Duckula*, I think.' She caught the barman's eye. 'A gin and tonic and three of those,' she said, pointing at the kamikazes.

I noticed that she'd only ordered one drink. 'Who are you here with?'

'Just me,' she said. 'I came to Europe for the summer, after my junior year in college.'

'That's brave.'

'Really? Should I be scared here, all on my own? I'm a grown-up. Besides, all my friends had summer jobs and I really wanted to do some travelling. It might be the last chance I get. And it was just something I needed to do.'

The barman put the drinks on the bar and she handed over a

credit card. 'You want to join me and my friends?' I said. 'I can't promise much in the way of wit and sparkling conversation, but it's probably better – just about – than being alone.'

'Sure,' she said. 'Why not? I'm Sherry, by the way.'

When I came back to the table with Sherry, Jerry and Paul nearly fell off their chairs. She had that effect on people. Without blowing my own trumpet, I'd been out with some good-looking girls, but she was something else.

I don't believe in love at first sight. I don't think it's possible. Love is too complicated. It requires knowledge, and trust and a sense of security. However, you can feel something at first sight, something more than lust or interest or whatever else people talk about. For us it was the feeling that we somehow fitted together; we were comfortable with each other immediately. It just felt right.

Very soon after we sat at the table, we were lost in each other. I don't really remember what happened – where Paul and Jerry went, what we talked about, what we drank. All I can remember is the sensation of being at opposite ends of a thick elastic band, stretched taut between us and pulling us closer and closer. We kept getting caught in these long, visual embraces, in which we would start looking at each other's eyes and then be unable to stop.

Sometime in the small hours, Sherry yawned.

'I have to get back.'

'I'll walk you home.'

'It's okay. I can manage.'

I shook my head. 'No way. I'll come with you. Just drop you off, then I'll be on my way.'

We left, walking side by side, close enough so that our hands periodically brushed against each other. Each time they did, the touch was thrilling, but I didn't dare take her hand; I didn't want to crush whatever we might have with a clumsy or misplaced gesture, however innocent holding someone's hand might have been. It was hardly putting the moves on, but it was still a risk I didn't want to take.

Eventually, though, our fingers caught, and like a fly in a web, they stuck and then laced themselves together. It was awkward, that first physical contact; even though it was only a touch of our hands it was the first step along a path, and it was a step we had taken together. It made us, in a small way, a couple.

We both ignored it, however, and carried on talking; we'd been jabbering non-stop since we left the bar, spilling out our stories to each other in a rush to deepen our relationship as fast as we could.

She was staying in a hotel a little out of town. It was smart, much better than ours, and we stopped outside the revolving doors.

She faced me and took my other hand in hers.

'Thanks,' she said. 'That was fun.'

'It was. You're a cracking lass.'

She tilted her head. 'Is that a good thing?'

'It is. It's about as good as it gets in the north of England.'

She couldn't stop herself grinning at the compliment. I took advantage of the pause. 'Do you want to meet up again?'

'Sure. When were you thinking?'

'Tomorrow?' I said, then blushed at how keen it sounded. I decided to joke it away. 'Or maybe sooner?'

She bit her top lip. 'Tomorrow it is.'

'I'll meet you here. Midday?'

She looked at her watch. It was four in the morning. 'Will you be up?'

I'd be up all right. In any case, I didn't think I was going to be able to sleep.

'Midday,' I said and stepped backwards. For once I'd decided to be a gentleman. That was what American girls expected from us Brits, right? I was rewarded by a flicker of disappointment on her face.

'Midday,' she said, and stepped inside the revolving doors.

At midday the next day I was outside her hotel, standing in the shade of a bus stop opposite and swigging from a bottle of water to clear my head. Each time the revolving door started to move I got ready to wave and smile and call to her; each time it was not Sherry I slumped back against the wall.

By twenty past midday I had given up hope. It wasn't like she had far to go; she could hardly have got lost in the lift on the way down to the hotel's front door. For a second I considered going in to ask for her, but I decided not to bother. What was I thinking? There was nothing special between us. I was just getting carried away because a beautiful girl had spent the evening with me. She probably regretted it and was looking out of her window waiting for me to bugger off. It was ridiculous, and when I told Paul and Jerry I was pretty sure they'd let me know just *how* ridiculous.

I decided to take a bus back to town. I didn't fancy the walk in the heat, especially not with a hangover. However, I didn't want to wait here too long, in case she *did* come out. She'd think I was a stalker. If the bus was more than ten minutes away, I'd walk. As it was, there was one in five minutes, which was perfect.

A few minutes later, the dusty green bus came into view, the heat haze shimmering above it. I watched it approach, my heart sinking. This really was it.

Someone tapped me on the shoulder.

'You're not leaving, are you?'

A woman's voice. An American voice. I turned round and there she was.

'I'm sorry,' Sherry said. 'I thought we could go to the beach so I went to get some food for a picnic, but it took longer than I thought.'

She was wearing a black beach dress, which showed off her long, tanned legs. Despite little sleep and no make up, she looked even better than the night before.

Sometimes life hinges on tiny moments. Had the bus been due in twenty minutes, I would already have set off and the rest of my life would have been different.

'Don't worry about it,' I said. 'So we're having a picnic?'

'Hey,' Sherry said. 'Wake up.'

I was face down on my beach towel; she had her hand on my shoulder and was gently pressing it. I kept my eyes closed. I was enjoying the feel of her hand on me.

'Hey,' she said. 'Come on. It's time to go. I'm hungry.'

We'd been on the beach all afternoon and the sun and sleepless night had caught up with me.

I opened one eye and looked up at her. 'How long have I been asleep?'

'A couple of hours. You lay down and passed out after we got off the pedalo.'

Two hours. I was sad and glad at the same time. Sad, because I'd wasted two hours I could have spent with her, and even at that early stage I knew time was precious, and glad because I needed some sleep.

'Did I snore?' I said.

She shook her head. 'No. But you drooled. And you tried to roll on me.'

'I did *not*.' I hoped I had. I liked the thought of rolling on her and if I had, it didn't seem she minded. 'You want to go and eat?'

'What about your friends?'

What about them? They'd seen Sherry; they'd understand why I'd ditched them. 'They'll be okay.'

'I feel bad, taking you away from them.'

Don't, I wanted to shout. *I want you to take me away from them.*
'Honestly, they'll be fine.'

'Why don't we meet later? I'll go to my hotel, eat, get some rest,
get cleaned up, and I'll see you after that.'

I was reluctant to let her go, in case she didn't come back. 'Okay.
Same bar as last night? What time?'

'Ten p.m.?'

Ten p.m.? I looked at my watch. That was four hours away.
That was almost next year. 'Don't want to make it nine?' I said.

She rolled her eyes. 'Ten,' she said. 'I need my beauty sleep.'

'Fuck me,' Paul said. 'She is way out of your league.'

'You're just jealous,' I said, although if pushed I would have
agreed.

'Fucking right I'm jealous.'

Sherry was at the bar, buying us a round of drinks. She was
wearing a patterned silk dress that stopped halfway up her thigh.
Every male head – and some female – had watched her leave our
table, and walk to the bar. It was finally her round. We'd been there
a few hours, and after we'd refused her endless attempts to pay,
she'd insisted.

'She's got company,' Paul said.

A tall, dark-haired guy was talking to her. From the angle we
were sitting at I could see her face: she was smiling a half-smile,
her head cocked as though listening. When he had finished speaking, she shook her head.

'Some numbnuts asking her out,' I said.

'Occupational hazard of having a fit girlfriend,' Jerry said.

Paul laughed. 'Not that you'd know.'

I was only half-listening. I was watching Sherry; the guy was still
there and still talking, only this time she wasn't smiling. There was

something aggressive in his posture and when she turned to leave the bar, he blocked her path.

'Shit,' I said, and got to my feet. 'I'd better sort this out.' A few strides later I had my hand on Sherry's arm.

'Hey,' I said. 'What's up? Want a hand with those drinks?'

She looked at me with some relief. 'Thanks. I was just looking for you.'

The guy moved so that he was in front of me. 'Who the bloody hell are you?' he said. He was over six foot, a good few inches taller than me, and well built, but whatever muscle he had once had was now turning to fat. His eyes were glazed with drink.

'Come on, Sherry,' I said. 'Let's sit down.'

He shuffled forwards. 'I asked you a question.' He had a nasal, public school accent, which I identified with snobbery and arrogance; like a lot of northerners, I had a chip on my shoulder about class. He and I were not going to be friends. He winked at Sherry. 'You want to find yourself a real Englishman. Remind you of what you're missing over there in the colonies.'

'Let's go,' I said. 'Leave this dipshit to use his charm on some other lucky girl.'

'*Leave this dipshit to yoose 'is charm on some other loocky girl,*' he said, mimicking my accent. 'You fucking northern oik.' He stared at Sherry, his eyes running up and down her body. 'Is she really with you or are you doing that thing where you go and "rescue" a girl so she owes you a favour? Did you see it on *Coronation Street*?'

It was all I could do to keep my hands by my side. 'Enjoy your evening,' I said, and put my arm around Sherry's waist. 'Most of the hotels have the porn on channel nine. But then you probably know that already. See you later, flower.'

I guided her back to the table and we sat down. She was pale, and shaking. A few drinks later, Paul and Jerry stood up. We'd arranged it beforehand; around midnight they'd go off somewhere else and leave us alone. I think they were glad; having Sherry around was guaranteed to put off any women they tried it on with. 'We're off down the strip,' Jerry said. 'See you later.'

We watched them leave. 'Drink?' I said. 'Or try somewhere else?'

Sherry put her hand on mine. 'How about a drink somewhere else? I've had enough of this place.' She was still subdued for a while; I guessed it was something to do with the incident by the bar.

'Sure.'

'I'll just go to the bathroom,' she said.

The bathrooms were in the far corner of the room. To get there you skirted the dance floor, which had a concrete pillar at each corner. As she walked past the first pillar, I saw her stop, then shake her head. She was talking to someone, who was hidden from my view by the pillar.

I knew who it was, though.

I jumped up and pushed my way through the crowd. The guy from before was standing on the far side of the pillar, his hand gripping her bicep. He was grinning and very drunk and with at least one other person, a similar looking guy who was leaning against the pillar and smiling. Sherry was trying to free her arm from his grip but she was trapped. She was pale, terrified.

As I approached, the guy reached behind Sherry with his other hand and pulled up the back of her dress.

In the second before she snapped his hand away, I saw her buttocks, white against the tan of her legs, and her black thong. I couldn't believe that this guy thought he could do this. I was shaking with rage.

'Ow,' she was shouting, as I got there. 'Let go! You're hurting my arm!'

He saw me arrive and released his grip. 'Here he is,' he said.

'Your knight in shining armour.' His friend stood up next to him. 'Not so cocky now there's two of us, are you?'

I sized them up. They were bigger than me – taller, at least – but they were not in any kind of shape, and, more to the point, they were soft. I'm no Rambo, but in the course of a career as a professional rugby player you learn how to handle yourself, and these two were not up to much at all.

I wasn't thinking that, though. I was just fucking murderous.

Without speaking, I grabbed the first guy – the one from the bar – by the back of his head and yanked his face towards the floor. With my right hand I threw an uppercut, which smashed into his cheek. It was a strange sensation; normally when you hit someone they see it coming and get out of the way, or lift their hands to protect themselves. He did neither. Either he was too drunk, or he didn't expect to get hit. Whichever, there was a loud crack and something in his face broke. He slumped to the floor.

I glanced at his friend, who looked shocked and terrified. My anger fell away. These two might have been dickheads, and they might have been asking for it, but if the police showed up I was in trouble, even in a Spanish holiday resort. We had to get out of there. I wished I'd just grabbed Sherry and walked away, but then walking away has never been my strong point.

'Come on,' I said, and took Sherry's hand. 'Let's go.' Once we were outside we'd just be faces in the crowd, and as long as we didn't go back to that bar, I thought we'd be okay.

She didn't move; she had a lost look on her face that made her look like a little girl, and tears were streaming down her face.

'Come on,' I said. 'It's not that bad. We need to go.'

She gulped, and nodded, and let me pull her through the small crowd that had gathered. Outside, I put my arm round her, my hand pulling her head onto my shoulder, and we mingled into the crowd.

*

When we got to her hotel she had stopped crying, but she was silent and withdrawn. We sat on a sofa in the bar and ordered gin and tonics.

'I'm sorry,' I said. 'I shouldn't have done that. I just lost my temper.' I felt sick; I couldn't believe that I'd hit that bloke in front of her. It was out of character for me, but I didn't know how to make her see that.

She didn't reply.

'Listen. That's not like me. It's just – what he did – it just got to me.' I tried to catch her eye. 'I'm not some kind of thug, I promise.'

She closed her eyes. The tears had started again. I could see why she was shaken up but this seemed a bit of an over-reaction. 'Hold me,' she said. 'Please.'

I shifted closer to her and put my arm around her shoulder, pulling her close. She didn't sound angry; it was worse. She sounded hollow. 'Are you okay?'

She didn't speak for a long time. When she did, she sounded much calmer. 'I'm fine,' she said. 'I was just shaken up.' She shuddered. 'The way he grabbed me. It was awful. And I don't think you're a thug. I'm glad you hit him.' Her voice hardened. 'He deserved it.'

Thank God for that. 'Well,' I said, feeling like John Wayne. 'You're safe now.'

She looked up at me. 'Let's get out of here,' she said. 'Let's go somewhere else.'

'You want to go back out to the bars?' I nodded at the clock above the door. 'It's gone two.'

'No,' she said. 'Somewhere else entirely. I don't want to see that guy again. Let's go to Paris. I have a friend who has an apartment there. It's empty in summer. All of Paris is.'

I hesitated. 'Isn't it a bit much, to leave town because of a scuffle? And I don't think you'll see him again' – it felt good to say it – 'unless you go to the hospital.'

'I don't care. Just knowing he – or his friends – are around makes me feel sick. I want to go. This place is ruined now. I don't feel safe.'

It was extreme, and I had to admit I liked the idea, but it was never going to happen. For one thing, there were my friends, for another, I'd paid for the holiday and I didn't have the cash to just abandon it and go to Paris.

'I'll pay,' she said. 'We can take the train.'

'No. I can't let you pay.' I shook my head. 'I hardly know you. No way.'

'Please. I want to go, and I want you to come with me. You can pay me back. Please. It'll be fun.'

We got the overnight train the next evening. A second class sleeper cabin for two, in which we sat up drinking and talking until we passed out, huddled together on the bottom bed.

Paris in Summer

Paris in summer is strange; at least, so said the guidebook. I had no idea whether it was always like this or not, having never been. Apparently most of the city decamped to the beaches of the south for the summer months. Whatever; it was certainly quiet.

Not that it mattered to Sherry and me. We spent our days walking the city, stopping in at quiet cafes for bitter coffees and glasses of wine and bowls of soup and rare steaks. I spent a lot of the time wondering when and how I could make a move; given that we spent twenty-four hours a day in each other's company, I was hoping for an opportunity, but somehow it didn't come. Partly it was because we were always busy; partly because Sherry never let me get close. Holding hands that first night was as far as it had gone.

By the fourth night, I was starting to get worried. She was probably just a good girl, but it was driving me crazy.

It was around nine p.m. and we were sitting outside a restaurant by the River Seine, our chairs turned out to face the water. Sherry was wearing a summer dress and as she reached for her wine her bare knee brushed mine. She left it there, her skin hot against mine. At that moment I was happy. There was no past and no future and I realized I was falling in love with her.

The thing with falling in love, at least in the way we did, is that it blocks out the rest of the world. It's a kind of madness, an obsessive, compulsive desire to be with one person and one person alone. I had never felt this way before, never felt that the simple fact of being with someone, whatever the other circumstances we were in, was enough to make me happy.

The feeling bubbled over.

'I think I love you,' I said. Did I blurt it out because we were in Paris? Because it was a holiday romance and going nowhere? Had we been back home in a pub would I have blurted that out? I don't know. All I know is that she looked at me for a long time, then smiled.

'Me too,' she said.

And there it was. We were in love. It was joyous, absurd, intoxicating.

I laughed. 'We've never even kissed!'

'Do you want to?'

'I didn't mean that,' I said. 'I was just saying—'

She shushed me, and put her hand on my cheek. We kissed, a long, deep kiss. I was lost in it, simultaneously disbelieving that it was happening and noticing the details: the softness of her lips, the taste of wine and garlic, the feel of her cheeks brushing my nose. Sometimes a first kiss is an awkward stumbling for a rhythm that works; this was instinct and it was perfect.

The waiter coughed. 'L'addition, monsieur?'

We broke apart and I nodded.

The sex was everything the kiss had promised; the first time a little hesitant, and then incessant. We barely left the apartment. It was as though we were trying to work it out of our system, as though the knowledge that this was a holiday fling which had an end-by date gave everything we did an added intensity. Each time we had sex, each time we showered, each time we shared a meal was one of a numbered series that was coming to an end. We didn't have the luxury of the rest of our lives to fill with each other. We only had the rest of that holiday.

We fell into an easy routine. We'd known each other days, but it already felt like – I wouldn't say a lifetime, but much, much longer. Sometimes it's like that. You meet someone and it's all so natural between you.

Anyway, every morning I went out to get breakfast – a pretty late breakfast, by the time we'd woken up and had sex, but just about early enough not to be lunch, which in any case we skipped on the way to *steak frites* and red wine for dinner – and brought it back. Sherry made fresh coffee and we sat, often naked, at the small, ornate dining table and ate.

The fifth day after we arrived the lift wasn't working, so I traipsed up the narrow stairs. The lift was a noisy, clanking thing with one of those grille-type doors that you slide back. There was no way of making a silent approach in the lift; if the clanking didn't give you away, the rattle of the door as you pulled it back would.

But I wasn't in the lift, and as I opened the apartment door I heard Sherry's voice.

She was agitated, that much was obvious, and at first I thought there was someone in the flat with her, until I realized that it was only her voice. I was uncomfortable listening in – for all the ease we had in each other's company, it reminded me that we were basically still strangers – and so I stood in the doorway, breathing in the smell of fresh coffee, uncertain what I should do.

Her voice rose.

'No!' she said. 'I'm not ungrateful! I—'

Whoever was on the other end of the line must have interrupted as she was quiet for a minute. Ungrateful for what, I wondered? Was she speaking to the owner of the flat? It seemed very emotional for something like that.

45

'Daniel!' she said. 'Drop it, please! Just—'

There was another pause, then she spoke again.

'I'm fine! I promise. I just came to Paris for a change of scene. You don't need to worry about me—'

Another pause, short this time. When she spoke, she sounded calmer.

'I know you do, and I'm lucky to have a friend like you, but there's nothing to worry about, honestly.'

This was weird. I put the paper bag from the bakery down, making sure it rustled and banged the door shut behind me.

'Hi,' I said. 'I'm back.'

She fell silent. I opened the door to the bedroom; she was sitting in her underwear on the bed, the phone to her ear, her mouth and eyes open wide enough that I could see I'd surprised her.

'I've got to go,' she said, into the phone. 'Bye.' She listened. 'It's no one. A friend. I've got to go.'

She put the phone down.

'Who was that?' I said.

'A university friend,' she said. 'Worried because I'm in Europe on my own.' She rolled her eyes. 'Nothing, really.' She stood up and kissed me, her tongue flicking into my mouth. 'I missed you.'

'I was only gone twenty minutes.' I wanted to ask her more about the mystery phone call, but the movement of her hand under the waistband of my shorts distracted me, and after all, it wasn't really any of my business, was it?

'That's long enough,' she said. 'I don't like you to be gone at all.'

'Then I'll stay,' I said, and pulled her onto the bed.

Separation

The day before I left we were lying on the bed. Sherry had her back against the headboard, hugging her knees to her chest. I was lying on my back, my forehead against her hip.

'So what will you do when you get home?' she said.

Home. My two-up two-down terraced house in Stockton Heath. The thought of arriving there alone, opening the door to a pile of junk mail, going to the shop to buy stuff to make a meal, filled me with dread. How could I go back to that after this? After this moment in the sun?

'Work. You know. The usual.'

'Will you see Paul and Jerry?'

'Yeah, probably.' They'd be back. Perhaps I'd meet them for a pint and tell them about Sherry.

She stroked my hair. 'Don't be sad,' she said. 'It'll be okay.'

'Why don't I come with you?' I said. 'To the US.' It came from nowhere; I hadn't been aware of the thought before the words were out of my mouth.

'What about your job?'

My job. Life at the hospital helping geriatrics recover from hip operations. Worthy, and admirable, of course. But it just seemed so dull after the last few days.

'I'll pack it in.'

She laughed. 'Could you do that?'

'I could.' I hesitated. Could I? I had a mortgage to pay, a life to live. Could I just leave it? A week ago it would have seemed unthinkable, but now we were discussing it, and if we were discussing it, it must be possible, right? 'It wouldn't be easy, but I could.'

'I don't want you to make sacrifices for me.'

'I wouldn't be. And I can always come back.' I was about to say *if it doesn't work out*, but I stopped myself. I didn't want the words to be said. I didn't want to acknowledge that we might ever break apart. 'And whatever I was leaving behind, I'd be getting something better.' I said. 'You. I don't want to lose you. I love you.'

She looked at her fingernails. I was suddenly conscious that I was naked, and baring my soul. I felt vulnerable. I pulled the sheet up over my hips.

'I love you too,' she said. 'I didn't want to. It makes things awkward, but I do.' She slid down the bed and put her head on my shoulder. 'I love you, Tom, and it scares me. I don't know what we should do.'

'Then let's stay together,' I said.

'How? You'll be in England, I'll be at college in America.'

With lots of handsome American college boys, I thought, all trying to get into your pants.

'I don't know. But first comes the decision. If we decide to stay together then we can figure out how afterwards.' I propped myself up on my elbow. 'So should we? Stay together?'

'Yes,' she said. 'Yes.'

'Okay. So you have one year to go in college?'

'I'm done May next year.'

'That's ten months. It's not that bad.' She looked at me like I was mad. We struggled with ten minutes apart; ten months seemed ridiculous. 'Let's think about it,' I said. 'Let's think about the details.'

'Fuck the details.' Sherry rolled on top of me. 'I just want you. That's all.'

I slid inside her, my eyes closed.

Afterwards we made a plan.

'What will you do when you finish college?'

'Graduate school. Social work, maybe.'

I got the impression she wasn't planning to qualify as a social worker because she felt a calling to help others, but because she couldn't think of anything else to do.

'And you'll be twenty-three when you finish?'

She nodded. 'I took a year out. I did my freshman and sophomore years in Boston, but I transferred.'

'Didn't like it?'

She looked at me in silence. Her eyes were very, very dark, but they seemed to darken further still. People say the eyes are the window to the soul, but if that's true, it's only true in the sense that a window in a house looks into only one room. You can see inside the house, but there's a lot more going on in there than that one window lets you see.

'It wasn't for me,' she said, eventually.

'Did you do anything good on the year out? Travel?'

'Worked a bit. Drove cross-country. The usual US things.'

Clearly she didn't want to talk about it; that was fine. She didn't have to. Whatever she'd done, there was no reason she had to share that stuff with me. I certainly wouldn't have wanted her to know all the embarrassing shit I'd done.

'Look,' I said. 'I don't know how to do this. I just know that I want to be with you. Why don't you come and live with me? We'll figure it out.'

She shook her head. 'I have to finish college,' she said. 'I have to.' She kissed me. 'I'll come and visit you at Christmas and at Easter. I'll be done in May, then we can see what's what.'

She was more sensible than me. I would have dropped everything and moved to Bali if she'd suggested it, but I could tell this was the best I was going to get.

'All right,' I said. 'Let's see how we go.'

We moved to the US at the end of her senior year, having tied the knot in a civil ceremony so that I could get a visa.

Her mother, Lauren, tried hard to hide her disappointment, but it was obvious. I didn't blame her – her daughter was fresh out of college and marrying some British guy – and I left it to Sherry to do the convincing. Her father had died when she was in high school, so at least there wasn't a paternal obstacle for me to overcome, but the hostility from her mother still made me uncomfortable.

Likewise, my parents were less than impressed, and I had some difficulty convincing them it was a good idea. My track record with girlfriends was mixed, to say the least, and had been characterized to that point by volume, rather than by the longevity of any particular girlfriend. Reasonably enough, they assumed that Sherry would be the same, so when I told them we were marrying so I could move to Barrow, Maine, they were a little taken aback.

'I'm sure she's a lovely girl,' Mum said. 'But you don't want to be hasty. You do like to chop and change your girlfriends.'

'I used to.' There wasn't much else I could say. I could hardly deny it.

'And she's quite a bit younger than you. You don't think she's rushing into it?'

I shrugged. 'It's up to her. And – I don't know, Mum, it's just different.'

Dad coughed. 'Well,' he said. 'I've been thinking about this, and there's a question I'd like to ask.'

If it seemed an effort for him to talk it was probably because it was. Dad *never* said anything. I mean it: he never spoke. When I was a kid days, weeks could go by without him saying anything. He got up, made his tea and toast in silence, left for work, came home, ate his dinner, read the paper in the bath with a cigarette (which he did every night), then went to bed. My brother, Jonathan, and I used to lay bets on how long it would be before we heard him speak. Jonathan once asked Mum if he spoke at work. She said he did, and I suppose he must have done, but we couldn't picture it.

'Go on,' I said, wondering what wisdom, what insight from his own marriage, he was finally going to share

He sipped his cup of tea. 'Are you sure?'

That was it. That was the best he could do. But then, I suppose I'm more like my dad than I think, because, instead of giving the answer I wanted to give – no, I'm not, I'll be leaving my home, my job, my country, my friends and my family and who knows what'll happen, but I can't face the thought of life without Sherry, it's just unbearable, so what choice do I have – I just nodded and said what he would have said.

'Pretty much.'

And so it was done.

A Week's a Long Time

Since becoming a father I've become a crier. Before, I rarely, if ever, cried. I suppose I must have done, but I can't remember it, excepting a few outbursts of teenage angst. I wasn't being tough; it was simply that nothing seemed to warrant tears. I could see how, in an objective sense, a news story or a movie or a book was sad, but they just didn't affect me. They had no way of getting a hook into me, of pulling me in. Likewise, I had no way of really comprehending the emotions involved.

All that changed when Peggy was born. For a while, in the first few years of her life, I was forever crying, or at least choking up. If I saw a father and child enjoying a tender moment in the park, my throat would constrict, if I looked at my sleeping daughter, her mouth wide open and her arms and legs flopped through the bars of her cot, tears would fill my eyes; heaven forbid, I should see or read or watch something actually sad, like the death of a child. Just the thought that someone, somewhere had lost a child, that that kind of thing was possible, that it might happen to me . . . I'd have to stop reading or look away. On a flight once I watched some awful movie in which a father and son get caught up in a war against zombie aliens, or something like that, and the father gets killed, leaving the son howling over his body. The acting was terrible, the script melodramatic, the film risible, but I had tears running down my face. That poor boy was going to have to live *without his father*. The flight attendants must have wondered what the hell was going on, but the answer was simple – however terrible the movie, that scene tapped into the love a father has for his child, which is endless and frightening.

Of course, it makes you rethink your relationship with your own parents. Before I left the UK I never really considered that they would miss me. Just as I objectively understood why a book or movie was sad but didn't really feel it, I knew they probably missed me a bit, but I didn't really get how much. It was only when Peggy came along – when it was too late – that I understood. I also understood something else: grandparents don't differentiate between their children and their grandchildren, so however much they missed me, they missed Peggy just as much.

And now my mother was ill.

I'd always dreaded this moment. There was the risk I was going to lose a parent, which was bad enough in itself, but there was also the knowledge that, once she was gone, the sacrifice I had made in coming here was going to claim its prize. Because once she was gone, I could never make up for the last few years, in which she had hardly seen me or her granddaughter.

Of course, she would have said – and she would have meant it – that she wanted me to be happy, and she knew that Sherry made me happy. If the price of my happiness was her happiness, then she would have paid it. I knew that, being a parent myself, but also knew that she would have preferred it if I'd been happy *near her*. It was human nature, and I had no doubt that, all along, she harboured a hope that, however unlikely, I and Sherry and Peggy might move to be close to her. When – if – she died, that door would be shut, I would have to live with the guilt.

Which is why, while I could, I wanted to do all I could for her.

We sat on the couch alone. After the phone call everyone had left. Peggy had gone to Sherry's mum's so we could talk it through. We were eating the rest of her mother's strawberry pie. It was as delicious as ever; the memory of what we'd been doing when it was delivered made it more delicious still.

'How's your dad?' she said.

'Upset. He didn't say so, but I could tell. That's the worst thing about it. If he's upset it must be bad.'

'Want to talk about it?'

'Not really. We have to go and visit. We can book tickets later.' I poured a glass of wine. I felt like I needed it. It had been a draining day. 'By the way, I remembered something earlier, something from when we were in Paris.'

'Oh? Sounds intriguing.'

'Do you remember someone phoning, when I was out getting breakfast one morning?'

I thought she stiffened, just a little, but I couldn't be sure. It could have been my imagination.

'No,' she said. 'Not really.'

'I came back and you were on the phone. I heard you talking when I was in the corridor—'

'You were eavesdropping?' There was definitely an edge in her voice.

'No. I came in, heard you speaking and shouted out to let you know I was back. I was careful *not* to eavesdrop. Anyway' – I stroked her hair: I didn't want her to think I was angry about this – 'I think I heard you call the person you were speaking to

"Daniel". And then today I met Daniel and wondered whether it was the same person.'

'It could have been,' she said. 'We were still quite close friends back then.'

'So was it him?'

She thought for a moment. 'I don't know, Tom. I don't remember. It was a long time ago. But it could have been.'

I dropped it. She was right – it was a long time ago, and so what if it was Daniel? I didn't want to have an argument, and besides, we had more important things to discuss.

'We should be able to get flights tomorrow,' I said. 'Go for two weeks, maybe more. I'm sure work will give me time off.'

Sherry did this side to side thing with her head. She always did it when she was about to disagree. 'You should stay. Peggy and I need to be back after a week. School starts next Monday. It's important Peggy's there.'

'It's important she's in England. This could be her last chance to see her grandmother.'

'I'm not saying she – we – shouldn't go. I'm just saying she needs to be back in time for school to start. It's the first week of real school. It's important to be there. Friendships are made, groups are formed. It's not good to miss out on all that.'

'She's five. She'll be okay.'

'The friendships I made when I was five have lasted all my life. Lisa, Mike, Daniel. They're important, Tom.'

I tensed. Whatever the rights and wrongs of this I felt she shouldn't be making it more difficult than it already was. 'Look,' I said. 'I'd rather get over there and play it by ear.'

'A week is plenty, Tom.' Sherry cuddled up to me and stroked my chest. 'I know this is hard for you and I'm not trying to be difficult, but I think it's reasonable for Peggy to spend a week there and then come back in time for school to start. She can do both things.'

'A week's nothing. Mum is dying, Sherry. This is the last chance we'll have to see her.'

'*You* should stay. As long as it takes.'

'So should Peggy. You go home after a week. I'll stay on with her. This is more important than school.'

She shook her head, her copper hair brushing my cheek. 'She can do both. Besides, the school doesn't like pupils to miss too much.'

This was becoming an argument. I knew because I was about to repeat myself. 'She's five, Sherry. She'll be okay.' I pulled back from her. 'What's she going to miss? Mud pie making? Nose picking 101?'

'There's no need to be sarcastic. They do a lot at that age. That's why we sent her there, remember?'

That's why you sent her there, I thought. Peggy went to an expensive and exclusive Catholic junior school – St. Mark's – that promised to prepare her for the best academies and universities. She had started the year before in pre-school and was already spouting platitudes about the Baby Jesus while she prayed before bed.

I shook my head. 'She can miss it.'

'I don't want her to. I know how important it is that she sees your mum, but she can do both. Don't you see that?'

'No.' There was a long silence. We both knew we were at the crossroads of a major argument; we both also knew that this was not the time. There was enough to deal with without us fighting.

'Look,' I said. 'Let's just go. We'll get open return tickets and we can decide when we get there.'

Sherry kissed me. 'Okay. Let's not fight. I'll book tickets tomorrow.'

But we should have resolved it, there and then. In a marriage it's rare that you can't adjust to whatever agreement you make with your partner. It's when that agreement is unclear that the problems arise.

Being Fine

There's something about airports that sucks the life out of me. They remind me, in a way, of the casinos in Las Vegas, unchanging night or day, their forced cheeriness and bright lights designed to cut you off from the outside world as you make the transit from wherever you are to your destination. The whole experience takes your mind off the bizarreness of what you are doing: you enter and sit in a metal capsule, distract yourself for eight hours, then climb out *three thousand* miles away. To earlier generations this would look like teleporting does to us: a journey of unimaginable speed.

We arrived at my parents' house late, having driven up to Warrington from Heathrow. The next morning I went downstairs. The house smelled of old people, that slightly stale, not quite unpleasant smell of inaction. It was the first time I had noticed it. A lot had changed in the years since I was last here. The smell reminded me of how long it had been – since Peggy was one – and I felt the needling pinch of guilt.

Dad was in his sagging brown armchair by the window, reading the *Daily Mail*.

'Morning,' I said.

He lowered the paper and nodded. His eyes were surrounded

by dark circles, and had a filmy look I had not seen before. I wondered whether it was old age or sadness.

'Tea?' I started to fill the kettle.

'Just had one,' he said. 'But I'll have a refill.'

There were only two teabags left, and not much more than a splash of milk. Men of my father's generation rarely even entered the kitchen, never mind stocking it with groceries or, heaven forbid, cooking. I cooked a lot, as did most of my friends, but it was a new thing for men, certainly in the north of England. For the first time I wondered what he would do if Mum died. Once, when I was about sixteen, and old enough to be trusted to my father's care, she'd gone on a rare – I think the only ever – holiday with friends. She'd made lasagnes and pies and all sorts of food, frozen them and left instructions for how to heat them up. Dad took me to the pub or chip shop every night (where we ate in silence), and, the day before she came home, he threw the food she'd made out and told me to tell Mum that we'd eaten it. Cooking – even heating up frozen food – was a mystery to him, and he relied on Mum for everything. But he could hardly eat three meals a day in the pub. I didn't know what he would do.

I made the tea, handed him a mug and sat on the couch.

'So how's Mum?'

'Not so clever.'

'And you?'

'Fine.'

I might as well not have asked. He could have had two broken legs and been bleeding from his ears and he would have answered the same way. If you'd asked my dad whether there had ever been a time in his life when he was anything other than fine, he would have thought for a second, then shaken his head.

'Sherry and Peggy are still sleeping,' I said. 'Jet lag.'

He nodded.

'You know, they'll probably be asleep for a while. Maybe we should go and see Mum? I'll leave a note.'

He nodded again, and then smiled. 'She'd like that.'

Mum was asleep when we arrived. I settled my father in the chair by the bed and studied her.

I was shocked by what I saw. Illness had rarely intruded into my life. The occasional cold, a bout of flu, a trip to the doctor with Peggy, a session with the club doctor for a rugby injury: this was the extent of my interaction with the medical community. Peggy's birth was the last time I had spent any significant time in a hospital, and that didn't feel like illness.

So I was not prepared for the changes in my mother. She had always been robust, with a strong build and a heavy frame, which, as she had got older, had carried a bit of extra weight. Her hair was thick, and she kept it neat; getting her hair done was her one concession to vanity.

Now, though, it was lank and plastered to her head, revealing the bumps and ridges of her skull. She had lost a lot of weight on her face and the skin was pale and paper thin, the blue veins visible underneath, which gave the impression that she was fading away, already see-through. It wasn't that she was hardly there; she was hardly her. Illness was stripping her bare.

I looked at Dad. His eyes were fixed on her, slightly narrowed, as though not sure what he was looking at. He blinked, and gulped, and I realized that he was near tears. That was as shocking as anything else.

'Mr Harding?'

Both Dad and I turned round.

'I'm Doctor Singh.'

I shook his hand. 'I'm her son. Tom Harding.'

'Pleased to make your acquaintance.' He looked in his late fifties

and spoke the slightly antiquated English of many of the immigrants from the sub-continent of his generation.

'How is she? Will she recover?'

He wagged his head left and right in a so-so gesture.

'She is quite poorly.' He tapped the pen in his top pocket.
'It is likely she will suffer some physical disabilities as a result of
the stroke. Perhaps trouble walking. Some speech problems,
but with physical and speech therapy she should make some
progress.' He looked at me, fixing his eyes on mine. It was what
doctors often did when they were going to give you bad news.
They made sure they looked you in the eye, rather than looking
away. If they couldn't deal with it head on, what hope did you
have? 'But she will not recover fully. And there is a chance of
another stroke.'

'How long? Dad said a year, maybe.'

A year, maybe.

He nodded. 'It's impossible to tell. Maybe even more than a
year.'

My jaw started to quiver. I'd known this was the case, but confronting it was much harder than I'd expected. I looked out of the
window and clamped my teeth together. I didn't want my dad to
see me cry. Stupid, I know. But still, I didn't want him to see.

It's always strange talking to doctors. They say such big things
– *your mother has a year to live, your son is brain-damaged, your
daughter has leukaemia* – in such a matter-of-fact way. I suppose
they're trained to do so. I wondered whether Dr Singh ever got
used to it.

'Will she be able to come home?' I said. *Come home*, I'd said,
not *go home*. As though I still lived there, as though it was still
home for me. In a way it was; in a way your childhood home is
always your home.

'In a few weeks,' Dr Singh said. 'We try to situate patients in the

61

home environment as much as possible these days. It helps with their recovery to have their loved ones around.'

Except Mum wouldn't have hers – at least not all of them – because I and Peggy and Sherry would be in the US.

The doctor backed into the doorway. 'If you have any questions or concerns, please, don't hesitate.'

I picked up Mum's hand and squeezed it gently. Her fingers were limp and cool. As I raised it to my lips, my phone rang.

The noise was shatteringly loud in the quiet room. I snatched it from my pocket and answered.

It was Sherry. 'Hi, darling. Are you with your mum?'

'Yes. I thought I'd come while you two were still in bed.'

'How's she doing?'

'Okay. She's sleeping.'

Mum coughed. 'Not any more,' she said, and smiled at me. 'The phone woke me. Hello, love. Thanks for coming.'

Her eyes were open, and in contrast to the rest of her, were bright and alert. I thought it was a mixed blessing. Being aware of your situation is not always a good thing.

'Mum. I'm sorry to wake you.' I bent over and kissed her. 'It's Sherry.'

'Say hello from me,' she said. 'Is Peggy there?'

I spoke into the phone. 'Sherry? Mum's awake. Is Peggy up?'

Sherry called Peggy and told her it was her grandma on the phone. I put it on speaker and held it near my mum's head.

'Hello Grammy Margaret,' Peggy said. 'How are you? I went on an airplane. A big one.'

My mother's smile wiped away, for an instant, all the traces of illness on her face. I had to look away, my guilt at the sight of the joy she felt at the simple sound of her granddaughter's voice too great to bear.

'That sounds lovely,' she said. 'Did they let you have a drive of the plane?'

'Yes,' Peggy lied. 'I drove all the way here.'

'Really, love?' Mum said. 'Almost drove or really drove?'

Peggy hesitated. 'Almost drove. I'm coming to see you, Grammy. That's why I went on the airplane.'

'That's wonderful,' Mum said. 'You come as soon as you can. I can't wait to see you.'

I put the phone to my ear. 'Are you guys ready?'

'We can be,' Sherry said. 'Ten minutes?'

'Okay. I'll call a cab to come and get you.'

'Why are you in the hospital, Grandma?' Peggy said. She was perched on the edge of the bed, swinging her legs back and forth. Mum was holding a photo frame we'd brought with a picture of grinning Peggy in her dance uniform.

'I'm not feeling too well,' she said. 'So the doctors want me to be in here where they can keep an eye on me.'

'Have you had pukies?' In Peggy's world there were 'ouchies', for minor complaints and 'pukies', which came along when things got really bad.

'No,' Mum said. 'It's not as bad as that.'

'Can you eat the chocolates?' Peggy had brought a box of chocolates, which were now on the mobile table that the nurses served lunch on. Peggy looked at them.

'Not right now,' Mum said.

'I can,' Peggy said, guilelessly.

'Do you want to open them?' Mum smiled. 'Go on, then.'

Peggy looked at me. 'Can I, Daddy?'

Before I could say no, my father picked up the box and unwrapped it. ''Course you can. Dig in, petal.'

Peggy put one in her mouth, then took one in each hand. I

glanced at Sherry, who gave me a little nod. We were quite strict on stuff like chocolates, but this was an unusual situation.

'Aren't you going to offer them around?' I said.

Peggy held out her hands to my father. The chocolates she had taken were already starting to melt.

'It's all right,' Dad said. 'You have them. I'll get one later.'

His eyes were fixed on Peggy, a half-smile on his face as he soaked up every detail of her enjoyment. He would have fed her the entire box if she'd wanted.

Peggy shook her head. 'I want you to have it,' she said. 'It's a present.'

Dad looked at her, his hands folded in his lap, for a few seconds.

'Well, if it's a present I'd love to eat it,' he said. He picked up the chocolate and ate it. He leaned forward and took her face in his hands. His wrinkled fingers looked enormous against her smooth skin. 'Thank you. That was delicious. The best chocolate I've ever eaten.'

Peggy laughed and did a little jump, bouncing on the bed. She held out the other chocolate. 'And you, Grammy? Do you want one?'

'I shouldn't,' Mum said. 'But how could I resist that face?' She took a small bite – little more than a lick – and put the chocolate on the table. 'I'll finish it later.'

'If you don't,' Peggy said. 'Can *I* eat it?'

'Would you like it now?'

Peggy nodded.

Mum looked sideways at her, as though considering it. 'Go on, then,' she said, as Peggy pounced. 'Just this once.'

British BBQ

We left my mum late in the afternoon and headed home for a nap. We were all exhausted; flying east is so much worse than flying west. With the travel from Maine to Boston to London to Warrington, and with the emotion of seeing Mum, we were wiped out.

We had to go out that evening, though. The following day Paul and Jerry were heading with their families off to a villa they rented each year in Turkey for two weeks, so if we wanted to see them, tonight was the night.

We pulled into Paul's drive. He had a new house since I'd last been over, a large barn conversion on the edge of Culcheth, a smart village north of Warrington. Jerry lived in Kent, and was staying at Paul's before they left. As we stopped, the front door opened and my two oldest friends stepped outside.

When you haven't seen someone for a while you notice two things when you finally get together: the first is how little they've changed. The second is how *much* they've changed. It's a disconcerting feeling – from a distance they look the same, but when you get closer you see the small ways in which they are different: a tired look in the eyes, some grey hairs, a rounding belly.

Still, the overwhelming feeling was how great it was to see them.

Jerry's wife, Sarah, came out, their infant girl in her arms and a three-year-old boy at her feet. The boy was Trevor, a name I remembered easily as it was Jerry's dad's name, and because it seemed incongruous on a small child. I couldn't remember the girl's name, having only seen it in occasional emails, but Sherry saved me.

'This must be Isabella,' she said. 'How beautiful. The name and the girl.' She hugged Jerry, and then kissed Sarah. 'And Paul,' she said. 'Do we get to meet Ruth?'

Ruth was Paul's second wife, recently acquired. He nodded. 'She's inside, making some drinks. Come on in.'

We sat around a table in the back garden. Trevor tried to interest Peggy in the collection of dump trucks and other construction equipment he kept in his sand box, but she was too tired to pretend interest, and took up station on Sherry's lap.

A small, dark-haired woman came outside. 'Now then,' she said. 'Who wants a drink?' She looked at us, her eyes flickering from one person to the next. She had a nervous energy that was already exhausting.

'You must be Ruth.' Sherry stood up. 'I'm Sherry. This is my daughter, Peggy.'

'Welcome,' Ruth said. 'And if you want anything, anything at all, just ask me. Okay?'

I got to my feet and held out my hand. 'Tom.'

'I've heard all about you, Tom. Would you like a drink?'

'Get him one of those nice beers,' Paul said. He lit a cigarette. Beside me, Sherry tensed. 'It'll be better than that muck they drink in the US. You must miss decent beer.'

'There's some that's not so bad,' I said. 'Microbrewery stuff.'

'But most of it's piss, right? When I was in Florida I couldn't believe what they drank. I wouldn't even have fed it to my dog, if I had one.' He paused. 'I finally figured out a use for it, though. It was good to wash your feet in.'

'The salads are in the kitchen,' Ruth said. 'Grab a plate and some salad, and then head over to the barbecue. The steaks should be ready. If anyone doesn't want meat, there's salmon in the tin foil.'

'Great, isn't she?' Paul said, exhaling smoke. 'Does everything for me.'

I risked a look at Sherry. She was staring ahead, unblinking. The two things she hated most were the kind of unthinking male chauvinism that Paul was in the process of displaying and people smoking, especially around Peggy. Among the liberal middle classes of the US it was an almost unpardonable sin; basically, they viewed it as someone murdering their child. The fact that they themselves had smoked as teenagers and college students, and had given up after a long struggle, and that their children would in turn do the same, didn't register, but then it wasn't a rational reaction. It was a kind of tribal identification, and all the more powerful for it.

'She's too good to you,' Sarah said. 'You don't deserve it. I hope you make it up to her.'

Paul swept his hand around to indicate the large garden and house. 'She gets all this,' he said, and then flicked his tongue in and out of his lips in an obscene gesture. 'And more.'

Jerry and I laughed. Even Sarah giggled; but then, we knew Paul, and knew that, despite his crassness, and tastelessness, he was at heart a pretty decent bloke. Besides, when someone is one of your gang, you make exceptions for them. He was just one of us, just Paul, with all his faults. Sherry, however, barely knew him, and saw no reason to extend such forgiveness.

It was strange for me to be there with someone who was so important in my life – my wife, no less – and yet have her be a stranger to my best friends. It saddened me. It reminded me of another thing I had given away by leaving my home. It also gave the meeting an odd dynamic. At the heart of it were Jerry, Paul and me, three childhood friends, who'd grown up together and who, even now, could predict each other's thoughts and reactions with near total accuracy. Then there was Sarah, who knew Paul well, and me a bit, and then there were Ruth and Sherry, who knew no one very well at all.

'So,' Jerry said, when we were sitting at the table with our plates of food. 'How's your mum?'

'Probably near the end.' I glanced at Peggy and shook my head. 'But I'll tell you more later.'

Paul clapped his hand on my shoulder. 'Anything I can do, let me know. Anything. I know some people at the hospital so if you're not happy let me know. Anything at all. Marge was great to me growing up.'

'Thanks, mate, but I think we're fine.'

Peggy reached for a glass. 'Could I have some water, please?'

'Listen to that,' Paul said. 'She's got a little American accent. *Warder*, not water, with a "t". It's weird, eh?'

'It's not weird to me,' Sherry said. 'She is American, after all.'

'I know, but she's *Tom's* kid. A little Warringtonian with a Yankee accent.' He looked at me. 'You know what I mean?'

I did. You assume your kids will grow up as you did, that they'll take after you, and to hear her speak with her accent was a very visible sign that she was growing up as an American. Not that I minded, but I did notice it. I wasn't going to say that, though. With Sherry tired and in a bad mood, this conversation was already on dangerous ground.

'Kind of. But I don't really think about it.'

'She does have an American accent, though.' Paul said.

'She does.'

'You'll have to stamp it out. Get her talking proper English. Like what the Queen speaks.'

I knew what Sherry was about to say – that Paul, with his broad Warrington accent, hardly reminded her of the Queen – and, as she sat forward to speak, I kicked her ankle under the table. Thankfully she stayed silent.

'I'll see what I can do,' I said.

'So tell me about America,' Jerry said. 'You enjoying life over there?'

'Yeah,' I said. 'Same as anywhere, really. Keep your head down, make a living. Spend time with the family.'

'When I was there,' Paul said, 'I couldn't believe how shit the coffee was.'

'First the beer and now the coffee. It can be a bit hit and miss.'

'And it's full of fat fuckers.'

Sherry coughed. 'Would you mind not dropping the "f-bomb" in front of my daughter.' There was ice in her voice.

'The what?' Paul laughed.

'The f-bomb.' She evidently didn't feel the need to explain.

'The what? That's very American, that, to have a delicate little word for it.'

'Yes,' Sherry said. 'It is. And I would prefer it if you didn't say it in front of Peggy. Or, for that matter, any of the other curse words you like to say. She's at an age when she repeats everything.'

Lots of Brits indulged in the unthinking anti-Americanism that Paul was displaying – yes there were plenty of obese people in the US, yes there was a lot of shit beer and even shitter coffee, but to characterize a nation of three hundred million people like that was just lazy, and more to the point offensive. It was rooted in insecurity – the oft-quoted statistic that only five per cent of Americans had a passport, whether it was true or not, was a good example. *Look at them,* we could say, *they don't even have passports, whereas we leave our homes and see the world.* We *are outward looking and interesting;* they *are insular and boring.* No one pointed out that, if you lived in England, you could hardly avoid leaving your country if you wanted to do anything, like get some sun or go skiing. To fly from Edinburgh to Istanbul – that is, from one end of Europe to the other – took about four hours; a similar journey in the US – New York to Los Angeles, say – took five and a half hours. If you lived in the US, you didn't need to leave the country, because the country was a continent.

Although at first Paul may have been indulging in a lazy stereotyping of Americans, now, though, he was having fun. He could never resist winding someone up.

'Sorry,' Paul said, and grinned. 'When I went to Florida, I was astonished at how many fat *people* there were. They were everywhere. Porker city.'

'Florida is not the US,' Sherry said. 'Just like Warrington is not the UK. I mean, if this was all you saw of the UK you'd hardly be impressed, would you?'

'I dunno,' Paul said. 'Wouldn't you?'

I had to stop this. Paul was an argumentative bastard. He would get into a row about anything – blazing, terrible rows in which awful things were said, normally by him – then afterwards he would just carry on as though nothing had happened. That was the thing with him – he never took offence at what people said to or about him, and he saw no reason why anyone should take offence at what he said. That, however, did not stop them taking it.

'Well,' I said. 'You know, up in our part of the US things are pretty good.' I was speaking quickly. 'It's not like the rest of the US.'

Adding that was a mistake and I knew it as soon as I'd said it. 'What's wrong with the rest of the US?' Sherry said. Now *I* was in trouble, which felt a little unfair.

'Nothing. Absolutely nothing. I love the US. That's why I live there.'

Sherry glared at me. Before she could speak, I looked at Jerry, the one neutral I could talk to. 'Anyway, how've you been, Jerry?'

'Good,' Jerry said. 'Busy. Looking forward to holidays tomorrow. Right, Paul?'

Even Paul knew when the subject was being changed.

'Should be good,' he said. 'Sun, sand, beer. And Turkish food's decent.'

I relaxed and put my arm around Sherry. She was bolt upright in her chair, Peggy dropping crumbs onto her knee. She gave a half-shrug to get my arm off her and took a small bite of her steak, which she chewed slowly and without relish.

Not much later, she folded her napkin on the table and arranged her knife and fork on her plate. 'Ruth,' she said. 'That was lovely. But Peggy – and I – have to go to bed. You know how it is when you travel. Jet lag.'

'So soon?' Paul said. 'We're just getting started. You can let Tom stay, though?' He peered at my forehead. 'Or is that a thumbprint I see there, Tommy?'

'It isn't,' Sherry said, her smile genuine now that she was on her way out. 'Tom can stay as late as he likes.' She kissed me on the cheek. 'See you at your parents', darling. And thank you again, Ruth.'

The Tickets

The day after the barbecue I woke up from a dream in which I had a headache to find that I *had* a headache, along with a dry mouth, a delicate stomach and a raw feeling in my eyes. It wasn't helped by the manner of my awakening: Peggy was lifting my eyelids and telling me to wake up.

'Come on, Daddy,' she said, when she saw that I was conscious. 'We have to see Grammy.'

I have never been good with a hangover. I think it is what has kept me from alcoholism, as I like a drink and come from a culture in which there is no taboo on drinking, or, more specifically, on being drunk. In the US, staggering about in the streets late at night is seen as a sign of a problem. In the UK it is seen as good, clean fun.

So I could easily have slipped down the path to a functioning, middle-class, low-level alcoholism, with a drink before dinner, some wine with the food and a small whisky before bed, were it not for the fact that, however much or little I drank the night before, the morning after I felt terrible. Even a couple of beers or a glass of wine was enough – my sleep was poor, I woke up tired and I couldn't function. I sometimes wondered whether it was because

I had been a sportsman, so I was in tune with the state of my body; perhaps, though, it was simply an accident of birth.

I swung my legs out of the bed and rubbed my eyes. I was wearing one black sock. I saw the other one out of the corner of my eye. It was on my pillow. I tried to remember how that had happened, but couldn't. I couldn't even remember coming home. Had I walked? Taken a taxi?

I did remember that it had been a lot easier after Sherry had left. She didn't fit in with my friends, which meant that we didn't fit in as a couple. If she was feeling awkward, then so was I. Warrington might have been home for me, but it would never be home for us.

'Get ready, Daddy,' Peggy said. 'Mommy said she's ready to go.'

'Okay,' I said. My voice was a rasp, and I coughed. I was reminded of the cigars we'd smoked the night before. 'Tell her I'll be down in ten minutes.'

Peggy nodded. 'I'll give you some privacy.'

She had started saying that when we were potty training her. Sherry would close the bathroom door and say that she was giving her some privacy so she could do her poop. Sherry had read something about not watching kids shit as it shamed them. It seemed to me that they weren't in the slightest bothered who saw them go about their business, until the day their parents introduced the idea of privacy.

I rummaged in the suitcase for some clothes and the toiletry case. It was underneath the travel documents. Sherry dealt with those kinds of things – passports, documents, taxes – whatever organizing needed doing, she took care of it. It was why Peggy didn't have an English passport yet – I hadn't got round to it, and Sherry didn't care, so it hadn't happened. I had her birth certificate though, and I planned to go to the passport office and get one on this trip.

As I moved the travel documents something caught my eye.

There was only one name on the paper – mine. I read it – it had the details of the flight we'd taken, and no return flight. That was fine, an open return, as we'd discussed. We'd get to the UK, see how Mum was, and make a decision about when to go home then.

So where were the other names?

I rifled through the papers. There was another booking, in Sherry and Peggy's names. With a return flight, in four days.

Four days. They'd be back in time for school.

The paper shook in my hands and I put it back in the case. I couldn't believe she had done this. Apart from the fact that we should be taking decisions together, this was my mother – my dying mother – we were talking about. I pulled on a pair of shorts and marched downstairs.

Sherry was at the kitchen table, reading the *Daily Mail*. Peggy was lying on her stomach on the floor, head in hands, watching the television.

'I can't believe anybody reads this garbage,' Sherry said. 'It's all celebrities and titillation.' She folded it and put it down. 'I guess you're feeling a bit delicate? What time did you get in last night?'

I ignored her question. 'Where's Dad?'

She looked at me for a while before she answered. 'He's at the hospital. Everything okay?'

'Fine. Come upstairs. We need to talk.'

'We have to go to the hospital. Your mum's waiting.'

'You're very concerned about my mum all of a sudden. What changed?'

She frowned. 'What do you mean?' The blood draining from her face gave me the impression she knew what was coming.

'If you cared about my mother you wouldn't be planning to leave in a few days. That's not what we talked about.'

'Peggy starts school on Monday.'

I pointed upwards. 'Let's talk upstairs.'

74

In the bedroom, I closed the door. 'Mum's ill. You saw how much she loves Peggy. It's not too much to ask for her – and you – to hang around for another week.'

Sherry shook her head. 'The main thing is that she's been here. She's seen your mum, and we've got four more days.'

'It'll make Mum happy. She doesn't see much of Peggy.'

'There has to be a balance, Tom. Peggy'll see her for a week. That's a lot.'

I felt the argument slipping away from me, like it always did with Sherry. 'Please. For me. I just want Mum to see her grand-daughter.' I repeated my only argument. 'You've seen how happy it makes her.'

'I know. But think about Peggy. Forget about school for a second. There are things she's better off not seeing. It's not a great environment for a kid. She's five, Tom. She doesn't need to be around hospitals and illness and thoughts about people dying. This is the best way, trust me. Peggy gets to see Margaret; Margaret sees Peggy, and Peggy starts school with the other kids, filled with pleasant memories of her grandma. Life goes on, Tom. And Peggy can always come back another time.'

We both knew she wouldn't, but I could tell I'd lost the argument.

'When were you going to tell me about your plan?'

'When the time was right.'

'Which was?'

'From your reaction, obviously not now.'

'You just don't get it, do you? This is my mum. I gave up a lot to be with you – and I don't regret it for a second. But I still gave it up. And this is what you give me in return?'

She stared at me and shook her head. 'You didn't give it up. It was a joint decision. And you're not alone. We're not special; every marriage involves sacrifice. I raised a hand. 'Okay. I'm sorry.

But, joint decision or not, I still left my home, my family, my friends.'

'Having seen what your friends have become you're better off having left.'

'They're my friends. They might not be perfect – none of us are, you included – but they're my friends.'

This had been a discussion about something; it was becoming a slanging match.

'I mean, look at last night. Paul, with his little wife running around after him.' She shook her head. 'Anyway, it changes nothing. I still think we should go home.'

I closed my eyes. She was convinced that she was right, that this was the best, most balanced decision. That was how she operated: simply demanding something because that was what she wanted was uncomfortable for her; it made her feel that she was stamping her feet and being unyielding. Instead, she built up a steady, secure and logical case around her desires which gave them the appearance – to her at least – of being neutral conclusions derived from the evidence.

In my case, it was all about emotion. I just wanted Peggy to be there. I wanted my daughter to be near my mother, even if she was only five and so she only saw her for five minutes a day. It was about raw emotion, and that was what Sherry didn't see. She was convinced she was right, that her rationality and reasoned arguments were all there was to it, but she was wrong, and her mistake was robbing me of the last thing I would ever be able to give my mother.

The next day my brother came with his wife, Iris. It was some years since I had spoken to him; probably a decade since we had seen each other. Jonathan and I were not close, not because we didn't get on, but because we were many years apart. He was nine years older than me, so we had never spent any time together. When he was a teenager, I was just a pain in the backside who he occasionally had to look after. By the time I was a teenager he had left home to live in Carlisle, where he was a partner in a small law firm that specialized in immigration cases.

'Oh,' he said, when I opened the door. 'I didn't know you were here.'

'Got here a few days ago.' He was shorter than me, and chubbier than I remembered, with the unhealthy sheen of someone who spends their time at a desk under artificial light. He reminded me of the outsized tomatoes you see in US supermarkets, pumped full of water under their shiny red skins.

'I suppose that means we need to find a place to stay,' he said, and glanced at Iris, who was standing beside him.

'We can move out, if you want,' I said, spluttering a bit.

'Are you sure?' Iris, a softly spoken, brown-haired Cumbrian woman who wore the thickest glasses I had ever seen, said.

I wasn't sure at all – in fact, I couldn't believe they were going to throw us out – but I had never been good at demanding things from people in this kind of situation.

'I suppose we could find a B & B,' I said. 'How long will you be here for?'

'That's very kind,' Iris said. 'Jonathan will get our things from the car.'

God. How the hell was I going to explain this to Sherry? She was going to think I was a complete patsy, although I doubted we'd have a row about it. We'd not spoken much since she'd declared that she and Peggy were going home. I decided to deal with it later; in any case at that moment they were out buying some clothes for Peggy.

'Make yourselves at home,' I said. 'I was just heading to the hospital. Perhaps I'll see you there.'

*

In the end she wasn't that bothered, either because she felt a bit sheepish about leaving so didn't feel like complaining, or because she was happy to be out of the house, where the atmosphere could be a little on the heavy side. The B & B set up a small bed for Peggy, but she didn't use it. She crawled in with us and slept sideways, which meant I ended up on the floor, my cheek against an old, dusty carpet which had doubtless had the full gamut of human bodily fluids spilt on it over the years. I put my coat down and tried not to think about it.

We established a pretty steady rhythm in the next few days: breakfast (Peggy loved the full English), a visit to the hospital, lunch somewhere in town or at a country pub, another visit, and then dinner at home.

The day before the girls left Dad and I were sharing a sandwich at the hospital.

'I thought we might get everyone in the room for a picnic tomorrow night, with your mother,' he said. It was an uncharacteristically romantic gesture from my father, which just reminded me of how strongly he loved her, a love that I had neither suspected he felt nor thought him capable of. 'She'd like that.'

I hadn't told him they were leaving. Every time I tried my mouth dried up and I found a reason to postpone. 'How about tonight?'

'I've not bought the stuff. Besides, Jonathan isn't here. He and Iris are eating in Manchester with some friends.'

No doubt on their friends' tab, I thought. I didn't know Jonathan well, but what I had learned since he had arrived was that he was the most tight-fisted bastard imaginable. He had a way of letting people suggest things and then going along with it – like when I had offered to let him kick us out of the house – and avoiding paying. Somehow it was always me or Sherry who went to pick up a takeaway or buy something to cook. *I'll set the table*, he or Iris would say, or *I'll get some wine*, and they'd come back with a bottle of Albanian plonk that you would struggle to persuade a tramp to drink.

'I'm not sure tomorrow will work.' I looked at Dad, sheepish. 'The thing is, Sherry and Peggy are heading back tomorrow. To the US.'

'Sorry?'

'They're going home. Tomorrow.'

'Does your mum know?'

I shook my head. Words were beyond me.

'She'll be sad.'

'I wanted them to stay, but Peggy has to start school.'

'She's five years old.'

I took the easy way out and hid behind the foreignness of my family. It was the vaguest of excuses. 'I know. I would have let her miss it, but you know what the Yanks are like.'

'No,' he said. 'I don't.' He looked away. 'Anyway, you can tell your mother this afternoon. She needs to know.'

'I will. I'm sorry.'

He didn't flinch. 'Well, that's that for the picnic,' he said. 'Shame we didn't do it earlier.'

'Let's do it tonight anyway.'

'It's okay,' he said. 'You don't need to bother. It was just an idea.'

To the guilt about them leaving was added the guilt of denying my father the chance of organizing a family picnic for his dying wife, because I hadn't had the courage to tell him earlier. I wished I could have shrunk to a point and disappeared.

The Last Day

We pulled into the hospital car park. Sherry and Peggy were on their way to the airport and we were dropping in so they could say their farewells. The mood between us had been heavy, and I didn't want it to squat there, unresolved, while we were apart. As we got out of the car I took her hand.

'Hey,' I said. 'Let's not be in a mood with each other.'

She smiled. 'I'm not. It's you.'

It wasn't true. She had been just as much part of the tension as I had, stalking around silently and making no effort to patch things up. Now, though, was no time for a fresh disagreement.

'I know. I'm sorry. I don't want you to leave like this.' I didn't say it, but part of me was thinking about the plane crashing with this still between us.

'Okay. Thanks for saying something.' The speed with which she accepted the apology suggested she was thinking the same thing. She kissed me, her hands on my cheeks. 'I love you. You're a great father and husband. And son.'

I was glad she thought so. Right then I felt deficient in all three areas. I opened the back door and unbuckled Peggy. 'Let's go in.'

*

I'd told Mum the day before. She'd pretended that the tears that formed in her eyes were because of the pain she was in. They probably were, but it wasn't the physical pain.

'Hello, Peggy,' she said, when we entered the room. She smiled at me; she didn't look at Sherry. Peggy let go of my hand and went to kiss her. 'It's been lovely to see you this week. Come back, won't you?'

'I will, Grammy,' Peggy said.

Mum reached under the bedclothes and pulled out a small, red-velvet jewellery box. Her hands shook with the effort; she had weakened considerably over the last few days.

'I want you to have this,' she said. 'It's for my princess.'

Peggy took the box. She looked at me.

'Go on,' I said. 'You can open it.'

Peggy flipped open the box and gasped. She took out a ring. 'Is it for me, Grammy?'

My lips started to quiver and I blinked to stop the tears. Peggy was holding Mum's engagement ring. I glanced at Dad; he smiled and gave a small nod.

'It is.' Mum held out her hand. 'Let me help you put it on.'

Her hands were shaking too much, so I took the ring, feeling the warmth of the worn, yellow gold between my fingers, and slipped it onto Peggy's finger. The small diamond glinted even under the harsh, institutional light.

'Is it a diamond?' Peggy said. 'A real one?'

'It is,' Mum said. Tears were running down her face. 'Grandpa gave it to me when he asked me to marry him. I've worn it every day since. And now it's yours.'

I took the box. It had *Howard's the Jewellers* stamped on it in gold letters. I remembered the shop from my childhood; it was closed now. Mum had kept the original box, although I suppose when you don't receive much in the way of jewellery you keep whatever you get.

'I *love* it,' Peggy said, breathlessly. 'And I love *you*, Grammy.'

Mum's shaking hands brushed the tears clumsily from her face. 'I love you too. I'll miss you.'

'I'll miss you,' Peggy said, and hugged Mum. 'I'll come and visit soon.'

'You do that,' Mum said, her words choked off and indistinct. 'You do that.' She pressed her lips to Peggy's head. 'I love you. You're my special little girl and I love you. Now, haven't you got a flight to catch?'

Sherry was crying as well; it was hard not to. She stepped forward and took Mum's hand in hers.

'Goodbye,' she said. 'I'll miss you.'

Mum didn't look her in the eyes. 'Take care of them, Sherry,' she said. 'And yourself.'

Dad walked with us to the car. I opened the back door and started to lift Peggy into her car seat.

'I'll do it,' Dad said. He picked her up and, his arms round her waist, held her so that they were face to face. His arms, even at his age, were thick iron bands.

'Cheerio, Peggy,' he said. 'You be a good girl on that plane.'

Peggy nodded.

'And you look after that ring.' He slipped it off her finger and handed it to me. 'Your dad'll keep that for you, 'til you get home.'

'I will,' Peggy said. 'Grandpa, will you and Grammy come to my house?'

Dad pursed his lips. 'Maybe we will. In the meantime, I'll miss you.'

'I'll miss you too,' Peggy said. 'And Grammy.'

He kissed her. 'I love you.'

I was shocked. Not that he loved her, but that he said it. I had never heard him say it to anyone – not me, not Mum, not Jonathan.

He put her in the car and buckled her in. 'Bye, petal,' he said. 'You be a good girl. Take care.' It sounded very final.

I watched them disappear through the security check and into the airport. I felt rootless, and very alone. I no longer knew the town I'd grown up in and I no longer felt like I had a place there; the town I now lived in would never be home.

I stayed for another week. I thought about checking out of the bed and breakfast and sleeping on the couch but I decided not to. It didn't feel right somehow. I didn't belong at my parents' house anymore; it felt as though my claim on it as my home had expired.

I saw Mum every day. She made some progress. The day I was leaving, Dr Singh said he thought she'd be home in a month.

'There you go, Mum,' I said, when he left the room, with a forced jolliness in my voice. 'You'll be back in no time.'

'Aye,' she said. 'But I'll be stuck in bed most of the day.'

'You'll be able to get around. They'll send people. And Dad'll be there.' I grinned. 'He can make your meals. Think about that, eh? You'll get to eat Dad's cooking. Every cloud has a silver lining, right?'

She lifted her hand to her forehead. It took a while. 'Takeaway,' she said. 'Normally I wouldn't touch it, but it has to be better than what your dad'll put on a plate. I remember the last time he cooked for me.'

'Really?' I looked at Dad, who shrugged. 'I didn't know you'd ever cooked for Mum.'

'It was Valentine's day. Before you were born. Your dad made me a risotto. Very fancy, it was.'

'Well, well,' I said. 'Was it good?'

Mum paused, then shook her head. 'Not really. It reminded me of wet cement.'

'Not that you've ever eaten wet cement,' Dad said. 'So I don't know how you'd know.' This was clearly an old conversation, part of the brickwork of their relationship.

'It was a lovely gesture, mind,' Mum said. 'But never again.'

'Not until now, anyway,' Dad said. 'I'll look up that recipe, if you like. Cement risotto. It's a delicacy at the Savoy.'

Mum laughed; it was a light, sparkling laugh that made her sound like a young girl who was falling in love. This was an aspect of their marriage which I had never even suspected existed, and it made me feel better about leaving. At least I knew Mum was in good hands. The best hands.

At the airport, Dad shook my hand.

'See you then, son,' he said.

'See you, Dad.'

He nodded, his eyes blinking.

'Will you be okay?'

'Of course we will.' He looked at me like I'd just asked him the most stupid question he'd ever heard. 'We've got this far, haven't we? Now go and take care of your family.' He patted my elbow. 'And remember to enjoy it, son. It'll be gone before you know it.'

PART TWO

Home

Barrow hadn't changed. I felt it should have, given what had happened while I was away, but the same people sat on the same porches, the same Subarus were parked in the same driveways and the same sensation of relief at being back home washed over me as I opened the front door and walked into my house to be greeted by the thunder of Peggy's bare feet on the wooden floor as she charged out of the kitchen.

'Daddy!' she shouted and jumped into my arms. She was dressed in her pyjamas. 'You're home!'

'Hi, petal.' I realized that I called her that because my dad did. You picked up lots of things from your parents without knowing it at the time. 'I missed you.'

'Will you read me a book, Daddy?'

Sherry came out of the kitchen and put her arms around me. 'I'm so glad you're home.' She kissed me. 'When you're not here I realize how much I love you.'

'Can I stay up, Daddy?'

I looked at the clock. It was past her bedtime. 'No. But I'll read you some books before bed.'

As Peggy fell asleep, I lay next to her and smiled. It was good to be home, to be back together with my family. When she was asleep I came downstairs and sat next to Sherry on the couch. She slid next to me and rested her head on my shoulder.

'We missed you.' She kissed my cheek. '*I* missed you,' she said. 'A lot. It was hard to sleep, thinking of you over there. And the bed felt empty without you.'

'I missed you. All the time. I felt a bit lost, to be honest.'

'I know. It was – I don't know – incomplete without you. Our little family was broken up. It felt wrong.'

I stroked her hair for a while. Its texture and smell were so familiar.

'I love you, Sherry,' I said. She didn't reply. She was asleep.

My job was a dream. After a few years of doing whatever came my way – waiting tables, labouring, teaching English to Somali immigrants in Portland – I'd applied for, and got, a job as strength and conditioning coach at Hardy College. Basically, I worked with the different sports teams on fitness programmes, each tailored to the demands of their game. With my background in sports science and as an ex-professional rugby league player it was the perfect fit, and I loved it. The sports facilities were incredible, the kids were responsive and the hours were pretty forgiving. I walked to work, could have lunch at home when I wanted (although more often than not I took advantage of the excellent, and free, canteen), and was back by five at the latest. In the holidays it was even less of a strain; with no kids to coach I worked on programmes and attended courses to learn about the latest training techniques. It was no wonder American college sports were so good; it was effectively a professional set-up.

The Wednesday after I'd come home, a morning strength training session with the lacrosse team overran and I missed the college lunch, so I jogged back home. When I got to the house there was a silver Mazda convertible in the driveway. I recognised it from the day we'd been at church; it was Daniel's hairdresser-mobile.

From the back garden I heard the sound of laughter.

I opened the side gate and walked round. Peggy was in her paddling pool, back from school for the afternoon, crouched on her haunches. She put her hands in the water, scooped some up and leaped to her feet, sending the water in the direction of the house. 'Splashy, splashy!' she shouted.

I recognized Sherry's laugh, alongside another, definitely male, laugh.

Jealousy is a strange emotion. It's a mixture of anger and love and fear, and it consumes you. The mildest, most upstanding man in the universe could kill because he was jealous. And when I heard that laugh, my jealousy flared up.

I knew it was wrong, and stupid, and that I should have trusted Sherry, but I couldn't help it. There was just something about Daniel, something that I didn't like. Never mind trusting Sherry; I didn't trust him, and now the little fucker was in my house, with my wife, without my knowledge.

'Okay, Peggy,' Sherry said. 'I'm soaked! That's enough splashing for now.'

'Sure is,' I said, and closed the gate as though I'd just arrived. 'What's going on here?'

Peggy sat in the water. 'I'm *splashing*!'

'You sure are.' I walked round the side of the house so I could see Sherry and Daniel. They were sitting on the stone patio, which I had put in two summers before, on the two Adirondack chairs I had made the year we'd arrived, drinking some kind of sparkling wine.

'Oh,' I said. 'Daniel. I wasn't expecting to see you.'

'Hey,' he said. 'I was just passing by.'

Sherry stood up, her face slightly flushed from the alcohol and the sunshine. I scanned it for any trace of embarrassment or concern, but there was none.

'Hi darling,' she said. 'Not at work?'

'I missed lunch. Thought I'd pop back for a quick sandwich.'

Sherry raised the glass. 'Champagne,' she said. 'The real stuff.'

'I didn't know we had any.' I hid my hands behind my back and clenched them. 'What's the special occasion?'

'Just old friends catching up.' Daniel got to his feet. 'I had it in the car. There's more in the fridge. Have a drink.'

'No thanks. I have to get back to work. Can't have the strength and conditioning coach turn up smelling of booze!' I looked at my watch. 'Actually, I have to get back. I've got a meeting.'

'You've not eaten.' Sherry stood up and joined me by the kitchen door. 'I'll make you a quick sandwich.'

'It's all right.' My throat was tight and I didn't want to speak in case I shouted. 'I really have to go.'

'Okay.' She frowned. 'Have a good day.' She tilted her head up and kissed me. 'Love you.'

'Bye.' I pulled back and walked round the house. As I reached the gate, Daniel called out.

'See you later, Tom.' I looked back. He was leaning back in the chair, glass in hand, his forearm perched on the arm rest. He raised his other hand in a casual salute. For a moment our eyes locked, then he turned and smiled at Peggy.

On my way back to the campus I bought a turkey and cheese sub at the local deli. I couldn't eat it, and on my way out later that afternoon I threw it in the bin.

Champagne and Margaritas

When I got home, Sherry was sprawled on the couch, the blinds down. In the kitchen, the empty champagne bottle was next to the sink, alongside two cocktail glasses and a bottle of lime concentrate. Margaritas as well; it had been quite the afternoon. I poured myself a glass of water and went into the living room.

The blinds gave a loud report as they snapped up. Sherry groaned.

'Leave them down. It's too bright.'

'I've been in meetings all afternoon. I want some sunshine.'

She rolled over and buried her head in a cushion. 'I've got a headache.'

'You're drunk.'

She shook her head. 'Not drunk. I'm *hung-over*.' It was not much of a joke and neither of us laughed.

'Where's Peggy?'

'Mum took her. She's having dinner there.'

'What did your mother think of this?'

'Of what?' Her voice was muffled by the cushion.

'Of you getting pissed in the afternoon with some bloke and farming out your daughter on her?'

'She didn't think anything. And she knows Daniel. She was glad to see him.'

'Well, I think it's a fucking disgrace.'

There was a long silence. When she spoke it was just one word. 'Sorry.' I could tell from her tone she didn't mean it. She just wanted the conversation to be over.

'Is that it?'

'What do you want me to say? Jesus,' she looked at me, her eyes red. 'It was just a bit of fun. Two old friends catching up.'

'By getting smashed in the afternoon?'

'I didn't plan to. It was Daniel who showed up with the champagne. I just had a glass or two and—'

'And the margaritas?'

'He made them.' She motioned for me to lower the blinds. 'Lighten up. You know how it is, in the heat. Before you know it you've had one too many.'

Lightening up was not on the menu. 'I don't know how it is, as it happens. I don't have much experience of getting drunk in the afternoon with other women.'

'Daniel is not another man. Give me a break. He's a friend from high school. Trust me, there's nothing between us.'

'You think? I happen to come home in the day and find my wife at home with her high school boyfriend? That's nothing?'

'My high school boyfriend? Where did you get that from? God, I didn't date every guy in Barrow.'

Where did I get it from? It had just come out, but now it made perfect sense. 'You and Daniel, Lisa and Mike, the old crew. The crazy gang.'

'Is that what this is about? You think Daniel is my ex?'

'Is he?'

'No! And so what if he was? High school was a long time ago.'

'You don't think it's strange to be drinking in the afternoon with your ex?'

'He's not my ex!' She clasped her hands to her forehead. 'You need to relax.'

'He's still a man. A single man.'

'We're just friends.'

'There's no such thing as just friends. Not with men and women. Trust me. I know what men are like. I am one.' Men didn't show up with booze at a woman's house – high school friends, recent acquaintances, colleagues, whatever – just because they were friends. Up until that point I'd not been sure that Daniel was interested in my wife – I'd considered it, even been a bit jealous, which was only natural – but now I was convinced. And I was going to put a stop to it.

'And I'm a woman. And there is such a thing. I'm not interested in him.' She gave a high little laugh. 'I can't tell you how unthinkable it is that there would be anything between me and Daniel. Think about it for a second. I've known him since I was twelve. Twelve. If it was going to happen it would have done by now. Don't you have friends – girls – that you've known all your life?'

I did. And from her point of view I could see why she thought I was being unreasonable. Why should she not see an old friend? But Daniel wasn't just an old friend; that was obvious to me. The problem was she couldn't see it.

'Look,' Sherry said. 'Don't worry, okay?'

'I'm not worried. Just disappointed.'

'What are you, my fucking parents? I love you. You're my husband. Stop being so insecure.'

She looked at me as though studying something she'd just seen for the first time. 'You know, I thought you trusted me.'

'Don't turn this on me. I wasn't the one drinking it up all afternoon with some woman.'

'I know, and I've said I'm sorry. I just didn't expect that reaction.'

'What the hell reaction *did* you expect?'

'I don't know. Nothing, really. Maybe interest in someone from your wife's past? Maybe that you'd be pleased to see me reconnect with an old friend? But not this. Not jealousy.'

So I was in the wrong. As per fucking usual. I knew this should stop here, but I couldn't help myself. 'So it's just me being jealous, is it? Not you giving me a reason to be jealous?'

'Maybe, at first, I can understand a bit of jealousy. But I've explained the situation – Daniel's just a friend and you have nothing to worry about. The fact you're still jealous—'

'I'm not. I'm angry now.'

'Or angry, the fact you're still angry when there's nothing to be angry about, well, that worries me. It makes me think you don't trust me, either with other men, or what I tell you. And that's a problem.'

'I do trust you—'

'Then what's the problem? I've told you that you have nothing to worry about, you trust me, so you know there's nothing to worry about. So why are you worrying, or angry, or jealous, or anything?'

She'd always been able to do this, to tie me in knots. We'd argue and, once I'd got through the initial emotion, she'd find some way of turning it on me, and making her argument so obvious, so *reasonable*, that I couldn't disagree without feeling like an idiot. I was left without a rhetorical leg to stand on; what she didn't see was that there was more to it than rhetoric. She might have proved me wrong, logically, but I still felt like shit, and that feeling was going to go somewhere.

'Okay?' she said. 'We're friends again?'

I nodded, the wind gone from my sails. 'Sure.'

'Great.' She groaned and lay back on the couch. 'Would you pass me some water?'

I gave her my glass. She gripped my hand and kissed it. 'Thank you. I love you, Tom. And I need a nap.' She closed her eyes. 'Could you pick up Pegs? Seven p.m.'

'Fine.'

Small Towns

Barrow was a small town, in both size and mentality. It was one of the first things I'd noticed when we arrived and one of the last I'd got used to. In truth, I still didn't like it. I was used to a more reserved way of interacting, in which you didn't ask people too many questions, 'too many' being more than one or two, and sometimes not even that. It applied just as much to friends, even close ones: if they volunteered information you might discuss it with them, otherwise, you kept your mouth shut. A friend of my father, Reg – a good friend, whom he saw to play bowls every Sunday, and had done for as long as I could remember – got divorced. They never mentioned it to each other. Reg didn't bring it up, so Dad didn't ask. That would have been prying.

Here, though, people thought nothing of grilling you about every detail of your life. I no longer found it rude, just off-putting, and I had learned to deal with it by giving enough information to satisfy my inquisitor without encouraging them to prolong the inquisition. It was better than when we arrived, at which point I had sometimes been so alarmed by the questioning that I simply made up answers. There were probably still people around who thought I was an ex-special forces soldier from New Zealand or a Swedish mackerel fishing champion.

I had also been shocked by how much of my business people knew. It was, however, a very small town, which I realized a few weeks after we moved there. I was in the house alone. That morning, a couch had been delivered and Sherry was out buying cushions for it. There was a knock on the door.

An old lady smiled at me. She was dressed in cream, high-waisted slacks, a silk blouse and a blue jacket. A small dog accompanied her.

'Hello,' she said, and held out her veiny, fleshy hand. 'I'm Martha.'

'Tom,' I said. 'How can I help you?'

'I heard you have a new couch.'

'We do.' I was, frankly, bewildered. Since no one knew about the new couch, I assumed she was from the shop and had come to check, in person, on the delivery. 'It came this morning. Thank you. Everything's fine. We're very pleased with it.'

'That's wonderful. What colour is it?'

'Sort of red. Dark red.' Shouldn't she have known this? She knew everything else.

'Hmm. The walls in your living room are pale yellow, aren't they? I'm sure it looks lovely against them.'

'That's why we bought it.'

She stood on the porch, her smile morphing into a fixed grin. I don't think her expression actually changed – none of her facial muscles moved – but it took on a frozen quality.

'You're not from the furniture shop, are you?'

She shook her head, which meant that she was an interested – well, an interested what? Passer-by? Journalist?

'I heard you had a new couch, and thought I might come to see it. I am a friend of the family.'

'Well,' I said. 'Come on in.'

It wasn't the last time that I was surprised by how word spread – one day I was out at the supermarket buying a bag of potatoes and a man my father's age pointed at them and said he was surprised I needed them as the potatoes I'd planted in my vegetable garden were nearly ready for harvest – but it was the one I remembered most.

What this meant was that I could not avoid Daniel. Everywhere I went, people mentioned him to me. *Sherry must be pleased, they were good friends, you know* or *have you met him? We had him over for dinner. He's so charming, but then he always was* or, most ironically, *I bet you two get on like a house on fire, don't you?* I learned a bit about him though: he'd gone to New York after college, worked in the city on some esoteric and complicated financial product, then set up an ethical commodity trading firm that made sure the farmers and growers of the commodities they traded got a fair deal. Not as fair a deal as him, though: by all accounts he was very wealthy, which in America meant he could do no harm. In the American imagination only the good got rich.

After one such exchange, I was about to wander off when the lady I was talking to – an ex-teacher at the Junior High, who knew Lisa, Mike, Daniel and Sherry – reached into her bag and pulled out an envelope.

'Oh,' she said. 'I almost forgot. Could you give this to Sherry?'

'Sure,' I said. 'What is it?'

'It's a birthday card.'

It was Sherry's birthday that Saturday. When we'd found out that Peggy's due date was so close to Sherry's birthday we'd hoped that they would end up sharing it – or rather, I'd hoped while Sherry had been convinced that it was going to happen, having read into it some cosmic destiny which was going to forever link her to her daughter. Peggy, having failed to consult her horoscope, arrived early.

I thanked her for the card and set off for the car. It was a good thing she'd reminded me, as I'd totally forgotten. On the way home I stopped to pick up one or two things.

Sherry didn't like much fuss on her birthday; every year she claimed that she would rather no one mentioned it, which I had realized she did not mean literally fairly early on in our relationship when one year I had neglected do so. Her reaction had taught me that 'not much fuss' was not the same thing as 'no fuss at all', and since then I had been scrupulous about the observance of her special day.

On this special day, Peggy and I were making her breakfast in bed. I'd got up early so that when Peggy awoke I could whisk her downstairs before she roused her mum, and we'd started on our menu.

I had a good idea of what I wanted to prepare: half a grapefruit, a bowl of creamy oatmeal and blueberries, a lightly poached egg on an English muffin (which is what Americans called muffins; a muffin here was one of those small sweet cakes; either way, Sherry loved them. English ones, that is), and a shot of espresso made from beans I had ground myself the evening before.

Peggy had other ideas.

She put her hands on her hips and pouted. It was amazing how womanly her gestures had already become. 'Mummy needs something *nice*, Daddy.'

'This is nice.'

'No, it's not. She has oatmeal all the time.'

'But today she gets to have it in bed. *That's* the treat.'

Peggy shook her head. 'It's her *birthday*. We have to make her a special breakfast.'

'Well,' I said. 'What do you suggest?'

Peggy sucked on her bottom lip, which she had done since she was a toddler when she was thinking.

'Marshmallows,' she said. 'And chocolate.'

'I'm not sure that's what Mummy would like for breakfast.'

Peggy frowned. It was, of course, inconceivable to a five-year old that anyone, even an adult, would not want marshmallows and chocolate for breakfast, lunch and dinner, seven days a week.

'Daddy,' she said. 'Don't be silly.' She opened the pantry cupboard in the corner of the kitchen. 'Look,' she said. 'Look! Cheddar Bunnies! We should put *those* in the oatmeal.'

I pictured Sherry's reaction at the breakfast from hell.

'Maybe we should hold off on the Cheddar Bunnies,' I said. 'Save them for another day.'

Peggy took the packet out. 'She wants them. Mommy *likes* them.'

She dumped a handful of crispy Cheddar Bunnies into the bowl. They sank into the oatmeal, like buoys on a riverbed when the tide is out.

'I tell you what,' I said. 'You make that and I'll make some eggs. Mum can have both. But we should make *your* breakfast really memorable for Mummy.' I looked at my daughter. 'What else does she like?'

Peggy thought for a moment, her bottom lip trapped between her teeth.

'Wine. Mummy likes wine.' She looked around and her eyes settled on the cup of milk I'd given her. 'And milk.'

I nodded. 'She does. Okay, so a cup of wine and milk. In the same cup, you think?'

Peggy nodded. 'And how about … a cheese straw? On the plate with the marshmallows and chocolate.'

'Should I cook them all together? Maybe in an omelette?'

'Yes. Yes, you should.'

I got to work on the breakfast. While the chocolate, marshmallows and cheese straw melted and combined with the eggs into an almost unimaginably unappetising omelette, I poached two eggs, cut up some fruit and poured two cups of coffee. When it was all ready, we assembled it on two trays – one holding Peggy's breakfast offering and one holding mine – and headed upstairs. Peggy threw the bedroom door open.

'Surprise, Mommy!' Sherry rolled over and opened her eyes. 'Happy Birthday!'

Peggy and I broke into a rendition of 'Happy Birthday'. When it was done, she carried her tray over and set it down on the quilt.

Sherry tilted her head and looked at it with an expression that suggested mild disgust.

'Well,' she said. 'This looks – ' she glanced at her grinning daughter – 'lovely.'

'It's all for you, Mommy.' Peggy started to detail what was on the plate. 'There's a chocolate and marshmallow and cheese straw omelette and some oatmeal with Cheddar Bunnies and some milk—'

'With a little wine mixed in,' I said. 'White, of course. Red wine and milk don't go well together at all.'

Sherry grimaced, then laughed. 'And I have to eat all of it? I'm not that hungry this morning, and there's a lot.'

Peggy frowned. 'Mommy! It's your birthday breakfast! We made it specially for you. You *have* to eat it.'

I coughed and placed my tray in front of her. 'You can, of course, save it for later, when you're really hungry, and try this breakfast now?'

Sherry pursed her lips and stared at me with a wicked look in her eyes.

'No,' she said. 'That's fine. I'll eat the one Peggy made. It looks delicious. I *love* it.'

Peggy's face flushed with pride.

Sherry looked at me. 'But I love it so much I want to share it with Daddy. Is that okay?'

Peggy nodded. 'Okay, Mommy. Daddy can have some.'

Sherry smiled at me. She took a small bite of the omelette then sliced off about a third of it and handed it to me on a fork. 'Here you go, darling,' she said. 'It's delicious. Make sure you eat it all.'

A few hours later, with the breakfast still swilling around in us and the taste of milky-wine on our lips, we went out for part two of Sherry's special treat: a morning strawberry picking.

There is something absorbing, almost therapeutic, about picking strawberries; in fact about picking or harvesting any fruit or vegetable. Food is, of course, vital to our existence, yet we rarely see it in its natural state. You could be forgiven for thinking that milk and cheese and meat and potatoes came from supermarkets. The link to the land is gone.

I saw it in Peggy's response when she spotted a strawberry hanging from a plant. It was a blend of excitement and surprise. It says a lot when a child is surprised to see a strawberry on a plant and not in a plastic carton; it should be the other way round.

But then, this was why we lived here, and not back where I came from: this kind of life was available in Barrow, along with the local swimming holes, beaches, mountains, kayaking in the summer and ski resorts in the winter. I had left a lot behind; my parents, friends and family, the opportunity to see my kids grow up and play rugby and cricket (women's rugby, if it was Peggy) for the teams I had played for, speak with the same accent as me. It was a lot to sacrifice, but it was worth it for a life that was, in many ways, little short of idyllic.

And I had to think of it in those terms. It was our decision, taken jointly. It couldn't be me giving up everything so that Sherry could have what she wanted; that was the road to resentment and bitterness. It had to be a positive decision – this is the life we chose, the life we wanted.

Baskets full of strawberries, we pulled up in the drive. I saw Sherry's expression before I saw what was on the porch.

'Tom,' she said, and kissed me. 'That's so sweet.'

I followed her gaze. There was an enormous – and I mean enormous, probably two metres round – bunch of flowers on the porch, although to call it a bunch of flowers didn't do it justice. It was a work of art, a riot of colours and shapes and textures, all perfectly dovetailed together.

I climbed out of the car to see who it was from, although I already had my suspicions. There was no card. That bastard had sent her anonymous flowers, so that she'd start guessing who they were from, spend her time thinking it through, make the present larger in her mind even than it was in reality.

Well, two could play at that game.

'They're even nicer than I'd hoped,' I said. They weren't anonymous flowers any more; they were from me. Thanks, Daniel.

'What did they cost? It must have been a fortune.' She stopped. 'No, forget the cost. I'm just going to enjoy them. Thank you, darling. You're the sweetest husband.'

'I'm just glad you like them.'

'I *love* them. But you shouldn't have.'

I didn't, I thought, *but you don't know that. I get all the credit and none of the cost. The perfect crime. I don't know what Daniel thinks he's up to, but he's lost this one.*

It was a big mistake, although at the time I didn't know that. At the time I was too busy feeling smug to see what was coming.

Flowers

At lunchtime the next day the three of us were sitting on a rug on the lawn having a picnic lunch.

'Those flowers are beautiful,' Sherry said. She'd put them on the kitchen counter; it was the only surface large enough for them. 'Thanks.'

I didn't want to talk about it. I was glad to hear the side gate bang open.

'Hi,' Daniel said, appearing round the side of the house. He was wearing a pair of shorts and a Nike running vest. I couldn't help notice that, despite the slim fit, his stomach was not filling out the material. I, on the other hand, despite working out constantly, had started to wear loose fitting clothes to disguise the beginnings of a gut. It was the fate of lots of big guys; at twenty-five, the size of your frame meant you could hang a lot of muscle on it. At thirty-five it was a struggle to keep that muscle from turning into fat. Daniel, a slimmer build, had no such problem, although there was no way he was as strong as me. In a gym I'd have kicked his skinny arse.

'Hope I'm not interrupting.' He swept his sunglasses up from his eyes.

'Not at all,' Sherry said. She looked at me, a warning in her eyes. I smiled. After the flower incident, I felt I could be generous.

'Of course not,' I said. 'Come on in. Would you like a drink? It's a warm day.'

'No thanks. Maybe on the way back. I'm thinking of running out to Shear Point.'

'Shear Point?' Sherry said. 'You're crazy. How far is that?'

'Eight miles, or so. But I don't run that fast.'

There it was, that false modesty again. I'd have preferred boasting. If you were in good shape say so: a sixteen-mile run was a decent haul. It was far better to acknowledge it than to pretend it was nothing. Everyone knew it wasn't fucking nothing. My dislike of him hardened. Still, there were always the flowers. I glanced at them in the kitchen and smiled.

'I thought it was only mad dogs and us Englishmen who went out in the midday sun?' I said. 'Seems like we're not alone.'

'No,' he said. 'I like to run at this time of the day. I'm not a morning person, and in the evening I'm normally feeling a bit lethargic. Lunchtime's perfect. I don't mind the heat too much.'

'I suppose it's not too bad for a guy your build,' I said, making the point that I was bigger than him.

'Oh?' he said. 'Why's that?'

'Heat generation is a function of body mass but heat dissipation is skin surface area. Since for every additional unit of mass you only get a quarter of a unit of skin surface area, the bigger you are, the more heat is a problem.'

'Right,' he said, then paused. 'That's very interesting.' He looked at Sherry and raised his eyebrows. 'Your husband knows a lot of stuff.'

My neck prickled and I felt sweat bead on my forehead. Now I felt stupid for saying it; I'd learned it during my sports science degree and I told it to the students at Hardy when they were working out, to make sure they drank enough water and kept cool.

Then Sherry looked at him and rolled her eyes. *She rolled her eyes.* The way kids do when their parents embarrass them; the way friends do when someone who's not cool tries to impress them; the way you do when you're saying to someone *I know, I know, he's a pain but I can put up with it.* It was a gesture that put me on the outside of their relationship; I was stunned.

'Anyway,' she said. 'Don't let us stop your run.'

'No problem. Actually, I did stop in for a reason. I wanted to drop this off.' Daniel reached behind his back and pulled out an envelope. He must have had some kind of pocket in the back of his running shirt for food or water or whatever. 'For your birthday. Sorry I didn't get it to you yesterday.'

I was further from him, but he handed it to me.

Sherry smiled. 'Thanks, Dan. That's really kind of you.'

He caught my eye and a faint, mocking grin played over his lips. He held my gaze for a second while he spoke.

'Actually, it's a shame it didn't come yesterday,' he said. 'I wanted it to be with the flowers I sent.'

'Which flowers?' Sherry said. 'I didn't see any other than the ones Tom bought.'

I was frozen, the envelope pinched in between my fingers.

'Mind you,' she said. 'There wasn't much room for any other flowers. Tom's were quite an impressive bunch.'

I had to stop this. I stepped towards Daniel, about to take his arm and steer him out of the garden. I'd explain it to Sherry afterwards, somehow.

He saw my move and sidestepped next to the house so that his face was next to the window.

'There they are,' he said. 'On the kitchen counter.'

'But those are—' Sherry started to speak, then caught herself. 'Thank you, Daniel. They're lovely.' Her voice was thin and tight.

Daniel seemed not to have noticed. 'No problem. The least I could do.' He looked at her, then at me. 'And Tom bought you flowers as well. Quite the lucky day for you.'

Neither I nor my wife replied. Daniel – who knew exactly what was going on, I was sure of it – sat back and enjoyed the silence.

It lasted for a while. When Daniel spoke, his voice was innocent and questioning.

'Are Tom's in there as well? You said they were an impressive bunch.'

Sherry looked at me. 'Tom?'

I stared at the flower bed. I had two options: say nothing and run the risk of looking a fool or speak up and remove all doubt. I chose the former.

'Tom?' Sherry was leaning forwards now. 'The flowers you bought?'

'There was a kind of a mix-up,' I said.

'That's right, there *was* a kind of a mix up.' I realized that Sherry's voice was not angry; I looked up to see her smiling. This was a joke to her, and it made it worse.

She pointed through the window. 'Tom told me *those* were his flowers. I guess his are on the way.'

I should have laughed it off – at that moment I still could have – and made some comment about taking your opportunities when you see them. I could have grinned and sent Daniel packing. I should have done that from the start, from the first day Daniel showed up, should have been the big man, secure, king in his castle: *who was that? Seemed a nice guy. Invite him over some time.* It was just another occasion when I should have walked away.

But I couldn't. I couldn't then, I couldn't the first time and I couldn't at the end. It was just too humiliating. The thing with humiliation is that it's not inherent in a situation; it's in how you respond, and once people see that you feel it, it gets worse and worse, until it's all you can see. You feel diminished, and it takes a long time to wipe it away.

Daniel raised his palms in a gesture of mock apology. 'Sorry about that, buddy,' he said. 'My bad. If I'd made sure the card was there in the first place none of this would have happened.'

'It's hardly *your* fault,' Sherry said. 'And I'm glad you came over. Otherwise I wouldn't have known to thank you for the flowers. Thank you. They're lovely.'

Was it deliberate on his part? I've wondered about that many times since. Was he already playing a game then, or did that come later? Whatever it was, I didn't see it coming until it was too late and I was well and truly sucked in.

Oana's Brunch

'Come on, Tom. Hurry up.'

We had been invited to a birthday brunch at the house of an old school friend of Sherry, Oana. Oana was a serious, earnest lady whose Romanian parents had made it to the US in the sixties, refugees from the regime in their homeland. They had endured years of poverty in New York City, until, by dint of sheer hard work and thrift, they had made a modest life for themselves in Barrow. I wasn't sure what they had done but I knew it involved both parents having multiple jobs, and Oana and her sister going to school in ragged clothes that made them the target of teenage abuse.

Sherry had been – and still was – her only friend. Oana was very protective of the time they had, and would plan it minutely. A drive out to this place, a lunch at this café, a visit to this museum. Sherry, as was her way, just went along with it.

Now that I was around, however, it was much harder for Oana to have Sherry to herself. If she came to our place then I'd find an excuse to go out as it was obvious that she didn't want me there, but it was an uneasy compromise: Oana wanted a full allotment of time with Sherry; Sherry didn't have that time to give. When I came home, Oana was polite, but it was awkward between us.

Oana couldn't just hang out and have fun; she wanted her fun to be *organized*.

As I pulled on my boots I tried one more time to get out of it.

'Are you sure you want me to come? Oana might prefer it if it was just you and Pegs.'

'I'm sure she would,' Sherry said. 'But she invited all of us. And it's about time you started being nice to her. She tries her best to accommodate you. The least you could do is be kind to her.'

'I am kind to her. Kind enough.'

'She's scared of you. She wants your approval.'

'And she can have it. Oana's great. She works hard, she's honest. Anyway, who cares what I think?'

The thing was that Oana cared. She cared what *everyone* thought. One of the consequences of her upbringing was that, while she didn't have much, what she did have she valued. Which in itself was fine, but, when mixed with her insecurity and earnestness, made her incapable of just enjoying things. She had to showcase them.

She paused. 'And anyway, it wouldn't be just me and Pegs. Daniel's going to be there.'

'Oh.' I bit my lip. We hadn't talked about Daniel since the flowers. Neither of us had brought it up. I think we knew it would be a sore topic. 'I didn't know Oana knew him.'

'She doesn't. I invited him.'

'Really? Did he suggest it?'

'No, he didn't.' Sherry sat next to me on the step. 'Tom. Daniel's a friend. An old friend, and I thought it might be nice to introduce him to Oana. She's single, after all. There's nothing to be jealous of. You should be glad. Maybe he'll hook up with Oana.'

'I'm not jealous.' My teeth were clenched; I felt stupid that she'd called me out on my jealousy. It was so embarrassing, so *teenage*. I slammed my foot into my boot. 'Come on. Let's go.'

*

'Hi!' Oana opened her door, her apron carefully dotted with flour. 'I'm just making pancakes. Come in! Daniel's already at the table.' She was more wild-eyed than usual, the panic of having a man – a *single* man – in her house clearly almost more than she could take. Sherry gave her a little flick of the eyebrows as if to say *how's it going with Daniel?*; Oana replied with a nervous, uncertain expression, as if to say *aaargh, I don't know, help me.*

She kissed Peggy, hugged Sherry, and then grabbed me in a quick, awkward embrace. Neither of us wanted it, but hugging was what you did with your friend's husband, and an awkward, unwanted hug was better than no hug at all. At least the hug had happened and there were no questions about why not. It was like the diplomatic niceties between enemy countries. They may have been a sham, but it was better to go on with the sham than stop it and reveal the truth of their relations. Oana, with her antenna for the real meaning of what people were saying, tuned over years of sensitivity to the digs and slights, real and imagined, that people had made at her, would have made an excellent ambassador.

The table was stacked with food; Daniel was almost hidden behind it. There was more than the five of us could have eaten in a week, but that was Oana's thing: she had prepared everything anyone could have wanted, and in quantities sufficient to cover any permutation. If we all wanted scrambled eggs and only scrambled eggs, there were enough for all of us. Likewise pancakes, bacon, orange juice, muffins, thin sausages, fat sausages, coffee, bagels, smoked salmon and cream cheese, hash browns, melon, grapefruit, strawberries, blueberries and yogurt. The shopping alone must have taken hours, never mind the preparation.

'So,' Oana said. 'There's bacon, pancakes . . .' I drifted off while she pointed at each item and explained why it was special. The bacon was from some local farm where the pigs were fed on cloudberries and moonjuice, the sausages were made from the finest blah blah blah, the maple syrup was from some special tree in Canada that only produced one jar of the stuff when the full moon was out and twenty virgins danced naked around it at midnight. This was the thing with Oana: you couldn't just enjoy what was undoubtedly an excellent spread. No, you had to itemize it, understand it, appreciate it in some dry, intellectual sense. You couldn't even praise it – apart from the fact that Oana had already praised it for you, you could never have found words to do it justice. From being an object of salivating wonder, the breakfast became intimidating.

'Right.' Oana appeared by the table and ushered us into our seats and handed out plates. 'What would you like? Tom?'

'No, no,' I muttered. 'Ladies first.'

'That's okay.' Oana was looking at me, an intense, fixed expression on her face. 'What would you like?'

Oana wouldn't be deflected from her purpose. I knew what she wanted. She wanted me to smile and groan with pleasure at the choices on offer, to umm and ahh and give her the chance to impress.

Her hand, serving spoon clutched in her fingers, hovered over the table.

I made a show of scanning the vast selection of food. I lingered over the pancakes, then moved on to the bacon, then the fruit and maple syrup and cream, then the eggs. Finally, I looked up at her.

'Got any toast?' I said.

I don't know why I said it. It was a joke, and in the way that jokes have, it just came out.

Oana tried to smile, but she looked horrified. She gave a tiny, unconscious, shake of her head. 'I could make some.'

I felt awful. 'It's okay. I was just joking. This looks lovely. I'll take the pancakes.'

It was too late. Oana knew it was a joke, but she couldn't see the humour in it. Like the breakfast, she got it on an intellectual level, but she'd been on the receiving end of too many jokes to really find them funny.

The smile faded. 'No. But I'll make some. It'll only be a minute.'

Sherry, tight-mouthed, glared at me. 'That's not necessary. He's just being stupid.' *Being stupid.* Not *he's just joking.*

I wished I hadn't said it.

'Sorry. You know us Brits. Always joking.' I pronged some pancakes onto my plate, followed by some eggs. The awkwardness abated. It reminded me of the barbecue at Paul's house; just as Sherry didn't quite fit in the place I came from, I didn't fit where she came from, which meant that as a couple we didn't fit in either place. There were too many times we both felt awkward because one of us did. I hadn't meant to offend Oana; it really had been a joke, and back home it would have been taken that way. But not here.

Oana turned to Daniel.

'Daniel? Something for you?' She said it in a clipped, brisk tone designed, as far as I could tell, to be as businesslike as possible. If Daniel was interested in her and looking for signals that she reciprocated his affection before he made a move then nothing would ever happen.

But he wasn't interested in her. I could see that plain as day. He was polite, and charming, and attentive, but it was a sham. There was no warmth there. It was when he looked at Sherry that his eyes lit up.

'A bit of everything, please Oana,' he said. 'This is amazing. You must have spent all morning on this.' Now I saw how to do it. Sincerity – even as false as Daniel's – was always okay. He fitted in here, all right. There was no doubt about that.

Oana blushed. Not slightly, not a gentle reddening of the cheeks, but a full bloom. Daniel pretended he hadn't seen and took a bite.

'Delicious,' he said. 'What a treat.'

Sherry smiled, pleased for her friend, and handed Peggy a spoon. 'Here, Pegs. You get started.'

Peggy loaded her plate with five times more food than she would be able to eat. At least she wasn't hiding her enjoyment at Oana's brunch. I hoped it made up for me.

'Well, Peggy,' Daniel said. 'You sure have a good appetite. Will you eat all that?'

Peggy nodded. She couldn't answer; her mouth was too full.

'I'll be impressed if you can.'

Up until now Daniel had hardly paid any attention to Peggy; in fact, I could hardly remember a time when he'd spoken to her at all. I didn't want him to start. Watching him lean towards her made me feel sick. I wanted to shove him away and yell at him to leave my daughter alone, but that would hardly have helped Oana's brunch recover as a social occasion.

Peggy swallowed enough of the huge mouthful so that she could speak, albeit in a voice muffled by pancake.

'I can.'

'I bet you could eat a horse, couldn't you?'

Peggy nodded.

'I hear you like horses.'

'I love them.'

'Well, I happen to have a friend who has some at a stables in Wiscasset. I asked him and he said you can have one.'

Peggy's mouth gaped open. A crumb dropped onto the table. Oana flinched. 'To keep?' Peggy said.

Daniel laughed. 'Not to keep.' He leaned even closer to her. 'But to adopt. You can go and ride it any time you like. They'll teach you how to ride and how to take care of a horse. Then, if you really like it, maybe you can get one of your own.' He looked at me. 'Although that depends on what your daddy says.'

Peggy clapped her hands together and squealed. 'That's the best present ever! A horse!'

'A horse you can adopt,' Daniel said. 'Not quite the real thing.'

'But almost,' Oana said. 'How kind. How generous.'

'Can I go and see it today?' Peggy said, looking back and forth between me and Sherry.

'We'll think about it,' I said. I looked at Daniel. 'Thanks. We'll let you know.'

When she got home Peggy fell asleep. I went into the living room with a cup of tea and sat on the couch. A few minutes later Sherry appeared in the doorway. She had her hair tucked behind her ears and her hands on her hips.

'I hope you're pleased. That was cruel.'

'What was?'

'Your little performance at Oana's.'

'It was a joke,' I said. 'Just a joke. You know what it's like. I can't deal with the earnestness. It's irresistible to burst the bubble.'

'You can't hide behind your British sense of humour every time you offend someone.' Sherry shook her head. 'It's not acceptable. It's just mean. Oana put a lot of effort into this and you just ruined it for some shitty joke. It would be bad enough with anyone, but Oana? You know what this means to her.' She shook her head more vigorously. 'And in front of Daniel. She was hoping to impress him. You knew that.'

'I'm sorry.'

'I hope so. That was really embarrassing for me.'

'Come on. It's not the end of the world.'

'No, it's not. But that doesn't mean it's okay. I don't want my friends to think you're like that. I love you, and I want them to see why.'

'So you're embarrassed because Daniel won't like me?'

'No. This isn't about Daniel. It's about you.' She paused and looked at me. 'Is that why you were mean to Oana? Because you were pissed that Daniel was there?'

Sherry was extremely perceptive, especially when it came to me. Okay – then there was no point in hiding what I thought, so I launched right in.

'I think he's interested in you.'

'You're not serious. Don't be stupid. You don't think I'd know by now?'

'I've seen how he looks at you. And then he comes here, with champagne? And the flowers? You don't think he's interested in you?'

'He's a friend. I don't know how many more times I have to say that. If he wants to come and visit, he can.'

I shook my head. 'No, he can't. I don't think you should see him. Not on your own.'

'Are you serious?'

'Yes.' I tapped my hand on my thigh. 'Why's that a problem? You want to hang out with Daniel? You have plans I don't know about?'

'No, I don't. It's the principle. Since when did you get to pick my friends?'

'We're married. I don't think it's too much to ask you not to hang out with another man.'

'Any man, or just Daniel?' Her voice was strained, on the verge of hysteria. 'What about Mike? What if you come back from work and Mike happens to be here? Or Gerard? Am I not to be in a room with a man without a chaperone, is that it? How about you fit me with a chastity belt?'

I kept my voice calm. 'You're being ridiculous. Mike is different. Gerard is different. I trust them. Daniel is trying to come between us. I'm just stopping him.'

'He's what?'

'Trying to come between us.'

'So not only does he have a crush on me – a crush he's managed to hide for more than a decade – he's also trying to break us up. Do you have any idea how weird you sound? What if he isn't? What if this is just your paranoia? Have you thought about that?'

I had, and it wasn't paranoia. 'More to the point, I don't want Peggy going to see this horse.'

'So Peggy has to miss out now, as well?'

'No, she doesn't. I bought her some horse riding lessons on Popham Beach.'

'That's not as good, and you know it! Daniel's offering her a great opportunity!'

'No, he isn't. I'll tell you what he's doing: he's putting me over a barrel. If I agree to it then he's a hero, if I say no then I'm a villain. I can't win.'

'It's all about you, is it? Don't you think it might be a generous gesture to a friend?'

'No, I don't. And even if I did I still wouldn't accept.' I said it, and I said it like I meant it, but I wasn't sure it was true. Never mind; I carried on. 'If we can't afford a horse then I don't plan on taking charity. There's plenty of other things we – Peggy – can do.'

'Don't do this,' Sherry said. 'Don't make an issue out of this. Out of Daniel. He's just a friend. Accept it and move on.'

I looked at her for a long time. 'There's an even easier solution.' I took a deep breath. 'Like I mentioned earlier, just don't see him alone.'

'I don't believe this. You're actually serious?'

'Deadly. Don't hang out with him in our back garden drinking. If we see him out and about, no problem, but don't see him one on one. That's not such a big deal, is it?'

'It's ridiculous, is what it is.'

'And I want you to tell him. I want you to tell him that you can't see him alone.' That would teach him, show him that I wasn't going to allow him to wheedle his way into my wife's affections.

She folded her arms. 'What else should I tell him? That my husband is a jealous idiot?'

'There's no need to be offensive.' There was a long, heavy silence. 'Tell him it's inappropriate.'

She laughed, a short mocking burst, and put on a shrill English accent. 'I can't see you because my husband deems it inappropriate.' She turned to look at me. 'Do you have any idea, any idea at all, how this makes you look?'

'I don't care. I don't care how I look to Daniel. I don't care what he thinks of me.'

'What about how you look to me?'

I suppose I knew that this was hurting our relationship, but I could live with that. I just wanted Daniel out of the way; once that was done I could repair the damage.

'I still want you to tell him.'

Her shoulders slumped. 'Fine. I'll tell him.' She grabbed her car keys. 'I'm going out.'

The next morning she called me at work. *It's done,* she told me. *Happy now?*

In that second, I was.

The Institutional Approach: School

One morning a week later I was running past the Hardy College Athletic Centre, where I had my office. The lights were on. I looked at my watch. My pulse was one forty; I switched the screen to the time. It was just after seven-thirty a.m. It was strange; I was normally the first in at around eight-thirty.

I jogged towards the door to see what was going on. When I was about twenty yards away, the door opened and Daniel stepped out.

I ducked behind a tree. He was wearing a dark suit. I guessed he was on his way to a meeting somewhere, which explained the early start. No one in Barrow, whatever their job, wore a suit in summer.

He was followed out by Stephanie Loeb, the Athletics Director and my boss. She shook his hand and said something, her face arranged in the serious look that people who are not used to business meetings use when they have a business meeting.

Daniel handed her a card and got into his Mazda. He unclipped the convertible top and put it down.

'Thanks,' he called out. 'And think about it. Let me know.'

I studied his face as he drove past me. He had a kind of satisfied smile. For the life of me I couldn't work out why.

When I got into work, Stephanie wasn't there, and she didn't show up until lunchtime. I was about to ask her what was going on – I planned to tell the truth, that I'd seen Daniel leaving as I ran by; I could leave out the hiding behind a tree part – when the phone rang.

It was one of the football alumni asking when the games were; when I hung up, Stephanie was standing in my office doorway. She was in her fifties, with entirely grey hair that had started to go grey in her twenties. For years she had dyed it, but a few years back she had stopped. I thought it was a good idea; it made her look distinguished. It also took your attention from her height. She'd been a top college basketball player, and was a few inches at least over six foot.

'Hey,' she said. 'Welcome back.'

'Thanks. It's good to be here.'

'Sorry to hear about your mom.'

I shrugged. 'Thanks. About the leave,' I said. 'I know I used up more than I'm entitled to, but I guess we can figure something out.'

She waved a hand as if to dismiss my concern. 'Don't worry about that. Just make up the time when you get a chance.' She was a good boss, Stephanie.

I was about to mention Daniel when she spoke again.

'By the way, I wanted to run something by you.'

I shut up. This had to be it. 'Yeah?'

'I received an interesting offer this morning. For some funding.'

My heart rate quickened. 'Really?'

'For quite a lot of funding. Enough to relay the AstroTurf pitch and refit the weights room.'

That was serious cash. Daniel had that kind of money? 'Who from?'

'They asked to remain anonymous. Even to you. The only stipulation was that I keep them informed on a one-on-one basis of the progress of Hardy Athletics. How recruitment's going, if we have any stars, all that kind of stuff.'

What the fuck was Daniel up to? Why was he so interested in Hardy Athletics? 'Is this guy – if it is a guy – a Hardy alumnus?'

'No, which is kinda weird. But he's from Barrow.' She made an oops face. 'Which probably narrows it down. Not too many folk around here with that kind of money.'

'Good job I'm an outsider then,' I said. 'I've got no idea. But what's in it for him?'

'He likes sport.' She shrugged. 'That's what he said. Doesn't want any publicity, no sponsorship, nothing. He said that he knows how important Hardy is to Barrow and that he loves Barrow, so he wants to help in any way he can.'

'Sounds like a great guy,' I said, struggling to keep the bitterness from my voice.

'So what do you think?'

Tell him to piss off, was what I thought, but I could hardly say that. I'd have to give my reasons, and I had none other than that I didn't like the mystery donor. 'Sounds good. Take the cash. We could certainly do with it.'

Fucking Daniel. I was sure he was up to something. I had no reason to be; he was remaining anonymous, so I couldn't see how he was going to gain from this. No one was going to know, so it wasn't like he was after adoration. Perhaps he really did just love Barrow and love sports and want to help out. Maybe it was me. Maybe I was just being paranoid and jealous. I resolved to stop thinking about Daniel. He could do what he wanted. I had my wife, my job, my home, and he couldn't touch them.

Still, it pissed me off. I've never been good at letting go. I find it near impossible to walk away, even when walking away is the best thing to do.

The Institutional Approach: Church

The pews were nearly full, as usual. Sherry told me that they had been almost deserted when she was growing up; now the faithful of St. John's included a large number of young couples and families. It seemed that the appeal of the church, at least in Barrow, Maine, was growing. I didn't see what it was, myself. I was there for a different reason, a reason that had nothing to do with the divine or the salvation of my soul or the beauty of the eternal.

I was there because Daniel was there, and because I didn't want him alone – even surrounded by the flock of Jesus – with my wife.

At the end of the service we gathered in a large room in the next building where the tea and coffee was served. The priest (at least I think it was a priest; maybe it was a vicar, or a reverend. Whatever, it was the man in black at the front who handed out the wine) clapped his hands and coughed. We fell silent.

'Some Church business,' he said. 'One of our community would like to say a few words about a project he is starting.' He held out his hand, palm up, fingers pointing to Daniel.

I was standing at the back. I took Sherry's hand in mine as Daniel stepped forward.

'Thank you for the opportunity to speak today, Father Mike,' he said, and turned to face us. 'I wanted to share something with you all, and ask for your help. As you know, there are many people in the US who live with what is called, euphemistically, food insecurity. We know it as poverty, and it is, frankly, ludicrous that in the world's richest country as many as a quarter of the population are in such dire straits.'

He paused and looked around. There was a hush in the room.

'Of course, there is no need for this to continue. When you consider how much food is wasted – think of how much you yourself throw away in food bought and allowed to go off, or cooked and not eaten – it is clear that there is plenty to go around. Even here in Barrow this problem exists. Think about it: there are families that worry about where their next meal is coming from, while, in the same small town, another family throws food away. If, as you opened the garbage can to cast out that food, one of those families was passing by and asked for it, you would hand it over, grateful that the Lord had given you the opportunity to do so. And yet, because you – we – do not see them, we do not help them. So the fact that some of our fellow Barrovians go without is not just a moral outrage' – he put a special emphasis on outrage, like a good politician – 'but a logistical problem. And logistical problems' – here he smiled – 'have logistical solutions.'

Daniel reached behind himself and took a glass of water from the table. He sipped it and looked thoughtfully at the congregation.

'So, as a start, I have reached an agreement with Hardy College that I will arrange to take the food they do not eat – food that would otherwise be thrown away – and transport it to a food distribution centre in Barrow. I have arranged finance for all of this; what I need is volunteers – people – to staff it. To drive the vans, sort and package and distribute the food. And that is where you come in.'

There was a murmur in the room, a murmur that was a mixture of admiration and wonder, a murmur that became a swelling round of applause. Daniel held up his hands in a gesture designed to calm the crowd, as though he was a rock star announcing an Aid to Africa package at Wembley Stadium.

As the silence gathered, an elderly woman in front of us turned round and shook her head.

'What a marvellous man,' she said. 'This is incredible.'

'It is,' Sherry replied. 'Incredible.'

'Remarkable,' I muttered. 'Truly.'

'There is a book on the table behind me,' Daniel continued. 'Please, if you can spare some time, put your details in it and I'll contact you.' He beamed at us. 'And thank you.'

On the way out Sherry signed her name in the book.

Later that day, Peggy and I sat at the local diner eating ice cream. It was our Sunday afternoon activity; walk downtown for grilled cheese and sundaes. Sundaes on Sunday, we called it. I wondered how old she would be before the joke wore thin.

'How was Sunday School?' I said.

'We're giving food to the poor people,' she replied. 'It's Mr Faber's idea.'

'Oh?' So they'd announced it to the Sunday School as well. War on two fronts from Daniel. Get 'em young. I stopped myself. I hated thinking this way; why was I so annoyed? The guy was doing something good. I didn't have to like him to recognize that. And I had no real reason to dislike him, other than my childishness. 'That's great. Well done, Mr Faber.'

She nodded. 'It is. And we're saying prayers for them as well.'

'Shame they can't eat the prayers.'

'Miss Norman says they can. She says prayers will feed their soul as much as food feeds their bodies.' She looked at me, her face earnest in the unselfconscious way only a child's face can be. 'She said Mr Faber is a good Dalmatian.'

I assumed she meant Samaritan. 'Well, I suppose that's true.'

'She said we have a duty to help the poor. We're all God's children.'

'Then maybe He could help them Himself,' I said. 'If He's such a great guy it's strange that so many people need help, right?'

Peggy looked at me thoughtfully as she spooned a huge lump of ice cream into her mouth. I often marvelled at how much she could fit in there. She was quiet while she worked on it. A trickle of ice cream leaked out of the corner of her mouth.

'Daddy,' she said eventually. 'What are souls?'

'Well,' I said. 'It's what' – I didn't really know how to answer – 'it's what God gives you when you're born.'

'Does everyone have one?'

'Some people think so.'

'Do you think so?'

I pursed my lips. Up until now I'd gone along with the God and Jesus and Heaven stuff, but she was old enough to hear a more sophisticated view. Besides, it might take some of the sheen off Daniel.

'I'm not sure,' I said. 'But not really. Personally, I don't think they really exist. But lots of people do, and you should make up your own mind.'

'Miss Norman says everyone has one.'

'Miss Norman thinks that, so she should say it, but not everyone agrees.'

'Oh,' Peggy said. 'I see.'

I looked at my daughter, a human being who five years ago had been little more than a shrimp that I could fit in one arm, and who was now contemplating the mysteries of the universe, and I wondered where that tiny baby had gone. How had it happened? How could she have grown up so goddamn quickly?

Peggy

A few years after we'd moved to Barrow I came home after a base-ball tournament one Friday night – I had just joined Hardy as an Athletics Co-ordinator – and found a glass of red wine on the kitchen table, next to a small white pill.

'Sherry?' I called. 'You home?'

There was no reply. Only the click and whirr of the CD player and the opening bars of Barry White's 'Can't Get Enough Of Your Love, Babe'. For a second I didn't know what was going on, then I burst into laughter.

'Sherry! Where are you?'

I heard her footsteps. As Barry got into his stride, she appeared at the bottom of the stairs. She was totally naked.

'Hi,' she said, then, with a look of mock surprise: 'Oops. I think I forgot to get dressed.'

'So this is it,' I said. 'Friday night, glass of wine, some Barry White on the stereo—'

She finished it for me. 'And nine months later Bob's your uncle.'

It was what I said when people asked if we were planning to have kids. *Oh, I'll know when the time has come. I'll get back on Friday night, Sherry'll feed me red wine and put some Barry White on the stereo, and nine months later, Bob's your uncle.* I would then explain that *Bob's your uncle* was a British phrase that meant something like the American expression *you're all set.* Where it came from I had no idea; at least *you're all set* made some kind of sense. Either way, it had entered the vocabulary of our marriage.

'You sure you're ready?'

She nodded. 'Of course. We have a house, some money. Why wait?' She padded over to me and pressed her body against mine. 'But most of all, we've got each other. You're going to be the best dad ever. I knew it when I met you.'

'You think?' I said. 'I'm warning you. I'll be a British dad.' I put on a strict face. 'Child! Get to bed. And no crying or I'll get the cane out!'

'Yeah, right. You're an old softy. It'll be me who provides the discipline.' She slapped my buttock. 'And that's enough talking. It's time to get to work.'

I took a sip of the wine. 'And what's this pill?'

'Zinc,' she said. 'It helps with sperm production.'

I have never liked the phrase *trying for a baby.* Whenever friends announced that they were in the midst of it, it always called to mind sweaty, slightly desperate couplings which I would rather not have imagined. I enjoyed even less the advice friends gave when they found out. *Fill her up with sperm and keep her topped up,* Paul told me. It was a horrid image.

I have to admit, however, that actually doing it was a very pleasant experience.

It is as though your body instinctively understands that getting pregnant is a numbers game. It's like darts – if you have only one dart then, however carefully you aim it, the chances of a bullseye are limited. If, however, you have a hundred darts, then eventually any idiot will come up trumps. I hated to agree with him, but

Paul's advice was actually pretty good. I didn't pass it on to Sherry, though.

I didn't need to. Morning, noon and night. We had a pretty adventurous sex life as it was – I was a typical bloke who had few inhibitions and Sherry was, well, at least imaginative, if not out and out kinky. Dressing up, role play, handcuffs: they all found their way into our bedroom during that period. After all, when you're doing it three times a day, you need a bit of flavour.

A few months later I was at my desk, staring into space.

'You look tired,' Stephanie said. 'Everything okay?'

I couldn't tell her the truth: I'd fallen asleep on the couch at one a.m. after having been tied to it by Sherry and then woken at four and crawled into bed, only to be woken at six for another bout.

'You know how it is. End of term. Got a lot on.'

'Take it easy,' she said. 'You've only just started. I don't want you to burn out already.'

I was exhausted. Thank God the weekend was coming up and I could get some sleep.

The phone on my desk rang.

'Hi.' Sherry sounded odd. I knew immediately what she was going to say.

'Are you?'

There was a long pause. 'I am.'

I think I screamed. Whatever I did got Stephanie's attention.

'Are you sure everything is okay?' she said.

'Better than okay,' I said. 'Sherry's pregnant.'

She hugged me; it was clear that her joy was genuine. 'Congratulations.' She wagged a finger. 'Now I know why you're so tired. Tell me next time. I'll let you go home during lunch.'

*

All the doctors and books and internet articles advise you not to tell anyone about the pregnancy until twelve weeks have passed. Apparently, after that there is a much reduced chance of miscarriage. In any case, it becomes hard to hide the bump.

We couldn't keep our mouths shut. Every time I saw someone I blurted it out; soon, the Barrow grapevine had ensured that our news was no longer news to anyone. People I barely knew congratulated me in the street. It was marvellous, fantastic, exciting; it was like being a celebrity.

I could not leave Sherry alone. I made meals that contained the recommended amounts of calories, made sure she took the correct dietary supplements – I was a trained nutritionist, and I was delighted to use my training at home for once – and made her take it easy in the evening. After a few days she started to hate me.

'I'm not an invalid,' she said. 'I can't put up with this for another thirty or so weeks.'

'How many weeks, exactly?'

'I don't know. The doctor said the baby will come when it's ready.'

'I know, but what are you now?' I started to work it out. 'Eight weeks and three days, right?' I put my hand to my forehead. 'God. Thirty more weeks seems like forever.'

'It *will* be forever, if you carry on like this.' She stood up. 'I'm going for a run.'

I put my hands on her shoulders and pushed her back down. 'What? You can't do that. You're pregnant.'

'I'm fine. I can run, bike, swim, whatever I want, until it becomes uncomfortable.'

'No, no. It'll shake the baby around.'

Sherry glared at me. 'Stop fussing.' She escaped my grasp and grabbed her running shoes from the basket by the back door. 'If you want to be useful, do the laundry.'

*

The next morning I woke early. Sherry was nudging my shoulder. I looked at the alarm clock. Six a.m. Was she waking me up for sex? Surely now she was pregnant those days were gone?

'I feel a bit sick,' she mumbled. 'Crampy.'

I turned on my back and held her to me, her head on my chest. At the slightest hint of anything bad related to a pregnancy – or children, for that matter – people immediately assume the worst. Thankfully, the worst rarely comes to pass.

'It's probably just morning sickness,' I said. 'Try and go to sleep.'

She nestled against me and I listened to her breathing deepen. When she was asleep, I climbed out of bed. I've never been able to go back to sleep once I wake up. I used to try, lying in bed frustrated for hours, but by that time in my life I had learned to accept my fate.

I sat downstairs with a mug of coffee and a slice of toast. We had a small house – small that is, by US standards; it was big compared to the terraced houses I was used to, and moreover it had a garden large enough to kick a football around in – bought and paid for with the money Sherry's father had left her. Sometimes – often – I couldn't believe my good fortune. Married to a beautiful woman, expecting a kid, a job in sports, no financial pressure. It was a world away from what I'd grown up with.

Still, though, I worried. It was just the way I was made, I guess. Sherry never did. She had the gift of living in the moment, not thinking about what might come next. She had an unfailing confidence that whatever happened she had the tools to deal with it and that, in the end it would work out okay.

I was the opposite. Always making plans for the possible outcomes, rehearsing them in my head, getting used to the idea that things might go wrong. I tried to make sure that I had every option covered; *if this happens then I can do that; if the other happens then*

I have a plan b, if x happens I can do y. I ran through them over and over; sometimes I wondered if this was what madness felt like.

In the end, though, I would ask myself, 'What's the worst that could happen?' If I had a plan for that, then I felt at least a little bit safe.

At around ten a.m. Sherry called me at work.

'Hi,' she said. Her voice was quiet; it sounded like she wasn't quite there.

'You okay?'

'I'm at the doctor.'

I tensed. 'What for? I didn't know you had an appointment.'

'I didn't. The cramps got worse so I came in. I thought it was food poisoning, or something.'

'And? What did the doctor say?'

She started to cry. 'He said I'm having a miscarriage.'

By the time I reached the doctor's office it was all over.

Sherry was in the nurse's room, sitting on the examination table with her hands around her knees. The nurse, a large woman in her late fifties, was standing beside her, stroking her shoulder. When I came in Sherry looked up at me. Her face was swollen and blotchy.

'I want to go home,' she said.

I held out my hands and pulled her into a hug. She buried her face in my neck and clung to me like a child. As I took her out of the room, the nurse caught my eye.

'She's booked in at the hospital for tomorrow morning. For a D and C.' She handed me a leaflet. 'This has all the information you need. And Mr Harding – she'll be okay. This happens more than you'd think. I lost two in between my first and second children. It gets better.'

The whole thing felt unreal. This morning we'd been prospective parents, full of all the joy and nerves and excitement that that brings; now we were grieving for a child we'd never even met, for a future that we'd imagined was ours but which had just receded sharply into the distance.

It was the loss of the future that was the worst thing; the sense that the path we were on had suddenly crumbled was horrifying. Being human, you looked for a reason, an explanation of why this had happened. Blind chance was not enough. Did we do something wrong? Was there something wrong with us? What was to blame here? All the certainty of youth, that feeling of invulnerability, was swept away in an instant.

Sherry clearly felt the same. As soon as we got home, she lay on the couch, she buried her head in the cushion and started to weep. When she spoke, her voice was hollow.

'What if we can't have babies?' she said. She looked terrified. 'I mean it. What if this keeps happening?'

'It won't.' I don't think I was very convincing, not least because I was thinking exactly the same thing.

D and C stands for dilation and curettage. It is also called uterine scraping; in essence the contents of the uterus are scraped out. Apart from anything else – the distress, the pain, the grief – the procedure has the effect of demystifying pregnancy. Until then I had seen pregnancy as almost a magical process – the giving of life – but, when I saw Sherry on an operating table and listened to a doctor explain, in that matter-of-fact way that doctors have, what was about to happen, I saw pregnancy for what it was: a physical process, which, when it goes wrong, leaves behind a mess that has to be cleaned up.

The doctors and nurses and internet articles all agreed on one thing: there is no one reason for a miscarriage. A lot of people held the opinion that it was the body expelling a weak or damaged embryo – survival of the fittest – which made sense. We are, after all, animals; although, unlike animals we get attached to the idea of the unborn child, we think about it, imagine it, fall in love with it, and so when it dies, even though not yet met and still unknown, it is as though we have lost a child.

It also happens more than you think. As soon as word spread there was a steady procession of messages from women who had themselves gone through it. It was a very common, yet very private, experience. It felt like we had joined a club in which every member wished they had never had to join. Still, it was comforting to know that so many other women – couples – had been through the same thing. If it was that common, it couldn't be that bad, could it?

The worst thing about it was watching Sherry fall apart. I felt so helpless; all I could do was sit with her, hold her, tell her it would be okay, none of which seemed to make the slightest difference. She just could not stop crying. We'd be in the middle of a meal, or out for a walk, or in the supermarket, and she'd suddenly stop whatever she was doing, her face would crease up and she'd start crying. Anything could set it off; the sight of a mother and child, a sad song on the radio, a brief moment when she was distracted from whatever she was doing and the tears had time to rise.

Sometimes, in the middle of these crying fits, she would shrink into herself, her eyes focused on some far away, indistinct point, and mutter to herself. *What if I'm damaged? What if something got broken?*

I'd tell her she wasn't, that, sad as it all was, it was routine, but it made no difference. She was lost in some private reverie, where those questions were forever unanswered.

What if I'm damaged? What if something got broken?

It chilled me to hear her say that, to hear that despair. And there was simply nothing I could do.

I did decide, however, that next time we'd wait the twelve weeks before saying anything.

Slowly, she got better. Came out of herself, started to laugh, started to eat and exercise and make love to me. About six months later, I came home on a Friday night and there was a glass of red wine on the table next to a little white pill. I heard the click and whirr of the CD player, and Barry started to sing.

It was funny, and we laughed, but the sex that followed was a nervous, timid affair. We were as fearful as we were hopeful of her getting pregnant. Neither of us wanted to go through that again; the fear was almost strong enough for us to give up on the idea of having a family. But we wanted a baby more. It was just that now the stakes were higher.

Ironically, given how paranoid we were about it, Sherry's pregnancy went smoothly. Peggy grew inside her at regulation speed, Sherry had sickness and veins in her legs and mood swings, all things that were a pain, but which we welcomed. They were signs that it was working out. So it was pretty easy: had it been the first pregnancy we would have enjoyed it, but after what had happened there was little enjoyment. We just wanted it over with. Wanted that baby in our hands.

We didn't find out the sex. I think we didn't want to risk getting too close to the unborn child. If we knew whether it was a boy or a girl it would somehow make it more real, make it a person. The less we knew about him or her, the better.

So when she was born, ten fingers, ten toes, pink and healthy, I couldn't stop crying. I was just so relieved.

Making it Difficult

I had just picked up the phone on my desk when Stephanie put her head around the door of the office.

'Good news,' she said. 'The donation came through!'

I gave her a thumbs up and pointed at the phone. *Sherry*, I mouthed.

'One more thing,' she said. 'The donor's joining the staff. It's Daniel Faber.'

I stared at her, blinking. 'It's Daniel?'

'Joining the team. Great news, right! Details to follow.' She gave me a double thumbs up and ducked out of the room.

'Tom?' Sherry said. She sounded serious. 'Are you there?'

'Yes. Just finishing something up with Stephanie. What's up?'

'It's Peggy.'

A series of tragic images spun through my mind.

'What about her?'

'She's in trouble at school. They want to see us there this evening.'

'Oh,' I said 'Thank God.'

'Sorry?'

'Oh. Nothing. I just thought it was something worse, that's all.'

'Whatever. Can you be there at five o'clock?'

I pulled into the school car park and turned sharply into a space. As soon as I'd put the phone down on Sherry I'd gone into Stephanie's office to find out what the hell she'd meant when she'd said Daniel was joining the team. She told me.

He was our new Student Welfare Liaison for the Athletic Department. Part-time, of course; Daniel had other important things to be doing. When he was available, he'd be there for any athletes that had welfare issues – social, sexual, health, academic, whatever. I didn't think he was going to be too busy. In my experience the biggest problem most of our athletes had was finding their way home when they were drunk. One of them kept breaking into and then waking up on the floor of the houses of the good people of Barrow; he'd been nick-named Jehovah because he turned up unannounced and unwelcome at people's front doors.

All afternoon I'd wondered why Daniel was doing this, why he wanted this in his life. It was driving me mad. And now I had to deal with Peggy. It was the last thing I needed.

Peggy was sitting on a bench outside the head teacher's office, talking to the secretary. I kissed her on the head and followed the secretary's directions into the office.

There were three people in the room: Sherry, a young lady and an older lady.

'Thank you for coming,' the older lady said. 'I'm Ms Perry, the head. This is Miss Kennedy, Peggy's homeroom teacher.'

'Tom,' I said, and shook their hands. 'Tom Harding.'

Ms Perry steepled her hands and touched her index fingers to her nose. It was a gesture that teachers used the world over. Perhaps they learned it in teacher school.

'Allow me to cut to the chase, if you will,' she said. 'I'm afraid that Peggy has not been behaving herself very well in the confines of the classroom.'

She had the habit of using ten words when one would do. I suspected she enjoyed the sound of her own voice. 'Cut away,' I said. 'What's she done?'

Ms Perry nodded at her colleague. 'Miss Kennedy?' Their actions felt choreographed, like a piece of theatre. I found it irritating.

'Peggy expressed some – controversial – opinions in class, both yesterday and today.'

'Oh?' Sherry said. 'Like what?'

Miss Kennedy smiled. 'After morning reception Peggy announced there was no point in praying for the poor and hungry as you can't eat prayers.'

Ms Perry leaned forwards. 'According to Miss Kennedy, she also said that if God was such a great guy then there would be no poor or hungry people in the first place.'

I recognized those words; they were mine. I hadn't expected Peggy to take them on board so completely, nor to start sharing them with her classmates. I could see why it was a problem for the school, but still, it was hardly the end of the world.

'It's not that bad,' I said. 'And Peggy does have a point.'

The two teachers glanced at each other.

'It's very disturbing for the other pupils,' Ms Perry said. 'This is not the kind of thing that we wish to expose them to.'

'Peggy's entitled to an opinion, isn't she?'

'Of course.' The head teacher sat back in her chair. 'But is it *her* opinion? Or someone else's?'

'Sounds like it's hers. She said it. Look. This is ridiculous. You brought us in for *this*? She's five. Who cares? She'll make up her own mind in time.'

'We care. And I wonder if perhaps she has picked up these opinions at home?'

'What do you mean, picked up? You make them sound like a disease.' I was starting to get angry. It had been a long day and I wasn't in the mood to put up with this.

Sherry put her hand on my arm and started to speak. 'I'm sure we can talk to her.'

'Please do. It is unpleasant to see a young mind corrupted—'

I exploded. I was furious; more than I should have been, perhaps, but I couldn't help it. I felt like a pot of water boiling out of control.

'Corrupted? If what you mean by corrupted is have I told her that there is no reason she has to believe in a bunch of two-thousand-year-old fairy tales, then the answer is yes. She doesn't have to believe in it, any more that she has to believe in witches or ghosts or astrology.

'They are not the same thing,' Ms Perry said, her mouth pinched. 'Astrology is – I hate to say it – bunkum, but religion is a matter of *scripture*.'

'We agree on one thing, then,' I said. 'Astrology *is*, to use your word, bunkum. But your opinion that God exists and that scripture is important—'

'It is not an opinion,' Ms Perry said. 'I *know* that God exists.'

'And I *know* that He doesn't.' She stared at me. 'But we can't *both* know it, can we? It's all just opinion. And you can have yours, and I can have mine, and Peggy can have hers. And if you're so threatened by a five-year-old girl disagreeing with you, then you need to think about why your beliefs are so fragile.'

'Mr Harding—'

'Tom, please.'

'We have to consider the welfare—'

'The indoctrination.'

This time Sherry spoke. It sounded like her teeth were clenched. 'Stop interrupting, Tom.'

'Thank you, Mrs Harding,' the head teacher said. 'We have to consider the welfare of the other pupils. I would like you to talk to your daughter – you can say whatever you like – and explain to her that this is not the kind of behaviour we can tolerate here.'

Sherry stood up. Her face was bloodless. 'Thank you. We will do that.' She shook their hands. 'It's been a pleasure.'

In the car Sherry sat totally still.

'Well,' she said. 'That went well.'

'I was just saying what I thought.' I shook my head. 'I know I shouldn't lose my temper, but it's so annoying. How dare they tell me what I can teach my daughter?'

'You have to be careful, Tom. You can't go around saying those things.'

'Why not? This is just typical of the way the religious community claims some kind of special status for their beliefs. You're not allowed to argue with them. You can't even disagree; it's like you're insulting their ancestors.'

'Do it for Peggy. You'll just make her life harder.'

'If she doesn't conform, you mean?' I laughed. 'Well, there we have it. The American Way. Fit in, at all costs.'

'There's always the British Way, I suppose. Sit around in silence repressing your feelings.'

'I just want her to think for herself.'

'Tom, why are you so angry? Don't you think this is a bit of an over-reaction?'

'I'm fine,' I said, eventually.

'Fine. Just like your dad.'

I didn't reply.

140

'So will you speak to Peggy in the morning?' Sherry said.

'No.'

'I don't know why you have to make this so difficult.'

I didn't reply.

'Tom. I'm trying to talk to you.'

'You're trying to nag me.'

Sherry rolled her eyes in frustration. 'Why are you doing this?'

'Doing what, exactly? Sticking to my beliefs?'

'Peggy's five. Let her believe in all that for a while. There's plenty of time for cynicism and reality later. I don't know why you're making an issue of it.'

'It's the way the school rams it down your throat. I can't stand it.'

'It's a *Catholic* school, Tom. What do you expect?'

'I'm just sick of it. Sick of the bullshit.'

'Then let's drop it for now. This doesn't need to be such a big deal. She's five.'

'As you keep saying. Five's quite old, though, isn't it? Old enough to need to start school when your grandmother's in the last year of her life.'

I watched as Sherry bit her lip. 'Is that what's behind all this aggression? All this anger?' She shook her head. 'Tom, don't let this get to you. It won't end well.'

'She's my *mother*, Sherry. She just wanted to see her grand-daughter.'

'And she saw her.'

'For a few days. It wouldn't have hurt if she'd stayed another few.'

Sherry didn't reply. The silence between us thickened.

'I gave up everything for you,' I said, pausing after every word. I was aware that I was about to break an unspoken understanding that underpinned our marriage: moving here was our decision, and we would both face the consequences. There is no room for a martyr in a marriage. 'My country, my friends, my family. And you couldn't even give me that.'

Sherry closed her eyes. 'You want to know something? Sometimes I wish we'd never met.' She paused. 'No, that's not true, because I love you and Peggy, but sometimes I think it would have been easier if we hadn't met. One of us was always going to have to do this. And sometimes I would prefer it if it was me. At least then I'd only feel guilty for myself. Now I have to feel guilty for you as well.'

I don't regret meeting you, I wanted to say. *You're the best thing that could have happened to me. Before you, I was drifting, never really had a serious relationship, just playing at life. Without you I'd be Paul, and, much as I love him, that's not what I want. I want this, I want us, Peggy, our family.*

Instead, I said: 'You wish we'd never met. That's nice.'

I was feeling hurt, and alone, and I wanted her to tell me it wasn't so. That I was the most important thing in the world to her and that we'd be okay. That whatever price we had to pay to be together it was worth it.

Instead, she said: 'You're making this impossible.'

'Of course I am. It's all me, right?'

She sighed. 'Tom, I know you feel bad. I would in your position. But you need to work through it. Don't take it out on me or Peggy. I'm going to talk to Peggy about school, and I don't want you to contradict me, okay?'

I didn't reply.

'Okay?'

'Fine. You just tell me what you want me to do, and I'll do it. That's how our relationship works, I guess?'

'If it has to, yes.'

I knew there was no point making a stand. I could hardly

change the way people in small-town Barrow thought about religion, but I wasn't going to change my view just because it didn't fit in. Right, wrong or indifferent, it was now a matter of principle.

'Okay. Thanks for supporting me.' Sherry looked away. 'Then I'll talk to her.'

A matter of principle. Through history much has been lost, damaged or destroyed over matters of principle. I should have wondered how often they had been worth it.

Self-inflicted

'So all's well then, Dad?'

The conversation was thirty seconds old and I had asked him the same question three times in three different ways: 'How are you?', 'You getting on okay, then?', and finally 'So all's well then, Dad?' He had answered them all identically.

'Fine,' followed by a long silence in which I wondered if there was another way of asking him how he was, and how many more I could try before it became ridiculous; that is, more ridiculous than it already was.

What I wanted to say, of course, was: 'Dad, I love you, I miss you, I'm worried about you and I wish I could see you more, but that's the way life has come out for me and I regret it, but how could I live without Sherry? You see that, don't you? And you know that it's not that I don't want to be near you and if it was anything – anything – other than Sherry and Peggy then I would put you first.'

'And Mum,' I said, instead. 'How's she?'

'Fine.'

'Can I talk to her?'

'She's asleep.'

'And is her rehab going well?'

'Aye, not too bad.'

'Well,' I said. 'That's good. I'm glad you're okay. I'll call you next week, okay?'

As I put the phone down, the back door opened and Lisa came in.

I knew immediately from the look on her face that she had come to borrow something. It was a kind of half-thoughtful, half-conspiratorial look, which she always had on her face when she came over and was about to steal our stuff.

I knew the expression well. I saw it most days.

Now, I realize that Lisa was a friend and neighbour and that friends and neighbours help each other out, but Lisa, frankly, took the piss. She borrowed – I say borrowed, but that's not the right word, as none of it ever came back – something almost every day, normally something to eat. I'd grown sick, then tired, then accustomed to the back door opening and her head appearing round it followed by a request for bread / coffee / milk / cheese / cereal / wine (mainly, but not exclusively, in the evenings) / oatmeal. It drove me mad. Often she didn't even bother disguising her pilfering behind a specific request, for say, a banana, or a cup of sugar, or a bit of cheese, which at least gave a veneer of respectability, as though she really needed that one thing and there was nowhere else she could get it. Sometimes she would just ask whether we had any food. *I'm making dinner and I've got no food. Do you have any?* The thing is, you're brought up to be polite so you say something – as grudgingly as possible – like *I'm not sure, have a look in the fridge*, and before you know it she's rummaging around your groceries. A couple of weeks back she emerged holding a packet of cod. *There's some cod. Mind if I take a piece?* Did I *mind*? I wanted to fucking kill her, but instead I nodded dumbly and watched her carve off a healthy slice of my dinner. I mean, for fuck's sake. What was next? *Got any money I could have?*

That morning I looked at her and waited to hear what she had come for.

'Hi,' she said. 'Do you have any fruit?'

'Probably,' I said. For some reason – perhaps my mother, perhaps just the cumulative effect of having my food stolen – this time anger and frustration welled up inside me. 'But you know – they have loads in the shop. That's where I get mine. It's a great system. You give them some money and in return you get whatever you want.'

One of the benefits of the English knack for deadpan delivery is that non-English people don't always pick up on the subtext. That means, of course, that many of your jokes go un-laughed at or cause, sometimes serious, offence; thankfully, like this time, it also means that you can get away with the occasional insult.

Lisa looked at me uncertainly and carried on. 'I was thinking bananas, apples, oranges? Anything, really. I'm making a fruit salad for the cook-out at our place this afternoon.'

'Sure,' I said. 'Take whatever you want. I think we've got some pineapple and melon in the fridge.'

'Thank you,' Lisa said. 'I'm *so* busy and you've saved me a trip to the grocery store.'

Saved *her* a trip, but I'd be back there later, buying more fruit. I helped her put it in a bag and watched, shaking my head, as she beetled off.

'What's got into you?' Sherry appeared in the kitchen door.

'Nothing. Just watching our food disappear next door, as usual.'

Sherry sighed. We'd argued about this many – too many – times. 'I've told you. People here help each other out.'

'Glad to see we've helped,' I said. 'I can't believe the cheek of that woman.'

'"That woman" is my oldest friend. She's busy, she needs some help – what's the big deal?'

'The big deal is that she uses our house like a free supermarket.'

'I often borrow from her. And she looks after Peggy whenever I need her to, remember? What's that worth in child care?' She drummed her fingers on the counter top. 'I don't know what's got into you recently, but you need to snap out of it.'

'Nothing's got into me.'

'Good,' she said. 'Then I'll see you later. Remember, the cook-out is at three.'

I threw out the anchor and the let the current pull the boat back until the line was taut. Gerard and I were drifting in a channel between two islands in the Casco Bay, the only sound that of the water lapping at my ten-year-old Boston Whaler's hull.

Gerard baited a hook and passed me the fishing rod.

'Watch 'em jump aboard,' he said. 'The mackerel run here. It's a deep water channel.' He said *deep water channel* in a grave, sonorous voice as though we were in some kind of danger. You'd have thought we were on the verge of diving into the Mariana Trench or about to set off from Everest Base Camp on a windy day.

'Is it?' I didn't have much faith in Gerard's wisdom when it came to fish. His homespun wisdom was enough to impress one-time tourists from 'away', but after a few times you started to wonder if it was all bullshit. A few times after that you *knew* it was all bullshit.

'Sure is. We're in deep water.'

'I am, I know that.' I cast the line into the dark water. 'I keep having arguments with Sherry.'

Gerard passed me a beer. 'That's no good.'

'Right.'

'Just agree with her.'

I sipped the beer. 'What if I don't agree?'

'Agree anyway. Then do what you want. That's the secret of my success with women.'

I raised an eyebrow. Gerard's wife had left him when their son was two. She'd found him in bed with the neighbour's twenty-year-old cousin.

'That's not how it works for us. And anyway, I can't help arguing. I get sucked in.'

'Well, that's women for you.'

'And then I say something and there's a mood between us and the next time we talk it's awkward.'

Gerard sniffed. 'Well, just pretend it never happened.'

I always felt better for talking to Gerard. Despite the fact that his advice was useless he did have a way of simplifying things. He would have got on with my dad; both of them shared the basic belief that the answer to any crisis was to say you were fine and carry on with what you were doing.

'Woah,' he said. 'You've got one.'

There was a tug on the line and I reeled it in. I fully expected to see a plastic bag or an old shoe on the hook, but, astonishingly, there was a mackerel, glistening blue-grey in the sun.

'Fuck,' Gerard said, jumping to his feet. 'I've got one too! The mackerel are running!'

It was an epic, mythic few hours. You get one occasion like this in your life, if you're lucky. It's like a hacking golfer who hits a hot streak and comes down the back nine in thirty-two, or a Sunday bowler who picks up a hat-trick with three unstoppable reverse-swinging yorkers. For one blessed moment you are picked out by Fortune to be the winner in Her lottery. Enjoy it while it lasts, because it'll never come again.

We must have hauled in twenty mackerel that afternoon. It was as though they were trying to get aboard. While they wanted to, we let them. By the time it stopped, it felt as though the boat was covered in fish.

Gerard threw me another beer as I piloted us towards the marina. If we'd caught twenty fish, we weren't far behind that in the number of beers we'd drunk and now the thrill of the fishing had died down, I was reeling from their effect.

'Jacob's Bar?' Gerard said. 'Quick drink before you go home?'

I looked at my watch. It was nearly three p.m. 'I'd love to, but I have to go to a cook-out at Lisa's.' I rolled my eyes. 'But what can I do?'

Gerard shrugged. 'Another time. I'll drop you off at home.'

The cook-out was in full swing by the time I showered and changed. Sherry glared at me when I arrived.

'Sorry,' I said. 'The mackerel were running. Can't miss that.'

'Of course not.'

There was a table covered with bottles of beer and wine. I pointed at it. 'Drink?'

Sherry shook her head. 'Already got one. And from the smell of you, you've had enough.'

'I have.' I leaned towards her and whispered in her ear. 'But I'm not missing this. Free booze from Lisa? It's not often *I* take something from *her*.'

Sherry pushed me away. 'I can't believe you're still going on about that.'

I went to the table and poured myself a large glass of the most expensive looking wine. I knew I should eat something or drink some water, but I was at the point in drunkenness when you still know what you should do, but you can't force yourself to do it.

Daniel was there. He waved, but didn't come over. Good; it seemed he was getting the message to stay away.

Lisa's downstairs bathroom was at the front of the house, and you have to walk past the dining room – which is an annexe off the main living room – to get to it. As I passed it, the door was open, and I saw the fruit salad on the dining room table. For some reason, I went in and looked at it.

It was an excellent fruit salad, colourful and filled with bright, exotic fruits. I picked out a piece of apple and ate it. It was lovely, fresh and full of sweet syrup. I pictured her carrying it out into the garden and glorying in the compliments from her guests. I imagined myself shouting out *that's my fruit*, and Sherry's appalled reaction. I'd never do that. I was in enough trouble with her as it was.

Anyway, it wasn't that big a deal. It was just some fruit, after all. There was no point in getting uptight about it.

'Thinking of getting in ahead of the others?'

I turned round to see Daniel leaning against the doorframe.

'Just looking. Admiring Lisa's handiwork.' He didn't say anything. 'Is that what *you* were hoping for? Get in early?'

He didn't move. His eyes were hard and cold, the warm smile and solicitous expression gone.

'Well,' I said. 'Bathroom for me.'

He moved aside so I could pass him. As I did he grabbed my bicep. His grip was surprisingly strong. I turned to look at him.

'What?' I said.

He stayed silent, staring at me. I got the impression he was going to say something but thought better of it, then he let go. For a second I considered pushing him or hitting him or doing something, but I backed away. I wasn't scared of him – he was half my size – but there was a strange intensity in his eyes that made me wary.

*

On my way back from the bathroom Lisa was coming out of the dining room with the fruit salad. It was very large, and she looked like she was struggling, so I offered to help carry it.

'It looks wonderful,' I said. 'Really wonderful.'

She smiled. 'Thank you for the fruit. It was very kind.'

'My pleasure.' In that moment I was filled with a kind of, if not love, then deep affection for Lisa. She was, when all was said and done, a kind and considerate friend and neighbour. We were lucky to have her and Mike.

I set the fruit salad on the table in the garden. Mike was serving food so I grabbed a burger and went to find Sherry.

She was talking to Betsy, an elderly lady who lived down our street.

'Hello, Tom,' Betsy said. 'How are you?'

'Well. You?' I was conscious that I was still a bit drunk and I wanted to keep the number of words I said to a minimum.

'Oh, not too bad.' She looked at my paper plate. 'Is the food good?'

'Delicious. I was late. Been on the boat all day; I was hungry.'

'Well,' Betsy said. 'I might go and get some more.'

'Have the fruit salad,' Sherry said. 'It's on the table.'

'Oh,' Betsy said. 'I think I will. Lisa makes such a good fruit salad.'

'So,' Sherry said. 'You seem in a better mood.'

I put my arm around her waist and kissed her on the cheek. Her skin was warm from the sun. 'I am. I was just thinking about how lucky I am. You, Peggy, our lives together. More than that, though, people like Lisa and Mike and Gerard. We have good friends here. I'm learning to appreciate them.'

'I'm glad,' Sherry said. 'I love you.'

'And there was the burger. I needed to eat. That put me in a good mood as well.'

She rolled her eyes. 'You always have to joke, don't you? Never serious.' She put her hand on my lower back and slipped her fingers under my belt and onto the top of my buttocks. 'I've got something *serious* to discuss with you later.'

'Crikey,' I said. 'Sounds like I'm in trouble.'

She squeezed, hard. '*Big* trouble.'

'Okay,' Lisa announced. 'Here it is,' she said. 'The pièce de résistance!'

There were some oohs and ahhs. She'd scattered some flowers on the top. It did look impressive.

Sherry looked at me. 'You want some?'

'Sure,' I said. 'Looks really good.'

'And,' Lisa said, 'I must say that Tom and Sherry kindly gave me the fruit this morning. Here's to good neighbours!'

'Our pleasure,' Sherry called out. 'All we want is to be first to eat some.'

'Of course,' Lisa said. 'Come and get it!'

She dipped a ladle into the fruit salad and started to fill up the bowls. Sherry joined the line and passed one to me.

I knew from the first bite that there was something wrong. I could tell from the look on Sherry's face that she could tell it too.

'Is this alcoholic?' she said.

I nodded. The fruit salad tasted of alcohol, and not just a bit. It was overpowering. It was weird; I was sure it hadn't tasted like this when I tried it in the dining room. I looked around. It was clear that other people had the same reaction as we did; parents were grabbing the bowls back from their children.

'That's weird.' Sherry put the bowl on the table and tapped Lisa on the shoulder. 'Is this supposed to be like this?'

Lisa frowned. 'What do you mean?'

Sherry didn't have time to answer. Sarah Birch, who lived a few doors down the street and had two boys, slammed two bowls of the fruit salad onto the table.

'Are you for real?' she said.

Lisa looked completely dumbfounded. It was at that point that I realized what had happened. Sometime between when I had tasted it and Lisa had brought it out the fruit salad had been spiked, but not just spiked; it had been sabotaged.

And I thought I knew who had done it. It was Daniel. I'd left him there when I went to the bathroom. Who else would have had time to do it?

'I'm not sure I understand,' Lisa said, white-faced. 'What's wrong with it?'

'What's wrong with it?' Sarah was purple, apoplectic with rage. 'You don't see anything wrong with serving this to kids? Serving alcohol to kids? Maybe I should call the cops and they can explain it to you.'

Lisa's hand was shaking as she lifted a spoonful of the fruit salad to her mouth. She paled even further when she tasted it.

'Oh my God,' she said, in a quiet, shocked voice. 'I'm so sorry. I had no idea.'

'Whatever,' Sarah said. 'We're leaving. You should be ashamed of yourself.'

Sherry had evidently come to the same conclusion as me about what had happened. She put her arm around Lisa and addressed the guests. 'Sorry, folks,' she said. 'I don't know how this has happened, but there's a problem with the fruit salad. It seems there's been a mix-up and somehow some alcohol's gotten into it. Just put your bowls back on the table and we'll clear it up.'

'It's okay,' John, one of the dads, said. 'I prefer it like this. He held up his empty bowl. Any more?'

There were a few laughs; most people returned their bowls to the table, and the party continued. Sarah stomped off, shaking her head. Lisa just stared at the bowl, motionless, her face drained of blood.

'Hey.' It was Mike. 'What happened?'

'I don't know.' Lisa looked at him, biting her bottom lip. 'I just don't know.' Her mouth started to quiver and tears came to her eyes. 'I gave alcohol to the kids!'

Mike put his hand on her shoulder. 'No you didn't,' he said. 'Whatever happened, it wasn't that. Go sit down. Take a break. I'll hold the fort here.'

Lisa nodded, and went upstairs. Sherry followed her. I looked at Mike and raised an eyebrow. 'Somebody wanted to get the party started.'

Mike nodded. 'Yeah. And if I find out who it was –' He didn't finish his threat. He didn't need to. He was a gentle guy, but the look of fury on his face left no room for doubt about what he would do.

I settled into an Adirondack chair. About half an hour later, Sherry came down. She was on her own.

'No Lisa?' I said.

She shook her head. 'Poor thing. She's devastated.'

'It's not that bad. Nobody died.'

'I know, but this is kind of her thing, you know? Cooking and baking and that kind of stuff. She'll get over it; she's just embarrassed. I feel terrible for her.' She shook her head. 'I wonder who did it? I mean, who would do that kind of a thing?'

'I don't know.' Could I tell her my suspicions? I didn't think so. There was no point. Firstly, she wouldn't believe me and secondly, she'd think I was just trying to get at Daniel. 'Mean trick, though, whoever did it.'

'Let's go home,' she said. 'I've had enough.'

Our gardens shared a fence, but we had not put a gate in between, so to get from Lisa and Mike's garden to our house, you had to go out onto the road. Our garage door was open and we walked in.

I should have realized what was going on when I saw that my fishing bag had moved. It was a big green canvas thing I'd bought from Army surplus years ago and when I'd come home from fishing that afternoon I'd left it in the corner of the garage, where I always left it. Now, though, it was next to the door to the mud room.

Sherry picked it up to move it to one side. Something inside it clinked. It was unzipped – I never left it unzipped – and, as she put it down, it fell open.

'What's that?' Sherry said, her voice high and taut.

'What's what?'

She pointed at the bag, and I saw it.

There was a bottle of vodka. It was big – one and a half litres – with a yellow label and a red cap. And it was empty.

'What's that?' Sherry said again. She grabbed it and pulled it out of the bag. 'Was it *you*?'

I shook my head. All I could do was stare at the bottle.

'Answer me. Was it you who spiked the fruit salad? Is that where you went?'

My mouth dried up. Even though I was innocent I couldn't look her in the eyes. I knew how it seemed.

She waved the bottle at me, her eyes wide and wild. 'Did you spike it? With this?'

'No. I-I' I stammered, 'I've never seen that before.'

'Really? Then how did it get in your bag?'

'I don't know.' I did know, though. So this was what Daniel had done.

'You need to come up with some answers, and soon.'

'It was Daniel.'

Her eyes narrowed. 'What?'

'It was Daniel. I saw him near the dining room when I went to the bathroom.'

'Why would he do that?'

'To frame me.'

'Right. So he spiked the fruit salad – his oldest friend's fruit salad – then crept round here and put this in your fishing bag, which he knew, somehow, that I would look in. And all to make you look bad? This is ludicrous, Tom.'

'Why would I do it?'

'I don't know. I don't know why anyone would, but maybe, just maybe, someone who was annoyed at the person who had made it and who had been out all day drinking with his friend might have thought it was a good idea.'

'So you think it was me?'

She didn't answer. She just looked at me like I was a piece of shit she'd had to scrape off the sole of her shoe. That look stayed with me for a long time.

Number Two

'Daddy,' Peggy said. 'Do you love Mommy?'

I was lying next to her in bed, her book folded open over my stomach. I'd nearly nodded off; she liked me to lie with her while she fell asleep, and I often woke up a few hours later. Normally I'd stay there and look at her for a while, marvel at my daughter, sprawled out, mouth open, Sammy the horse clutched in her hands.

I thought she was asleep; she normally was by now, and the idea that she was being kept awake by a worry about me and Sherry broke my heart.

'Of course,' I said. 'Of course I do. And I love you.'

'Does Mommy love you?'

'Yes. Yes, she does.'

She paused. 'Are you going to get divorced?'

Where the hell had she learned about divorce? 'No.'

'Never?'

'Never.'

She rolled on her side. 'Okay,' she said. She seemed satisfied; a few minutes later her breathing deepened and I went downstairs.

*

Sherry was stacking the dishwasher. I stood in the doorway and watched her. When she finished she started to arrange the magazines and letters on the countertop. She always did this when she wanted to avoid something; she distracted herself with pointless activity.

'Stop,' I said. 'Let's talk.'

'I need to tidy this up.'

'No you don't. We need to talk, though.'

'You got drunk and spiked my friend's fruit salad and the entire neighbourhood ate it. What's to talk about?'

'I didn't do that.'

She looked away. We'd had days of arguments about this. She was convinced that I had done it; I knew I hadn't. *Why can't you just admit it? The bottles were hidden in your bag. You'd been drinking. You'd been complaining about Lisa that morning. I won't be angry; I just want you to be honest. I just want to move on.*

But I hadn't admitted it. How could I admit something I hadn't done?

'Fine,' she said. 'Then there's nothing to talk about.'

'There is, Sherry. Peggy just asked me if we love each other. Clearly she's picking up on our arguing. It's not fair.'

She paused. 'What did you tell her?'

'I told her that of course we did. And we love her as well.' I took her by the wrists. 'We do, don't we? Love each other?'

'Do we? I wonder, sometimes.'

'I don't. Wonder, that is. You and Peggy are everything to me.' I pulled her close. 'Everything.'

'I've been worried about you.' She had tears in her eyes now. 'The stuff with Daniel, and the school, and now the fruit salad. It's not like you. Is it because of your Mom?'

I closed my eyes. I said nothing. There was no point denying it again. It was incredible how totally – and how quickly – something like this could infest and poison a relationship, but then I guess Daniel knew that.

'Is that it, Tom? You're worried about your mom?'

It wasn't. It was Daniel, but this looked like a way out. 'Maybe. Maybe it's the thought of her over there. It makes me sad. I'm sorry if I took it out on you. It's not your fault.'

'I feel so guilty knowing how it affects you. If it wasn't for me you'd be back home, married to someone else and without all this to worry about.'

'And I wouldn't have you, or Peggy.' I paused. I wasn't sure I wanted to admit this, but the conversation was going well. 'I guess that's why I was so anti-Daniel. I feel exposed, you know? I've already given up so much to be here with you – my friends, my family, my home – and he seemed like a threat to what I *do* have, which is you and Pegs.'

Sherry kissed me. 'I'm not interested in Daniel. Honestly. And he's not interested in me. He never has been. We're just friends. There's nothing between us.'

I believed her. I really did. 'I'm glad we talked,' I said. 'We needed that.' I slipped my hand around her waist and under the waistband of her jeans. 'How about we do some work on that brother or sister?'

Sherry pulled away. 'That's something else I want to talk to you about. I want to go for tests. It's been five years; I think something might be wrong. I want to find out now so there's time to do something.'

'What do you mean, tests?'

'Fertility tests. It's taking too long.'

The desire fizzled out. 'There's nothing wrong. We've done it before. Twice, if you count the miscarriage.'

'Things change. I want us to get checked.'

'Us? You want me to go as well?'

159

She nodded. 'Just in case.'

I didn't like the thought of having my sperm tested, mainly because I didn't want to find out if there was something wrong. Like a lot of men my medical strategy was to ignore things until they either went away of their own accord or ended in a trip to the emergency room. For a while, I'd been seeing blood on the toilet paper when I wiped my backside – not every time, but enough to prompt me to type 'blood in stool' into Google. The fifteen minutes I had spent looking at the possible diagnoses before I had forced myself to switch the computer off had convinced me that I had colon cancer and that I needed to get it checked asap; nonetheless I had adopted my 'ignore it and hope for the best' strategy. The blood had remained, though.

Still, tonight was not the night to argue. It was the night to make concessions. And, after all, a sperm test was one of the more pleasurable ways to experience the medical system. I'd donated sperm once at university – if it was still the same then you went into a cubicle with a jazz mag and knocked one out into a jar. Not as good as the privacy of your own bathroom, but not that bad, especially when compared to some of the other things doctors did to you.

'Okay. And what if there *is* a problem?'

'We can adopt.' She said it with a lot of certainty; she'd evidently given it some thought. 'I'd be okay with that.'

'Me too,' I said. I wasn't sure that I was okay with it, but it was easier not to argue. It was unlikely it would ever be an issue, and if it was, we could cross that bridge when we arrived at it. 'Whatever it takes for us to be a family.'

Sherry pressed against me. 'I love you,' she said, and started to unbutton my jeans. 'And in the meantime, we should keep trying the traditional way.'

Colonoscopy

I woke around three in the morning. Sherry had stolen the covers and I was cold. I pulled them over me, and went back to sleep.

Except I couldn't.

The idea of fertility treatment had opened up the possibility of more children, a possibility that I suppose I had given up on. It wasn't happening, for whatever reason, and I was okay with that. Now, though, we were going to make it happen. We were going to have another child. A larger family.

And I had colon cancer.

Well, not exactly. I didn't know for a *fact* that I had colon cancer, but it was a possibility. And that was enough to terrify me.

Under the covers I started to sweat. God, I was stupid. I'd had the bleeding for a month, at least, and I'd just ignored it. A month lost. If it turned out to be cancer – well, I'd only have myself to blame.

I got out of bed and went onto the landing. Peggy's door was open, her nightlight spilling out over the wooden floor. I went in and looked at her. What if I died? How would she take it? Would she have psychological problems in later life? I pictured her at thirty in some shrink's office, unburdening herself of the load she'd carried since childhood.

161

He knew. He ignored the signs. If only he'd gone to the doctor earlier I might have my daddy today. A pause. *Unless he wanted to die. Wanted to escape me*.

I shook my head. This was crazy. I didn't have cancer. I had to stop my mind whirring like this. *Just go to bed,* I told myself. *Go to bed*.

But what if you do have cancer? a little voice said. *What then, eh?*

I got an emergency appointment the next day.

'How often is the bleeding?' the doctor, a woman of about forty called Dr Allison, asked. When I'd seen her my blood had run cold. Why did it have to be a woman? And a youngish one at that? It was much harder to say the words *I have anal bleeding* to a woman than a man.

'Every other day,' I said. 'Something like that.'

'And how much blood is there?' She didn't seem concerned, which comforted me; she just asked her questions and made notes. Having said that, they were probably trained not to show emotion. For all I knew she could have been thinking *he's on the way out, poor bastard. No point in making it harder for him*. My worry returned.

'Not too much. Just a few spots, normally.'

'Is it in the stool, or on the paper?'

'On the paper.' I thought about it. 'I suppose it could be in the stool as well. I haven't looked too closely.'

She gave me a contemptuous look that said *you're bleeding from your arse and you don't check your shit?*

'What colour is the blood?'

I paused. Was this a trick question? 'Red,' I said. 'Are there other options?'

She closed her eyes briefly, not much more than a slow blink.

Had she sighed loudly, blown out her cheeks and rubbed her temples she could not have expressed her contempt better. 'Dark red? Or bright red?'

'Red like a – ' I tried to think of something red. It was harder than I expected. Normally when you wanted to say something was red you said it was red as blood, but that was out of the equation. Red as a robin's breast? A fire? In the end I decided to stick with what I knew. 'Red like the blood when you cut yourself.'

'Fresh blood, then. From the lower end of the colon.'

God. It was fresh. That meant I was bleeding now. *Right now inside me I was bleeding.* I felt faint.

'Is that bad?' I said.

'Normally it's better than older blood, but it's hard to say without taking a look.' She gave a smile, which with hindsight I remember as a little sinister. 'Take off your pants and lie face down on the examination table.'

'You're going to take a look? Right now? In my – ' I didn't know what to call it. Arse sounded vulgar; anus almost sexual. 'Bottom?'

'Yes, I am. I need to examine your bottom.'

A few minutes later I was lying on my front listening to the snap of rubber gloves. I felt the cool plastic spread my buttocks then a finger probe my anus. I tensed.

'Relax,' she said, then: 'Hmmm.' Seconds later it was over.

When I got dressed she was behind her desk. 'Well, I can't see anything. I'm going to refer you for a colonoscopy. They'll have a proper look.'

I started to regret coming. *A proper look.* That meant there was something to look for, and as far as I could tell from the internet that meant cancer, which meant death, probably in about three weeks.

'What – what might they find?'

'Probably one of three things. Haemorrhoids, a polyp, which is a little growth on the bowel wall, neither of which is a problem. Or it could be something a little more worrying.'

Oh my God. 'Like cancer?'

'Yes. Like cancer.' She smiled. 'But don't worry about that just yet. It's not that likely.'

I didn't manage not to worry. All the way home I was convinced I was dying and everything I saw reminded me of it. A pretty flower, sunlight on a puddle, the thought of Peggy: they all made me see how precious life was and how much I'd been taking it for granted. If I survived, I swore to be a better man.

I called Gerard and arranged to meet him at a bar that evening. I needed to get out.

He was waiting there when I arrived.

'Hi,' he said. 'Want a beer?'

I'd been meaning to bring it up later, but now that I saw him I couldn't stop myself.

'I think I'm dying.'

He looked at me for a while. I suppose it must have taken a while for the words to sink in; it was quite unusual for a friend to march up to you and announce his imminent demise.

'Well, you'll definitely want a beer then,' he said. 'What're you dying of?'

'Bowel cancer.'

He raised his eyebrows. 'Really?'

'Probably.'

'Better make it Guinness,' he said, and gestured to the barman. 'That'll clean you out. How probably is probably?'

'Probably enough that I have to have a colonoscopy.'

He winced. 'Ouch.'

'Are they bad?'

He nodded. 'You know what they use, right? You have seen the scope?'

'No.'

'Oh.' He smiled a faint, forced little smile. 'Then don't worry. You'll be okay.'

'What are you hiding? What's the scope like?'

'Nothing really. Just a little camera they pop up there.'

'Just tell me what it is. I can take it. I'm a big boy.'

'You'll need to be,' he said. 'The damn thing's about six feet long.'

It was. Maybe even longer; although the doctor told me it was not quite six feet, I wasn't sure I believed him. He held a coil of thick black tubing containing a camera and a light.

I had opted not to have a general anaesthetic. Now I saw the colonoscope I was wondering whether it was a good decision. Once you've seen it, there's really no decision to make.

'About that general anaesthetic . . .' I began.

'You'll be fine.' The doctor was a thin, precise man in his early thirties. He looked like he lived on bran, vegetables and exercise; perhaps he was a health freak, or perhaps he just knew what a colonoscopy involved so steered clear of a lifestyle that might result in one. 'Let me outline the procedure. There's really nothing to it.'

I pointed at the scope. 'Doesn't seem that way.'

'You'll hardly feel it. The nurse will pump you full of air to inflate the colon. This thing will barely touch the sides. Unless we see a polyp, in which case we'll snip it off, which you might notice.'

I wondered what made a young doctor train in this speciality. Cardiologist, I could understand; gynaecologist, the appeal was obvious. But arse-doctor? Who wanted to spend their career looking at people's colons?

It's the giving of pain, I realized. They're sadists.

'Right,' he said. 'If there are no questions, you can go through to the exam room.'

In the kind of daze where you find yourself going along with things – really, I wanted to run screaming from there – I went into the examination room. A nurse, young and pretty with large teeth and the most luxurious hair I'd ever seen, handed me a backless hospital gown.

'Change behind the screen and lie on your side on the table,' she said. 'You're very brave, not having the anaesthetic.'

I didn't want to be brave. I wanted to be unconscious. 'Do most people have it?'

'Oh, yes. Most people prefer to be asleep.'

'Does it hurt?'

'I don't know, but I guess you're about to find out. Let me know!'

She attached something to my anus and I felt my stomach inflate.

'Is that okay?' she said.

'Sure.' It was uncomfortable, but hardly painful. It was the sensation of really, really needing to fart.

'Okay. You're ready.'

The next ten minutes – was it twenty? Half an hour? – passed in a blur. The doctor fed the tube up into my colon and started his poking around. It was horrible. Not painful, exactly, but horrible. There was a six foot tube slowly making its way up my colon. If that sounds weird, and alien, then that was how it felt. Mainly, I wanted to pass wind.

When, eventually, it was over, the doctor sat back.

'Well,' he said. 'Get changed and come through to the consulting room. We can discuss it in there.'

There was something to discuss. The pain of the colonoscopy vanished, replaced by the panic of my impending diagnosis. It was cancer. I knew it.

I put my clothes on slowly. This could be the last time I dressed as a healthy man. The last thing I did in my pre-cancer life. I opened the door to the consulting room, my heart heavy. What was I going to tell Sherry? We couldn't have more kids now. It wasn't fair.

'Well,' the doctor said. 'Take a seat.'

I sat down. It was uncomfortable, the air they had pumped into me still trapped in my bowels.

'Good news,' he said. 'Clean as a whistle. I must say, you have a very nice bowel.'

A nice *bowel*? These people were weird.

'So there's nothing? No cancer?'

'Nope.'

I almost didn't believe him; I wanted to jump up and down.

'Then where is the blood from?'

'You have a small haemorrhoid on the inside of the anus. That's all.' For a second I thought he was disappointed. Still, he could console himself with the thought he'd seen a nice bowel. He scribbled on a pad. 'Here's a prescription for some cream. See you again.'

'I hope not.' It was a well-worn joke, but I enjoyed it.

There were two other people in the reception area, an old lady and her son. I suspected that they might not be on the verge of such good news. Still, nothing could dampen my spirits. I was free! My death sentence lifted!

'So,' the nurse, who doubled as the receptionist, said. 'Good news.'

'That's right.' I grinned at her; a movie-star grin, the grin of a survivor. I realized I was flirting. 'And the pain wasn't that bad.'

'Just a haemorrhoid.'

'Just a haemorrhoid.' Even the fact that she knew I had piles couldn't deflate my euphoria. 'See you around.'

I took a step away from the counter and towards the exit door.

Perhaps it was because I was relaxed; perhaps it was just that it took that long, but at that moment the air they had pumped in obeyed whatever laws of physics governed it, and out it came, noisily, and at length.

Behind me, the old lady sniggered.

I froze, and it stopped. I took another step and it came again, and again, and again. Each time I took a step I let out the most monumental fart, and there was nothing I could do to stop them.

I looked back at the receptionist. She had covered her mouth with her hand, her face red with the effort of containing her laughter.

'Cheerio,' I said.

She clearly didn't trust herself to speak; she just gave a little wave. I closed the door to the sound of gales of laughter.

Boating

I lifted Peggy and handed her to her mum, then stepped from the boat into the canoe.

'Right,' I said. 'Time for an adventure.'

I untied the canoe from the stern of the boat – we'd towed it out with us – and pushed off. We were anchored at Whaleboat Island, a long, thin spit of land in the Casco Bay. Ten yards away was a narrow, rocky beach where we were planning to have a picnic; first, we were going to circumnavigate the island.

'Watch out for pirates,' I said. 'Peggy, you're in charge of pirate spotting. I'll paddle. Mum's the navigator.'

'Okay,' Peggy said. 'I'm looking.'

'Okay *captain*,' I said. 'You have to call me captain.'

'*I* want to be the captain.' She peered at me. 'Me and Mom will be the captain. *You* can be the pirate.'

'The pirates are not on our boat. They'll be on their own boat. A big one. A big pirate ship.'

'Can we go on it?'

'No. We don't want to go on it. If we go on it, that means they've captured us.'

'But I want to go on it.'

Sherry laughed. 'Looks like Peggy has her own ideas about this.'

'Let's discuss that later, Pegs,' I said. 'For now, keep a look out.' I dug the paddle into the water and we began to make our way along the shoreline. It was beautiful; the early fall sun striking the water and dappling the damp rocks, seabirds diving for fish, seals barking. After all the difficulties, the stresses, of the past few weeks, this was just what we needed. Something we could do as a family, something new and fresh and invigorating.

'I can't see the pirates,' Peggy said.

'Keep looking.'

Peggy looked for five more seconds. 'I still don't see them.'

'Maybe they won't be here today,' Sherry said. 'They're probably having a day off. It's too nice a day for pirating, anyway. I bet they're on the beach somewhere.'

'Hmmm.' Peggy had one last look around, then pointed at my oar. 'Can I paddle?'

'No,' I said. 'You might drop it.'

'I won't!'

'Later. Have a go later.'

'Can I have a go now?'

I bit my bottom lip. 'Sure. Hold it like this. Use two hands.'

Peggy thrust it into the water. It trailed behind us. When she tried to move it forwards it caught on the water and jerked out of her grip.

In a canoe it is wise not to make any sudden movements; certainly a lunge sideways in order to grab a passing paddle is likely to result in disaster. So it was that I watched as the paddle drifted beyond my reach.

'Great,' I said. 'That's just great.' It was the only paddle we had; it had come with the canoe when we bought it at a yard sale. I had been meaning to buy another, but hadn't got round to it.

'Sorry, Daddy.' Peggy looked at me, her expression a mixture of worry and fear. She was probably putting it on but it worked. I leaned forward and kissed her.

'Don't worry, darling. It was an accident.' I shrugged. 'So what do we do now?'

'Good job it's a nice day,' Sherry said. 'You'll warm up quick enough after a swim.'

I stripped off my shirt and got ready to exit the canoe. I didn't mind; no one minds the chance to be a hero for his wife and daughter.

It *was* a good job it was a warm day. To call the Atlantic Ocean off the Maine coast cold would be like describing being kicked in the balls as a bit uncomfortable; that is, a massive understatement. It is bitingly, unthinkably, shockingly freezing.

When I got my breath back I grabbed the paddle and passed it to Sherry.

'Jesus,' I gasped. 'Jesus Christ.' I circled my legs frantically. I was worried that if I stopped moving them they might freeze and snap off. 'Help me get in.'

Sherry raised an eyebrow. 'Good luck.'

'What do you mean?'

'Good luck climbing into a canoe without tipping it over.'

'I can't risk that. There's no way Peggy can fall in this.'

'Exactly.' She smiled. 'That's why I suggest you start swimming for the beach. I'll paddle us in.'

It took me an hour to warm up, by which time we had eaten and were ready to head back to the marina. We paddled back to the boat and climbed aboard.

It was about five miles back to the marina, and we were back on our mooring twenty minutes later.

'Look at that,' I said. 'What a mess.'

Tied to the dock was a new addition to the marina: a large, flashy powerboat of the type loved by rock stars and teenage boys. It was probably forty foot long and had two huge outboard engines on the back. Whoever bought it had more money than sense, more money than taste, at any rate.

'Not my kind of thing,' Sherry said. 'But each to their own.'

'Exactly.' I pointed to a wooden cutter on a mooring a few down from ours. I hadn't seen her before and she was gorgeous, painted navy blue with dark wood trim. Polished brass letters spelled her name. *Phoebe*. 'That's the kind of boat I'd like. I'd love the chance just to sit on it. Even got a pretty name.'

'I'll buy you one, Daddy,' Peggy said. 'For your birthday.'

I didn't want to point out the obvious flaw in her plan; there was no need to squash the impulse to generosity with a heavy dose of reality.

'Thank you, darling,' I said. 'I can't wait.'

The launch pulled up alongside us and we climbed aboard. I gestured to the new powerboat.

'Quite the machine, isn't she?' I said to the middle-aged guy who ran the launch.

He laughed. 'Yeah. Some new guy in town bought her.' He shook his head. 'Thing's a disaster. Expensive to run, ugly.'

'I know. I don't know why anyone would spend their money on something like that.'

'It's a lot of money. Three hundred g's at least. I *think* that I wouldn't buy something like that if I had the money, but you never know.' He grinned at me. 'But I'd sure like to find out.'

When we reached the dock I climbed off the launch. Sherry picked up Peggy and handed her to me.

'Can I get some candy, Dad?'

The marina had a small shop which sold penny candy. June, the lady who ran it, would sit with the kids and help them figure out how much they could get for a quarter or a dime. It was an educational experience, she told us; it seemed to me like a chance for her to be the most popular lady in town.

'I suppose so.'

'Carry me.'

I picked her up – she was tired, and limp like a doll – and walked up the steps to the shop.

Inside, Daniel was sitting at the counter, sipping a coffee.

It was awkward; he knew that I'd asked Sherry not to see him. It made me feel stupid, as though I was scared of him hanging around with my wife.

Still, I could afford to ignore it; hell, I could even afford to be friendly. I was holding Sherry's hand and had Peggy in my arms and we had just had the best time together we'd had in ages.

'Hi,' I said. 'Good to see you.'

'You know Daniel?' June said. 'He's back in town.'

'That's right.' Daniel's face was set in a broad grin. 'Back in town and back on the water.'

Of course, the flashy power boat was Daniel's. What an arsehole; Maine wasn't the kind of place where you splashed money around like that.

'New boat?' I said.

Daniel looked out at the water. 'Sort of.'

I pointed at the powerboat. 'That yours? She's nice.' Sherry gave my hand a warning squeeze, but I was enjoying this. 'A bit understated, but that's no bad thing.'

Daniel frowned. 'That thing? No. Mine's on a mooring. I bought her a few years ago and had her restored. They just finished and put her in the water.'

Had her *restored*? What the hell was he talking about?

'Which one is it?' Sherry said.

'The cutter. I called her *Phoebe*, after my mom.'

'Daddy,' Peggy said. 'That's the one you said you like.'

I froze. 'That's right,' I said. 'She's lovely.'

'Really?' Daniel said. 'You think so?' He smiled. 'Thanks. Come on her any time.' He looked at Peggy, then at me, then at Sherry. His eyes rested on her. 'Bring the family. You're always welcome.'

'Thanks,' I said. It was a hell of an effort to get that one little word out. 'We'd better be going. Peggy's tired.'

'I'm not.' She pointed at *Phoebe*. 'Can we go on Daniel's boat now, Daddy? It's much nicer than ours. Ours is noisy.'

'Old two-stroke,' I muttered. 'Not the quietest. But it's okay.'

Daniel waved a hand, magnanimously brushing my explanation aside.

'Like I say,' he said. 'Any time.'

Doctor Two

The medical experience that followed the colonoscopy was a lot more pleasant.

The day it took place Sherry looked at the kitchen clock. It was just past nine in the morning.

'What time is your appointment?'

'Ten.' Sherry had already been for whatever tests she had to do and was waiting for the results. In the meantime I was due to give my sperm sample. It turned out that things had moved on from the last time I had donated sperm and you now provided the sample in the comfort of your own home and then rushed it to the doctor's office; provided you got it there within an hour it was okay. 'I'll do the sample in a bit.'

'You just do it in a bottle?'

'A kind of cup. They gave it to me when I made the appointment.'

'You want a hand with it?' She uncrossed her legs and sat forward. 'Or a mouth?'

I had also been advised not to indulge in any sexual activity in the five days leading up to it; my mouth dried up and I got an immediate erection.

'Sure,' I said. 'The cup's upstairs.'

Thirty minutes later I was pulling into the doctor's office, the sample nestled in one of the cup holders in the central console of the car. We had got a bit carried away and the blowjob had turned into sex; fortunately I had remembered to pull out at the last minute and managed to grab the cup and aim the sperm just in time.

'It should be ready this afternoon,' the nurse said, as I handed her my sperm. In the medical world the normal rules of social interaction really were turned on their heads. 'I've scheduled you in at four to discuss the results with Dr Mantel.'

'Okay,' I said. 'See you later.'

Dr Mantel was a grey-haired man in his fifties. He wore a wedding band and there were photos of three teenagers on his desk. No sperm problems for him, it seemed. It was a bit insensitive to advertise the fact given the nature of his work.

'Right,' he said, as I came in. 'Take a seat. We've got the results.'

I am always nervous in medical situations. Most of your life you go along ignoring the physical fact of your body; you don't think of it decaying or going wrong. It's like your car: until it fails you assume it will start every morning. Visiting a doctor reminds you that a) you're a very complicated machine and there's a lot that can go wrong and b) you're eventually going to die. Still, I'd learned from the colonoscopy. There was no point working yourself up beforehand; you couldn't do anything about it anyway (other than visit the doctor, which you were already doing) and in any case, there was probably nothing wrong.

Hadn't someone said that worry was a dividend paid to disaster before it was due? Good advice, that, so I took a deep breath, smiled and sat down.

'Well, Mr Harding.' Dr Mantel looked at the notes. 'It seems there are one or two abnormalities.'

Abnormalities? What the hell did he mean? Hearing that from a doctor meant there was something wrong. Some official medical problem, linked to my sperm. My heart started to thump in my chest. Despite my nervousness, I'd not really expected anything to be wrong. This was crazy – his next words were going to have an impact on the rest of my life. It looked like this time I *should* have fucking worried.

'You have low motility,' he said. 'Or rather, your sperm do.'

'What does that mean?'

'It means your sperm are not very active, which makes it harder for them to reach and fertilize the egg.'

'Not impossible, though?' It couldn't be; I had Peggy.

'No. But unlikely.'

'How unlikely?'

'Very unlikely.'

'But not impossible?'

'No, but if you want to have children I suggest you consider some fertility assistance.'

It wasn't future children I was worried about. 'I have a daughter. You know that, right?'

'As I said, it's possible.'

'You said it was unlikely.'

He bit his lower lip. 'It is entirely possible that your sperm have become less active over time. It's quite normal.'

I put my thumb and forefinger to my temples and pressed on them. There was a mistake here. There was nothing wrong with my sperm; I had a daughter. 'Is there any chance that the sample was damaged? Took too long to get here? I think the results aren't right.'

'Mr Harding, I understand your reluctance to accept the results. But this is not uncommon in men.'

'Fine, I get it. But are you sure there's not been an error?'

'We can re-run the test, if you like, but from what I see here there is no indication of any error.'

'Right,' I said. 'We'll re-do it. Tomorrow morning, I'll come here. That way we'll know it's a good sample.'

He nodded. I could see he felt sorry for me. 'Okay. I'll see you tomorrow.'

I stared at Peggy as she ate her spaghetti. There was no way she wasn't my daughter; she looked like me, she always had. My eyes were a kind of murky green colour, which she shared. It had been that way since soon after she was born. There was no way that could be a coincidence. No way.

'Daddy, stop looking at me.' She slurped up a piece of spaghetti which was dangling from her mouth. It left a red splodge on her chin and I leaned forward and wiped it off.

'Sorry, petal. I was just thinking how beautiful you are.'

She smiled. One of the great things about five-year-old kids is that they haven't learned yet to be bashful about taking compliments. I *am* beautiful, she was thinking, and it made her happy. If only kids could retain that simple confidence the world would be full of happier adults.

When she was in bed I looked through the photo album Mum had made. I had a photo of Peggy on the beach at six months and I was pretty sure there was one of me at a similar age. I wanted to compare us as babies, before the vagaries of gender and upbringing hid the resemblances.

When I put the photos side by side there was no doubt. There could be no doubt. It could have been the same baby. Which meant I *could* father children, which meant that the test was wrong.

In bed, Sherry cuddled up to me. I'd not told her the result. I'd just said the results were delayed and would be available tomorrow. *No need to hold back tonight,* she murmured. *The test is over.* I rolled away. I wanted to give it my best shot in the morning.

Whatever semblance of calm I'd managed to adopt the previous day was long gone. I sat in the waiting room, my legs jiggling up and down. The nerves had made it hard to produce a sample that morning, almost as if my body didn't want to know, and I had been in there for about twenty minutes. Eventually, though, I'd squirted a thimbleful of sperm into the cup and handed it to the nurse.

'Dr Mantel will see you now.' The receptionist smiled at me and gestured towards the consulting room door. 'You can go through.'

This was it. I went in and sat down.

I knew as soon as I saw his face what the result was, and he knew that I knew. He told me anyway, though.

'I'm afraid it's the same result,' he said.

I stood up. I knew there'd be more visits, discussions of options, IVF, possible treatments, all that stuff, but I didn't want to talk about it now. Now I just wanted to go away and lick my wounds.

'Thanks,' I said.

He nodded. 'We'll be in touch.'

When I got home Sherry was standing behind the island in the middle of the kitchen. There was a bottle of champagne and two glasses in front of her, which she filled as soon as I came in.

Before I could speak she raised her finger to her lips and shushed me.

'The results came,' she said, and held up an envelope. 'I'm fine. There's nothing wrong. No endometriosis, nothing. I can have babies.'

She pushed one of the glasses towards me. 'Let's celebrate.' She smiled. 'I'm so relieved. I was so worried.'

'That's great news.' I didn't pick up the glass. 'Congratulations.'
She frowned. 'Are you okay?'

'Fine.' I sounded like my dad. 'Actually, not fine.' I looked at the
bottle of champagne. 'Not really in the mood for celebrating.
Maybe for drowning my sorrows, though.'

'What's wrong?'

'I got *my* results, as well.'

She paled, and put the glass on the island. She leant on the
granite top for support.

'And?'

I couldn't look at her. 'Low sperm motility. I have lazy sperm,
apparently.' That *apparently* made it seem somehow better, as
though it was something happening outside my life, something not
associated with me.

'What does that mean, exactly? We can still have kids, right?
There's Peggy?'

Despite the photos I'd looked at the night before I searched her
face for any trace of guilt. She just looked concerned, or heart-
broken.

'It's unlikely. My sperm could have deteriorated since Peggy.'

I couldn't believe I was saying these things to my wife. I couldn't
believe I *had* to. I knew it was stupid and irrational, but I couldn't
help associate my sperm with my manliness, with my virility. Finding out they were lazy bastards made me feel emasculated.

'Don't worry, darling. It's fine. Lots of people go through this,
and they find a way. We will too,' she said. I could tell she didn't
believe it. There was a rigidity in her smile that screamed disappointment. She'd been planning a few glasses of champagne then
a night of baby-making; no point now, was there?

She continued, feeling some need to fill the silence. 'There are
treatments. Or we can adopt. You want to adopt?'

'It's a bit early to make a decision about that now.'

'But we could, right?' She was drowning, grasping at straws.

I swallowed the champagne in one gulp. 'Just have a drink,' I said. 'We'll talk about it later.'

Twin Path

Sherry threw herself into baby-making contingency planning. Her American training came to the fore: she was relentlessly upbeat about the situation, convincing herself that the other options – basically IVF or adoption – were equally good. I was less optimistic; IVF was expensive and even then it wasn't a sure thing, and adoption didn't appeal at all. I wanted more kids, but I was happy enough with Peggy; I didn't see the need for a huge effort to find a solution, because I didn't really see the problem. I would have preferred to wait for a while, let the dust settle, and then make a decision.

Sherry, on the other hand, was in the grip of a kind of baby-making fervour, partly as a displacement activity for her disappointment and partly as a result of her hormones. I knew better than to stand in the way, so I went along with her planning.

One night I was reading to Peggy – she was a big fan of *The Witches* by Roald Dahl. Personally I found it quite frightening and worried she was too young for it, but she found the whole thing hilarious. If she ever met a witch the poor thing wouldn't know what to do; witches were presumably used to children being at least a little bit scared of them.

We'd just got to her favourite part, about the square-toed shoes, a chilling detail which Peggy chuckled at, when the door cracked open.

'Hi, popsicle,' Sherry said. 'Can I come and say goodnight?'

Peggy shifted on her bed so there was room for Sherry to lie down.

'Are you enjoying the bedtime story?'

Peggy nodded. 'It's *The Witches*,' she said. 'They're so funny. Daddy does a funny voice.'

'Does he? Can I hear it, Daddy?'

'Oh, it's only for when I'm reading,' I said. I had a cackling voice I used for the Grand High Witch. Peggy loved it.

'I'd like to hear it. Would you like Daddy to speak in his funny voice, Pegs?'

'Go on, Daddy,' Peggy said. 'Say something.'

'Okay, but don't be too frightened.' I scrunched up my face. It helped me get in character. 'Who's this in Peggy's bed?' I said, in my best witch's cackle. 'It looks like Mummy. I think I'll put her in my pot and boil her up for dinner.'

My girls laughed; Peggy because she was five and Sherry because Peggy was. When they stopped, Sherry rolled on her side.

'How would you like a little sister? Or brother?' she said.

Peggy thought for a while. 'I don't think I'd like it,' she said. 'Could we get a pony instead?'

I stifled a laugh. Sherry continued.

'Maybe. But at the moment Mommy and Daddy are thinking of getting a baby.' She put her arms around Peggy. 'I just thought I'd let you know. We can talk about it more some other time.' She kissed her and got to her feet. 'Good night, popsicle. I love you.'

When she had gone, Peggy turned to me. 'Are we really getting a baby?'

'Not right now.' I looked at her eyes, the same colour as mine. I kissed her on the nose. Her skin was so smooth; she smelled of bath soap and babies. 'Don't worry about it, poppet. You have a good night's sleep.'

'That was a bit premature, wasn't it?'

Sherry shook her head. 'I don't think so. We have to get her used to the idea.'

'We can start when you're pregnant. Nine months is a long time. And there's no guarantee IVF will work.'

'If it doesn't, then there's adoption. I've applied for the forms.'

'Can't it wait? Until we get through the IVF?'

'Adoption takes a long time, Tom. Two or three years. I want to get it started now. If the IVF works then we can cancel it.'

'You know, Sherry, I think you're getting a bit carried away with this. Let's just take one step at a time.'

She glared at me. 'Don't you want to do this? I thought you wanted kids?'

Not like this, I wanted to say. *Not in this pressure cooker. I want to think it through.* But I could hardly say that, could I? I knew what she was thinking – it's you that has the defective sperm and now you want to go slow on the other options?

'Okay,' I said, staring down the twin paths she'd outlined for us. 'Let's do it.'

Daniel at Work

I started to hate walking to work. Originally it had been one of the best things about my job; no daily grind up the freeway or fight to get on a subway for me; my commute was a stroll through the leafy grounds of a New England liberal arts school. Now, though, it exposed me to a succession of young men – tutors, students, maintenance men – and all I could think when I saw them was that they most likely had normal sperm. The deep-seated male urges towards competition and sexual jealousy are impossible to ignore and I felt as though I was losing on both counts. I could not reproduce; they could. I felt incomplete.

A few weeks went by and I started to come to terms with it, mainly because we had Peggy, which meant that no one knew or would guess about my defective sperm. I realized that so much of our happiness is tied up with what people think; as long as people think well of us we can ignore the reality. If no one knew about something it was almost as though it didn't exist. Provided that every one *thought* that a judge was a pillar of the community, then he was a pillar of the community, whether he went home and watched porn while dressed as a woman or not. It was only when people found out about your habits that they became embarrassing. Likewise, I learned, for defective sperm.

I settled at my desk and started to go through the day's emails. There was one from Stephanie – she was not coming in until nine-thirty – but other than that nothing worth dwelling on. Around nine o'clock I was pretty much done, and I went to make a coffee.

I poured the coffee and added milk – actually, a powdered substance of uncertain constitution called *non-dairy creamer*, which didn't dissolve into the coffee so much as clump together like flour in water – and turned to go back to my desk.

I heard footsteps in the corridor and the door opened.

It was Daniel.

It was the first time I'd seen him since the marina. I assumed he was here about the money. I'd heard nothing from Stephanie about his offer of funding, but then I'd not seen that much of her. Often at this time of the year she wasn't around – one of her major functions was to be out and about meeting people to drum up funds or discuss recruitment.

'Oh,' he said, and smiled. 'I was looking for Stephanie.'

'Not here.'

'How've you been?'

'Fine.'

'The family?'

'Fine as well.'

He waited for me to ask after him. The conventions that govern polite conversation are very strong; it was hard not to enquire how he was but it was an easy way of letting him know what I thought of him.

'I'm well,' he said. 'Been busy.'

He was determined, I'd give him that. If he wanted to have a conversation all on his own, then so be it. I nodded.

'Sorry to hear your news.'

He really was persistent, although I didn't think for a second that his concern for my mum was genuine. 'Thanks. She's doing ok, though.' She wasn't, but I was damned if I was going to discuss it with him.

He frowned, puzzled. 'Sorry?'

'My mum. She's been ill.'

'Oh. I'm sorry to hear it.' He paused, just long enough for me to wonder what he was originally sorry for. 'I meant your difficulties with, you know, a brother or sister for Peggy.'

I tensed. 'What difficulties?'

He raised his hands, palms up. 'I shouldn't have said anything. It's none of my business.'

'Damn right it's none of your business.'

'I just wanted to pass on my sympathies.'

'I don't want your fucking sympathies. And I don't need them.' He couldn't know about my sperm test, it was impossible. Sherry wouldn't have said anything, and the doctor, even in Barrow, wouldn't have disclosed personal medical records. He was just guessing, trying to get under my skin. 'And there is no problem. We're fine.'

A broad smile spread over his face. 'Really? I heard you had – ' he nodded at my crotch – 'some laziness issues.'

I felt the blood drain from my face. How did he know? How the *fuck* did he know? My head swam; I couldn't think of anything to say, which was fortunate, as by the time my head cleared I'd had time to calm down.

Walk away, I thought. *Just walk away.*

I smiled. This was the way to do it; relax, don't get involved. I wished I'd learned this lesson earlier in my life. 'Is that right?' I shook my head. 'I think you must have your wires crossed. But thanks anyway.' For the moment, how he knew didn't matter; I just didn't want to let him get under my skin.

His smile didn't waver.

'Anything else I can help you with?' I said.

'And Peggy?' he replied. 'Is she yours?'

Hearing him ask was a shock. It was obvious why he did; no one would ask me that unless they were trying to antagonize me, make me question myself or Sherry or now Peggy. He needn't have bothered. It took a lot of effort, but I managed to smile.

'Don't you have anything better to do, Daniel, than try and wind me up?'

He frowned a little, and looked at me with an expression of false sincerity. 'Look, there's no need for us to be at loggerheads.'

'We're not.'

'Really? You seem – if I may say so – a little hostile towards me.'

'So what? Why do you care? We don't need to be friends.'

'It makes things a little awkward. Sherry and I share a lot of the same friends.'

I shrugged. 'Not my problem. I can live with that.' I disliked him with a deep, thrumming intensity.

'I don't understand what I've done to antagonize you?'

'Nothing. Don't worry about it.'

'There must be something. I just want to clear the air, that's all. If I've done something, let me know and I'll apologize.'

I wanted this conversation to be over. 'Maybe I just don't like you. Did you think of that? Maybe I just think you're a smarmy bastard who can't be trusted.'

He nodded slowly. 'Is that what it is? You think I can't be trusted? With Sherry, I take it?'

'Yeah, maybe. You've been sniffing around.'

He laughed. 'Come on, buddy. We're just friends. You know that. I'm not interested in Sherry.'

I wished I hadn't said anything. Now I was in a conversation. ''Course you're not. Anyway, I'm busy. I'll tell Stephanie you stopped in.'

He carried on. 'Look, Sherry and I go back a long way. We were at high school together.'

'I know. You were just one of her many friends, ten years ago. You might have had a crush on her; I understand, she's a good-looking girl, but she wasn't interested in you then and she isn't now. Get over it.'

He tilted his head and looked at me with narrowed eyes. A sly grin flickered over his lips.

'Is that what she told you?' he said. 'Very interesting.'

The tone in his voice was suddenly confident, almost mocking.

I should have ignored him, but I couldn't help myself. 'What else would she have told me?'

'You should ask her that.'

The anger I thought I'd suppressed returned. 'What the fuck are you talking about?'

'I think that should be between you and her.'

'You guys dated? Is that it?'

He shook his head. 'No. She never told you? About the year out from college?'

I wanted to stop this. I didn't want to give him the satisfaction he was evidently getting from this, but I was sucked along, unable to stop myself. 'She quit university in Boston and took a year off. Then she restarted in Vermont. Is that it?'

'Ask her about that year out. And how she spent it; *who* she spent it with.'

We stared at each other in the silence.

'Get out,' I said. 'Get out of my office and get out of my life.' I'd sort this out with Sherry later; we'd be okay. I just wanted him gone.

He leaned against the wall in a gesture that said he had no intentions of leaving.

'We lived together for a year,' he said. 'Not as boyfriend and girlfriend; we were closer than that. As close as you could be.'

'I don't want to know. I don't give a shit.' I didn't want to hear this. I knew my wife, knew everything about her. I didn't want to find out that wasn't the case, didn't want to know that she had some past that I hadn't suspected. Whatever it was, I would be fine just to leave it there, where it had been for so long, untouched and unable to hurt us, especially if it involved Daniel. I wanted him out of my life, not further in it.

'You think you know her,' he said. 'But you don't, not as well as I do. I know her as well as anyone could, because I made her. I put her back together.' He mimed someone picking up pieces. 'Like Humpty-Dumpty. All the King's horses and all the King's men couldn't help her, but I did.'

I felt sick; my fists clenched. 'Just leave.'

'She never told you, in all these years? Never told you what happened? About the most important thing in her life? How does that make you feel, Tom?'

It made me feel like I wanted to kick the shit out of him. I kept my hands on my knees, under the table. 'I'm the most important thing in her life. Me and Peggy.'

'I wonder what else she's not told you? If there's one thing there might well be some others. Did she tell you about her time at school in Boston? About her reputation? She was quite – how should I put it – quite sought after. Very popular with the boys.'

I rubbed my cheeks with the thumb and forefinger of my right hand. I needed something to do. 'I don't care.' My voice was strained. 'That's her business.'

'She enjoyed herself, let me put it that way. A very liberated woman. She's always enjoyed a good time. Can't imagine she's any different now.' He grinned at me. He had a strange light in his eyes. 'With your problems, you ever worry about Peggy?'

That was it. The anger – rage, really – had been building. I knew he was trying to provoke me and I knew that I should ignore him but that was irrelevant, because I wasn't thinking. Another part of my brain had taken over. A part that was beyond reason.

I jumped up and grabbed him by the throat, slamming him against the wall. He was surprisingly light, and I lifted him onto his toes.

I kept him shoved against the wall and held my right hand, clenched into a fist, to his face. 'Stay the fuck away from me and my family.' The words came out like bullets, each one relieving the anger. 'Or I swear I will kick seven shades of shit out of you. Understand?'

He glared at me, unresponding.

'You understand?'

There was the sound of footsteps in the corridor. Daniel leaned forward so his face was pressed up against mine, then slammed his head back against the wall. We were under a shelf and he directed his head against the bracket; it made a sickening sound and I saw the smear of blood on the wall as his head bounced forwards.

The door opened and Stephanie walked in. Daniel glanced at the clock above the window. Just past nine-thirty. He gave me an almost imperceptible wink. He'd known she was coming. The bastard had played me like a puppeteer.

Stephanie didn't say anything for a few seconds. She just stood there with her mouth open, taking in the scene, a scene which consisted of her strength and conditioning coach holding a wealthy donor against a bloodied wall, just after she'd heard an almighty bang.

I let go of Daniel, who slumped to the floor. It was a performance worthy of Woody Allen.

'What the hell is going on here?' she said, eventually. 'Tom?'

I couldn't think of what to say. The anger was gone, replaced by a sense of dread.

She knelt by Daniel's side. 'Are you okay?'

Daniel nodded, and looked up at me nervously, as though worried I might assault him again. Had I not known better my heart would have gone out to him.

'Fine. Just a bit shaken up.' He touched his fingers to the back of his head. When he looked at them, they were covered in blood. 'Nothing too serious.'

Stephanie glared at me. 'Wait in my office,' she said. 'I'll deal with you later.'

After the Fact

I heard them murmuring through the door, but I couldn't make out their words; it didn't matter, I was pretty sure what was being said: Daniel expressing his bafflement at what I had done and why, Stephanie expressing her shock and disappointment, both of them indulging in head-shaking, hers genuine, his forced.

Of course, all sorts of emotions and thoughts whirled around in my head, but the strongest was shock. Not at what had happened, per se. After all, two men pushing and shoving over a woman was hardly news, but at *how* it had happened. Daniel had *set me up*. He had known Stephanie was coming and he had pushed my buttons until I reacted. It didn't really matter what the reaction was – if she had come in to find a full-blown shouting match I would still have been in some trouble. As it was, I couldn't have played my part any better. It would have been better to walk away; the story of my life.

There were so many questions. How he knew about the sperm test, what he had meant by all the babble about Sherry's reputation. *I know her as well as anyone could, because I made her. I put her back together. Like Humpty-Dumpty.* What the fuck was that all about? At the heart of all of this was fear: there was more going on than I knew about, a part of my wife's story that I didn't understand and had never suspected. And I knew he was telling the truth, or some *kind* of truth – if not, then what the hell had that phone call in Paris been about? I felt nauseous. Whatever this was, it had been there all along. Ever since the day we met.

I was also frightened, both of what came next but more that I had an enemy who was prepared, it seemed, to do whatever he could to hurt me. He was the first enemy – real enemy – I had ever had, and all that remained was to find out what he had planned next.

I didn't have to wait long. A few minutes later the door opened and Stephanie came in. She was white, her hands trembling.

'Well,' she said. 'I don't know what to say.' She sat down. 'The good news – if there is any – is that he isn't going to press charges – which he could, Tom. What you did was assault.'

This was getting worse. Now he was being magnanimous, not pressing charges against the man who had assaulted him.

'I didn't do it,' I said. 'I know you won't believe me – I know how it looks – but for the record I didn't hit him.'

'He didn't say you did. He said you grabbed him and pushed him against the wall, which is when he banged his head. That's why he isn't pressing charges; he's prepared to accept it was a mistake and you just meant to shake him up.'

'I did grab him. But that wasn't why he banged his head. He did that himself.'

She shook her head. 'I can't believe I'm hearing this, Tom.'

'It's true.' I looked at her. She stared back, a look of utter disbelief on her face. 'He's trying to set me up.'

'You're saying – seriously – that after you grabbed him and pushed him against the wall he banged his own head against it? And why? To make what you had done look worse?' She sighed. 'Why would he do that? He didn't need to, Tom. You'd already attacked our soon-to-be largest donor – which you can hardly deny, since I saw you with your hands round his neck – which on its own is bad enough. Why would he add to that?' She leaned forwards. 'I've known you for a while, Tom. Tell me, what the hell were you thinking?'

I looked at the floor. There was nothing I could say; I had no words. And there was no point anyway; whether or not he had banged his own head against the wall didn't matter. I had attacked him in the office, in front of my boss. Game over, no high score.

Which left the question of why he had done it. The only answer I could think of chilled me. He wanted to show me how serious he was.

'He told me you feel threatened by his friendship with Sherry and you got into an argument.'

I think I groaned. It was so embarrassing; so teenage.

'Nothing to say?' I shook my head. 'Okay, Tom. I'm going to have to decide what to do about this. You should go home. I'll let you know what's going to happen.' She took a deep breath. 'But I don't see how it's going to be anything other than bad news.'

I walked home in a state of shock. It was a warm day and the campus was busy. I heard a shout from behind me.

'Yo, Coach Harding!' I still found the habit of calling sports coaches 'Coach' amusing, but that day it barely registered.

It was a lacrosse player, Phil Turner, a slight, sandy-haired boy who I had put on a training regime designed to bulk him up. I turned round.

'I can't make it to practice today,' he said. 'I've done something to my shoulder. In the gym yesterday.' He lifted his arm and grimaced. 'When I do that it's wicked painful.'

'Keep it still,' I said. 'Go and see one of the physios. They'll strap it up.'

He grinned. 'Cheers, coach.' Nothing got these kids down. Up to now most of them had known nothing but success, academically and athletically, and a Hardy College education was the result of that. They had the whole of their lives to come, and they assumed that success would heap upon success: jobs, houses, families, retirement all reached in a state of bliss. Life was rarely like that, though; the tragedy of college was that when your parents told you to enjoy it, as it was the best years of your life, they were right.

When he was gone I took a side path that led to a trail through the woods that surrounded the campus. I didn't want to see anyone else. I sat on a log and tried to order my thoughts, grasp some of the questions that popped up one after another. I was there a long time, but there were a lot of questions. What was going to happen next? Would I lose my job? What was Daniel up to? What about the sperm test? How did Daniel know? *Did* Daniel know, or had he been guessing and got lucky? Most pressing of all, what would I say to Sherry? After all, it wasn't just me that had some explaining to do.

Revelation

When I got home a few hours later Sherry was sitting on the couch. She had her arms folded. I knew immediately that she had heard.

'So,' she said. 'What the fuck?' I realized she was a little drunk.

'Who told you?'

'What does that matter?'

'I'm interested. Was it Daniel?' I saw from the guilt that flickered over her face that it was.

'Yes. He called to talk to you, but you weren't home. I could tell from his voice something was wrong and I made him tell me. Don't blame him.'

'What did he tell you?' I couldn't hide the jealousy in my voice.

'He told me what happened.' She shook her head. 'He also asked me to tell you he's not pressing charges. That's why he called, Tom. Not to get me into bed. You ought to be grateful.'

I'd have preferred it if he had pressed charges; at least then I wouldn't have owed him anything. I looked at Sherry. 'So did he mention why it happened?'

'You had an argument. About me. It's pathetic, Tom, it really is. You should know better.'

At every moment of your life you face decisions. You don't always know it; often it seems like you have no choice what you do, but those decisions are there, and they all lead to different versions of the future. Some of them are big – do you go to Paris with the girl who goes on to be your wife and with whom you move to Barrow, Maine, or do you go home and marry someone from your home town – and some of them are small, but they are all there, a myriad forking paths that your life could take.

It's quite unusual that you know when you face one, but at that moment I did.

I could admit what had happened, apologize, and try to pick up the pieces, or I could challenge her with what Daniel had told me about their shared past – they had lived together, for fuck's sake – a shared past that she had explicitly denied, and face whatever the consequences of that were.

To be honest, I didn't know which was the better option. I either lived with the knowledge – or suspicion – that she had lied to me, which would corrode me from the inside, or I pulled whatever secret she had from where it lay in her past, however much better it would have been to leave it there, dormant. All I knew was that I had to know. I couldn't not ask the question.

'Did he say why we had the argument?'

'Because of your jealousy!'

'Not quite.' I decided not to dive in; I could peel the onion layer by layer. That way, if he was bullshitting the damage would be limited. 'He mentioned a few things about you.'

'Like what?' Was the look of uncertainty on her face proof that what Daniel had been getting at – whatever it was – was true? Or was it just uncertainty because she was in an uncertain situation?

'He talked a bit about the year you took out of college.'

This was more than a passing uncertainty; the blood drained from her face. 'What did he say?'

'You told me you were never a couple.'

'We weren't. Is that what he said? That we were a couple?'

'He said you lived together, for a year.'

She looked almost relieved. 'We did. But not as a couple. As housemates.'

'You didn't tell me that.'

'I didn't think I needed to. I stayed in Boston for a year. Had a few jobs, hung out. He was a student there as well and we shared a house. No big deal.'

I remembered the intense look he had, the fierceness he had spoken with. *Not as boyfriend and girlfriend; we were closer than that. As close as you could be . . . I put her back together. Like Humpty-Dumpty.*

'No big deal? He made it sound like one. He said you were closer than boyfriend and girlfriend.'

'We were friends. Good friends.'

She looked worried, and I drove on. 'He seemed to think you had some kind of special bond.'

'Not really. No. Nothing.'

'He said he knows you as well as anyone could. That sounds like something.'

Her voice was quieter now. 'What else did he say?'

'He said he knows you so well because he made you. He put you back together.'

She paled a little and closed her eyes. 'Oh,' she whispered. 'He said that?'

Whatever tension there was between us, whatever anger and fight had been in the room had gone. We both knew we were at a crossroads. 'Sherry, you need to tell me what happened between you two.'

'Okay,' she said, her voice a whisper. 'But I'd like a drink.'

College Days

I made it a stiff one. When I handed it to Sherry she looked ten years older, her face lined. I hadn't looked at her for a while; she was thinner than I remembered.

'So,' I said. 'Shoot.'

She took a large swig of the drink. 'It's not really about what happened between us,' she said. 'It's what happened to me. Daniel was – is – just part of that story.' She laughed, a brittle, dry laugh. 'You know, I haven't talked about – thought about, really – all this for years, so I don't really know where to start. I guess I'll start at the beginning.'

I sensed that she needed to order her thoughts, and I let the silence grow. Eventually she spoke again.

'I suppose it started at high school. There was a group of us who hung out together. Me, Lisa, Daniel, Mike and a guy called Nate, who lives now in Florida, of all places. He was my boyfriend, by the way. Looking back I can't believe it, but at the time he was the one. The first guy I slept with, the first guy whose heart I broke and who broke my heart. It was all so intense. You know how it is.'

I did. My first girlfriend and I were convinced – more than that, we *knew*, absolutely – that we would marry and have babies. I believed that until a friend told me he'd seen her kissing an older boy at a St Valentine's disco in the town centre. I confronted her; she didn't deny it, and our relationship went the way of all the others.

'After Dad died, I went through a rough patch. For a few months I pretty much withdrew. I broke up with Nate, didn't go out much, didn't really talk to anyone, not even my friends. I also put on a lot of weight, and between that and the isolation and the grief I lost my confidence. I used to look at myself in the mirror and hate what I saw, hate the fat face that leered back at me, which was difficult for me, it really was. I don't want to sound vain, but I knew I was attractive – I got a lot of attention from guys – and to lose that, at seventeen, was a nightmare. I thought I'd never get it back.'

I listened. So far, so ordinary. I didn't want to be cynical, but at that point I didn't see exactly what the loss of her father – sad as it was – had to do with Daniel and the year they had spent together during college.

She took another swig of her vodka and tonic. 'Mum didn't help much; she was struggling herself and I don't think she really noticed what I was going through. My friends kind of drifted away from me, the way kids do. I ignored them and after the tenth rejection even Lisa stopped calling. The only one who didn't was Daniel.'

'Of course,' I said. 'Like a vulture, hanging around the damaged animals.'

She looked pained. 'I know what you think, but it wasn't like that. He helped me.'

'Fine,' I said. 'Whatever.'

'So anyway, I got back on my feet, went to university in Boston.'

'With Daniel.'

'No. He came later. He took a year out. Went volunteering in South America, building schools or something.'

'He came to the same university? He followed you. The guy's a stalker.'

'We were just friends, Tom. Nothing had happened between us. I don't know why it's so hard for you to accept that.'

Because I'd seen guys do what he did before, seen them hang around the girls they secretly loved, waiting for a chance to move in, hoping that if they were there long enough and stayed close enough, their opportunity would come. He must have loved it when her dad died; it gave him the chance to play the hero. I could hear him: *I'm here for you, we're best friends, I'm happy just to be with you.* She'd have been feeling guilty, worried that she was taking advantage of him, but it would be too easy just to keep on doing it, and besides, he really didn't mind – he said so all the time.

And I'd seen the way he looked at her, but there was no point in my telling her. She'd been blind to it for a decade; she wasn't going to wake up now.

'Go on,' I said.

She looked out of the window. 'I had a pretty wild time those two years in Boston. I was the girl at the party with a joint between my lips and a bottle of tequila in my hands. I was also the girl – well, I wasn't promiscuous, exactly. I wouldn't sleep with anyone, but I slept with more people than I wish I had. Any good-looking, long-haired type who showed up had a chance.'

I hated hearing this. Even though we hadn't met then, so she owed nothing to me, just the thought of her with another man – or men, as it seemed – was painful. I wanted her to have been a virgin when we met.

Daniel, also, could not have liked this. Everybody got a piece of his girl apart from him. My glee at the thought of how he must have felt balanced, a little, my jealousy. 'And where was Daniel through all this? He must have *hated* it.'

'He was – ' she shook her head. 'I don't know. Doing his thing. Working hard. I think he had a girlfriend, Meredith.'

He'd probably given up. I'd seen that, as well. Guys like that operate by keeping the object of their obsession close; when the girl gets away then they realize the game is up. Normally, they move on, marry some girl they don't like and treat her like shit, resenting the fact that she's not their one and only true love. It would be romantic if it wasn't so fucking pathetic.

She held out her glass. She looked tired. 'Would you mind?'

I handed it back to her, refilled.

'And then,' she said, her eyes seeing something else. 'It all went wrong.'

You're His Type

She seemed to have withdrawn, her shoulders slumped and shrunken back into the couch. Her voice was quiet and emotionless; had I not been looking at her I'm not sure I would have known who was speaking. It didn't sound like her at all.

'I met a guy, a hockey player. He'd left a few years back and was visiting college. In the days before he arrived there was a buzz about him; he was a star in his college days and there were a lot of stories about him – his athletic feats, his partying, his eye for the ladies. *He'll like you,* I was told. *You're his type,* others said. It made me feel good, like I was the chosen one, the girl that could hook the alpha guy.

'Anyway, he showed up, I went to a party at a bar and we were introduced. He was handsome – really, really handsome – and he was huge, larger than life. The way you picture a cartoon superhero.' She gave a little shake of her head. 'I was entranced, as much by the situation as anything – he was like a celebrity, surrounded by all these people, and he was flirting with me. I just got caught up in the whole thing.

'We ended up back at someone's house, someone I didn't know. None of my friends were there – I'd kind of lost them in the bar –

but I didn't care. I was all wrapped up with this guy, smoking joints in the kitchen and getting drunker and drunker.

'After a while I realized that it was only guys left in the house, older guys who I didn't know. There had been some girls but they'd ignored me and now they were gone, either with guys or on their own; I didn't know.

'Still, I didn't mind. The guy, the hockey player, had his arms round me now – we were both stoned and drunk – and we were swaying together, making out a bit, talking a bit. He was muttering about how college was the best time you'd ever have, how when you left it was all downhill. He worked in some office in Atlanta. I don't think he liked it much.'

I knew a few people like that: superstars in the limited world of college who left to find that the world outside didn't value them as they were used to; good looks and hockey skills didn't cut it in corporate America. They had to work hard to earn promotions and accolades. Just being a college star wasn't enough and for some of them it was hard to adjust, which was why they were hanging around their alma mater years later. There were plenty at Hardy.

'I said something stupid, about how I'd remind him of the good times, and he said, yeah, I hear you're a good time girl, then he started to grope me, his hands under my top and down my jeans. He changed, became more aggressive and I remember thinking it was a good job I wasn't wearing a skirt. Drunk as I was, I wanted to get out of there. I made up my mind to leave as soon as I got the chance.'

I was starting to feel bad about where this was going. Part of me wanted to stop her so that she didn't have to go back there, but I said nothing. I'm not sure I *could* have stopped her even if I'd tried; she didn't look like she even knew I was there.

'The chance never came. I thought about that for so long afterwards, those four words echoing around my skull. *The chance never came*. He grabbed my wrists and pushed me against the wall, his face close to mine. His eyes were bloodshot and his breath stank of alcohol and pot. I retched and he put a hand over my mouth, turning my head away from him. With the other hand he grabbed the waistband of my jeans and pulled. The button flew off and he shoved his hand inside my underwear.'

'It's okay,' I said. 'You don't have to tell me this.'

She ignored me. 'I was totally powerless. I'd never felt like that before – normally there's something you can do, but right then I had no options. He was so strong. The worst thing was that the adrenalin had sobered me up and so I no longer had the drunkenness to protect me from what was happening.

'I shouted out; screamed at him to stop, but he just looked at me. *You want this. That's why you're here,* he said. *Come on. We'll go upstairs.* He kind of wrestled me upstairs, through the room where his friends were. I remember them watching us, disinterested, apart from one scrawny guy with a beard and long hair, who followed me with his eyes.

'Upstairs, he threw me on the bed on my stomach. With one hand he held my face against the pillow – there was no way I could cry out, or scream, it was all I could do to breathe. More than once I thought I was going to suffocate, which was a relief, as it took my mind off what was happening.

'With his other hand he pulled my jeans down. I was wearing lingerie, just in case I hooked up with him and I remember him pulling it aside and saying see, you want this.'

She paused for a long time. 'And then he raped me.'

'I'm sorry,' I said. 'I'm sorry.'

She was crying now. 'And when it was over he left the room. I heard him downstairs, laughing with the others. I lay on my stomach, still wearing my underwear, my jeans hanging from one leg, and heard him laughing.'

'Stop,' I said. 'That's enough.'

She looked at me, her eyes red and unfocused. 'You wanted to know. So listen.' She finished her drink. 'I was wondering how to get out of there when the door opened again. It was the scrawny guy.'

'Sherry, stop. You don't—'

'He raped me, too.'

I had to stop it. I thought of the only question I could. 'Who was it? Did you tell the police?'

She laughed. 'They wouldn't have believed me. I was drunk, everyone had seen me go home with him. I was known as an easy lay so they would have said I consented and who was to say they were lying? Date rape; happens all the time.'

'It's still rape.'

'Sure is. Try telling the police that.'

'Tell me who did it. I'll make the fuckers pay.'

'No need,' she said. 'That was taken care of.'

'What do you mean?'

'Someone paid for them to get hurt, the hockey player, at least. Apparently it's quite easy to arrange.'

'Who?'

She didn't reply. She didn't need to. I already knew the answer.

Therapy

I put my arms around her. She was stiff and she barely reacted to my touch. She just looked at her watch.

'Someone has to pick up Peggy,' she said.

'I'll go.' I got to my feet and picked up the car keys. Her face was blotchy and streaked with tears. 'Have a shower or something. Don't let her see you like this.'

'Okay,' she said.

'I love you,' I said.

She nodded.

I didn't see the jogger approaching the crosswalk until she was in front of the car. In Maine people always stop for people to cross the road, so much so that pedestrians assume drivers will come to a halt and just step out. I'm surprised more of them don't get run over when they leave Maine and go, for example, to Paris, where drivers never stop.

The jogger shared this assumption, and, had I been looking, she would have been right. As it was I was miles away, somewhere in an anonymous house in Boston watching my wife get raped.

I missed her by about six inches, which was fortunate: today was bad enough, without killing a jogger.

She screamed at me and banged on the roof of the car. On another day I might have apologized – and I was sorry – but I had enough on my plate. I forced myself to concentrate for the last mile or so until I pulled up in front of the school.

It's strange how tears make you feel better. They act as a kind of reset button, but it's hard to see how water leaking from your eyes has any bearing on your mental state. Why the eyes? It doesn't seem to offer any obvious evolutionary advantage; quite the opposite, you'd think. The last thing you need when in a state of high emotion with a sabre-toothed tiger nipping at your heels is a problem with your vision. It's not like there aren't other orifices available: you could cry from the nose, or the mouth, or the anus, which would, for men at least, have the advantage of hiding the emasculating fact that you were crying.

I could have used some hidden anal crying then; quite a few of the parents (mainly mums but with a few dads sprinkled among them) saw me blubbing and must have wondered what was going on. Anyway, after a minute or two the tears stopped and I found that, incredibly, I did feel better.

I was a few minutes early, which gave me a chance to reflect, although it was hard to grasp any particular thought; each time I tried a new one muscled in. Sorrow at what had happened to Sherry was replaced by anger (and dreams of revenge) at the people who had done it, which was shoved aside by admiration at the way she had put it behind her, far enough that she went travelling alone in Europe. I remembered her description of her trip as something she *had* to do; not an extended holiday, but, as she'd said, *something I needed to do.* The whole thing explained a lot about the early days of our relationship: her reaction to the guy who had grabbed her in the bar and her happiness that I had, as she saw it, protected her; her initial reluctance – near fear – of sex, and then the intensity of her desire for us to stay together. I guess she felt she'd found – in me – someone she felt safe with, and wanted to keep me close.

And Daniel. A man who was, it seemed, prepared to arrange retribution on behalf of Sherry – presumably he'd paid someone to beat up the guy, which would have seemed incredible were it not for my first-hand knowledge of how far he would go. How she didn't see that he was obsessed with her was beyond me, which led to the final thought, the one that lurked in the background of everything else: the sense that she had lied to me. That she had been lying all these years.

I felt selfish for thinking that way, but I couldn't help it. I suppose she had no obligation to tell me about her past, but when Daniel had shown up she had lied about their relationship. I could understand why, but it didn't change the fact that a guy had reappeared and started hanging around my wife, a guy who was obviously in love with her, which I had told her, but which she had denied. They were just friends; nothing to worry about. I suppose she could say she hadn't lied technically – I had asked if they had been boyfriend and girlfriend, not if they had lived together after she suffered a multiple rape – but, while a lawyer could get you off on a technicality, the trust required to fuel a marriage was not awarded by a judge in a courtroom, and my trust had been betrayed.

When Peggy and I got home Sherry was upstairs in bed. Peggy and I played with her 'magic' easel, which worked on some principle of magnetism and could be wiped clean at the press of a button. She drew fairies, one after another; she also read books about them, wore clothes with them on and looked for them in the garden. I had no idea where this obsession had come from, but come it had, and there was no way to divert her from it.

'Can you draw me a fairy, Daddy?' she said, and handed me the magnetic pen.

I scrawled something that looked like a triangle with legs and a distorted head.

'That's not one,' she said. 'Fairies are pretty.'

'That's pretty.' I looked at it. 'For a mushroom. It's a fairy mushroom.'

'There's no such thing!' She wiped it from the easel and her face took on a serious expression. '*Are* there fairy mushrooms?'

'Maybe. I don't see why not. Fairies have to eat too.'

She shook her head. 'They don't eat mushrooms. They eat honey and candy.'

'Oh. Then maybe not.'

'Maybe they sit on them.'

'No,' I said. 'You're thinking of gnomes. They sit on mushrooms and fish.'

'Why do they sit on fish?'

'They don't. They sit on mushrooms.'

'You said they sit on fish. Mushrooms and fish.'

'I meant they sit on mushrooms while they fish. Like you sit on a chair and read. Gnomes sit on mushrooms and fish.'

She didn't look convinced.

'Can I see a gnome, Daddy? Or a fairy?'

'We could have a look.'

We spent the next half an hour engaged in an unsuccessful gnome and fairy hunt in the garden. I decided to buy one – if they sold them in America, which I was sure they did – put it in a variety of places in the garden and take some photos, which I would show to her from time to time as proof of the existence of the nether world.

'Is Mommy ok?' she said.

We were lying on her bed together, books read, teeth brushed, ready for sleep.

'Of course,' I said. Peggy was the kind of kid who kept herself to herself, even at that age. It was hard to know what she was thinking and it always worried me when I got an inkling that something bothered her, as I assumed it must run deep. 'She's fine. Just a little tired.'

She looked at me for a while. I took the chance to study her face. She had a kind of notch at the top of her ears, which my mother had had. She'd noticed it the first time she saw Peggy. *That's my granddaughter,* she'd said. *Look at those ears.* I'd forgotten about it but seeing it now comforted me. And then there were the eyes; she was mine, there was no doubt about it. That was one thing I could be sure of. Whatever Daniel said, I didn't need any confirmation of that. In any case, whether she was mine or not, there was no way I could love her any less.

I leaned over and kissed her on the forehead. 'Sleep tight. I love you.'

On my way out I heard my phone ring downstairs. When I got to it, it had stopped. The display said it was Stephanie.

I'd almost forgotten about Stephanie and the incident at work; it seemed to have happened in another life. Talking to her was the last thing I wanted to do, but I felt I had to. She deserved that, at least. I dialled her number.

She picked up immediately.

'Tom. Thanks for calling back.'

'Sorry I missed your call.' I said. 'I was putting Peggy to bed.'

'Well,' she said. 'I have some good news.'

'You told me. Daniel's not pressing charges.'

'More than that. He asked me not to even start any internal proceedings – disciplinary proceedings, Tom – against you. I have to say I'm surprised. If you'd done that to me I'd be after your ass.'

'That's great. I'm very pleased.' I paused. 'I want you to know, or I want to have said it, for the record – that he banged his own head against the wall. I just want you to hear that.'

'Tom. I don't know why you persist . . .' She stopped, frustrated. 'Look. Whether that's true – which I have reservations about – or not, it makes no difference. What you admit you did is enough to lose your job, but that's not going to happen. Just be grateful.'

'I am.'

'There's one more thing. This will have to go on your employee record. Daniel might not want to take it further, but I can't let it pass. You'll keep your job, but it's on probation. One more incident and you're out.'

The harshness of the words made them sound odd coming from Stephanie's mouth. She was so gentle, normally. I'd thought she was my friend; perhaps I'd made a mistake and she'd been my boss all along.

I grabbed a bottle of beer from the fridge. I needed something wet and cold and uncomplicated and substantial. I drank half and put the bottle on the counter. I went upstairs. I didn't want to disturb Sherry but my clothes felt grubby and I wanted to change them.

The bedroom was dark. I could just make out the hump of Sherry's sleeping form in the bed. I padded to the bureau and pulled out a fresh T-shirt and shorts. I could change downstairs.

Her voice was flat; in the darkness it seemed disembodied. It didn't sound like she'd been asleep.

'You want to hear the rest?' she said.

Quite a Bit

'Sit down.' She patted the bed. 'There's quite a bit.'

'Okay,' I said. 'If you feel up to it.'

'I'm fine.' She sounded remarkably calm. Either drunk or in shock, I guessed. 'Really. It was a long time ago. The memories are unpleasant, but I moved on. It took a lot of work, but I did it.'

Or maybe she really was calm. I tried to take her hand, but she pulled it away.

'What Daniel said was true, after a fashion. He did put me together again. I wouldn't have used those words to describe it, but it's not far from the truth.'

'So you and he do go way back.'

She ignored my dig, her voice staying calm. 'I moved in with him. It was either that or come home, and I couldn't face that. I felt safe with Daniel – I could call on him any time of the day or night and he'd come. He was a great friend.'

'Don't you see it?' I said. 'He was – is – in love with you. No one does that for someone unless they love them.'

'You keep saying that.' She shrugged. 'I don't agree. He never tried anything with me. Never tried to kiss me, never hinted at anything else. He was just a wonderful, selfless friend.' She paused and looked at me. 'That's why I *know* you're wrong about him. He could have made his move on me back then, when I was at my most vulnerable, but he didn't. He just looked after me, like a bird with a broken wing, and when I was better he let me fly away.'

Jesus. I really was up against it with Daniel. No wonder she was so convinced of his innocence. I had to try anyway.

'Because he was scared you'd reject him and then it would be over.'

'You've already made up your mind, Tom. You think he loved me so you see everything through that lens. I was there, though, and I see it differently.'

She sat up a little.

'You need to understand the state I was in back then. I was broken. I couldn't sleep, I didn't want to sleep, because of night-mares – horrible, vivid nightmares in which I relived every moment of the . . . of what had happened in slow motion, over and over. Every day was a fucking rollercoaster. I either felt guilty, like it was my fault, or was enraged, with a deep, murderous rage, or trapped in an endless despair. I couldn't leave the house on my own, yet I didn't want to stay there because it made me feel trapped. I thought I was a sitting duck. It was months – months – before I would answer the door.

'I was so scared. Scared of everything. And at the heart of it all was an emptiness. I was convinced that it would never end, that this was my life from now on. Twice I tried to kill myself, once with sleeping pills and whisky and once by injecting an air bubble into my veins. Both times Daniel saved me.

'In the early days he never spent more than two hours away from me – that was his rule, the promise he made to me. He went to class, or the library, did what he needed and came back. Both times I tried to kill myself it was that two-hour rule that meant he got there in time.

215

'I saw a therapist, although I didn't call her that. Every time I saw or heard the word therapist it appeared to me as "the rapist", so she became my counsellor. Bit by bit, day by day, it got better.

'It always does. That was probably the most important lesson I learned: people are resilient. They heal. The most awful things happen to people all the time – think of the holocaust, 9/11, Cambodia – but you can get through it. Daniel used to say, ten times a day: *in five years we'll look back on this and it'll be history. The further away it gets, the smaller it'll look, so we'll just keep on putting distance between us and it.*'

I didn't like the sound of 'we' or 'us'. They were like little knives, stabbing at me.

'And he was right. It works. You can rebuild, and rebuilding is what it is. When everything has been broken you need new foundations, new walls, a new roof. Nothing is the same – your values, your beliefs, the way you see the world, how you interact with people – they're all different. It's like you're not the same person.'

And she'd rebuilt with Daniel. They must have had an incredible bond, which raised a question. 'So what happened? To you and Daniel?'

'When I felt up to it I signed up to finish college at a Catholic school in Vermont. It was the perfect place for me. Small, on a campus, outdoorsy, safe. Daniel wanted to transfer as well, but I insisted he didn't. I needed a fresh start. He came to visit a few times, but I started to make excuses. Once I was there, I just didn't want to see him. It reminded me of what had happened. I was ready to move on.'

'He can't have been very happy, after what he'd done for you.' I think I managed to keep the glee out of my voice. He must have been devastated. A second chance to get his girl and, despite him sacrificing everything for her, she took what she needed and walked away. I almost – but not quite – felt sorry for him; mostly, I was glad that the little shit had suffered.

216

'I know. I felt awful about it. But the counsellor told me that it was okay; if he was a true friend he'd want me to be happy whichever way I could.'

I could imagine what Daniel's reaction to that would have been. *That's right, Sherry. I just want you to be happy,* when he was thinking, *are you fucking kidding, Sherry? You need a new counsellor.*

'And so I finished college, came to Europe. I wanted to prove to myself I could do it, alone, but I couldn't. I was terrified, every day. And then I met you. I didn't let on how I was feeling – I didn't want to scare you away. You were exactly what I was looking for, the man I needed. Strong, decisive, older, no associations with my past. You told me I was "head to wind" – you remember that?'

I nodded. It was a phrase my parents' generation used to use, to mean that someone was on track, had their head screwed on. 'You seemed to have it together pretty well,' I said. 'I was impressed.'

'It was an act. But the more time we spent together, the more I started to feel it was true. I've remembered it ever since. Keep head to wind.' She lifted her hands, palms upwards. 'And that's it.'

I had only one question. 'Why did you never tell me this, over the years?'

She shrugged. 'It was the past. You were a new start.'

Not any more, thanks to Daniel.

'And when Daniel showed up? Why say nothing then?'

She hesitated. 'I didn't dare. I could see that you didn't like him, and I didn't want to make things worse. I just hoped it would pass.'

I laughed, bitterly. 'Well that didn't work. Now look what he's done.'

'What *has* he done?' Sherry said softly. 'It seems to me he hasn't done anything much. We're friends; he's acted like a friend. It's you who has a problem, you who is the cause of all the tension.'

'Because he loves you. I told you. He loves you and he's trying to come between us. He couldn't have you back then and so now he's come, with his big city money, to try again.'

'What if you're wrong? Your whole crazy thing is based on the idea he's in love with me – an idea which has no basis in fact.'

'It's true. I can tell.'

'You can *tell*? I've known him for twenty years and he's never once come on to me. Never once. There's plenty of guys who I *know* don't give a shit about me who've tried it on, just to see if they can get some. Don't you think, if he was as desperate as you make out, he would have at least tried something, once?'

'I told you. He's scared of rejection.'

'Tom, we were at high school together. I rejected most of the boys in my year, the year above and the year below at some point. Trust me, it doesn't end your friendship, or every school in the country would be a war zone.'

'So how do you explain what he did today? What about the money he gave to Hardy, the money that just happened to be in my department?'

'Maybe he wants to help his hometown college? Is that so ridiculous? And what *did* he do today? It was you who assaulted him, no?'

'After he insulted me.' I paused. 'He hinted that Peggy wasn't mine.'

'So you *attacked* him?' She raised her hands. I could see that whatever I said she wouldn't believe it. Everything flowed from whether or not he was in love with her; I knew he was, which made me the victim; she couldn't see it, and while she couldn't I was the villain.

'That's enough. I don't know what we're going to do about this, Tom. He's a friend. Now you know why. If you can't deal with that, then I don't know what we'll do.'

'He's trying to break us up.'

'No, he isn't. But you're doing a good job of that yourself. You've fallen out with a lot of people – Peggy's school, my friends, Daniel – and now you have a problem at work.'

'It's not my problem. I told you I did nothing.'

She groaned. 'Jesus, Tom. You know what I think? I think you resent living here since your mom got sick and you're taking it out on Barrow. All this stuff with Daniel is just a smokescreen, so that you feel you have a justification for your anger.'

'Is that what your counsellor would have told you? Because it sounds like the kind of pop psychology bullshit those people spout.' I paused. 'One last thing. He knew about my sperm test. He commiserated with me on it. How the hell did he know about that if he isn't taking some weird interest in my life?'

She rubbed her temples with her index fingers. 'The problem here is that you see everything he does as proof of your theory, but let me try and help you. He commiserated with you because that's what people do when they hear that people they know have some bad news. And he knew because I told him.'

'*You* told him?'

'Not exactly. I told Lisa – she mentioned it to Daniel and he called to say he was sorry. And he offered to help. He knows a lot of people in the medical world.'

I stood blinking at her for quite a while. When you hear something that you never thought you would hear – that you didn't consider possible – it takes some time for it to sink in. It requires a readjustment of your view of the world. It's like when you save a huge file on a computer; all the other functions of the machine slow down while it focuses on processing that one indigestible task.

And I never thought she would have discussed it with Daniel. I had assumed that he had paid a corrupt doctor, or something. But never, not once, had I considered that she might have told him. It was a question of simple loyalty; I had assumed I had hers. It appeared that we didn't see things the same way. How could she and I be so far apart? We were supposed to be married, for fuck's sake. Apart from anything else I'd been under the impression that she had agreed not to see him.

'You talked to him about this? You don't see anything wrong with that?'

'No. It's the biggest thing in my life, and he's my friend. And I didn't talk to him about it. He'd heard – from Lisa, or someone – and we offered to help. Let me say it again. Friend. And he offered to help. Get that? Help. Why would he help us have a baby if he wanted to break us up?'

I didn't answer; there was no point, although it was obvious to me. It was an easy offer to make. He knew I would never accept it so why not make himself look magnanimous?

'And the not seeing him thing?'

'I didn't. I told you I wouldn't – although I wish I hadn't. I shouldn't be letting you choose my friends – and I haven't. We talked on the phone.'

'That's all right, then.'

She stared at me, as though daring me to carry on, to attack her, but I didn't, of course I didn't. We shouldn't have been having this argument, not after what she had told me about her past. I should have been holding her, comforting her, but instead of sympathy I felt anger because the revelation she'd been raped was also a revelation of a relationship with Daniel, a relationship she'd denied, or at the least hidden. Just at the moment I should have been her rock, I was wondering whether she'd betrayed me.

Which was exactly as Daniel would have wanted it when he set this whole thing in motion.

I had already heard too much; my head was spinning and I had to get away. I left without a word and went downstairs.

In the kitchen I picked up my half drunk bottle of beer. The damn thing was warm. I tipped it in the sink and poured a scotch.

Getting Away

An image of her talking to Daniel about my faulty sperm pounded in my mind as I ran through the forest trails that surrounded Barrow. It was early – I had spent the night on the couch and hadn't slept very well. Our couch was small and old and uncomfortable, but it was better than lying next to Sherry in a tense silence all night long, being careful not to accidentally touch.

I couldn't believe it. Okay, so there was something in her past – something painful – and I could just about accept that she had hidden it from me in an attempt to keep it buried. But now it wasn't about that, it was about what Daniel was trying to do. She needed to cut him out, make him keep his distance, but instead she was confiding in him, giving him the ammunition he needed to attack me.

The problem was that she saw me as the one at fault. Daniel was just her friend – why couldn't she talk to him? As far as she was concerned I was just jealous, and the jealousy made me interpret his actions as sinister when they were innocent. I pointed out that he'd told me about her past, and why would he do that unless he was trying to get at me somehow, but she just said he was trying to show how and why they were friends. Maybe she was right – maybe his being in love with her was an article of faith for me, maybe it did twist how I saw him, but the fact he was an innocent friend was just as much an article of faith for her, and she couldn't see him as anything other than that, whatever the evidence to the contrary.

It maddened me. He had us both exactly where he wanted. Me, angry and liable to do something stupid like attack him at work, Sherry convinced of his innocence – and therefore of my unreasonableness.

There was another thought, one that had been nagging away at me since the conversation the night before.

What if I was wrong? What if Daniel was just a genuine, loving friend?

Gerard handed me a coffee and a breakfast sandwich. 'It's on me,' he said. 'Tough times ahead for you.'

'Thanks.' I could always rely on Gerard for some calming words.

'So what happened?'

I told him. He whistled through his teeth. 'You really fucked that one up good, didn't you?' He pursed his lips. 'It'll pass, though.'

'And what about Daniel?'

He looked at me and shrugged. 'Fuck him. Just ignore the douchebag.'

I sipped my coffee. Talking to someone outside of it all really helped. When I was at home talking to Sherry the emotion was overpowering. There seemed no way out. Talking to Gerard it seemed obvious. Let it blow over and ignore Daniel.

'What do you mean, ignore him?'

'Just be polite. Say hello. Offer him a drink. If he tries to wind you up, just say thanks and pick up a newspaper.' Gerard tapped his fingers on the table. 'When my old man had a problem he used to say, "If you ignore it for long enough it'll go away." It works. I've tried it.' He grinned. 'Hell, I've lived my *life* by it.'

It was good advice, but I wasn't sure I could take it. I'd still have to put up with Daniel sniffing around. I'd always be wondering what he was up to, remembering what he'd done, knowing how he felt about my wife.

Unless I was wrong about that, in which case I was making an awfully big mess for no reason.

Gerard looked at me. 'Why don't you go camping?' he said. 'Get away from it for a few days. You could go to Baxter State Park. It's wild up there. You won't see no one for days. Place a man can do some good, hard thinking.'

I nodded. I felt in need of some good, hard thinking.

Baxter State Park

You don't have to walk very long to feel lost in northern Maine.

About an hour from where I left the car at the north entrance to Baxter State Park, I felt like I was on a different planet. The forest was thick, the trails hardly more than a gap in the undergrowth between the trees. The park, my guidebook told me, was just over two hundred thousand acres in size and got somewhere between fifty and seventy thousand visitors a year, which is around four acres per visitor, *if they all came at the same time.*

It was certainly a good place to be alone.

I had chosen a backcountry camp site called Boody Brook, a small tent site deep in the woods. It was hard-going to reach it and I was constantly checking my map and the GPS I had with me. I was used to the mountains of the Lake District or North Wales, where, assuming it wasn't pissing it down you could see the surrounding topography and work out where you were on the map. Here all you could see was forest, endless forest. Had I been dropped, with a map, onto Skiddaw in the Lake District, I could have worked out where I was in minutes; here that would have been impossible. I don't know how people found their way before the advent of handheld GPS systems; I guess Mainers were used to this kind of terrain. I wasn't, though, and getting horribly and irretrievably lost would have been the simplest thing in the world.

It was beautiful, however, an assault on all the senses. The lush foliage, dense undergrowth, gnarled, sentinel trees, birdsong; the fragrant smell of the woods all around. I got lost in the rhythm of walking, the noise of my boots stepping on twigs and dried earth.

Sherry had agreed silently to my plan to get away. I told her I would stay if she wanted, but she waved me away. *Just go,* she said. *It'll do you good. Give you a chance to think. Maybe you'll see things for what they are.*

Maybe you will too, I'd replied.

She'd looked at me, her expression a little sad. *Let's hope so.*

I hung my food some distance from the camp site. Supposedly there were bears around. They were only black bears, Gerard had told me, adding that black bears were vegetarians, but I neither trusted Gerard's knowledge of the dietary habits of large mammals nor wanted to take any chances.

Back at the tent, I took out a small bottle of whisky and a notebook. Since I was a kid I'd found it helpful to write down my thoughts.

It didn't take long; the situation was really quite simple. On one piece of paper I wrote Sherry's view: my mother was ill, I was upset and angry that I – and my family – had not been near her in the last few years, and this had made me resentful of Sherry in particular and my life in Barrow in general. My animus against Daniel was merely my subconscious finding a way to damage the things we had here so that they looked bad. It had already put my job in jeopardy.

On another page was my view – yes, my mother was ill and I had found it hard to know how much she missed me and Peggy, but that was a fact of our relationship. Wherever we lived we were away from one set of family. Of course I was frustrated and of course it made me sad, but I could live with it. What had complicated the situation was Daniel's arrival and his deliberate attempts to sabotage our relationship, get me fired, upset my friends. Without that none of this would have happened.

I turned to another page and wrote a heading: *Solutions*. I underlined it three times.

An hour later the page was still blank, apart from a red smear where a mosquito had landed and been squashed against the paper.

I couldn't think of any solutions. Whatever I did – accept Daniel, struggle against him – he was still going to be there, still going to be working against me. What else would he do? Frame me for a crime? He was the central fact of this whole situation, and while he was still around I was trapped.

And he wasn't going away. He was like the Terminator: he was just going to keep on going until he got what he wanted. Obsessed, relentless, implacable, terrifying, and no one else could see it. They just thought I was jealous and a bit unhinged because my mother was ill. The problem was that I wasn't sure I could stand up to him. He was mad, and I just didn't think I could beat him.

Which was why there was only one thing to do. Jesus, it was obvious. So obvious I couldn't believe I hadn't seen it sooner.

Barrow

I woke early and was briefly disoriented, partly because I was in a tent and it was damn cold this late in the year in Maine and partly because I had been more deeply asleep than for a long time. I had become used to the feeling of my troubles boring into my mind, a feeling that could be dispelled by activity but which reasserted itself as soon as you stopped, which made sleep unattainable. Now that I had a solution the weight had been lifted, and I had rediscovered sleep.

I packed up my tent and hiked back to the car. There was a chill in the morning air and the woods were silent; out here I could sense that summer was over and that winter was approaching.

By lunchtime I was back at the car and on my way. Not far from the park entrance I passed a handwritten sign announcing a yard sale half a mile up the road. I didn't want to buy anything – I was in a hurry to get home to share my news – but the impulse to look *just in case* is impossible to overcome and as I passed I slowed down.

And then I saw them.

There were half a dozen of them, standing on a table at the left-hand edge of the yard sale. They had been arranged to look as though they were standing in a circle talking, apart from one of them, which had his back to the others. He was sitting on a toad-stool, smoking a pipe and dangling his fishing rod over the edge of the table.

I pulled up and climbed out of the car. A boy of about eleven walked towards me.

'Hi,' he said. 'How can I help? I have books, CDs, collectibles and sundry.' As he told me each category he pointed to its location. My targets were in sundry.

On a bench between the tables and the house his parents smiled and gave me a little wave. The boy was running the show and he had evidently been schooled in the art of customer service.

'How much for the gnomes?'

'Ah,' he said. 'The gnomes.'

There was a flicker of disappointment in his eyes and I got the impression he was hoping they wouldn't sell.

'They'll be going to a good home.'

'They're four dollars each.'

'So for six that's . . .?'

I let him do the maths.

'Twenty-four bucks.'

'They're your gnomes?'

He nodded. 'I got them when I was a kid. I used to think they were real.'

'You sure you want to sell them?' I didn't need to take this kid's childhood friends. There'd be other gnomes.

'Yeah. I'd keep them if I could, but I want to buy a dirt bike.' He shrugged. 'Gotta make some sacrifices.'

That was true enough. If he could remember that lesson it would stand him in good stead in years to come. I pulled out my wallet and took out two twenties.

'I'll take them. There you go.' He pulled out a wad of cash from his pocket. 'It's okay. Keep the change. These are good gnomes. They're worth it.'

'Thanks,' he said. 'Cool.'

'Do they have names?'

'Uh-huh. Harry, Barry, Larry, Gary, Cary.' He pointed at each one in the circle and then indicated the one on the toadstool. 'And George. He's my favourite.'

'We'll take care of him,' I said. 'Thanks.'

Millinocket, Orono, Bangor, Waterville, Gardiner, Bowdoinham: the names appeared on the highway signs, until, after about four hours I saw the first mention of home. *Barrow, 14 miles.*

I looked at George. The others were in the back seat in a box but I had put him up front to keep me company. 'Nearly there,' I said. 'Nearly at your new home.'

When I arrived home the house was empty. I took Harry, Barry, Larry, Gary and George and lined them up behind the shed. Cary had an inquisitive face, so I propped him up at an angle so that he was peeping out from behind the shed. The others I tried to give an aspect of quiet contemplation. I had always thought they were the height of tweeness but I was starting to see why people got attached to their gnomes.

I took a photo of Cary from the kitchen window, as though I had happened upon him by accident, then took a few more of the gnomes behind the shed: one in which they were as I had left them, one in which they were running away, their backs turned (I hoped Peggy would ignore the fact that George was riding on a toadstool) and one in which they were gone, only the tip of Harry's red coat visible as they disappeared round the back of the shed.

Once the photos were taken I hid the gnomes in a thorn bush at the front of the house. It seemed a good home for them until the time came for Peggy to 'discover' them.

I uploaded the photos and made a cup of tea. On the kitchen counter was a pile of mail addressed to me. Amidst the usual junk mail and bills was a large brown envelope. The address was in my dad's handwriting.

Inside was a brief note – *This came for you. Looks official. Dad* – and another envelope marked *On Her Majesty's Service*. It was the British passport I had applied for for Peggy. I put it in my jacket pocket; I could put it in the file later.

Not long after that the car pulled up in the drive and Sherry and Peggy came through the kitchen door.

'Daddy!' Peggy ran to me and put her arms around my neck. She smelled faintly of chlorine. 'I went swimming.'

'I see that.' I looked at Sherry and winked. 'Guess what I saw in the garden.' I said it in my most serious voice.

'What?' Peggy's mouth dropped open. 'Was it fairies?'

I shook my head. 'Nope. It was gnomes.'

She gasped. 'Really? Can I see them?'

'Yep. I took some photos. They're on the computer.'

I was constantly amazed by how easily she used technology. She manipulated the mouse around and flicked through the photos on the screen.

'Daddy,' she said. 'They're *amazing*!'

'I know. And they live in our garden. You'd better watch out for them.'

'I will,' she said, and turned back to the photos. 'I will.'

I put my arms around Sherry and kissed her cheek. She was stiff and kept herself away from me. 'Everything okay?'

'You're in a good mood.'

'I am. I had time to think.'

'That's all it took?'

'Yep. Sometimes that's all you need.'

'And?'

'We need a fresh start. Put all this behind us – the stuff with Daniel, the fruit salad, the school – and just start again. It's been a shitty few months; let's just forget it and move on.'

'So you admit it? That you spiked the fruit salad?'

'I've been in a difficult place. Sorry.'

It wasn't an admission, but it sounded like one. What I'd realized in Baxter State Park was that whether I had or not wasn't the point. Sherry thought I'd done all this stuff, and it was corroding our relationship. Admitting it would allow us to move on, and it would be a powerful symbol of my willingness to do so. She would have to reciprocate.

If Daniel wanted to play games, then I might as well join in.

'I did it. I'm sorry. It was stupid and childish, but I was drunk. I wish I never had.' I held up a hand. 'And before you ask, I was too embarrassed to admit it. I mean, it was such a fucking idiotic thing to do.'

Sherry had tears in her eyes. 'Tom. I'm so glad you're saying all this. It's such a *relief*. I was so worried about you. About us.'

I took her in my arms. 'Don't be. I love you.'

'I love you too,' she said. 'So much.'

'And I trust you,' I said. 'With Daniel or Brad Pitt or George Clooney or whoever. That's all that matters. I trust you.'

She kissed me, her lips hot and wet from the tears. 'You know what we should do? We should have Thanksgiving here, with Lisa and Mike and Mum and Daniel. That really would be a fresh start, especially on Thanksgiving.'

I almost said no, but what was the point? It was just one meal, and I could put up with Daniel being here for one meal. Just ignore him, ignore what he was up to. That way he couldn't drag me into his bullshit.

I just had to stay close to my family, love them, keep us strong and tight and impregnable. Even Daniel wouldn't be able to breach that.

And then the phone rang.

Mum

It was Dad. 'Your mum's taken a turn for the worse.'

I felt myself pale. Sherry put her hand on my shoulder. *Everything okay?* she mouthed.

I shrugged. 'How bad?'

'Bad,' Dad said. 'She's unconscious.'

'Will she come round?'

The silence was all the answer I needed.

When Dad spoke he didn't answer my question. 'If you want to say your goodbyes in person you might want to hurry.'

There was a flight the next day. I clicked through the various screens until I came to the payment section.

Then I paused.

Did I really want to go? Of course, I *wanted* to go. Even if Mum didn't wake up I wanted to be there to hold her hand and kiss her goodbye, and to help Dad in the days that followed. But I didn't want to leave Barrow. I didn't want to leave Sherry alone. Not while Daniel was here.

I couldn't believe I was even considering not going, but who knew what Daniel would do in my absence? No one else could see it, but I knew how crazy he was; he didn't hide it from me. I knew what he'd been up to in my office; no one else did. But it didn't matter if I knew. He *wanted* me to know, wanted me to see how far he would go. Wanted me to be scared of him. He wanted to be so far in my head that I second-guessed a visit to my dying mother.

Sherry came into the study and looked over my shoulder.

'Find something?'

I nodded. 'It's expensive.'

'That doesn't matter. Not for your mum. And it's just you, right?'

No, I thought, *not it's not. Of course. That was how to deal with this. I'll just take them with me.*

'I thought you two might come.'

Sherry moved away from me. 'No, Tom. Your mum's not conscious. There's no point. And it'll just upset Peggy. I'm sorry.'

There was no way I was going to be able to convince her, mainly because she was right. But that meant leaving her with Daniel. And I couldn't do that.

'I might not go. Like you say, Mum's not even awake.'

There was a long pause. 'Really?'

'Uh-huh.'

'Tom, I . . .' She came round to stand in front of me. 'Are you sure? You don't think you'll regret it?'

I shook my head.

'What's going on, Tom? When we visited last time you were all for it. What's changed?'

'I'm not sure I want to leave you alone. Not right now. Not when we just started to sort everything out.'

'We'll be fine. This is your mum. And it's only a week or so.'

A week's a long time when Daniel's around, I wanted to say.

'I know, but . . .' I had nothing else I could say.

234

Sherry folded her arms. 'Is this about Daniel?' She'd always been very perceptive, and now was no exception. 'Is it?'

I stared at the screen. There was no point trying to lie to her, so I said nothing.

'Tom. You just said that you trusted me. With Brad Pitt or George Clooney or whoever. Was that just bullshit?'

No, it wasn't. It couldn't be. This was a test. I'd just declared that we were going to make a fresh start, decided to change the way I dealt with Daniel, sworn I trusted Sherry. And now the universe was asking me to prove it. And I would.

I clicked on *purchase*.

'Of course I trust you,' I said.

Mum died three days later. Dad and I were with her when she died; Jonathan had just left, when, without warning, her eyes opened.

Her cheeks were flushed, her eyes bright with a light that came from somewhere within her. Dad and I looked at each other. We knew this burst of energy was her final moment.

She couldn't speak, but she was aware of our presence. I kissed her forehead and told her I loved her; she squeezed my hand, and then I stepped back to let my dad say goodbye.

It had been a week of surprises from my old man. He climbed onto the bed and put his arms around her, turning her to face him. They looked into each other's eyes for the last time. He didn't speak. I don't think there was anything left for him to say.

After a few minutes Mum's eyelids fluttered and whatever light had been on went out. Dad pulled her closer, closed his eyes and rocked her back and forth.

I left the room, unwilling to intrude on his grief.

Calling Home

When I got back from the hospital I called Sherry. I looked at my watch. One p.m. It was morning in Barrow.

Peggy picked up the phone.

'Hi, darling,' I said. 'How are you?'

'Good. I'm getting ready to go to school.'

'Okay. Have a good day. I love you. Is Mum there?'

Sherry came to the phone.

'Hi,' I said. 'Mum died.' It was so easy to say, but so hard to believe.

'I'm sorry. When?'

'A couple of hours ago,' I said. 'It was painless.'

'I'm so sorry. I wish I was there.'

'I wish you were too.'

'Will there be a funeral?'

'Three days' time. I'll fly back Saturday.'

'How's your dad?'

'You know Dad. He's fine.'

On the other end of the line the doorbell rang. Our landline phone was in the hallway, on a table by the front door. I heard a voice call out.

'Sherry? You ready?'

It was a man's voice. It was hard to tell whose, but I had a pretty good idea.

My skin prickled. 'Who's that, at eight in the morning?'

Sherry paused. 'It's Daniel. He's giving us a lift to Peggy's school.'

'Are you kidding me?'

'My car won't start. It's the battery, or something.'

'Daniel's at our house? After all we talked about?' The shock was indescribable. I wasn't even angry, as such. Just in disbelief.

'What could I do? I need to get Peggy to school and there's no one else to call. Mum's away and Lisa's at work. It's just a lift.'

Daniel was behind this, I knew it. What were the odds that the minute I left the car broke down? That bastard had done it, I was sure of it. He'd come in the night and disconnected the battery or unscrewed something. I had to stop this. Once they were in the car with him who knew what he'd do? Abduction? Murder? Nothing was beyond him.

'Call Gerard. He'll take you.'

'Daniel's here now.'

'Call Gerard!' I was shouting; I didn't care.

'Tom. It's fine. I promise. I love you. And I'm sorry about your mum. And give my love to everyone. We're thinking of you over here. Call later; I'll be back in an hour.'

'I love you too.' Before I could say anything else she put the phone down. I looked at the handset, the dial tone faint, an image of a grinning Daniel behind the wheel, Sherry at his side, stuck in my mind.

I should have been thinking about Mum, soaking myself in memories of her, revelling in the grief that was her due. Instead, all I could think about was bloody Daniel.

The intensity of the jealousy and insecurity was increased in proportion to the distance between me and Sherry. If I was home I could do something – pop home at lunchtime, talk to my wife about it, seduce her – whatever, really. The point was I would be able to do something. Here, I was powerless. If she didn't pick up the phone then I had no link to her or my daughter. Anything could have been going on, and, in my mind, it probably was.

Except it wasn't. She wasn't having an affair – she couldn't have done. In Barrow everyone would have known and they would all have disapproved. Besides, despite the recent events, things were still good between us. Our story was a love story; it had been ever since we'd met. We had one kid and wanted more. We were committed to each other.

But I couldn't keep it from my mind. The thing is, when you become a father you become very vulnerable. Your children and their mother form a unit, which is quite self-contained, especially when the kids are young. They don't need *you*, specifically: any male could provide paternal support, finance, help with the housework, or whatever else you do. You are a bolt-on, replaceable part of the unit, and you know it, and that is the source of the vulnerability.

It was worse for me. I lived in her town, with her friends and her family. If we ever split up, what would I do? Go back to England and never see my daughter? Hardly. I'd want to go back to England – after all, the only reason I wasn't there already was because of Sherry – but I wouldn't be able to. I'd be stuck in Barrow, friendless and cast out. Whatever happened, I had to keep this marriage together. It was all I had.

I imagined her and Peggy and Daniel living in our house. It wasn't such a strange picture. After I was gone the waters would close over whatever trace I had left behind and I would be nothing more than a memory. Their lives would go on much as before; I would have lost everything.

Which was why it was a good job we *did* love each other. A good job that a large portion of the passion that had brought us together still remained. A good job that – despite these feelings I was having – I trusted her. I had to. This was a test.

I called an hour later. Sherry answered. She was alone, un-abducted and un-murdered, and we talked. About how we were lucky to have each other and Peggy, and about how we missed each other.

Still, though, I couldn't get that bastard Daniel out of my head.

The following morning we all sat – me, Dad, Jonathan and Iris – around a wooden trunk that we had lugged down from the attic.

The house felt different for Mum's death. Even though she hadn't been there since I'd arrived, the fact that she was no longer alive somehow changed the place. Perhaps it was that it was no longer her house; even when she had been in the hospital with no chance of ever coming back, this had been her home. Now, though, it was Dad's home, and it could well stay that way for a long time. He was in excellent health.

Not that you would have known it to look at him that morning. His eyes were raw with sleeplessness and his chin was covered with a rash of stubble, in which there was still some colour, unlike the white hair on his head. Worse than that though was the look in his eyes, a kind of stunned emptiness. I kept seeing him notice things in the house – photos, books, ornaments – which reminded him of his wife and of the barren years to come. He looked, if it was not absurd to describe a man of his age in these terms, as though he was suffering from a broken heart.

'Right,' Dad said, and nodded at the trunk. 'Dig in. Your mother sorted this stuff out a few weeks back. She wanted you to have it.'

'Don't you want it?' I said. 'To remind you of her.'

'I've got plenty. After forty years you do have.' He looked into the distance. 'And I don't need any objects to be reminded of her. She'll always be with me.'

Iris lifted the lid of the trunk. I wanted to ask her to leave it to us to go through Mum's belongings – really, I wanted her to leave the house while we did it – but I kept my mouth shut. There was no point arguing about it.

'Hmm,' she said. 'There's not that much.' She rummaged through the contents and started pulling things out. She handed Jonathan a photo album. 'This has your name on.' She pulled out another and handed it to me. 'Oh. And there's one for you.'

There were two photo albums, one with Jonathan stencilled on it and one with Tom on the cover. I opened mine. It was a collection of all the photos she had of us, from our earliest days in hospital to our wedding days. There was one of me and Dad on a beach, probably in North Yorkshire, sheltering from the wind. Dad had his arm round me, but was looking at something off to the left – Jonathan, maybe, or someone he knew – a wide grin on his face. There was one of Jonathan holding me as a baby, a scowl on his face. Under it Mum had written, in the handwriting that was so familiar to me and now would never be used again, *Not a Happy Big Brother But The Only Way is Up!*

There was one of me in the garden on my first day of school, arms straight to the side, cap jammed over my eyes, a serious look on my face. Next to it was one of me at the school gates, looking forlorn as Mum waved goodbye.

There were many more. By the time I reached the end I was crying, but not in sadness. I was crying in gratitude for what Mum had left us: these were not photo albums, but love letters, from a mother to her sons.

Iris took out a square box the size of a small novel. She opened it and held up a string of pearls.

'Remember those?' I said to Jonathan. 'Mum wore them when she was getting dressed up.'

'They're nice,' Iris said. She put the box by her feet. I noticed that there was another box there already.

'What's in that one?'

Iris shrugged as though she didn't know and handed it to me. It was a set of pearl earrings to go with the necklace.

'Bought those in Galway,' Dad said. 'I was fishing there and brought your mum a present.'

'Peggy might like them,' I said. 'Memories of her grandma. You mind, Jon?'

Iris coughed. 'Why don't we see what's in there and divide it up at the end? To make sure it's fair.'

There was a long silence. It wasn't really any of her business. 'I think we can just decide between us,' I said. 'We can just see what makes sense. It's not like there's that much stuff.'

'Right,' Jonathan said. 'Let's do that.'

I could tell Iris wanted to say something else but didn't dare; on another occasion I might have asked for her opinion, but I wasn't in the mood.

We sorted through some more things – books, letters, a set of old dolls, all stuff that Mum had thought we might either be interested in or want to keep. The last thing we took out was a thick, heavy bible.

'That was your mum's family bible. It's from the seventeen hundreds. Least that's what Margaret told me.' It was already odd to hear her name from his mouth. Dad ran his finger over the leather binding. It was in surprisingly good condition for its age.

He passed it to me and I opened the front page. In it was a list of names, with birth and death dates. The last entries read:

Margaret Briggs m. Roger Harding
Jonathan Trevor, b. June 4th 1963
Thomas Michael, b. March 9th 1972

I handed it to Jonathan. 'Look. All our ancestors. On Mum's side, at least.'

He gave it a quick look. 'Nice to see.' He closed it. 'Do you want it?'

Iris looked at him. 'If he takes that, you should take the pearls.'

What the fuck it had to do with her, I don't know, but Jonathan nodded. 'Sounds okay,' he said.

'Great,' Iris said, and scooped up the jewellery boxes. 'I think that's fair. Don't you?'

I didn't, but I didn't have the strength to argue. If she wanted them that badly, let her have them.

'Put those bloody boxes down.' Dad unfolded his arms and put his hands palm down on his thighs. He had always done that when he was angry. For a moment I thought he was going to lose his temper, but he just nodded at the boxes. I guess there was no point making things awkward between him and Iris. 'Tom. Take them for young Peggy, and make sure you tell her where they came from.'

Iris's eyes flickered from left to right. She couldn't meet my gaze as she handed them to me. I thanked her, and with that, the final act of Mum's life was over.

The motors whirred and the coffin disappeared into the furnace. Dad watched it go, stone-faced. The emotions he had showed in the days after her death were back in check, and he was the taciturn, imperturbable man I remembered. Still, he had changed. Something in him had relaxed, or broken, and I felt that I could see more of the man he had been to Mum, the man who had loved her, and his family, quietly and without demanding anything in return. Our entire relationship had always been based on minimal communication, but now I wasn't sure that it was his fault. I had interpreted his quietness as a lack of interest, but what if it was just that he thought I didn't want him to pry? If I had reached out to him, who knew how he would have responded?

I started to cry. It was too sad to think that we may have wasted our lives on some misunderstanding, too male, too northern, too fucking tragic. Worse, I was about to leave, again, and it could be years before the next time I saw him. Christ, the next time I was here could be *his* funeral.

It wasn't going to be. I was going to come and visit more often. I made a vow, but even as I made it, I wondered whether it would be honoured more in the breach than in the observance.

Dad patted my arm. 'She had a good life,' he said. 'Don't cry, lad. You've no need to. You did the best you could.'

I didn't, though. And now it was too late to change.

Thanksgiving

Although I have never quite figured out what Thanksgiving is for – it seems to celebrate the theft of most of the North American continent from its indigenous population – I have always liked it. It is a lot like the way older people in the UK describe how Christmas used to be; a warm, family occasion untainted by materialism and with a focus on eating and drinking and making merry.

In many American families, the minutes before the eating commences are spent in a round-table during which each guest says what he or she is thankful for. At first I had found this to be excruciatingly embarrassing – it didn't come naturally to me to tell people I was thankful for their love and friendship, so I would normally mutter some half-joke about being thankful for my turn now being over – but over the years I had come to, if not actively enjoy, at least appreciate the custom as something worthwhile.

This year, though, I was planning to jump in with both feet.

Since my return from Mum's funeral things had been going well. Summer – and all the events that had gone with it – seemed a distant memory. Peggy was settled, sparky and full of life; Sherry was cheerful and upbeat and our relationship was relaxed and loving. It might have been autumn – or fall, as it was called in the US, a name which I preferred – but it felt like spring.

Best of all, I'd not seen much of Daniel. He seemed to have gone to ground. I pictured him licking his wounds having failed to get what he wanted. Our paths crossed a few times at work – we'd had what were described as alcohol issues with the girls' rugby team and his job as Welfare Liaison meant he was involved. I left him to it. My job was to prepare them athletically. He was welcome to take care of their moral and spiritual wellbeing.

I had, however, invited him to our house for Thanksgiving, as I had promised to my wife. Now, with the turkey on the table and the food on the plates, it was time for us to declare what we were thankful for that year.

We all looked at each other, waiting for someone to start.

'I'll go,' I said. Sherry raised an eyebrow; normally I tried to go somewhere in the middle so I could hide away. Not this year, though.

'I'm thankful for many things this year,' I began. 'For old friends' – I gestured at Lisa and Mike – 'new friends' – I nodded at Daniel – 'family' – Sherry's mum got a smile – 'but most of all, for my beautiful daughter and my beautiful wife. I love every moment I spend with my family. We've never been happier. I feel like the luckiest man in America.'

'Well,' Lisa said. 'I'm not going next. Who wants to follow that?'

'I will,' Sherry said. 'I'm thankful for family and friends and the food on the table but more than anything I'm thankful for my husband.'

Eventually it was Daniel's turn. He kept it brief and to the point.

'I'm thankful to be back in Barrow,' he said. 'Thankful to be among such wonderful friends, and I'm thankful that God has blessed them all with such happiness. Long may it continue.'

*

After dinner I was washing the dishes when I felt a pair of hands slide around my waist.

'That was a lovely speech,' Sherry murmured into my ear, holding her body against mine. She ran her hand over my crotch. 'It made me think of something else we could be thankful for.'

I wriggled round to face her, pressing my erection against her stomach. Before I could reply there was a cough from the doorway. It was Daniel. Anyone else and I'd have been embarrassed to be caught making out like teenagers; as it was him I was glad. I wanted him to see how strong our bond was.

'I've got to run,' he said. 'Thanks for dinner.' He was smiling, but not with his usual smug, Hollywood smile; this one had something secretive, almost sinister about it. I remembered it later. It haunted me.

'See you,' I said. 'Thanks for coming.'

Sherry let go of me and went to give him a hug; I bent over slightly to conceal my erection.

When he was gone she came back and kissed me, her hands on my cheeks, her tongue flickering in and out of my mouth.

'Come on,' she said. 'Let's go and have a drink with the others. We'll see how soon we can get rid of them.'

It took longer than I'd hoped. Mike had a bottle of thirty-year-old port that he wanted to open and it took a while to decant it. We had to find a piece of cloth with a fine enough weave to strain it through; Mike wanted muslin; as Sherry pointed out, who the hell has muslin lying around their house? In the end we used an old work shirt of mine. It did the trick; the port was delicious. It was almost worth the delay.

I passed my glass to Mike for a refill.

'Which way do you pass the port?' I said. 'Isn't there some rule?'

'It's you Brits who are the masters of weird rules,' Mike said. 'I've got no idea.'

'Not all Brits,' I said. 'Maybe the ones who go to Eton and work in stripy suits in the City stealing people's money, but there wasn't too much port passing going on in my house.'

I heard some steps on the porch and then the doorbell rang.

'Wonder who that is?' I levered myself up from the chair. 'First person ever in Barrow not to just open the door and come in.'

It was Stephanie. She was dressed in smart slacks and a blouse, with a fleece jacket that looked as though it had been grabbed hastily as she left her house.

'Happy Thanksgiving,' I said. Stephanie and I had not spent much time together since the incident with Daniel. She had seemed to be angry at me, in the way a disappointed parent is angry. 'I didn't expect to see you.'

She didn't smile. 'Can I come in?'

'Sure.' I stepped back from the door and gestured her inside. 'Drink? Mike brought some vintage port.'

'No thanks.'

'Come through. Say hello.'

'No. I'm here to see you. Can we talk?'

She was pale, and her mouth was pinched.

'Everything okay, Stephanie? Is something wrong?'

'Yes,' she said. 'Something *is* wrong. Something is very wrong.'

An Unwelcome Guest

Stephanie put her hands on the kitchen counter. She was shaking.

'I will have a drink, actually,' she said.

I opened the fridge. 'White wine? Or something stronger?'

'That'll be fine.' She reached for the glass. 'So,' she said. 'I don't know how to say this.'

'Just say it.'

'We've had some complaints. About you.'

Focusing became a struggle and I leaned against the couch, my hand resting on the back.

'Complaints?'

She touched her thumb and middle finger to her temple. They fluttered there, covering her eyes.

'About what?'

'Inappropriate behaviour.'

The conversation – the whole scene – had taken on the feel of a nightmare. I felt like I knew exactly what was coming while at the same time I was struggling to keep up with it, struggling to understand the words.

'What kind of behaviour?'

Stephanie lowered her hand and drew herself upright, as though telling herself to pull herself together.

'Inappropriate touching,' she said. 'We've had complaints of inappropriate touching.'

This was unbelievable. Ridiculous. Crazy. This couldn't be happening.

'From who?'

'I can't say.'

'Come on, Stephanie! You can't let someone accuse me of that and then not tell me who it was! It's ridiculous! The whole thing is ridiculous. You know me better than that. Tell me who it was. Who was the person who said this nonsense?'

'I can't. We have an anonymous hotline for this kind of thing. Even I don't know who it was. And it's not a person. It's persons. There's more than one.' She paused. 'You see? If it was one I might be able to ignore it, but it isn't. There are multiple complaints.'

'From the office of the Welfare Liaison Officer?'

'This is nothing to do with Daniel,' Stephanie said. 'Please don't start that again.'

'But the complaints come via him, right?'

She shook her head. 'I'm not discussing that, Tom. That's not what's important here. What's important is what you've been doing.'

'I've been doing nothing! I could never do something like that!'

I could see in her eyes that she didn't believe me, that she thought I was perfectly capable of it. I could almost see her connecting the dots: she'd come across me assaulting Daniel, I was an outsider, a Brit, and there were multiple complaints. In her eyes it was pretty damning.

'Okay,' I said. 'Well, I guess the investigation will prove it one way or another.'

'No,' she said. 'There won't be an investigation. I've got an offer for you. You resign, with three months' pay, and we say we dealt with this internally. The girls involved will be happy with that.'

'Are you serious?'

'Deadly.'

'But that would be as good as admitting I did it!'

'Maybe. But it's better than it being proved that you did it, in the public eye.'

'It won't be proved.'

'Won't it? It's your word against theirs, and there are more of them than you. And your past record will be taken into account. If it was me, I'd believe the girls.' Her voice became angrier. 'Hell, I *do* believe the girls.'

'There's no evidence.'

'Look, Tom. The best you can hope for is a messy trial, at the end of which you get off because there's no evidence, but your reputation is in tatters. Worse, the girls have to go through a court case. Nobody wants that. Not even you. Either way, your career at Hardy – at any college in New England, if not the entire USA – is over. It's better to take what I'm offering.'

'Will you give me a reference? For other colleges?'

She didn't answer for a long time. 'Sorry, Tom. I can't.'

I was well and truly fucked. No reference was as good as a flashing sign saying *Steer Clear! Achtung! I left because of something really, really bad.*

But it might still be the best option I had.

'I need to think about it,' I said.

'Okay.' She stared at me like I had just puked on her shoes. 'You have twenty-four hours.'

250

Move to England

I'd miscalculated. Badly. I'd thought I could ignore him, kill him with kindness, that when he saw that his tactics weren't working he'd give up. But I was wrong. Daniel was like the colon cancer I hadn't had. Always there, day and night, lodged in your life, multiplying away. And what could I do now? Even if I got out of this, how would I ever get away from him?

I went upstairs and sat on our bed. In the glow from the street lighting I noticed that the sheets were rumpled; we'd made love on them after lunch when Peggy was having a nap.

I felt calm, contemplative almost, with the same sensation I'd had in the kitchen of being out of myself. It was useful; it allowed me to weigh up what was happening with a calmness and lucidity that would disappear over the next few days and weeks.

Could I be sure Daniel was behind this? He had to be. I didn't *know* that; all I knew for sure was that the complaints against me were completely fabricated. Whatever had happened, I'd done nothing wrong, although I already felt the security that that knowledge should have given me slipping away, felt myself becoming unanchored.

And whether Daniel was behind it or not, there was one thing that bothered me more than anything else. Who were these girls and why had they complained? If it was Daniel, how had he persuaded them to do so and if it wasn't, what was going on? In either case, they must have had something against me, which was a nasty shock.

I think I was aware of the front door opening and closing and the sounds of Lisa and Mike saying their goodbyes, but I was deep in thought, and it wasn't until Sherry came into the room that I realized how much time had passed.

'Everything okay?'

'Fine.'

'Just thought you'd get up here and be ready? Very keen, but a bit rude to our guests.'

'It was Stephanie who came to the door before,' I said. 'She had some news.'

'What kind of news?' She sounded alarmed. 'Is there a problem?'

'Yes.' I shifted on the bed so I was propped up against the headboard. 'Something's going on at work. Someone's been complaining about me.'

'Who?'

'I don't know. It's anonymous.'

'Anonymous? Can they do that?'

'Apparently. For this kind of complaint.'

I sensed her stiffen. Perhaps she'd guessed what was coming; perhaps it was just my tone of voice.

'What kind of complaint?'

'It's – complaints about inappropriate touching. Some of the female athletes.'

Just saying it made me feel guilty. It made me see how people would react when they found out. *No smoke without fire,* they'd say. I'd have said the same. The fact I was completely innocent made no difference at all.

Sherry gasped.

'Did you do it?'

'No!' I was offended she'd even asked.

She put her fingers to her lips. She couldn't look at me.

'Why would they say it?' It wasn't said as an accusation; it was a question.

'I don't know.'

'Is there something – that could have been misinterpreted? A hug?'

'Of course not! I'm ultra-careful about that stuff. I never have a female student in the office with the door shut, nothing like that.'

'Then what the hell is going on, Tom?'

I paused. 'I think it's Daniel.'

She groaned. 'Not this again, please, not now. You think he persuaded them to complain? How? The problem is you think he's some kind of evil genius, Tom, when he's just a nice guy.'

I knew better than to try and persuade her otherwise. 'Look. Whatever happened, I didn't do anything. Nothing. That's the most important thing.'

She stood at the side of the bed, staring at me.

'We need to talk,' she said, and went downstairs.

When I joined her in the kitchen she was pouring a gin and tonic and crying. It was an unusual kind of crying. She wasn't sobbing or heaving or sniffling, she just had tears coming out of her eyes and running down her cheeks.

She looked at me and her eyes were hard.

'I can't believe you've done this,' she said.

I was shocked. I hadn't really considered this moment, the moment when I had to tell my wife, but at the least I'd expected her sympathy. Not aggression.

'Sherry, I haven't *done* anything.'

'You must have done something. You might not have known it but you must have done something. People don't just make this kind of thing up. Not multiple people.'

'They do. They must do, or I wouldn't be in this situation.'

She looked away from me. I was glad; just before she did there was a look of disgust on her face.

'Sherry. Don't you believe me?'

She didn't answer.

'Sherry? I'm your husband. The father of your daughter. You think I would do something like that?'

'I don't know what to think.'

'Come on! Of all the people you should be the one who believes me! I can understand the neighbourhood gossips muttering that there's no smoke without fire – that's why this kind of allegation is so damaging. Everyone's always ready to believe that the older man did do something to the young girl. They love the thought of scandal, and that's why it's so important that you believe me. You know me best!'

'I know. And I just don't know, Tom. You've been so strange recently.'

'You think I did this?' I was shouting. 'Do you?'

'I don't know,' she said. 'But if this is true, it's the worst thing you could have done. The *worst* thing.'

I started to protest but she lifted her hand.

'After what I went through. After I was *raped*' – she spat out the word – 'if I find out my husband has been molesting young women – it – it'll be the end.'

And then I saw it, saw the full extent of what Daniel had done. He'd fitted me up for the one crime that Sherry could never forgive, and which she would always be ready to believe.

'No,' I said. 'Sherry, no. It's Daniel. Don't you see? What's the old legal saying? *Cui bono?* Who benefits? Only one person, in

254

this scenario. Daniel fucking Faber.' I remembered his sly smile as he left. He'd looked at me and known I'd been thinking I'd won, when he knew what was coming. 'It must be. I didn't do anything!'

'Is that it?' she said. 'All you can do is rant about Daniel, and quote Latin at me?' She was deflated, the anger gone. 'I thought this was all over. I thought we'd made a new start, that you'd made a new start. But it was all a front. Whether you did it or not, you lied to me about the new start. I see that now. Good night, Tom. See you in the morning.'

I slept on the couch.

What was I going to do? Take the money and get out of this with my reputation at least somewhat intact? Or fight it? I was innocent and my instinct was to fight, but how could I trust the system to get to the truth? If I couldn't convince my wife, who would I be able to convince? And either way, I risked losing Sherry.

Sometime in the wee hours the answer came to me. Not the answer as to whether I should fight, but the answer to the whole damn thing. Christ, I should have seen it before, months before. I went to wake up Sherry.

She wasn't asleep.

'Hey,' I said. 'I know what we need to do. It's so obvious. We should have thought of it before, but that's okay. Better late than never.'

She glared at me. 'What are you talking about?'

'The solution to our problems – my job, Daniel, all of that. It's so easy.'

'Okay? So what is it?' She looked unimpressed.

I smiled. 'We move to England.'

Her expression didn't change. She stared at me for a long time, then stood up and walked out of the room.

I followed her into the spare bedroom. She was looking out of the window. When I closed the door she kept her back turned.

'What's wrong?' I said. 'Why are you in here?'

Her voice was flat. 'Is that it?' she said. 'Is that what you think we should do? Move to *England*?'

I was surprised she was so strongly against it; perhaps if I explained the logic she would see my point of view.

'It makes perfect sense. A change of scene is what we need. A *true* fresh start.'

She lowered her forehead, rubbing it between her thumb and forefinger. 'This is unbelievable. I don't believe that you're even suggesting this.'

'Why? It solves everything. All our problems.'

'All the problems that you made!' She turned round and looked at me, her face wild. 'You made all this – shit – happen and now you want to run away from it. You want me and Peggy to give up everything to follow you!'

'I didn't make it happen.'

She groaned. 'Not this again. Not this rubbish about Daniel. For whatever reason – perhaps your mum, perhaps just because you've changed – you don't want to live here any more, and so you've created this situation where the only thing we can do is leave. Well, I'm not going to do it! You can forget it.'

'Okay,' I said. 'We'll find another way.'

Sherry looked at me, her expression fearful. She shook her head. 'I don't think so. I'm not happy, Tom. And neither are you. It's not working.'

'Don't, Sherry. It's just a blip. These things happen in a marriage.'

'A blip? It feels like more than a blip.'

'This is ridiculous.'

'Is it?'

It was, but it was also fucking smart of Daniel. He'd really done it this time. He knew how she'd react to even the whiff of sexual impropriety, of course he did. And now I was trapped: I could fight, and even if I won, lose my job and reputation, or I could accept the offer Stephanie had made and at least have something.

Either way, though, my wife thought I had been sexually abusing – however inadvertently, it seemed she would at least give me that – the young women in my care. And that, to her, was unforgivable.

'We've changed, Tom. I mean, we met young – at least I was young. You change a lot between your early twenties and thirties.'

I didn't bother replying.

'And now there's this – thing at work.' She turned away. 'I think we need some time apart,' she said. 'I'm sorry.'

PART THREE

All Over, Red Rover

'I know he's in there,' I said. 'I fucking know it.'

The front of Sherry's – my – house was dark, which from our vantage point was all Gerard and I could see. We were hiding in the garden of the house opposite, concealed behind a bush which was flanked by two tall trees. The house was home to an old man who was in bed by nine, and who in any case was both deaf and near-blind, so there was little chance of him finding us.

'I don't think he is,' Gerard said. 'His car's not there and the garage is empty.' He was right; the driveway was carless and the garage, which was open, was empty.

I finished my beer and opened another one. Gerard and I had started out early on the boat and I had lost track of how much I had drunk.

I had drunk a lot in the fortnight since Thanksgiving. I'd had plenty of time. I'd taken Stephanie's offer – "offer" was her word, to me it was an ultimatum – to resign so the days were empty, and the nights were not much better now that I wasn't living at home. I'd tried to talk Sherry out of it, then I'd begged, then I'd cried, but she wouldn't budge. She wanted me out of the house. This sounds bad, but I felt a deeper sense of loss after we broke up – I mean, started

261

our trial separation – than I did when Mum died. It might have been because the situation with Sherry was still uncertain whereas with Mum it was definite, but I found it harder to deal with.

I was living at Gerard's place. He had a flat over the garage which he used to rent out, but it had failed to live up to town code for a private residence and he had not got round to fixing it up, so it had been empty for a few years. I wiped away some cobwebs and moved in.

The other thing I had done a lot of was hiding in the garden opposite, mainly at night and after I'd been drinking. I had tried it in the day once, but it had felt too exposed. The last thing I needed was to get caught stalking Sherry; just about the only good thing in this otherwise sorry situation was that I had unlimited access to Peggy, and I didn't want that to be taken away.

I knew I shouldn't be spying on her, but after a few drinks it was an irresistible idea. When you're used to living with someone it's strange to suddenly have no idea what they are doing – for years I'd known where Sherry was, what she was eating, what clothes she was wearing, and not because I was tracking her, but because we lived together. Now I knew nothing, and it was driving me mad. Although I hadn't seen them together, I kept picturing her with Daniel.

'Come on,' Gerard said. 'Let's go. I don't want another repeat of the gnome incident.'

A week ago I had decided to creep into the garden and arrange the gnomes where Peggy could see them. I'd retrieved them from the thorn bush successfully but had been startled by an animal as I crossed the deck. George had slipped from my hands and broken off from his toadstool. I'd fled with the others, and now Larry, Barry, Harry, Gary and Cary were in the shower of Gerard's apartment. God knows what the little boy would have said had he found out.

'He's there,' I said. 'I just know it.' I had the one-track certainty you get when you're drunk. Everything I saw pointed to the conclusion I had already arrived at. 'Look at the back. There's a light on.' Through the rear window of the garage you could see a light at the back of the house, where we watched TV.

I sensed Gerard's confusion from the long silence. 'How does that mean Daniel's there?'

'Think about it,' I said. 'If—'

Gerard interrupted. 'Thinking about it might be a good idea.'

'If Daniel's there, they'll be watching TV in the back.' An image of them cuddled on the sofa watching a romantic comedy starring Hugh Grant flashed in front of my eyes. 'I'm going to look.'

'You sure that's a good idea?'

I should have learned by then that if Gerard wondered whether something was a good idea it was a sign that it wasn't. That one-track drunkenness can be persuasive, however, and I waved away his protest, finished my beer and rose unsteadily to my feet.

'Are you sure he's there?'

I was.

'You don't know that they've been seeing each other.'

Perhaps not, but I was about to have the proof I needed. I took a step towards the house.

'And what are you going to do if he *is* there?'

I stopped. That was a good question, one that I perhaps should have spent more time answering. Instead, I shrugged.

'I'll figure that out when I get there.'

Gerard sighed. 'What the fuck,' he said. 'You go round the back and I'll ring the doorbell. At least that'll distract them.' He stood up with a shake of the head. 'This is fucking stupid.'

I stepped into the shadow of the house and opened the side gate. The light was on and the curtains were shut, which meant I needed to get up close and peer through the gaps. Fortunately, all that was between me and the window was grass, so my approach was silent.

The window was open and I could hear the noise of the television, but I couldn't see into the room. The curtains overlapped the window and there was no gap in between them.

At the front of the house the doorbell rang. I heard shuffling, and then the sound of footsteps as someone – Sherry, presumably – went to the door. I pictured Daniel sitting on my couch, his feet up on my ottoman. This was my chance; the couch faced away from the window so I could twitch the curtain aside and get a quick look. Once I had seen him there I could get away.

I stretched my index and forefingers inside the window and gripped the curtain between them, pulling it apart until there was a crack. I tried to see through it but the angle was wrong and all I could make out was Peggy's play table. I opened it a fraction more.

In my pocket, my phone buzzed. With my other hand I took it out. It was Gerard. What the hell was he doing, calling me like this? It was a good job my phone was on silent – although he didn't know that – or I would have been discovered. I switched it off and put it back in my pocket.

I still couldn't see into the room. Another inch, maybe two and I'd have it. I eased the curtain apart, further and further until I could see most of the room.

I suppose by then the gap was four inches. Enough for me to see in, and enough for anybody inside to see me, which was a risk, but it didn't matter. The room was empty. No Daniel. Nobody at all.

Until the girl came in.

She was probably about fifteen; tall, brown hair, braces. I got a good look at her. All she saw of me was a face at the window.

I heard her screaming all the way round the house and halfway up the street. Gerard was nowhere to be seen; I assumed he'd worked out what was going to happen, which must have been why he was calling, and disappeared.

Sherry called about midnight.

'Was it you?' Those were her first words: no hello, no how are you, nothing.

'Was what me?'

'For fuck's sake, Tom. Was it you or not? I need to know if I need to call the police or if it was just my desperate, drunk ex-husband.'

'I'm not your ex-husband. This is a trial separation.'

'Right.' She sounded frustrated. 'I forgot. Either way, was it you?'

'It might have been.' I was too shocked by what she had called me to deny it.

'Well, thanks. You just cost me a babysitter. There's no *way* she's coming back here. You're an idiot, you know that? And what the fuck were you doing in the garden?'

I didn't reply. What could I have said?

A Kind of Madness

What followed was a kind of madness. I could not think of any-thing but Sherry. Even when I was with Peggy – which was quite often – I was thinking of her mum. I picked Peggy up and dropped her off at the times I said I would, took her to museums, went swimming with her, made sure she ate well when we were out. I never showed my frustration to Sherry; I was nothing but polite when I saw her or spoke to her, which was limited to when I called to arrange time with Peggy or arrived to pick Peggy up. In short, I did everything I could to prove I was a responsible dad and husband.

It didn't work. If anything, it had the opposite effect. It showed Sherry that we could make a separation work without too much impact on Peggy. I'd have been better off making it a bit difficult, a bit threatening for Peggy's well-being. Then at least I would have had available the argument that we should stay together for her sake. As it was, for the first time in a while everyone was happy. Everyone but me. By being the perfect, selfless separated father I made a permanent separation a valid option.

And all the while I was going mad, my mind capable of thoughts about only one topic: Sherry. Where she was, who she was with, what she was thinking; specifically, what she was thinking about me. I understood how those people who wander the streets muttering, covered in dirt, get the way they are: if my obsession deepened any further I would be like them, lost in a mono-maniacal reverie in which I had not got sufficient mental capacity to engage with any meaningful reality.

One day, I showed up for Peggy, but she was late getting back from swimming.

'Come in,' Sherry said. Manners are a wonderful thing; the last thing she wanted was me in the house, but leaving me on the door-step was too uncomfortable. 'Drink?'

I shook my head. Just being in the house was intoxicating. This was my house, my home; everything was so familiar. I belonged here. I drank it in.

'How've you been?' Sherry interrupted my reverie.

'Good.' I looked at her. She was beautiful, relaxed and well rested. She was wearing a pair of tight white pants; I knew she only wore them with the white lace underwear I'd bought from Agent Provocateur one year. Anything else showed. They were my favourite; she'd always worn them when we got dressed up and went out. My mouth went dry with desire for her and for our rela-tionship; it was impossible that it was over. We could work this out. I knew it. What had we been thinking? We were meant to be together.

'Sherry,' I said, my head full of the image of us having sex. 'This is daft.'

'What is?'

'That we're apart.' I looked her up and down, my thoughts obvious.

Her mouth tightened. She looked a lot less relaxed.

I realized I had badly misjudged the situation and my confi-dence evaporated, but now I had started I couldn't stop. 'I love you.' I sounded desperate.

'Don't,' she said. 'Things have been going so well.'

'No they haven't,' I said, the words a torrent now. 'I'm miserable. I think about you all the time. I can't think about anything else. I miss you. I just want to be back together.'

She grimaced and looked away. 'I'm sorry,' she said. 'Really, I'm sorry.'

'Sherry. Let's give it a chance. Come on. Please.'

'Tom. Let's not talk about this now.'

'Why not? We can try it. If it doesn't work I'll leave, I promise. What have you got to lose?' This seemed a convincing line of argument, so I pursued it further. 'You see what I mean? You have nothing to lose by trying. Just a week. Start with just a week. Why not?'

'Tom, I think you should leave.'

Her refusal to answer infuriated me. 'Just tell me why not, and I'll go. One week, that's all. Come on, why not?'

'Because I don't think it's a good idea.'

'That's not a reason!' There was a manic edge in my voice which I tried to contain. 'Just answer the question. Why not?'

'Tom. Let's talk about this later.'

'No. Why not?' I stared at her. 'Why not, Sherry?'

'I don't want to, not right now.'

'When then?'

'I don't know. Maybe never.'

'Then we're back to square one, aren't we? You still haven't given me a reason why we can't give it a try. If it doesn't work, I go. Nothing to lose, see? So I don't understand why not. Why not give it a try?'

'Because it won't work.'

'How do you know it won't? You can't know that.' I wasn't really listening, but the next words she said got my attention.

'Because I hate you.'

'Sorry?'

'I hate you.'

'What do you mean?' I was dumbfounded. A serious setback in our relationship; a major misunderstanding; a total breakdown in communication; all of these were possible. All of these were recoverable from. But I had assumed that, at the base of it all, we still loved each other. I certainly loved her; more, it seemed, than ever.

'I can't think of you without getting angry and frustrated and twisted up inside. That's hate, isn't it? The thought of – whatever you did to those girls and what it could do to their lives, their confidence. God, it just makes me so angry. I can't handle it, which means I can't handle you.'

'I didn't do anything.'

'I know. So you said. But how can I believe you, Tom? Why would those girls lie? And you've hardly showed yourself to be honest these last few months.'

And, as they say, on that bombshell our conversation was over. Peggy came home with her grandmother – who could barely look at me – and I took her to the drive-through diner for something to eat. I dropped her off afterwards and went back to Gerard's to get drunk.

Bombshell

'She'll change her mind,' I said. 'I'll give her some space and she'll come round. It won't be long before she starts regretting it, living there on her own with Peggy.'

Gerard nodded slowly, unconvinced. 'Try it.'

'It's been too easy for her. She's got the best of both worlds. If she needs me she knows I'll come running; she needs to think she's on her own.'

'You sure that's not what she wants?'

I shook my head. 'Nah. She needs me. She just doesn't know it. I'm going to back off for a while.'

Gerard passed me a beer. 'Sounds like a plan.'

I didn't get a chance; Sherry kept herself well away from me. A few days later when I picked up Peggy she was ready and waiting by the door. As I pulled up I saw Sherry in the window; seconds later my daughter was running down the driveway.

'Hi, Daddy,' she said. 'Mommy says can I be back by six-thirty? She has to go out.'

Sending messages through our little girl. Not good. I stored it up for future arguments.

270

'That's no way to greet me,' I said, and scooped her into the car and onto my lap. 'What happened to "Hi daddy, I love you?"' I kissed her on the cheek and hugged her.

'Mommy told me to tell you right away so I don't forget.' She kissed me back. 'Hi daddy, I love you.'

'I love you too. Where's Mommy going?' It must be something scheduled if she had to be gone by six-thirty. Maybe a concert? A movie? The kind of thing you went to on dates. My stomach lurched.

'I don't know. I have a new babysitter. You know Nicole Hendrickson? She's in high school. The other one won't come back. I heard Mom talking about it.' She looked at me and raised her eyebrows. 'She's scared.'

'What of?'

'I don't know.'

'Nothing to be scared of round here. Don't you worry about that. Anyway, guess where we're going.'

She thought for a second. 'Horse-riding?'

I had been hoping for a grand announcement and a look of ecstatic surprise. 'How did you know?'

'Is it really?' she said. Now I got the reaction I'd wanted. 'Daddy, that's *awesome*.'

I hate horses. I always have. The smell, that whinnying noise they make, the way they look at you with those dark, expressionless eyes; I hate them. Most of all, though, I hate how big they are. Any other animal that size – a bear, for example, or a crocodile, or a bull – we rightly avoid. I suppose there's cows, but I don't like them either, for exactly the same reason. They're too bloody big.

Not that either their size or my discomfort put Peggy off. I took her to a stables near Portland where they did lessons and watched her march over to the beasts, fit a saddle and the rein thingies, then climb aboard.

She looked so grown up.

It broke my heart. From a distance I could not tell her age; in jodhpurs and riding hat she could have been a woman. My little girl, out in the world, doing the things she wanted in the way she wanted. At that moment, if I could have clicked my fingers and had anything, anything at all – fame, riches, the promise of a long, happy life with Sherry – I would have chosen a few minutes with her in my arms as a baby, so that I could witness once again her beauty and innocence and perfection.

And then she was back with me, a sheen of sweat and a wide grin on her face.

'Thank you, Daddy. That was fun.'

The riding instructor, a red-haired girl in her late teens, handed me Peggy's crop. 'She's good. Not every kid is brave enough to ride like her at this age.'

I sensed that the instructor thought of herself as brave and that this was the greatest compliment she could pay one of her charges.

'Thank you. I'm very proud of her.'

'Where did she learn?'

'In riding school on Popham Beach. She went for a week.'

'Is that all?' She raised her eyebrows. 'I'd have thought she'd been riding for a while. She should have lessons.'

So my daughter had a talent for horse riding. I think I would have preferred just about anything else, but so be it.

Peggy grabbed my hand and squeezed it. 'Can I have lessons, Daddy?'

'We'll have to ask Mum, but I don't see why not.' Peggy did a little jump. I looked at the instructor. 'Could she do them here?'

'Sure. You can get the leaflets at the office where you paid on the way in. They'll explain everything.' She ruffled Peggy's hair. 'See you again, maybe.'

Peggy looked at her with the look of pure admiration that young kids have when they find an older kid to idolize. 'I hope so,' she said.

We drove back up the highway to Barrow. In the back Peggy fell asleep quite quickly; the day had tired her out. It was nearly six; we'd be home in time.

I fantasized about signing Peggy up for riding classes, then going to watch her with Sherry. I imagined us looking at each other, admiring our daughter, and realizing that this situation was crazy; we were a family. In among all the other bullshit we'd somehow forgotten that; all we needed was to remember it, and all the rest would follow, and perhaps it would take something new, like riding, to remind us.

I accompanied Peggy to the front door, leaflets in hand. It was the first time since I'd been in the house that I had not just let her out of the car and watched her to the door. Sherry opened it.

She was wearing a black, strapless dress that hugged her torso and flared out slightly below her waist, ending just above the knee. Her legs were slender, the skin golden brown. I had a sudden flash of how it would feel – cool – if I could touch it, and then all I wanted was to touch it.

'Daddy took me riding,' Peggy said, before either of us could speak. 'It was so much fun. The instructor – Mandy – said I was good and could take lessons.'

Sherry cocked her head to one side. 'Really? That sounds great.' She looked at me. 'Thanks for taking her.' She looked at her watch. 'I have to finish getting ready.'

She looked pretty damn ready to me. 'I'm not staying. I just wanted to give you these.' I handed her the leaflets. 'Take a look. If you want to, I'll sign her up.' She took them and I smelled the perfume I'd bought her a while back. I couldn't stop myself asking. 'Where are you going?'

'Out.'

I closed my eyes. 'Right. Have a good time.'

'And there'll be a babysitter here,' she said. 'Please don't do anything stupid.'

I walked away and climbed in the car. She looked fucking fabulous; it was painful to think of her. So recently she'd been mine. I couldn't stand the thought of losing her; for the first time I fully understood what it would mean to see her constantly for the rest of my life and not be with her. It would be unbearable, never mind if she was with another man; I shuddered. That was better left unconsidered.

I had to know where she was going. I knew enough about women to know that they didn't only get dressed up for dates – dinner with friends would do it – but I still had to know.

I drove away, turned left on the main road and pulled into a street opposite from where I could see her when she left. I knew it was a bad idea, but I had to know where she was going. I wished someone could have stopped me; I couldn't stop myself.

Not long later I saw her – our – car turn out of the street and head towards the highway. I waited until she was three cars ahead and pulled out behind her. That was how they did it in the movies, and I had no other point of reference. I just hoped they were accurate.

On the highway she went south; I assumed she was going to Portland. Who did she know there? Some high school friends, but she rarely saw them. What else was there in Portland?

Nothing, as it turned out. She pulled off at the exit for Falmouth.

I followed, still a few cars back. She turned off the main road into a residential area, then took a left and a right, taking us deeper and deeper into the houses. I hung back, no cars left for me to hide behind.

Up ahead, she stopped, then began to turn around. She was lost.

Mine was the only other car around. In a few seconds she'd be passing me, and, unless somehow she didn't look, she'd see me and know I'd followed her. It couldn't happen; it would destroy any chance I had of proving my reasonableness to her.

As she completed her turn I pulled into the nearest drive and slumped into my seat, keeping an eye on the side mirror as she passed. When I was sure she had gone I sat up. I doubted I'd find her again, but it was better than being caught stalking her.

I straightened in my seat. The front door of the house opened and an old man looked out. He gestured and I wound down the window.

'Can I help you?' he said

'Er, no,' I replied. I grabbed a map of New Hampshire from the side pocket. 'I was just, er – looking for my map. It was on the floor.'

'Oh. Are you lost?'

'Nope. Thanks anyway. Got the map now. All's well.'

'I suppose you're here for the Yacht Club Ball?'

The Yacht Club Ball. That must be where she was going.

'Er, yes, actually. Where is it?'

'At the Yacht Club.'

'Right. And the Yacht Club?'

He pointed towards the ocean. 'Head out onto Foreside Road and turn left. You'll see the signs.' He looked at my clothes and I could see him thinking that standards had slipped. 'Have a good night.'

The car park was nearly full, but I was glad of the opportunity to drive around looking as it allowed me to find Sherry's car. She was parked next to a Miata.

Daniel was here.

I found a vacant spot and pulled in. My heart was racing, my legs weak. Unless there was another Miata owner – which was possible – she was here with that fucking bastard Daniel.

The next few hours were torture. All I wanted to do was get out of the car, march into the Yacht Club and confront them, but that would have been totally stupid; even I knew that. Failing that I wanted to walk around and expend some of the nervous energy that was building up, but there was a crowd of smokers outside the door and I didn't want to draw attention to myself.

It was awful. I couldn't sit still, my physical discomfort matched by the churnings of my brain. I picked my fingernails, scratched my arms and legs, pulled at the skin on my face, picked the spots on my back.

Eventually people started to leave. I slumped in my seat and watched. Every time the door opened I thought it was them; it never was.

Until it was.

Sherry came first. She stepped outside, the door being held open for her by an older man, who studied her tits and arse as she passed. I felt a flare of jealousy, followed by a bitter feeling that it was no longer my problem. It was Daniel's.

If he was there. I hadn't actually seen him at that point.

Seconds later I had. He emerged from the door, dressed in a smart-looking tuxedo, slipped his arm into Sherry's and said something into her ear.

She laughed and glanced at the older man; Daniel raised an eyebrow. Evidently he had made some comment about the attention she was getting. I couldn't help noticing how his easy, confident way of dealing with it compared to my habit of getting into jealous rages.

They walked to the cars, arm in arm. Sherry reached into her bag for her keys and unlocked the door. Daniel opened it for her. As she passed him to get in, he put a hand on the bare skin of her shoulder and stopped her.

They looked at each other; he said something; she gave a tiny shake of her head, but she didn't break eye contact.

Then he leaned forward and kissed her. It lasted about ten seconds. When they broke apart she looked shocked; he looked hungry.

I started crying.

He stroked her face and said something; she looked at her watch and shook her head; he gave a delicate little shrug, then kissed her again, and guided her into the car.

I watched him watching her drive away, which meant I saw the little dance of joy he did when she was gone.

Lovely Mindy

You never know how you are going to react to something until it happens. I had played out a million scenarios in my head in which I caught Sherry and Daniel together – sometimes I hit him, others I shook my head sadly and made them feel bad, others I screamed and shouted and lost control, but in all of them I did something.

When it actually happened, I just sat there. I just could not believe it.

You'd think I would have been prepared for it, given how much time I'd spent thinking about it, but it was a massive shock. I learned then that surprise and shock are not the same things; had you been tracking its progress you would not be *surprised* by a meteor smashing into the earth, but it would be a hell of a shock.

I cannot remember the next few days that well; if I try I just think of the pain and ache and worry that the kiss triggered in me. Up to that point I'd seen her as being pushed away from our relationship by the problems we had. Now she was also being pulled away. It was no longer about me and Sherry, it was no longer a question of how I could patch things up with her; Daniel was now well and truly in the picture, but then I suppose he always had been. Sherry had just not seen it.

'You need to get out,' Gerard said. 'You look like a dirty dollar bill.'

'I don't feel so great.'

He opened the fridge and passed me a beer. 'We're going out,' he said. 'That's what you need. Beer and chicks.'

'That's the last thing I need.'

'Come on. Try it; you've got nothing to lose. If you don't like it you can always bail. That's what you said to Sherry when you tried to persuade her to let you move back in, right? If it's good enough for her, it's good enough for you.'

'Thanks for reminding me. That sensitivity training you went on really fucking worked.' I sipped my beer. 'And she said no, in case you don't remember.'

'Don't repeat the mistakes of the past,' he said. 'You're better than that. Isn't that what that guy said about history?'

'What guy?'

'The one who said don't repeat the mistakes of the past.' Gerard shrugged. 'Anyway, we're going out. Shit, shower, shave and I'll see you back here in ten minutes.'

I'd not been sleeping or eating much; it was a schoolboy error to flush my system with beer and tequila chasers. After about six I could barely see.

We were in Rosie's, a bar in downtown Portland that Gerard claimed was the best bar in America, and I was feeling alternately sorry for myself and pissed off.

'I just don't fucking believe it,' I said to Gerard, for maybe the tenth time. 'I never actually thought it was *over*. I never thought it *could be* over. You get what I'm saying? I mean, she's my girl, you know? I love her. And I know she loves me.'

Gerard pointed to the bar. 'Look at those two.'

'Are you listening to me?'

'Yeah, 'course I am. She's your girl, man. But look at those two.'

There were two women sitting at the bar. One was a redhead; the other had the kind of fluorescent blond hair that only comes from a bottle. The redhead was wearing a short leather skirt, the blonde was in low-slung jeans that showed off her underwear when she leaned forwards. Both were overweight and were bulging out of tops a size or two too small for them. They looked in their mid-to-late forties. Gerard couldn't stop smiling.

'You know what they say about the old ones,' he said. 'Don't smell, don't tell, grateful as all hell.'

'Fuck this, Gerard. They're hideous. I want to talk. Get some shit off my chest.'

'Sure,' he said. 'We'll do that.' He was looking at them, waiting for them to notice him. After a few seconds, the redhead glanced in our direction. Gerard smiled, and gestured for them to come over. My heart sank as they got to their feet.

'You ladies like a drink?' he said. 'Take a seat.'

They pulled out the stools and sat down.

'I'm Mindy,' the blonde said, 'and this is Crimson.'

'That's a beautiful name,' Gerard said. 'Crimson. I love it. I'm Gerard.' It was obvious which one of them Gerard had intentions towards. I didn't blame him; Crimson was a bit younger and was probably the better looking of the two, although that wasn't saying much.

'Who's your handsome friend?' Mindy said, turning her attentions to me, having clocked that her companion already had a suitor.

'I'm Tom.'

Mindy's eyes widened in mock surprise. 'Are you Australian?'

'British.'

'I *love* your accent. Say something.'

'Like what?'

'Anything.'

'I can't think of anything.'

Mindy put her hand on mine. 'I know you Brits are a little shy, but don't be. I'll take care of you. Now say, "Hi, Mindy, I'm Tom from England and I'm delighted to meet you."'

'Hi, Mindy, I'm Tom from England and I'm delighted to meet you.'

'I'm delighted to meet you too.' She signalled the bartender. 'Two rum and cokes and another round for these guys, please, Dickie.'

A glass of beer and shot of tequila appeared in front of me. Gerard had positioned his body so that he and Crimson could talk un-interrupted, leaving me with Mindy. She clinked her glass to mine and leaned towards me. 'Cheers,' she said. The way she took a long swig from her drink gave me the impression she was a lady of large appetites and somewhere inside me the beginnings of lust twitched. I drained the tequila glass.

She looked at my wedding ring. 'You're married?'

'Just about.'

'Oh? Trouble in paradise?'

'You could say that.'

She put her hand on my cheek and stroked it. 'You poor thing. Tell me all about it.'

So I did.

Somehow, hours later, I ended up in a taxi with Mindy. She had her hand in my flies; I remember thinking that it was incredible I had the beginnings of an erection given what I'd drunk. The body is capable of incredible things, it seems, and it has a mind of its own; in men this mind is often located in their genitals.

I had no idea where Gerard and Crimson were. At some point

they'd disappeared, I think around the time that I was telling Mindy how unfair it all was and how if it wasn't for Daniel I wouldn't be in this bar etc., etc. It was a testament to her patience, threshold for boredom and desperation that she hadn't wandered off earlier.

Mindy lived in a flat above an old shop in a low-rent part of town. I barely recall what happened when we got there; the only clear memory I have is that she was a screamer and her daughter, who must have been around seven, came downstairs when we were fucking on the couch to see what the noise was all about. I think she feared her mum was being murdered. Mindy reassured her - *Mom's got a friend to stay, that's all* – and told her to go back to bed, then we carried on.

The next morning I took a bus back to Barrow. I had the kind of hangover which is a mixture of pain, shame and remorse; the kind of hangover which only worsens as you remember fragments from the night before. At one point I groaned out loud; the lady next to me on the bus looked at me in alarm.

Mindy had offered to make me breakfast; I'd declined and fled the scene. She was younger than I'd thought and had the sad expression of someone who has realized that the life they have is how it's going to be for them. No more hopes, dreams; just mild disappointment stretching from now until the grave. I felt sorry for her, which was another ingredient in the toxic mix of my hangover.

Back home – well, at Gerard's house – I made a coffee and tried to escape my thoughts. Was this it? Nights out with Gerard, drunken sex followed by remorseful days? I wasn't much different to Mindy; was this how *my* life was going to be from now on? I flushed hot and broke out in a sweat, part hangover and part despair. My hands were shaking; I needed to eat, and sleep.

I opened the fridge. Some vegetables, about half a dozen condiment jars, a tube of mayonnaise and nothing else. Not even an egg I could boil. Gerard's bread bin was no more forthcoming. There was half a crust and some large crumbs. I spread a thick layer of mayonnaise on the crust and ate it. I wouldn't say I was satisfied, but I did feel better. Well enough to go out and buy something more substantial.

Barrow had half a dozen places to get some breakfast, an assortment of organic bakeries, fair trade coffee shops and vegan cafes. I'd never much liked them, with their blend of holier-than-thou preachiness and overpriced food, but today I was definitely not going near them. Firstly, I wanted something greasy, and secondly I couldn't stand the thought of the good citizens of Barrow looking at me sympathetically and muttering to each other. *There he is, he's living at his friend's house, you know. His wife asked him to leave. He was probably messing around. Such a shame for the daughter.* No, I was going to the mall on the outskirts of town where no one knew me.

Just in case, I pulled a baseball cap low over my eyes. I hated the mall, hated the way it pulled you in and made you consider buying things you neither wanted or needed, hated the hordes of listless people thinking they were on the cusp of purchasing happiness in the form of a new alarm clock or a solid gold necklace or dehumidifier. I never went there, unless, like today, it was absolutely necessary.

Sherry, of course, knew that. I would have been the last person she expected to see as she came out of the entrance to Target. Which was presumably why she thought it was a safe place to go with her new boyfriend.

On one side she was holding Peggy's hand; on the other she was holding Daniel's.

Peggy saw me first.

'Daddy?' she said, her expression a little confused.

'Pegs.' I crouched down and opened my arms. She hugged me and I stood up with her in my arms. A look of alarm flashed across Sherry's face.

'Well, well,' I said. 'Just friends, eh?'

Sherry didn't reply; Daniel looked away.

'Would that be friends with benefits or' – I covered Peggy's ears with my hands and spoke in a stage whisper – 'fuck-buddies?'

'Don't. Not in front of Peggy,' Sherry said. 'And the answer's neither. We're friends.'

'That's not what I heard. Someone saw you kissing in the car park at the Yacht Club.' It was true. Someone had seen them. They didn't need to know it was me.

She paled. 'That's rubbish.'

I ignored her and looked at Daniel. 'You got what you wanted in the end, didn't you, Danny boy?'

'It's not like that,' he said. 'This happened after you broke up.'

'I didn't know we broke up. We're on a trial separation, no? Although now shit-for-brains – that's you, Dan – has muscled in on the scene that looks like it's out of the window.' I was glad I was holding Peggy; the anger was bubbling up and having her in my arms stopped me from whacking Daniel.

'It's only just started,' Sherry said. 'It's nothing to do with me and you.'

'Come off it! He planned this from the start.'

Sherry shook her head. 'It isn't like that. We broke up because it wasn't working between us. Daniel had no influence on that. How could he?'

'Nothing to say, Dan? She's still married, you know. This is adultery. I could kick your ass from here into the middle of next week and plead temporary insanity.'

I was gratified to see fear on his face. It goaded me on.

'Maybe I will. Remember, I know where you live.'

'I know you feel bad,' he said. 'But please, don't threaten me.'

I put Peggy back down. 'See you around,' I said, and headed for my car. I was no longer hungry.

Was our relationship going to break down anyway or had Daniel caused it? Maybe the cracks were there and he had forced them open? I didn't know; I couldn't get a handle on things any more. I didn't see it; I thought we'd been happy, but maybe I was wrong. Whatever I thought was coloured by my bitterness and hurt, all my memories tainted by it. All I knew was that your life could fall apart in what felt like an instant.

A few days later the papers came. A letter from lawyers; Sherry wanted a divorce. I could see Peggy one weekend in two and Wednesday evenings. The words had no meaning, seemed unreal. What they signified was so alien to me: my marriage was over. My life as a father was over. Sure, I'd see her often enough, and plenty of fathers made it work, but that wasn't what I wanted. I wanted to be there for her every day, put her to bed, read her stories, listen to her concerns, watch her grow up. Now that was gone; some other man would do it and I would take her on sad little trips to keep her away from my apartment and the signs of my shitty life.

I read the papers again. Sign here, send them back. I didn't bother. Let them chase me. The game was over and I had lost.

Congratulations

Gerard piloted *The Money Pit* to the place where the mackerel had run when we had been fishing the last summer. He'd persuaded me to put the boat in the water for the afternoon; I was planning to get it winterized at Paul's, the local marina, and he'd suggested one more outing. It was unusual at this time of the year, but then Gerard was an unusual guy.

This time, though, the fish were not biting. I doubted they were even there this time of year. Gerard popped the tops off two bottles of Geary's Winter Ale and handed me one.

'So,' he said. 'How are you?'

'Fine.' Gerard was looking at me in a very odd way. Whatever we were here for it certainly wasn't fishing.

'Good. Heard some news the other day.'

'Oh?'

'Heard that Sherry and that fellow Daniel are getting married.'

My beer went down the wrong hole and I choked. When I finished spluttering I stared at Gerard. 'You heard what? We're not even fucking divorced.' The papers had come a week back; I hadn't even returned them yet.

'Unofficial engagement, that's what I heard. And you're getting divorced, ain't you?'

'Not as long as I can prevent it.' I swigged my beer. 'Is that why you brought me out here?'

He nodded. 'Thought it'd be better if you heard the news somewhere you couldn't smash too much stuff.'

I closed my eyes. 'Well, it's not good news, that's for sure. I mean, what's the fucking hurry? Is she pregnant or something?'

He hesitated. 'Heard that they're trying. Daniel wants to be a father. He's in a hurry. If they can't be married then at least they can be planning it. Apparently that's good enough for him.'

I'll bet it fucking was.

'Any other good news?'

He nodded and pointed to my line. 'Looks like you got a bite.'

Kids. Once she was pregnant I was pretty sure that the story about my failure and Daniel's success would leak out and give the good citizens of Barrow even greater reason to bestow their pitying glances on me.

Sherry, Daniel, Peggy and the kids. A perfect family. And what did I have? No job, a shitty apartment, no social life, Wednesday after school and one weekend a fortnight with Peggy.

It was the thought of that perfect family, of having to stand by and watch as they lived the perfect life that tipped me over the edge.

The following weekend I picked Peggy up on Saturday morning. I had it all planned and paid for. She got in the car and we headed to the highway.

'Aren't we going riding?' she said, as we passed the turn off for the riding school.

I shook my head. 'Not today.'

'Where are we going?'

'On a little trip,' I said. 'An adventure. It's a surprise.'

Three Thousand Miles

'Where *are* we going, Daddy?'

We were about an hour south of Portland, eating lunch in a roadside café.

'Boston,' I said. 'Then I thought we might take a trip to England. Go on a little holiday.'

She frowned. 'Does Mom know? I have school on Monday.'

I chose to lie. 'Sure she knows. She said it's okay to miss a bit of school. You'll learn a lot in England. We'll see some important sights.'

What I couldn't tell her was that it didn't matter how much school she missed because she wasn't going back.

Of course, looking back it seems crazy to have done it, but at the time it all made sense. I knew it was risky; I knew it was wrong, at least in a legal sense, but you have to understand my state of mind. I had no place in the world: my life in Barrow had collapsed, another man was living in my house with my family, I had no job. I was confused and lost and rudderless. All I knew was that I loved Peggy – I loved Sherry as well, but it was pointless dwelling on it, because I could see that I was no longer a factor in her life – and that I had no future where I was.

I was trapped. I suppose that's the risk when you have children; they tie you to the person you had them with for ever, and if you have set up home in a place three thousand miles of ocean away from your home, then when you break up you're more than a little exposed. We were in her home town, surrounded by her family and childhood friends. Whatever had happened, who had done what to whom, who was right or wrong; that was all irrelevant. Barrow was her town and they were her people. By definition I was on the outside.

In some ways I think her life had hardly changed. Same house, same town, same friends; just a different guy. I think she would have been quite happy if I had just disappeared. As it was I was just an embarrassing reminder of the mistake she had made. *Can you imagine,* I could hear her friends saying, *she used to be married to* him? *Have you seen the place he lives in?*

I couldn't stay in Barrow, I couldn't. And now they were getting married, planning a family, no doubt. I couldn't stay for that, couldn't bear the thought of seeing them out together, Daniel, Sherry, Peggy and a baby in a pram. But I couldn't leave, because of Peggy. So I decided to do the only thing I could; I'd clear out, leave town, give Sherry what she wanted, but I'd do it on my terms. I'd take my daughter with me.

That was fair, wasn't it? She had the house, the life, the husband, the future full of babies. I just wanted one thing. Just one. Peggy.

We were at the airport early. I'd checked in online and we only had hand luggage, so we went through security and sat in the food court on the other side. I put the passports in my jacket pocket.

Peggy pointed at them. 'Can I see?'

I handed it to her. It was brand new, an unused British passport. It was lucky I'd applied for it when we were last in the UK; Sherry had Peggy's US passport and I could hardly have asked for it. I took it as a sign that I was doing the right thing.

I'd been worried that Peggy would work out something was wrong or get homesick or kick up a fuss for some other reason, but she was fine. I suppose she was still at the age when new things happen all the time; besides, she had recently been to the airport and it wasn't as though I was some random stranger. I was, after all, still her father.

We boarded at five p.m. and took our seats. I looked at the map on the video screen in the seat-back in front of me. A quick hop over the Atlantic, skirt the coast of Ireland and into Paris.

I had decided that the point of entry should be France. We'd arrive at around six a.m. European time, which was midnight in Barrow, so we'd have about eighteen hours before Peggy was due home, at which point Sherry would start trying to phone me and would discover something was wrong. I wasn't sure what she would do so I wanted the traces of our voyage to be at least a bit misleading; if she called the police and they asked the airlines then they'd only know that we'd been in Paris about eighteen hours before. As far as they would know, we could be anywhere in Europe.

Peggy was asleep when the plane touched down, her head a dead weight against my shoulder. I let her sleep until we had taxied to the gate then gently woke her. I carried her off the plane, a bag over each shoulder. It was just possible that Sherry was already on our trail and so at immigration my heart was racing; I was glad of the jet lag as it gave me an excuse for the pale, haggard look on my face.

The border guard barely looked at our passports. A father and daughter, both British; nothing to see here. We walked out of the airport terminal into the chill air of an autumn morning in Paris. I smiled, for the first time in days. Free, and finally taking charge of my destiny.

And then I saw him and smiled even wider. This was going exactly as I had planned.

Friends Will be Friends

Jerry shook my hand. 'You made it.'

'Thanks for coming. Peggy, you remember Jerry.'

Peggy nodded, her eyes red and swollen with lack of sleep. 'Hi.'

'Hi, Peggy.' Jerry grabbed our bags. 'I'm parked in the short stay. At least I think I am. My French isn't up to much.'

We followed him to a lift and then into a car park. I saw his vehicle immediately; it was the reason why I had asked him to meet us. A white Ford Transit van with British plates. That had to be it.

He opened the back doors and put our bags inside. There was a double mattress laid out on the floor, with a quilt and pillows. He had put some stuffed animals on the pillow, along with some sandwiches and a bottle of water.

'Look, Pegs,' I said. 'A little bed. You want to lie down?'

She nodded again, a nod being about the only gesture she was capable of. I helped her in and lay her on the bed.

'I'll be back in a second,' I said, and climbed out. Jerry was leaning against the van, his arms folded. 'Thanks again,' I said. 'I wasn't sure you'd make it in time.'

'I drove through the night. Stayed at one of those Formule One hotels.' Jerry lived in Kent, so it wasn't such a long drive to Dover, and then to Paris. He rubbed his chin, the stubble rasping against his hand. 'You know, we're friends and I'm here to help, but are you sure this is a good idea?'

'Of course. It's not ideal, but I had no choice. Don't worry. It'll be fine.'

'Really? It's kidnapping.'

'No it isn't. She's my daughter, Jerry. You can't kidnap your own child.'

'I think you can. And I'm an accessory.'

'No one will ever know.'

He sighed. 'Whatever you want. But I think it's a bad idea. Come on. We'd better get going.'

I'd decided we should take the ferry; for some reason I thought it had more lax security that the Channel Tunnel. As we approached Calais I climbed in the back of the van, where Peggy was fast asleep. I'd told Jerry what had happened over the past few months, and I could see that he sympathized with me, but he still wasn't happy with what I was doing. That was okay; I knew it was a big ask of him to come and pick us up, but it was worth it, and I'd have done the same for him.

'Right,' Jerry said. 'We're here. We're just entering the ferry terminal. Keep it quiet back there.'

I listened to the clangs as we bumped slowly onto the boat. The smell of the sea mingled with the oily smell of the boat reminded me of childhood holidays and I felt a sudden connection to my youthful self. I imagined him boarding the ferry as a teenager, examining the girls his age and wondering about the possibility of a brief, ferry-based romance, his hormones seething around in his body. I wondered what he would have thought if I had appeared to him and said that the next time he was on a ferry he would be smuggling his daughter into the country while his wife slept in the

USA. In a way I wished it had happened; I could have warned him not to take up with American girls he met abroad. It might have saved me all the bother I was in now.

But then wasn't there some rule in time-travel books and movies about not interfering with the past because if you did you couldn't predict the consequences? I shook the thought from my head and lay next to Peggy. All she needed to do was sleep for another hour and we'd be in Dover.

Back in the UK. And no one would know where we were.

Jerry had to leave the van for the duration of the crossing. Even in the dark I could tell when we set sail; the whole feel of the ferry changed when it was cast-off and the slow pitch and roll motion of a boat on water began.

What if we sank? Sweat prickled my arms and torso at the thought. Assuming Jerry died, no one would know we were there, entombed in his van at the bottom of the sea. I didn't think he had told Sarah – it wasn't the kind of thing she would have approved of – and there was no other record of our being on the boat.

We would just have disappeared. Sherry would spend years searching for us, not knowing that it was pointless.

I felt a pang of longing for her, longing for the life we'd had. If only I had done things differently – I bit my lip. There was no point thinking like that. For whatever reason – Daniel, me, Sherry and I growing older and growing apart – it was over, and all I could do was move on, which was what I was doing now.

God, it was eerie down here, the thrum of the engines loud. Somewhere there were some lights on, but they didn't do much to dispel the gloom in the back of the van. It was all I could do to see Peggy's face.

Next to me, she stirred.

I stroked her head and shushed her. *Not now,* I thought, *don't wake now.*

Her eyes flickered open and she looked around.

'Daddy,' she said, her voice shockingly loud in the hold. 'Where are we?'

'Shhh.' I put a finger to her lips and whispered. 'We're on a boat. Go back to sleep.'

'On a boat?' Her face creased in puzzlement, but at least she was whispering now. 'Why?'

'To get to England. Don't worry.'

She sat upright, fully awake now. 'Daddy, I don't like it.'

I hugged her. 'Peggy. You have to stay quiet. I promise you it'll be okay, but you have to stay quiet.'

'Why? What's going on?'

She sounded just like her mother. 'We're not supposed to be here. We have to stay quiet so the police don't find us.'

Her eyes widened in alarm. 'Daddy! I'm frightened.'

'Don't be. I won't let anything happen to you. I love you.' I pulled her closer to me. 'Do you think you can do it? Stay quiet?'

I felt her nod her head against my chest and she fell silent. We stayed like that until the lights went on and the noise of people returning to their cars started up.

The front door of the van opened and Jerry climbed in. I looked at the back of his head.

'Peggy's awake,' I whispered. 'She knows to be quiet. Just so you're aware.'

He nodded slightly but didn't turn round. I could sense his nerves. If we got stopped going into the UK he – never mind me – would be in a lot of trouble. What was the penalty for people-smuggling and accessory to kidnap? I didn't know, but I was prepared to place a large bet that it was substantial. He was taking a real risk for me.

Ahead, drivers started their engines. The van shook and began to move.

I took a deep breath and lay next to Peggy, my arms still around her. This was it.

Customs

In thrillers there comes a time when the success or failure of whatever enterprise the protagonists are engaged in is in the balance, when the bomb must be defused or the hero must find a way out of whatever devilish trap he or she is in. It is the moment of highest tension, when all is at stake, and it is the moment at which the audience is most fully engaged, their backsides well and truly on the edge of their seats.

In life those moments are thankfully rare, because they are utterly terrifying.

The van rumbled forward, clanking over the ramp off the ferry and crawling towards the customs checkpoint. My arms tightened around Peggy; there was so much that could go wrong. She might speak or cough or sneeze at the wrong moment; some tremor or strain in Jerry's voice might pique the customs official's suspicion; we might just get unlucky and be picked out in a random check.

'Are you okay, Daddy?' she said.

'Shhh.' I relaxed my grip and whispered in her ear. 'Not a word. Not a sound. Close your eyes and pretend you're asleep.'

She did so; I kept mine open, looking at the back doors and imagining them opening to reveal a black-uniformed figure silhouetted against the light, a silhouette that would lean in, features appearing on its face, eyes, a nose, a mouth, lips that would speak.

Hello, what have we here then?

It was unlikely to be Dixon of Dock Green, but that was the image that came to me, followed by interrogation rooms, police stations, cells.

The van stopped and I heard the sound of the window descending. At that moment I understood that fear could literally make you shit yourself; my stomach felt like it had turned to liquid and I was overcome with an urge to let go. Somehow, I held it in.

'Here you go,' Jerry said. I thought I could hear a note of tension in his voice.

The officer's voice in reply was indistinct.

'Nothing much,' Jerry said. 'Just some beer, wine.' He paused, then added: 'It's for a wedding.'

Shit. Don't volunteer information; it makes you sound guilty. Just be calm.

'Yesterday. Stayed in one of those Formule One places. Bit of a shithole.'

There was a long pause. What was the officer doing? Checking something? Looking up something on a database? I looked at my watch. We had made good time from Paris, reaching Calais by nine a.m., followed by a bit of a wait for the ferry, then a ninety-minute crossing, which meant it was only eleven-thirty UK time, still early morning in Barrow. Surely Sherry hadn't contacted the authorities; she couldn't have. She wouldn't know Peggy was gone until six p.m. her time.

She wouldn't know Peggy was gone. Suddenly what I was doing hit me. Sweat prickled on my upper lip and I was filled, for some reason, with an urge to shout out. *We're here!* I wanted to shout. *We're in the back!*

I forced myself to breathe deeply; now was no time to panic.

Up front I heard the sound of the window going up.
'Cheers,' Jerry said. 'See you.'
The van started to move. We were through.

Bolt-hole

Jerry lived in a village in Kent called Chainhurst, but he headed for a small cottage in the countryside near Bewl Water that Sarah's parents had left them when they died. On the way we stopped at a supermarket.

'Can I have some bananas?' Peggy said.

'Sure. Have whatever you want. Special treat.'

She looked at me suspiciously. 'Whatever I want?'

'Whatever you want.'

'Can I have chocolate? And marshmallows? We can make s'mores.'

'Ok. S'mores it is. I'll get some other stuff as well, just in case.'

She shrugged. 'Okay. You get other stuff and I'll get the s'mores.'

We pushed the trolley into the confectionery aisle and Peggy began to load it up.

'We need some kind of biscuit for the s'mores,' I said to Jerry. 'Digestives, maybe?'

'Sure.' Jerry frowned. 'What are s'mores?'

'It's a kind of campfire food they have in the US. Chocolate and marshmallow melted between biscuits. They call them s'mores because you always want some more. You have to get the biscuits

right – they use Grahams, a kind of sweet cracker. I think digestives might be the closest we have.'

'Right.' He took my elbow and pulled me a step back from
Peggy, who was contemplating the unfamiliar chocolate choices.
'I'm sure that the biscuit choice is essential, but don't you think
you've got other stuff to be thinking about? What the hell are you
going to do?'

'Stay at the cottage for a while. Then we'll figure it out.'

Jerry was pale, his face strained. 'I don't think you understand.'

'Understand what?'

'In about ten hours Sherry is going to start looking for her daughter – who she has legal custody of – and at some point she's going to
find out that you've taken her to the UK, which means the police,
the CIA, the fucking Flying Squad for all I know are going to be
searching for her; the point is, you'd better have a plan, because
when she catches up with you you're going to be in shit street.'

'We'll work it out.'

'Good luck.' He shook his head. 'I'll see you at the van. I need
to pick some stuff up.'

When we got back to the van he handed me a mobile phone. He
had another in his other hand.

'They're pre-paid. Bought cash, untraceable. Call me on this. I
don't want any more links to this shit than I already have.'

I could see how worried he was, and it was starting to affect me.
I pushed the thought away. This was no time for doubts.

We didn't talk much on the drive to the cottage; I was tired and
Jerry looked lost in thought. The cottage wasn't far from the
supermarket, although it felt very remote, nestled away at the end
of a long drive. It was old, maybe two hundred and fifty years, and
had low ceilings with thick, dark beams in them. Every room had
a fireplace.

'You go upstairs and pick a room,' Jerry said to Peggy. 'I need to show your dad a few things.'

Peggy disappeared and Jerry led me to a room off the kitchen.

'This is the boiler,' he said. 'It can be a bit hit and miss—'

I interrupted him. 'I'll figure it out. Don't worry.'

Jerry rubbed his temples with the thumb and forefinger of his right hand. 'Look,' he said. 'I'm worried that this is a crazy situation. That you're not thinking it through.'

'I'm fine.'

'Are you? From what you told me it seems things have been tough the last few months. That can take its toll. And now – this. I don't see how this can end well.' He shook his head. 'I'm not sure you're thinking straight'

'Of course I am. It'll be okay.'

'You need to think about calling Sherry and telling her where you are. Then you can discuss it with her, apologize, tell her it was a last-minute trip and you'll be back in a week. If she thinks you kidnapped her . . .' He stopped, lost for words.

'Look. She has Daniel. Once she knows Peggy's safe we can come to some arrangement. She'll understand.'

I could see that he didn't agree, but I didn't need him to, and in the end how bad could it be? She was my daughter as much as she was Sherry's, after all. That was the crux of the matter; I had every right to see my daughter. Why shouldn't I take her on holiday?

'Look, Jerry,' I said. 'Thanks for everything you've done. We're good from now on.'

He closed his eyes. 'Good luck,' he said. 'I'll be in touch. Call me whenever.'

Peggy chose the smallest room; it was tiny, little more than a nook, and had a bed built into the corner. It was perfect for her and she had started to unpack the few things I had brought for her.

'So,' I said, sitting on her bed. 'This is fun.'

She nodded. 'I'm tired.'

'You want to go to sleep? How about some s'mores then you take a nap?'

When Peggy was in bed I called Dad.

'Hello?'

'Dad. It's me. Tom.'

'Tom.' I couldn't help feeling that he sounded disappointed.

'How've you been?'

'Fine. You?'

'Good. Look, I wanted to let you know I might be coming to visit. Next week.'

'With Peggy?'

'Yes. She's coming.'

His voice brightened. 'Excellent. I'll look forward to seeing her.' He paused. 'To seeing both of you.'

Peggy woke up a few hours later. She discovered a box full of toys, and, in the other guest bedroom, a doll's house that was taller than her and filled with the most detailed miniatures. Once we'd eaten I watched her play with it. She loved it, loved positioning the people in the different rooms and inventing stories about them. I'd get her one someday.

Around eleven p.m. my phone – the one from the US, not the one Jerry had bought – started to ring. I ran downstairs and grabbed it from my bag.

It was Sherry.

I hit the reject button and switched it off. I took out the battery and the SIM card. I wasn't sure if it could be traced when it was off, but I didn't want to risk it; after all, who knew what signals they emitted?

It was six p.m. in Barrow, so she'd be wondering where I was. How long before she hit the panic button? Not long, I thought. Not long.

In the end the call came early the next morning. Peggy and I hadn't gone to sleep until well after midnight, the jet lag keeping us awake. She was thrilled to be up so late; as far as she was concerned it was all a big adventure, and, to be honest, that's how I felt about it as well. I was just enjoying being with my daughter.

The phone call dragged me from sleep. It was Jerry.

'Morning,' he said.

'Morning.' I was groggy; it took me a while to fully regain consciousness. 'All well?'

'Not exactly. Sherry called me.'

I woke up a bit more. 'She called *you*?'

'Yup. Ten minutes ago. Wanted to know if I knew where you were. She sounded upset. Distressed. She said she'd called everyone she knew but you were nowhere to be found.'

'What did you say?'

'I gave her the address of the cottage and said I'd smuggled you in from France.'

'Really?'

'No, not really. I said I hadn't heard from you, but would let her know if I did.'

'Right. That's good. She doesn't know where I am.'

There was a silence on the line. 'You know that soon the whole world will be looking for you. You won't be able to go anywhere. Remember Madeleine McCann?'

'That's different. She was abducted. I'm Peggy's father.'

'And what do you think Sherry will say? That you're a level-headed, balanced bloke and she just wants to say hi, or that you're a bit fucking crazy and she's worried what you'll do?'

'I'm not crazy.'

'I didn't say you were, although I have my doubts. I said that's what she'll say. Your photos will be all over the place. You won't be able to go anywhere. Don't you see that?'

I started to speak but he interrupted.

'She gave me a message for you. A kind of offer.'

'And?'

'She said that if you did get in touch I was to tell you to call her. She said that the police don't know Peggy's missing, and she's not going to tell them for twelve hours. If by then you've called then you can sort it out with her – no need for them to get involved.'

'Forget it.'

'Listen, mate,' Jerry said. 'I think you need to at least call her. It's your last chance to keep a lid on this thing. If you don't it's going to go sky high.'

'No. I don't want to.'

'I don't care whether you want to or not. You need to.'

'I'm going to deal with this my own way.'

'I was hoping you'd see sense and I wouldn't have to do this.' He sighed. 'If you don't call her I will.'

I held the phone away from my ear. I couldn't believe what he'd said.

'Jerry,' I said. 'What the fuck? You're supposed to be my friend.'

'I am, and as a friend I can't let you do this. It has to stop.'

'Just stay the fuck out of it,' I said. 'We'll leave the cottage. You don't have to be involved. I don't want you involved.'

'I am involved, whether you like it or not. You involved me when you got me to pick you up—'

'So why did you, if you're not going to help me? If you're so against all this, why did you bother?'

'Because, Tom, you're my friend, and I thought it was better to have you close by than gallivanting around Europe with your kidnapped daughter. That's why I did it. That's why I broke God knows what laws to help you. Because I'm your friend.' In the background I heard one of his children cry and he muttered something away from the phone. When he came back his voice was grim. 'And that's why I'm going to do this. You've got two hours, Tom. Either you call her or I will.'

Betrayed

The bastard. I looked at the phone in shock, as though I couldn't believe that those words had come from it. It really shitted all over my plans; if he was going to betray me then I would have to get out of here, but I had nowhere to go, and in any case, I had no transportation to get there. In two hours Sherry would know where I was; I couldn't even arrange a car by then, and, with Peggy in tow, I wouldn't get very far on foot.

I was trapped. Well and truly trapped, just as I had been in Barrow.

And I'd be trapped wherever I went. I couldn't stay in Barrow but I couldn't leave, unless I kidnapped my daughter, in which case I was back in the shit, just somewhere else. That's the problem with having a kid, at least for me; I can't bear the thought of being away from her. If I could have left Barrow and started a new life in London or Paris or Bangkok and seen Peggy once a year, that would have been the answer to all my problems. But I had to be near her, and that meant Barrow – or this.

I walked into the garden, barefoot, the grass dewy and wet. I really had no choice. I tapped in Sherry's number on the phone and stared at it. I pressed the green button.

After a few seconds a metallic voice spoke:

You are not authorized to call this number. You are not authorized to call this number.

I smiled. Of course – it was a pre-paid phone, which didn't allow international calls. I took my US phone from the kitchen table and reassembled it. It didn't matter now if it was sending out signals or not.

Sherry picked up before the phone had rung on my end.

'Tom?'

'Hi.'

'Is Peggy with you? Is she okay?'

'Of course she is.'

She let out a huge, long sigh. 'Thank God for that.'

'You don't need to worry. I'm hardly going to let anything happen to her.'

'Where are you?'

'In England. Down south. I rented a little place.'

'England? Jesus, Tom. What on earth are you doing there?'

'It's where I'm from. I was going to visit Dad.' I didn't really know what to say; beyond the vague idea to head home and see my father, I had not really made any other plans.

She didn't reply for a long time. When she spoke she sounded almost sympathetic. 'Tom. You have to bring her home.'

I paused. 'She can stay with me for a while.'

'No. I'm sorry, but no.'

'She's my daughter, Sherry.'

'We can come to an arrangement, maybe. Some kind of escorted visit. But first she has to come home.'

'I don't think so.'

She spoke quickly, her voice nervous. In the background I heard Daniel say something and realized he was listening in, still hovering around my and Sherry's business. 'Tom. She has to come home. Immediately. This is kidnapping.'

'No, it isn't. You can't kidnap your own child.'

'Yes, you can. Believe me, I've made it my business to find out about that since you disappeared. It's a serious crime.'

I stared out of the window. None of this seemed real any more. The only thought I could keep hold of was *what have I done?*

Sherry continued.

'I have a proposal for you.' I heard Daniel's words in her phraseology. 'Send her home. Get her an escorted flight, and we'll leave it at that. The police don't know yet, and they don't need to. You can still see her – supervised, at first. We'll make this work, Tom. I understand what you're going through.'

No you don't, I thought, *you don't understand at all.* 'And if I say no?'

'Then it's the police. I don't know what they'll do, but I do know you'll never see Peggy again.'

'Okay,' I said. 'Let me think about it.' I put the phone down.

Peggy

Peggy was curled up in the corner of the bed, her back tucked up against the cottage wall. Her face was tilted upwards and her eyes were moving rapidly under her eyelids. As I watched they fell still; whatever dream she had been having had come to an end.

Despite all that had gone on in the last few months Peggy could still sleep the deep, replenishing sleep of childhood. That kind of sleep had come rarely to me as an adult, but when it had I felt invincible in the days that followed: I had the energy to do all the things I had been putting off; I loved Sherry and Peggy with a pinpoint intensity; I noticed details that I didn't normally notice. Life was fuller, richer, more rewarding. My mum used to say that a good sleep was nature's way of healing you. She often quoted something she had learned in school, which had stuck with me:

> *Tired nature's sweet restorer, balmy sleep*
> *He, like the world, his ready visit pays*
> *Where fortune smiles –*
> *the wretched he forsakes.*

311

Was that it? Was something as simple as sleep the difference between good fortune and wretchedness? Perhaps – and if so, how fortunate was Peggy, blessed as she was with the gift of sleep.

I sat on the bed. It creaked loudly and sagged towards me; Peggy moved and tensed and grunted and I held my breath, but she settled and her eyes stayed closed. I stroked her hair, rubbing a few strands between my fingers. She needed a bath; her hair was becoming greasy. She had always been a good sleeper, at least after the first few chaotic months when Sherry and I had been feeling our way into our roles as parents. In those days we had taken turns rocking her to sleep during the night, or pushing her around the neighbourhood in her pram, or strapping her into her car seat and driving her back and forth up our street. Sometimes, when she really wouldn't sleep, I drove to a speed bump near the school and went forwards then backwards over it. The bumping seemed to soothe her. Once, at about four in the morning, a police officer had pulled up and asked me what I was doing; I raised a finger to my lips and gestured into the back seat. He smiled and gave me the thumbs up, then pulled a photo from his wallet of a baby boy. *Good luck,* he mouthed, *she's beautiful.*

That was what life in a small town was like. It could be frustrating, with everyone in your business, and you could feel trapped, but the sense of community and belonging more than made up for it. Once, during the aftermath of one Maine's violent storms, we'd lost power and all our frozen food was in danger of spoiling. Normally we wouldn't have been bothered, but Sherry had expressed and frozen a load of breast milk, which had taken her a lot of time and effort. I went to the local market, Libby's – a kind of general store – to buy ice to fill the freezer with, and the owner asked what I needed it for. When I told him, he offered to let us keep our food in his freezers, which were still running thanks to his back-up generator. In England we remember that kind of thing with nostalgia and call it the Blitz spirit; in small-town Maine it's a way of life.

Peggy seemed so big to me now, lying there in the bed. When you have a child people always tell you how fast they grow up, and it's true. It seemed like – if not yesterday – mere weeks back that she had been a baby. Now she was a little girl, who had designs on being a teenager.

I'm probably not alone as a parent in saying this, but I don't think it's possible to love someone more than I loved Peggy. When I was with her or thought about her or dreamed about her it was as though every cell in my body was drawn towards her like a magnet attracted to a pole. If my being is made of fibres then every fibre of my being yearned for her. I couldn't have loved her more, because there was no part of me that wasn't already loving her at its maximum.

And because of that I'd wanted Sherry too, wanted us all to be together again, wanted our family to reunite. But Sherry didn't want me back, she never would, not when she thought I was guilty of 'inappropriate touching'. I knew that now. I think I'd been holding on to some hope that we could get back together but that had disappeared in the last couple of days. I don't know why; I couldn't remember any epiphany when I had seen the truth, but I knew that it was over even though I loved her as much as I ever had.

And now she was with Daniel. After all this, after all she'd said, she'd ended up with him. I wasn't sure I could forgive her that, even if I had the chance to. Had it been there all along between her and Daniel? I'd never know, because – and this was something else I'd realized – you can never really know another person. You think you do, but inside them there's always a secret place where they keep something of themselves hidden. Sometimes they're little things, like when a man is out at a romantic dinner with his wife and the waitress leans over to hand him a menu and down her blouse he sees her breasts cupped in a lace bra, what he says is *thank you, would you like a drink, darling*, but what he is thinking is how he would like to rip off the waitress's blouse and bury his face in her chest; likewise, when a wife is at a wedding and the groom is making a speech about the bride that is witty and charming and romantic and her husband is rolling his eyes and saying it's a bit soppy and he wouldn't make such an embarrassing speech, what she says is *I know, it's not the kind of thing that I like but I can see why other people do*, but what she is thinking is *God, I wish he would be more romantic, like he was when we met, I can't take another forty years of this boorish, inconsiderate behaviour, how does he think he can get away with taking me for granted like this.*

But that secret place is like a nursery; it's where the doubts form and grow and mature until, sometimes, they emerge fully formed and, without warning, a relationship is over.

And that was what had happened to me. I'd never seen it coming, but all the while it had been building in Sherry. Seen from her point of view this whole thing would have looked a lot different.

Fledging

'Are you coming, Daddy?'

I shook my head. 'In a few days. I'm going to visit Grandpa first.' She didn't need to know that I was staying for good. I had no idea what I'd be doing. I'd figure that out when the time came.

'Can I come?'

'Sorry, darling. Another time.'

'You promise?'

'I promise.'

The flight attendant – Lucy – picked up Peggy's bag. She was pretty, blonde and young, no more than twenty-five, and had the sparkling-eyed enthusiasm of a primary school teacher. I could see why they chose her to escort minors on flights. Peggy already idolized her.

'Time to go, Peggy,' she said. 'Are you ready?'

Peggy nodded. 'I am.' She looked up at me. 'Bye, Daddy.'

I sank onto my haunches and wrapped my arms around her. My tears were sudden and uncontrollable. 'I love you,' I whispered. 'I love you. Remember that.'

'Don't cry, Daddy,' Peggy kissed me. 'I love you too.'

I got to my feet. Lucy took Peggy's hand. 'You're a very lucky girl to have a daddy who loves you so much,' she said, then smiled at me. 'She'll be fine with us. Don't worry.'

I waved to Peggy. 'Bye, petal.'

Hand in hand with Lucy, she walked into the security screening area. Just before she disappeared I shouted out. 'Bye, Peggy,' then, at the top of my voice: 'I love you.'

She turned, and waved, and then was gone.

Back Home

She got home safely; Sherry sent me a terse text message to let me know. I got it just as I arrived at my dad's house.

Home. This would always be, in some way, home. I could have lived in Barrow for fifty years and it would never quite have replaced this house. You are formed in your childhood home; you become who you are. You grow and change and learn but at the centre of you there's a person you can never escape, and that person is made in the places you live as a child.

Dad was in his chair, watching *Countdown*.

'It's not the same since Richard Whiteley left,' he said. 'The new presenters aren't up to it.'

They could have been much better and Dad would never have admitted it. He liked things to stay just the way they were.

'Hi. Good to see you.'

He looked up. 'Where's Peggy?'

'She couldn't come.'

'Sherry want her at school, again?' He sounded bitter.

'No. That's not it.' I sat on the couch.

'So what are you doing here?'

'I've got something to tell you.'

*

317

I told him everything. The guilt when Mum died, Daniel's arrival on the scene, the episode with the vodka, the fight at school, the rape. I told him how I thought I'd fixed it all, how I thought Daniel was off the scene. I ended with Thanksgiving and the accusations of 'inappropriate touching', the subsequent collapse of our marriage, and Daniel's triumph.

'And you didn't do it, this inappropriate touching?'

'Of course not.'

He nodded. He believed me. It was such a relief; no one had had such unconditional faith in me for so long. This was what it meant to be home.

'Christ,' he said. 'It sounds like a right bloody mess.'

The next two days were brutal. I slept late, drank tea with Dad in silence, and went for long, wandering walks through the town.

I came back one evening to the smell of fish and chips.

'Thought you might like something to eat,' Dad said. 'Cheer you up a bit. You always liked fish and chips as a boy.'

'Thanks.' It was a kind thought, but it was going to take more than some greasy takeaway to cheer me up.

'You know, you need to sort this out, lad.'

I sprinkled some malt vinegar on my chips. 'Right.'

'You can't live here for ever.'

I readied myself for a speech about how I was wasting my life and I needed to pull my socks up. I was glad he was concerned for me, but I was a grown-up. Besides, I thought he might have liked to have his son around for a while.

'It's only been two days, Dad,' I said.

'I know.' He drank from his cheap, orange can of bitter. 'But you're so bloody miserable. It's a pain living with you.' He took another sip. 'And you can't stay here. You're wasting your life.'

'Where do I go, then?'

'Back to Barrow.'

'Right. And what am I going to do there?'

'Live near your daughter. See her at weekends. It's not perfect, but plenty do it.'

'And how about work?' I asked. 'No one will give me a job, not with the allegations against me.'

'I was thinking about that. You should fight them.'

'I told you. There's no point.'

'You didn't do it, right?'

'Of course not.'

'Then you have to stand up for yourself. If you didn't do it, then fight. The truth will come out.'

It was a nice thought, but I don't think I would have acted on it, had Gerard not sent some astonishing news.

Gerard

After we finished our fish and chips I sat with a can of bitter and checked my emails. There was one from Gerard.

Call me, it said. *Urgent. As soon as you get this, whatever time it is where you are.*

It was rare to get that kind of email from Gerard; it was rare to get any kind of email at all. I dialled his number on my phone. It rang twice and he picked up.

'Ayuh,' he said.

'Gerard. It's me. I got your email.'

'Tom. So, I've been working for Jeff Coffin – you know, the guy with the building firm, B & F Building. He needed someone to help on an attic conversion at a place out by the water.'

'Right.' I couldn't see what was so important about Gerard's building work. 'And?'

'And you need to get home, quick.'

'I'm not sure I see the connection, Gerard.'

'We were working at your boy Daniel's place. Amazing spot he's got out there. Private beach, you name it.'

This wasn't making me feel any better.

'Anyway, I had to re-route some plumbing, so I went into the spare room and moved a closet. There was a box behind it. I wondered what was in it – what he was hiding – and so I had a little look. And you wouldn't believe it.'

'What was it? Drugs? Porn? Child porn?' This could be useful. Even if I couldn't get my life back, I might be able to damage his.

'Worse. Or better, at least as far as you're concerned. It was full of photos. Hundreds of them.'

'Of what?'

'Of Sherry.' He paused. 'And there are recent ones, from the last few years. He must have got someone to take them. This guy's obsessed with your wife, buddy. And now you can prove it.'

I met Gerard at his flat. The flight back had taken about twenty hours; the only thing I could get went from Manchester to Madrid, from Madrid to New York and then from New York to Boston, from where I had to catch a bus up to Maine. It might as well have been twenty days. I don't think I have ever known time go so slowly.

'So,' he said. 'Take a look.'

I was exhausted. It was nearly midnight in Maine – which meant it was nearly five a.m. in the UK – and I had not had the most restful few days, but I took the glass of whisky he handed me and lifted the lid off the box.

It was an old wooden box – I think at one time it had contained twelve bottles of wine – and it was nearly full of photos. In among them were a few other objects: a faded Coke T-shirt that looked like it had belonged to Sherry – I assume it was hers – in the eighties, a woven friendship bracelet – I guessed made for him by a teenage Sherry –and a small box full of cheap jewellery.

It was the photos that were the mother lode, however. They went back years, to when Sherry was twelve or thirteen. Daniel was in a lot of the older ones, often in the background, along with Lisa and Mike and a bunch of other people I'd met over the years. In one, which looked like it had been taken before their last prom, there was a large group assembled outside Sherry's mum's house. The girls were dressed in ball gowns, the boys in tuxedos. Daniel was standing next to a thin, brown-haired girl who I didn't know; Sherry had her arm around someone. She looked incredible, already beautiful at eighteen. Her date didn't look so good, mainly because he'd had his face scratched out. Daniel was going to have difficulty explaining this.

'Well,' I said. 'This is fucking incredible. And this stuff – ' I picked up a photo of Sherry at a bakery in the town centre, an organic, gluten-free bakery which had only opened three years ago. 'This is just creepy. I mean, he must have been watching her – us – for years.'

'No shit,' Gerard said. 'I knew he was a weird fucker the first time I saw him.'

'You did?'

'Sure I did.'

'Thank God it wasn't just me.' I leafed through the box. A photo caught my eye – I think because unlike all the others Sherry was not in it – and I picked it out. It was taken in an office. It looked like a Friday night party, or something like that. In it were four people: Daniel, a tall, athletic looking guy and two women. All four of them were wearing suits and raising their glasses to the camera. 'I wonder who this lot are?' I said.

'There's some writing on the back.'

I flipped it over and read it, then read it again, to make sure I'd understood it correctly.

'You okay? You've gone white.'

'I guess,' I said.

'What is it?'

'Jesus, Gerard,' I said. 'You're not going to believe this.'

*

At dawn the next day, I got up and walked down to an old paper mill by the river. It had been abandoned years ago; some local artists had moved in and were trying to make it the focus of some regeneration efforts. It wasn't really working that well, but it was something. I walked through the car park, past the VW camper vans and old pick-up trucks, and onto the river bank. A little way along was a rocky outcrop where you could sit and watch the river churn by. The other bank was a forest, undeveloped. This view had been unchanged for a long time; it was one of the few that had.

I had breakfast on my own, then walked back to Gerard's flat. The box was on the kitchen table. It was really amazing to think Daniel had hoarded this stuff over the years, not to mention the more recent photos. It was also frightening to see the depth of his obsession; it was like peering over a cliff at the sea far below.

I smiled at the thought that it was Gerard who'd found it. Gerard, the guy Daniel had shunned the day I first met him, the guy he'd thought was beneath him. He should have paid a bit more attention.

I picked up the box. Peggy would be at school; Sherry should be home alone.

She opened the door an inch. I could see her eye through the crack in the door.

'What are you doing here?' There was trepidation in her voice; she was on her own and she thought I was crazy. I didn't blame her. I'd just kidnapped our daughter, and until two minutes ago she'd been under the impression I was in England.

'I've got something you need to see.'

'You shouldn't be here. I don't want to see you, Tom.' Her eye flickered downwards to the box. 'What's that?'

'Don't worry. It's not a bomb. It's something you should see.' I put it down on the porch and lifted the lid off. 'Take a look.'

'Go and stand on the road.'

I backed off and stood on the tarmac.

'Sit down,' she called.

I squatted and hugged my knees.

The door opened. She knelt down and leafed through the contents of the box. A few seconds later she dragged it inside and slammed the door shut.

It was a bit awkward waiting in the middle of the road. Despite the disdain my neighbours all felt for me now, I still had some pride, so I disobeyed Sherry and sat on the porch steps. I turned my face up to the sun. I was in no hurry. For the first time in my adult life I truly had nothing else to do.

It was only about ten minutes before she opened the door.

'Where the hell did you get this?'

'Gerard found it. At Daniel's house. He was working out there. He moved some furniture around, and there it was.'

She was pale. I got the impression a lot of things had clicked together in her mind.

'So,' I said. 'He's not in love with you, huh? What about the ones from the last few years? How does it feel to have been spied on, and lied to, by your fiancé?'

'This is crazy,' she said. 'He didn't really do this. You're making it up. Somehow, you're making it up.'

'Right. I got all those old photos of you – photos I would have no way of getting, but which I found in England – and put this together.'

'Tom.' I could see she was starting to wonder. 'What the hell is going on?'

'I told you, but you didn't believe me. He was behind it all. The fight, the vodka, the "inappropriate touching". It was all him. I'm going to fight them, by the way, the charges. And you know what we'll find? That there never was a complaint. He made it up, used the anonymity to fabricate the whole thing. He knew it was enough, knew that the threat of it was enough to turn you all against me. Stephanie was ready to think badly of me, after she'd found me pinning him against the wall, and he knew how you would react to the thought that your husband had been involved in any – however minor – kind of unwanted sexual advances towards students. He gave me a way out – to go quietly – and I took it. Well, I'm going to fight it.'

She closed her eyes and pushed the box at me. 'I don't want to know about this.'

'What are you going to do when the charges are shown to be false? You're going to have to face this sooner or later, Sherry.'

'Tom.' Sherry bit her nails and looked at me, looked at me the way she had when we first met and she was vulnerable and scared. 'What am I supposed to do?'

'That's not really my problem. I thought you should know.'

'Come inside,' she said. 'We need to talk.'

She sat on one side of the kitchen table, I sat on the other, the box between us like a loaded gun. It was strange to be home; it was so familiar, yet already it seemed to belong to a different part of my life.

'How bad is this really?' she said, after a long silence. 'I mean, so he lied about being in love with me. Is it really that bad?'

'You're going to let him off?' I said. 'After this? And he didn't just lie about being in love with you. What about the things he did to me? Are you really going to let him off the hook?'

The front door banged open.

'Off the hook for what?'

Daniel shrugged off his coat and hung it on the banister.

'Hi, Tom.' He nodded at me. 'I must say I'm surprised to see you here. I thought you were still in the UK.'

'I came back.'

'Evidently. But I don't think you should be in our house.' He turned to Sherry. 'Did he force his way in? Should I call 911?'

She shook her head. 'I let him in.'

'Oh?' I could see the uncertainty bloom in his eyes. There was something going on here that he didn't know about, and it worried him. His hand hovered over the phone by the stairs.

'Come in,' I said. 'There's something you should see.'

To his credit he did a good job of hiding his feelings when he saw the box. It must have been a hell of a shock; it must have been like confronting your worst nightmare. Daniel's tongue moistened his lips; that was about the extent of his reaction.

'Where did you get that?' he said.

'That's not the point, is it?' I said. 'It's what's in there that matters.'

'That's private property. You must have stolen it from the house.'

'Nope. Never been near your house in my life.'

His eyes narrowed. 'The workmen. You must know one of them.' He nodded. 'That fucking layabout Gerard. Small towns, eh?'

'You were in love with me all the time?' Sherry said. 'Since when?'

He threw his hands up in the air. 'So I love my wife to be? That's hardly a crime, is it?' He looked at Sherry. 'Sorry. I love you. I always have and I always will, but I hid it from you as a teenager because I was too nervous to do anything about it, and by the time I got over my nerves you were married, so I left you to your happiness. What's wrong with that?'

I looked at Sherry. She was staring at him. His outburst of honesty was working. I could see she was starting to believe him. He was convincing, I'd give him that.

He carried on. 'It was only after you'd broken up with Tom that we got together, remember? Nothing happened before that. I told you I loved you at the earliest possible opportunity, look at it like that.' He gestured dismissively at the box. 'As for that. That's just photos. I was in love with you, and it was the best thing I had. You can't blame me for that surely? I left you alone, but I had some photos. It's not that bad.'

'It's fucking weird,' I said. As soon as the words were out of my mouth I regretted them. It sounded like I was attacking him, and I saw Sherry stiffen.

'Thanks,' Daniel said. 'That's about what I'd expect from you. Now, can we throw him out and get on with the rest of our lives? I'll get rid of all that junk.'

'Okay,' she said. 'There's just one thing, Daniel. The recent photos? Was that you? Were you here, spying on me?'

'No.' He looked at the floor. 'I paid someone to do it. I couldn't resist.'

She picked up a handful of the photos. 'There's a lot of them.'

He pressed his lips together; he was becoming impatient. His strategy depended on getting this over with as quickly as possible.

'Look, let's just move on.' He moved towards the table and grabbed at the photos in her hand. 'Give me those. I'll get rid of them and we can forget all about this.'

'What about the rest of it?' I said. 'It's not just being in love with her. There's the fruit salad you spiked, the time you banged your head against the wall in the office so it looked like I hit you.'

'Right,' he said. 'Of course. All of those things I did. I think we've been over this. It's time for you to leave.'

I ignored him. 'And the inappropriate touching allegations that you made up. What about those?'

'What about them?'

'I'm going to contest them.'

His composure flickered, then he regained himself. 'Good luck.'

'I won't need it.'

'Sherry. I'm going to throw this guy out. Is that okay with you?'

Sherry nodded. 'Sorry, Tom. Bye.'

'Before I go,' I said. 'One more thing.'

I took out the photo of Daniel, the athletic-looking guy and the two girls in the office and handed it to Sherry. I took out a copy and handed it to Daniel.

'There are other copies,' I said. 'With a lawyer.'

'Get out,' Daniel said. He didn't look at the photo. 'Leave.'

'Wait,' Sherry said. She was very still, her eyes fixed the photo. Then, louder. 'Wait!'

'I've got all the time in the world,' I said.

'What's this?' she said. 'What the hell is this?'

For the first time Daniel looked at the photo. Even he could not hide his shock. His hand started to shake and he shoved it behind his back.

'Is that him?' Sherry said, her voice halfway between anger and disbelief.

Daniel didn't reply; he just stared at the photo.

'Is that *you*, with *him*?'

'Turn it over,' I said. 'There's some writing on the back.'

Daniel dived across the kitchen table. 'Give that to me,' he shouted. 'That's mine! You have no right to look at my stuff!'

Sherry snatched her hand away and he missed her; his other hand shot out and grabbed her wrist. He bent it back to try and dislodge the photo.

I grabbed his forearm and yanked it behind his back.

'Read it,' I said.

Sherry lifted the photo and read the words on the back. 'Oh my God,' she said, and held her hand to her mouth. 'Oh my God.'

She sank into her chair. 'How could you,' she said. 'How could anyone?'

I didn't need to look at the words to know what they said.

Dan, thought you might like this reminder of the good times in Atlanta. Looking forward to seeing you at alumni weekend. Thanks for the invite. The chick you told me about – Sherry, right? – sounds fun. I'll make sure I look her up!

My hand tightened around his forearm. I pushed him forward so that he bent over the table, his cheek against the wood. 'He set you up.' I said. 'This piece of shit set you up so he could be a hero.'

'Of course,' Sherry said. 'You met him in Atlanta, on that summer internship you did. And then you invited him to alumni weekend and invited him to rape me.'

'I didn't,' Daniel said. 'I didn't expect that to happen. Honestly. I thought you'd have a bad time with him, see him for the boorish fool he was, and then you'd think better of me.'

'Well, that's all right then,' Sherry said. 'You just thought he'd rough me up a bit.' She leaned close to his face. 'But you know what? I don't believe you. I think he'd done it before and you found out – hell, perhaps you did it together in Atlanta, found two girls who wouldn't complain to the cops just like I didn't and became rape buddies – and then you told him about someone else like that back at college.'

She was wild now, her pupils dilated, her fists clenched.

'It wasn't like that,' Daniel said. 'I promise. It wasn't like that.'

'Then what was it like? What did you think? That I'd be so fucked up I'd turn to you?' She looked away from him. 'My God, I can't believe you did this to me. And when you told me you'd had him sorted out, was that a lie too? Did you really just call him up and compare notes?' She ran her hand through her hair, clutching at her scalp. 'Did you have a good laugh about it?' she screamed. 'Did you?'

Then she slammed her fist into his jaw, hard enough that it bounced back. I heard something crack, and Daniel grunted; Sherry raised her hand, open like talons, and sunk her fingernails into his cheek. Blood started to trickle onto the table top.

'You bastard,' she screamed. 'You total fucking bastard!'

I would have happily let her rip his face to pieces; I had no love for him, but there was no point in her getting into trouble. I took her hand and pulled it from his face.

'Call the police,' I said. 'Just call the cops. Let them deal with it.'

'Did you do the other things?' she said. 'Was it you all along?'

Daniel didn't answer.

'Tell me!' she shouted. 'Did you spike the fruit salad? Did you set Tom up? Did you make me hate my husband?'

I turned his face so that his other cheek was facing upwards.

'I suggest you answer her question unless you want her to do the same to this side of your face,' I said. 'Although as far as I'm concerned you can keep quiet. It's no skin off my nose to see you in pain.'

Daniel grunted.

'So?' Sherry said. 'Was it you?'

Daniel didn't answer; Sherry let out a cry that was halfway between despair and hatred. She looked at me over the table; over our table.

'I'm sorry,' she said. 'I'm so sorry.'

'Go and call the cops. Wait outside. You don't need to see this turd any more.'

'Well, well,' I said, when she was gone. 'This is a bit of a bummer for you, Daniel.'

He still didn't reply.

'Nothing to say, old chap? I don't blame you. Let's enjoy the quiet before the cops show up, shall we? It's noisy inside, I hear. Accessory to rape must carry a custodial sentence, I guess? Either way, you won't be welcome back in Barrow. Word spreads in a small town, you know.'

'Fuck you,' he said.

I twisted his torn cheek against the table and he squirmed in pain.

'Careful. Don't move around so much.'

They were the last words I said to him; a few minutes later two burly cops arrived and bundled him out of the house. I walked out onto the porch and waved him goodbye. He wouldn't meet my eye.

'Hey.' Sherry said. She was standing at the side of the porch, watching the police car turn out of the street. 'You want to talk?'

I looked at her and shook my head. 'Not right now. Right now I owe the one guy who trusted me a night on the town.' I got to my feet. 'We can talk later. I'm going out in Portland with Gerard, and I'm going to get drunk.'

Rosie's

We went back to Rosie's. Gerard bought a round and we clinked glasses.

'Better than the last time we were in here,' he said.

'Sure as shit is.' I drained my beer. 'Another?'

'Does the Pope shit in the woods?'

'You mean either "is the Pope Catholic?" or "do bears shit in the woods?"'

'I mean, does the Pope shit in the woods? Anyway, you get what I'm trying to say. Now get the beers.'

We slid into a happy drunkenness. Later, Gerard, as he liked to do when he was full of beer, switched to tequila.

'So,' he said. 'What are you going to do? You going to go back to Sherry?'

'I'm not sure I can, after what happened. I'm not sure we can fix things up. There's too much damage been done. I could get a house, see Peggy at weekends. Or go back to England, visit from time to time.'

Gerard rolled his eyes. 'Don't be such a pussy. 'Course you can fix it. There was a problem, now he's gone. You two'll be love birds again in no time.'

'I don't know. There's a lot of water under the bridge.'

'And there'll be more, that's for certain. Anyway, you can stop all this umming and ahhing. You'll go back to her, I know you will. You're too soft to do anything else. You'll decide that it'd be a mistake not to at least give it a try and so you'll try it and a year from now it'll be like none of this ever happened.'

'I see. I'm glad you give so much weight to the agonies of my situation. This is a difficult decision.'

'No, it isn't. We're all the same, in the end, Tom. We think our situation is unique and we're the first person to wrestle with whatever shit life throws at us, but we're not. You two love each other and you'll find a way to make it work. It might not be easy, at times, but what relationship between a man and a woman ever was? If you want an easy life don't get married in the first place.'

'I think you're over-simplifying . . .'

'Sounds about right,' he said. 'I like to keep things simple. How about now we've got it nice and simple we keep it that way and get drunk?'

I lifted my shot glass. 'Cheers, Gerard. Here's to good friends.'

He didn't clink his glass against mine. He was staring at the door.

'Well, would you look at that,' he said. 'If it isn't Crimson and Mindy.'

Crimson and Gerard were long gone. I was leaning against Mindy, trying to keep on my feet as she walked me to a taxi.

'Sure you don't want to come back to my place?'

'No.' I was struggling even to get words of one syllable out. 'I'm marr—, marr—'

'You're married? So you're going to patch it up, then?' After Gerard and Crimson had left Rosie's I'd told her at length about my dilemma.

'Dunno. Gonna think about it.'

We reached the taxi stand and I opened the door.

'Good luck,' she said, and kissed me on the cheek. 'You're a good man, as much as any. I think you'll be fine. The thing is, it's all out in the open now, isn't it? There's no more secrets. You two can start again with a clean slate. At least you know where you stand. That puts you better off than most people. So go home.'

'Thanks, Mindy,' I mumbled. 'See you around.'

'Sure,' she said. 'Let me know how it goes.'

I told the taxi driver the name of my hotel.

'Up in Barrow?' he said. 'You on holiday there?'

'No,' I said, without thinking. 'I live there.'

As we pulled away I watched her walk across the street. She paused and delved into her bag for a cigarette. She lit it, then opened the door to her apartment, and disappeared.

Endings and Beginnings

The following morning Stephanie left a message at the hotel that she wanted to see me. I gave her a call and told her to come over.

She was there an hour later. We met in the bar and ordered coffee. I could see from her expression – a combination of shame and shock and horror – that she had heard at least something of what had happened.

'I'm sorry,' she said. 'I owe you an apology. More than an apology.'

I nodded. 'You do.'

'I got a call late last night from Daniel's lawyer. Daniel was in custody; the lawyer wouldn't give me any details – ' she paused, waiting for me to fill her in. I didn't. There was enough gossip in Barrow, Maine, without me adding some more – 'but she did say that the charges against you have been dropped. Daniel, apparently, has realized that he made a mistake.'

She said 'mistake' as though saying it tasted of shit.

'He did. If you think of fabricating the whole thing as a mistake. I think I may have mentioned that to you at the time.' I know you shouldn't rub people's noses in their errors; there's no moral high-ground in *I told you so*. But it felt fucking amazing to do it this time. And besides, I was annoyed. She was supposed to have been my friend, and, like many others, she had been all too ready to think I was guilty of molesting students. It was insulting, frankly, and I was enjoying her apology. I didn't feel ready to forgive just yet, either.

'I'm sorry. Truly sorry. For what we put you through.'

Now for the pleasures of magnanimity. 'You weren't to know.'

'It goes without saying that your job is yours, should you want it.'

'I'm not sure I'm ready to make that decision just yet. I'll think about it.'

'I understand if you don't come back. There'll be a reference – a glowing reference – if you need it.'

I sat in the bar and ordered a coffee, although I wasn't in the mood for celebrating, at least in part because I was so hungover. It was an odd feeling. I'd expected – what – triumph? Elation? Joy? But all I felt was a kind of emptiness, like it had all been for nothing. All the damage, all the pain, all the suffering – for nothing. Just so some man could get the girl he'd wanted since high school.

The bar was empty; the door opened and someone came in.

It was Sherry.

She looked awful. Eyes red with sleeplessness, hair lank, skin puffy. I gestured for her to sit down.

'Go on,' she said. 'Say I told you so.'

'It's not about that.' Now there really was no moral high ground – or pleasure – in *I told you so*. She'd suffered enough.

She closed her eyes. Her lips quivered and she started to cry.

'I'm sorry,' she whispered. 'I'm so sorry.'

'So am I.'

'I can't believe he would do that. Do all those things. I was such an idiot.'

'It's not your fault. You couldn't have seen through him. Christ, even *I* wondered whether I had it all wrong from time to time.'

'I should have trusted you. You deserved it.'

'You should have. But that doesn't matter now.'

'So what do we do?'

'What do you want to do?' I wanted to hear it from her first. I didn't want to say I wanted to try again only to be rebuffed. Childish? Yes. Selfish? Yes. But I didn't care. I think I'd earned the right to be both, at least for a moment.

'I want to go back to how it was. I know that's not possible, but we can try, right?'

'Where's Peggy?' Suddenly I wanted to see my – our – daughter. More than wanted; I needed to see her.

'At home.'

'Let's go.'

'Now?'

'Now.'

We walked urgently to the house. Once or twice Sherry started to speak but I didn't reply. When we arrived I opened the door and walked into the living room.

Sherry's mum stood up. 'Tom,' she said. 'I—'

She was interrupted by Peggy leaping to her feet.

'Daddy!' she shouted. 'You're here! Mommy said Daniel was gone away and you were coming home!'

'Did she?' I glanced at Sherry, who reddened. 'Do you want me home?'

Peggy nodded. 'I missed you.'

'I missed you too.' I picked her up and looked at Sherry. 'We can try,' I said. 'It might take a while, but it'll be okay. I love her – ' I kissed Peggy – 'too much for it not to be.'

'You think so?'

I nodded. 'I think so. But let's just give it a shot, and see what happens.'

Sherry nodded and put her arms round me, her forehead against mine. Peggy put her head against Sherry's then wriggled out of my arms and onto the floor.

'Come on, Daddy,' she said. 'Let's go and play. I built a fairy house in the yard.'

'A fairy house?' I said. 'How could I resist a fairy house?'

What Will Survive

The one thing he never expected to be was a single dad . . . Graham Melton was a normal fifteen-year-old until he met Charlotte Marshall over a can of warm lager at his best-friend's party in 1985. It was love at first sight, and teenage life was never going to be the same again.

Two decades later, Graham is a single father trying to protect his son from the rigours of the modern world. Everything has changed, and the innocence has long gone.

What happened in those years in between? How did something so perfect go so tragically wrong?

In a heart-warming and humorous tale of love, laughter and tears, Mark Gartside weaves a poignant story of one man's struggle to bring up his son whilst learning to love and smile all over again.

'Gartside's warm, thoughtful, emotionally honest treatment of the process of becoming a man, especially handling responsibility for others in the face of loss, is a promising debut from a writer not afraid to show his feminine side'   *Daily Mail*

www.panmacmillan.com